ESCAPE FROM ABUNDANCE

THE ABUNDANCE SERIES- BOOK 3

SHANNA SWENSON

Escape from Abundance
Shanna Swenson

Escape from Abundance is an original work of fiction. Names, characters, places, organizations and incidents either are the product of the author's imagination or are used fictitiously. Any resemblance to actual persons, living or dead, events, or locales is entirely coincidental.

www.shannaswenson.com

❀ Created with Vellum

FOREWORD

Dear Readers,

Believe it or not, *this* book was actually the first novel I ever wrote. I was sixteen years old and sitting in class when I got the brilliant thought, "What if a fugitive was on the run and decided to hide out on a horse ranch?" (The movies *The Horse Whisperer* and *The Fugitive* helped inspire me to think in this direction.) Before I knew it, it was halfway done, with pen and paper mind you. But then somehow, I lost it when I moved to Colorado. I can't describe how upsetting that was, but like everything else in life, it happened (for a reason). I didn't write for a long time, but these characters I created didn't leave me.

I kept thinking that Dallie and her parents deserved a back story. *Abundance* was born from that idea. After *Abundance*, the words just flowed, save for a small case of writer's block, but I always knew I would—at some point—be able to go back and finish this story, and 2019 was the year! So, without further ado, I give you Book 3 in the *Abundance* series, *Escape from Abundance*.

P.S. There will be 2 more books in this cowboy romance saga, so stayed tuned for those later in 2019 and 2020. Sign up for my newsletter to stay abreast of the latest updates and sneak peeks at www.shannaswenson.com.

THE ABUNDANCE SERIES

NOVELS BY SHANNA SWENSON

ABUNDANCE: AN ENDEARING ROMANCE

RETURN TO ABUNDANCE: THE ABUNDANCE SERIES-
BOOK 2

ESCAPE FROM ABUNDANCE: THE ABUNDANCE SERIES-
BOOK 3

STARLIGHT VALLEY: THE PREQUEL TO ABUNDANCE (FREE
EBOOK)

For my precious nephews, Trenton Gaige and Greyson Lake, you both make my life more fulfilling with your existence. You'll never know just how very much your Aunt Cookie loves you

PROLOGUE

Cole Callahan knew something was wrong the minute he walked into his shop, Burns and Callahan Automotives, on the corner of Windsor and Market Streets in downtown Austin, Texas. There was a faint metallic smell in the air and something just didn't feel right.

"Adam?" he called as he entered the office door, noticing that all the lights were on in there but not in the garage. He frowned. Adam's car was out in the parking lot, so he was here.

It was eerily quiet, he noted. *Maybe he's in the bathroom?* Cole thought, but the dread in his heart wouldn't be settled.

He looked down to see that the computer had been turned on already. Adam Burns had been there in the office at some point within the hour, so why hadn't he turned the rest of the lights on like every other morning? *Strange,* Cole thought.

Adam had always been the early bird. He usually got to the shop about an hour before Cole, around seven AM. He had volunteered to be the one to open the shop for the day, turn on all the lights and start the first pot of coffee. It had been done the exact same way since they'd bought the shop some three years ago. Adam was their

PR guy and customs designer, while Cole was the master mechanic. It had been a smart endeavor they'd sought out three years ago after graduating from college when they decided to go into business together. They were not only business partners but best friends.

"Adam?" Cole called a little louder this time, his voice more concerned as he saw Adam's phone sitting next to the laptop. Maybe he'd just stepped out for a minute.

Cole shrugged and picked up the heavy box of tools that sat in the metal chair across from the desk, surprised that Adam hadn't taken it into the garage yet. He couldn't shake the nagging feeling that something was amiss as he entered the garage. There, he heard the sound of metal scrapping beneath his shoe and felt his foot rise as he stepped on top of something in the heavy darkness of the closed garage. He instinctively looked down, trying hard to recognize the out of place object. He grimaced. Now, he *knew* something was wrong.

Cole had never left a tool on the ground before, not ever, and he was positive he didn't leave one last night before he closed up. He moved to the workbench against the back wall in the dim light and set the box down. He walked back over to the stray tool and knelt down, picking it up. It was heavy and round and he immediately dropped it, realizing suddenly what it was as his eyes adjusted in the dense darkness—Adam's gun. He ran to the side panel to turn the lights on. The scene before him slowly unfolded as his eyes were momentarily blinded by the florescent lights overhead. He stepped to the back of the car that sat on the lowered lift before him and felt his heart literally stop. Cole noticed first an extremely large pool of blood… then a pair of legs. He gulped, afraid to move any closer. His blood surged, loudly in his ears, but his fear didn't outweigh his curiosity. Cole held his breath as he came around the red sedan.

Much to his horror, Adam lay there in the dark viscous puddle, pale, eyes wide. As Cole inched closer, he saw a hollow, piercing wound to his friend's head.

"Oh God!" Cole cried and ran to his friend, squatting beside him.

Cole touched Adam's neck to check for a pulse as tears hit his eyes, knowing very well that he wouldn't find one. His best friend in the whole world, the man who had been like a brother to him, was lying dead in their shop. And he'd been murdered.

Cole swallowed hard and looked around. Was the assailant still there? Had it been a robbery gone bad? Who could *possibly* want to kill Adam?

Cole's eyes searched the garage and noted that nothing else seemed amiss.

Unexpectedly, he saw blue and red lights flashing beneath the closed door of the garage and felt panic rise in his throat, intense and crushing. *Oh no, they'll think I did it!* His mind raced in a million different directions as logic took hold of him. He'd touched Adam's lifeless body, he'd touched the gun. Now, he was going to be caught here at the scene of the crime next to the body, which wouldn't bode well with Cole's extensive criminal record.

He looked down once again at Adam lying lifeless on the floor and apologized as he raced like a bat out of hell out the back door.

"Forgive me, brother?"

He had no other choice!

He had to run!

CHAPTER 1

ole sighed, feeling both anger and sorrow, as he walked
down the road to the ranch deemed "Kinsen Ranch"
according to the iron archway above him. He was hungry, he was
tired and he was lost... lost in guilt and lost in confusion.

He'd miraculously been able to hop a ride with a trucker, who'd
been heading north, but not long into the journey, the rig had
broken down right in the middle of the dinky little town of Abundance, not far from Denton. It wasn't as far as he wanted to be from
Austin, but there were no other truckers around, and Cole didn't
have the proper tools or equipment to fix the big diesel himself, so
he'd walked down the sidewalk to look around, seeing as there
wasn't much else to do at the time but wait for a tow.

He'd grabbed a local newspaper that just happened to be sitting
on an empty bench there in the morning "rush" and browsed
through it. His attention was immediately drawn to the wanted ads
where someone had circled one post in particular. There it had lit up
at him like a beacon; a job working on a ranch. What better way to
hide than in a one-horse town on a ranch in the middle of nowhere?

It was brilliant! It would be a good gig for now then when he saved up enough money, he could head in any direction he wanted to.

He'd asked the mechanic, in the small garage where they'd towed the truck, what direction the ranch was, and the man had pointed and said it was a good twenty minutes outside of town. *Perfect!* An old man had piped in about that same time and said he was headed that way himself and would give Cole a ride there. *Even better!* It was as if the stars were aligning that morning as the sun rose higher on this hot June day.

But now as Cole walked the dirt road that led to the ranch ahead, his mind and heart drifted back to his poor dead friend. He felt the tears sting his eyes as bile rose in his throat.

Cole had been on the path to a lifetime of crime when Adam had come into his life. Adam had been his God-send when nothing else in the world was going right for him. Adam was kind and giving, one of the best people Cole had ever known, and they'd met on the bus one extremely rough day when they were both sophomores in high school. Cole had been considered a bully and a punk and his reputation had preceded him. He'd been arrested on multiple occasions for breaking and entering, vandalism, theft, even once for grand theft auto. He'd been a terror to his poor foster parents and had gone from home to home because he couldn't keep his mouth shut or his larcenous hands out of the cookie jars; he'd stolen so many times from them all. Thank God the last family had been incredibly patient with him. At the time, he was a troubled teen searching for answers as to why his biological mother had abandoned him. He had a lot of anger in him then...until Adam had helped fill the void.

Adam befriended Cole practically overnight. One day Cole had been contemplating running away from his current home, the next, he was having dinner with the Burns' and playing basketball in their driveway. Cole was able to have a genuine conversation with someone his own age for a change, and the entire experience opened his eyes to what a real family and a happy life was all about. He'd gone from being an absolute tyrant to a respectable young man in less than a year's time and he'd graduated with enough credits to go to technical school and make a living instead of going to prison as he knew he would've eventually done had his best friend not taken an interest in him. Cole had Adam to thank for so much...and now Adam was gone. In the blink of an eye. And at the hands of a killer.

Who could have wanted to kill him? He was an all-around boy scout. Everyone who met Adam absolutely loved him. He had parents and siblings and a wife who adored him. He was a volunteer, a city council member and the piano player of the First Baptist Church in Austin. It didn't make any sense. Why did Adam have to die? Who had done it? And of course, like a coward, instead of waiting to find out, Cole had run away when he was needed most. But he couldn't stay... They would never have believed him! Not in a million years.

Cole looked up at the beautiful three-story home before him in awe. It was a classic Cape Cod style house, looking like something straight out of a magazine, with its big porch and dormers, manicured lawn and flower beds. Wow, he'd had a totally different idea of the word "ranch" in his head. He waved at the man sitting out front, really hoping he was the owner then noticed the big growling, brown mastiff beside him.

"Howdy," the older man called to Cole as he stood from his seat in a wooden rocking chair—almost as if expecting him—and took the cell phone from his ear, sticking it into his back pocket as he firmly spoke to the dog. "Easy, Magnus."

"Good morning," Cole responded, eyeing the huge dog wearily.

"Can I help you?" The man asked, tipping the tan cowboy hat atop his head in Cole's direction.

He was a tall, broad-shouldered, muscular man who looked to be in his forties. He was dressed in what Cole assumed was the usual cowboy attire complete with a hat, blue button-down shirt, jeans and boots.

"Yes, sir. I'm Cole." *Damn! He'd used his real name.* "I saw your ad in

7

the paper. I just got into town and I'm looking for work as soon as possible." Cole grabbed the older man's work-hardened hand that suddenly extended before him.

"Well, how 'bout that!" The man gave a slight smile, making him seem less intimidating than he'd first appeared. "The name's Jack. Jack Kinsen. Welcome to my ranch."

Cole shook Jack's hand and smiled back. *Oh good, he's the owner.* Cole could get the formalities done and over with, get to work and start planning his next move.

"You look pretty tired, son," Jack noted, pulling his hand back and giving Cole the once over, taking in the younger man's appearance, as he crossed his arms over his big frame. Cole knew he probably didn't look all bright-eyed and bushy-tailed, not quite up to par for an interview, but this was as good as it was going to get considering. Jack's brows drew at him, trying to figure him out. "You got any work experience as a ranch hand?"

Cole knew it would be pointless to lie; Jack would see first-hand soon enough what experience—or lack thereof—he had. "No sir, I don't. I'm just lookin' for work and I'm used to hard labor, so I figured I could be of assistance." Jack just looked hard into his eyes, assessing him further for a few moments then he shrugged.

"Oh well, I guess that'll do… for now. You got a place to stay?" It was as if he could almost see into Cole's mind. Cole gulped, feeling transparent for a moment. "You a drifter?"

"You could say that. Aren't all ranch hands though?" Cole stammered and tried to laugh. Jack only half smiled in return.

"You're *not* a ranch hand…" Jack's brow cocked and his green eyes narrowed.

Damn! Cole thought. *I'm already mucking this up.*

"Alright," Jack said, "let's get a couple things straight real quick. First off, I'm fair if you are. I won't ask too many questions. I can see you're guarded. I'm fine with that. No worries on my end. I just ask that you work hard and don't take advantage. Respect me. I'll respect you."

"That's fair," Cole agreed and Jack smiled, taking some of the sudden tension away when he did.

"Good. You got any questions?"

"When can I start?"

"You're hired," Jack exclaimed with a laugh. "Well, first things first... you hungry?" When Cole nodded, Jack added, "Alright, let's get you fed and we'll talk business." With that, Jack led him into the house.

To say it was beautiful was an understatement. It was the nicest house that Cole had ever set foot in, and he'd stepped foot in quite a lot of houses over the years. Even Adam's family didn't have a home quite like this. It was big and roomy, but homey at the same time.

There were cathedral ceilings in the great room and a large stone fireplace that ran all the way up the wall. Hardwood floors and large leather couches and a huge kitchen with granite countertops. There was even a baby grand piano on the other side of the fireplace. These people had it all. Ranching must be a good business.

"Honey, I just filled the position I posted in the paper," Jack called as they stepped into the kitchen, walking over to a large breakfast nook table.

Cole laid eyes on one of the most beautiful women he'd ever seen. She had dark wavy hair, dazzling blue eyes and a smile that lit up the room. He liked her immediately. The woman smiled up at them from her position in the chair, and Cole presumed that she must be Jack's wife. The couple kissed then, confirming his suspicions, and Cole looked away, giving them some momentary privacy.

"Nat, meet Cole." Jack motioned over to him, and Cole extended his hand to the woman. "Cole, this is *Mrs.* Kinsen. My wife, Natalie."

"Mrs. Kinsen, it's nice to meet you." Cole smiled back at the pretty lady and shook her smaller hand.

"Please, call me Natalie," she said as she looked up at him.

"See babe," Jack stated as his hands went to his wife's shoulders, "I told you old school wasn't a complete waste of time and money." Natalie just gave him a crooked grin and shook her head slightly.

"Mama, na-na." Cole's eyes were drawn then to a highchair beside her, where a baby sat eating banana slices.

"This is our son, Jackson." Jack nodded over to a toddler with curly, sandy-blonde hair, who cooed and flapped his little arms at them.

Cole laughed. "Hey, little guy."

Cole waved over to him as the baby giggled and replied with, "Da-Da," as Jack walked over and kissed his little head.

"You'll meet the rest of the Kinsen gang shortly. Please have a seat." Jack motioned for Cole to sit down at the table and turned to Natalie then. "My love, would you be so kind as to grab Cole a plate while we talk shop?"

His wife just arched an eyebrow at him, an unspoken exchange between them, and moved to do as he'd asked. Jack smiled slyly as he watched her walk over to the stove and make a plate, his demeanor much more laid back that it'd been on the porch, and Cole got the impression that Jack and his wife had a playful relationship, despite that Jack seemed to be a pretty serious guy.

They discussed the basics of any job offering: salary, time off and job specifications while Jack fed and entertained the toddler for several minutes before Natalie returned with a massive sandwich and a steaming hot cup of soup. Cole's stomach immediately growled, and he looked down at the food with newfound interest... after all, he'd not eaten that morning—not that he would have been able to anyway.

Surprisingly, Cole hadn't had to search long for someone who looked even remotely interested in picking up a hitchhiker. He'd hopped right in with a good ol' boy trucker from Oklahoma, only to have the damn rig break down just three hours into their journey. He'd meandered around town a little while before getting a ride to the ranch. Just around five hours had passed, Cole realized, since he'd found his friend dead, but it felt like it'd been far longer. He tried to block out the painful vision as the smell of vegetable soup filled his nostrils.

He thanked Mrs. Kinsen profusely as he dug in and much to his astonishment, he scarfed down his lunch speedily. Jack and Natalie laughed as he sat back and sighed, his belly full.

"Been a while since you've had a good meal, huh?" Jack asked. Cole just nodded and smiled.

"Thank you, Mr. and Mrs. Kinsen. That was delicious." Cole patted his belly. "Maybe too much food before work though." The couple laughed.

"Oh, don't be so sure. You may change your mind come dinner time," Jack informed him and winked at his wife.

Natalie entertained the baby as he and the ranch owner talked more shop and once the specifics were settled upon and Cole was ready to start, they headed out the French doors and onto a screened-in back porch.

"...And don't worry, we can board you until you find a place, if you want. We have plenty of room in this house," Jack replied on their way down to the huge red barn in the back.

"I really appreciate that, Mr. Kinsen."

Jack just turned and nodded at him, smiling.

Wow! Cole was surprised by this family's benevolence towards him. He'd literally just met them and they'd fed him, given him a job and offered a roof over his head. He felt like he'd been adopted all over again...if only his first foster home had been this good to him.

The stables were as impressive as the house, extravagant and looked more like a training facility than any barn Cole had ever seen. Come to think of it; this would be the first barn he'd ever seen —up close and personal anyway—so what did he know about it?

They stopped at a circular corral out front where two men worked with a horse. Jack propped his boot on the fence rung and spoke to the men.

"Teddy. Craig. Come and meet our new rookie," Jack called out, and they ambled over to meet Cole, bringing the horse with them.

Teddy and Craig looked to be in their late twenties. Craig had on a wedding ring and both men wore cowboy hats, t-shirts, jeans and boots. Cole shook their hands and introduced himself. The ranch hands talked with Jack about the horses for a few minutes, using words that Cole was completely unfamiliar with—like green broke and hot horse and hard keeper—then he and Jack walked over to the fence on the opposite side of the barn.

"Hey, Mike." Jack tipped his hat as the man named Mike nodded to them and spoke up to another man on a horse. Mike then smiled and walked their way.

"Mornin', boss!" he said, tapping a clipboard in his hand.

"I want you to meet Cole, our new hand."

Mike smiled and grabbed Cole's hand, shaking it vigorously. "I'm Mike. It's a pleasure."

Cole couldn't help but notice how kind everyone was to him. They'd only just met him, but seemed overly happy for his presence and eager to meet him. It genuinely touched him. He smiled and shook the man's hand.

Mike was a little older than the other guys, in his thirties maybe. He, too, wore a tan cowboy hat, jeans and boots. Cole was going to need to go shopping. He felt ill-equipped in his black shirt, cargo pants and sneakers.

"Mike here will be the one teaching you the ropes. He's our foreman here. You'll answer to him and take orders from him. Any questions, you can catch me in my office. He'll take good care of you. Welcome to the crew, kid," Jack stated and slapped him on the back. Cole thanked him profusely, and Mike nodded for him to come on over.

Cole looked at the fence; it was too high to climb over. He noticed the spacing in the rungs. If he bent over, he could fit between the top and middle rungs, so that's what he did and awkwardly stepped through the fence, trying to regain his footing. He almost fell. Mike laughed and helped him.

"You're pretty green, huh?" he patted his back, and they walked toward the guy atop the horse.

He recognized the word "green" from watching a reality TV

show about fisherman and knew what it meant. "Yes sir. New to this business."

"Well, it takes some getting used to I reckon, but don't worry, we'll break you in just fine." The way Mike laughed at that had Cole a little nervous. He'd never worked with large animals or even small ones, really. Adam had a dog, but Cole's interaction with animals was limited beyond that. Maybe this wasn't such a good idea after all.

They stopped next to the brown horse and its rider, and Mike introduced him to Todd. Todd was younger than the rest of the gang; closer to Cole's age, he noted happily, and gave a swift nod up to him. That seemed to be the usual gesture for these cowboys. Todd nodded back and grinned at him.

Mike instructed Todd for a minute more before he slapped the horse's flank, and Todd was trotting off down the long corral. Mike then began telling Cole what he would be doing for the day. They needed to work on some fence repairs, shovel out some stalls in the barn then the hay truck was coming in later that afternoon. *Great!* Cole thought. He knew that hay bales were heavy as hell. He would be regretfully sore come tomorrow. *Oh well.* This is what he'd signed up for, right? Cole just nodded, his attention drawn to something in the distance. A running horse; he'd have to get used to that, he reckoned. He looked back to Mike, who handed him a pair of gloves and a hammer, and they walked toward the back of the fence.

Suddenly, there was a shout, "Look out!"

As if in slow motion, a white stallion shot through the fence beside them almost as if it were simply a blanket of fog. Cole barely had time to react as the horse came at them full speed. They both ran for the back of the fence; Mike jumping it as the horse gained on them. Cole wasn't so lucky, he attempted the leap but fell. The horse reared up, and Cole scooted back on his elbows, trying to get away, but there was nowhere to go. He was trapped and he was going to be crushed on his very first day on the job. He closed his eyes and waited for the pain to come.

He felt the vibration of the horse's hooves hit the ground and a spray of dust hit his face. He heard a, "Whoa," and some scuffling and when he noticed that he wasn't dead, he opened his eyes.

Welp, I'm indeed dead, he thought, for he was gazing up at an angel; a beautiful blonde angel in a cowboy hat. He didn't know angels wore cowboy hats and didn't care that she had no wings, for she had saved him. She stood, stroking the snow-white beast as he snorted and huffed, his nostrils flaring and his head flipping.

"Shh, easy boy. That's it, you're ok," her voice was so soothing that Cole sighed.

When she was satisfied with the horse's response, she turned to Cole and walked forward, extending her hand to him. That's when he saw her smile and he literally melted. She was even more beautiful than he'd originally thought. He felt gooey inside, kinda like the scorched marshmallow nestled next to a piece of chocolate smooshed in between two graham crackers. He grinned dreamily into her sparkling sapphire eyes and reached his hand up to hers.

"You ok?" She laughed as she helped haul him up. He couldn't respond as his voice lost its traction. He cleared his throat and tried again, but again he failed, so he just nodded. She smirked. "Hi, I'm Dallas Kinsen." Wow! She was Jack's *daughter? Holy shit!*

"I'm...gorgeous. I mean... You're gorgeous! I mean—" Cole gulped. *Get ahold of yourself, dude!* She laughed again; it was music to his ears. "I'm Cole! I'm new..." He blushed.

"Well, Cole, no offense, but I can kinda tell that." She winked and pulled her hand away, moving back to the stallion then. Cole noticed a rope around the horse's neck. Dallas was pulling it off of the beast and rolling it back up. She must have lassoed him. Impressive!

"Dallie?" Suddenly, Jack was jumping the other fence and coming towards them. Cole was going to have to learn to master that technique if he were to make it on this ranch. "You ok?"

"Yes, Daddy, we're fine. I got this hot boy under control now." She patted the horse's neck and looked down at his chest, frowning. "He's got some lacerations here. I'm gonna check him for splinters

14

and doctor him up. Mike, can you grab me a halter?" Mike, who'd now joined them too in the corral, ran to do as she'd asked as Jack joined them at the horse's side. He reached up and patted the horse, his other hand going to his daughter's back.

"He cause that?" Jack motioned over to the battered and broke fence rails, the remnants of the collision he must have heard from all the way in his office.

"Yeah, he got spooked real bad by somethin' out in the field and darted. I saw him and tried to catch up as fast as I could."

"I'm just glad everyone's ok." Jack sighed and looked over at Cole. "You alright, son?"

"Yes sir, just a little shaken up is all."

"I see that." Jack patted his back. "Why don't you go with Dallie? See how we bring the horses in then you can help with the fence later." Cole just nodded. "Mike, will you put Ameera up for Dallie? I gotta go into town and meet with a client." Mike—just arriving with the halter Dallie had requested—handed it over, nodded back at Jack and grabbed the black horse's reins. Cole's gaze went over to Dallie who smiled at him easily and motioned her head for him to follow her.

"Come up here beside me," Dallie firmly stated. "You don't ever want to be behind a horse." Cole ran to do as she said. She gave him the once over as they followed a good distance behind Mike and the other horse. "Looks like you'll need some proper attire if you're gonna be workin' here." Cole almost blushed, but simply nodded.

He followed Dallie through a wide doorframe into the large stables with row after row of horse stalls. She led him into a bay off to the side that looked a little like a small self-wash car wash bay. It had a nozzle on the wall as well as different kinds of brushes and a drain in the floor. Dallie hooked the halter up to a runner and stroked the stallion's cheek as she murmured to him. She then grabbed the stool next to the wall and the spray nozzle and took a seat in front of the horse.

"Would you mind brushin' him down while I check his wounds?"

she asked. Cole moved, only to hear, "Stop! Don't walk behind him." she corrected. *Dammit!* He must look like a total idiot to her.

"I'm sorry," Cole said and walked around the other way. He then stood dejectedly, gazing at the wall of various brushes. He looked back over at her in question. She just smiled and pointed to a big one. He took it and walked back over to the horse's side.

She laughed humorlessly. "It'll be *you* who's sorry if you ever get kicked…" she trailed off as she sprayed down the horse's chest gently and assessed the damage. "It looks like he's got a big cut here on the point of his shoulder. I may need to call Dr. Green out," she said, as much to herself as to him. "I could stitch it, but he has the drugs I need." She looked up suddenly, noticing that he wasn't brushing. Her brows went up.

"Oh, uh, sorry." He took the brush and tenderly began using it on the horse's back. He heard a giggle, and Dallas stood. She came up next to him and placed her hand under his in the brush handle.

"No. Like this." The gentle touch of her hand beneath his sent him into sensory overload. It was as if electricity shot through him, and he audibly gasped. She seemed to feel it too as she stopped and jerked her head up, gazing at him, momentarily frozen then looked back down. She cleared her throat and guided the brush down the horses back as if she didn't feel the spikes of energy sparking between their fingertips. "Long strokes from his withers," she instructed, "to his dock…like so." He simply nodded, his throat tight. He could do nothing else. She pulled her hand from under his and watched him do as she'd coached then turned toward him, assessing him. Cole felt the same scrutinous gaze he'd felt just a little while earlier from her father. He gulped. Like father, like daughter. "You're afraid of them, huh?" She motioned to the horse.

"Well, no, not really…maybe. I've never worked with livestock," he stammered.

"Makes sense," she replied and moved back to the horse's front. She grabbed a bottle and some towels from the shelf and used it on the cuts only she could see. "This will be much easier on you if you try not to let them scare you." Dallie stopped and looked up at him. "Think of them as big dogs." Cole just nodded as her blue eyes burned into his. She just smiled back and returned to her tasks. The horse flinched as she brushed the towel down his chest and pulled back on the rope. He and Dallie both froze. "Well, I'm gonna need some lidocaine, so I guess I'll call the vet." She sighed and motioned for him to follow as they walked into the center aisle of the massive structure, down several rows of bays that looked like they served various uses, and into a roomy office with a couple windows to the outside.

It was spacious and held a nice, big mahogany desk and executive chair along with a phone, computer, two adjacent leather seats, a water cooler and some book cases filled with various hardbacks, paperbacks, photos, trophies and ribbons.

Dallie picked up the phone and dialed the vet as Cole moved to the water cooler and helped himself to a cup of water. He drank it greedily and waited for Dallie to finish her conversation. She hung up the phone and sighed.

"He won't be here for another hour or so." She threw her hands on her hips and turned to look at him.

He drank her in then. Her long curly blonde ringlets were covered by a tan cowboy hat. A white tank top peeked out at him beneath a blue gingham button down shirt tucked into a well-worn pair of jeans tucked into tan cowboy boots. Her figure was slender and her breasts well-proportioned to her curvy hips. His eyes couldn't miss the little sliver of cleavage that called out to him. Her skin was creamy despite her work in the sun and her lips were pouty, complete with a perfect cupid's bow, but it was her eyes that he lost himself in. They were brilliant blue sapphires gazing into his hazel ones.

"Let's go into town and grab you some clothes then we'll meet Dr. Green back here and let him take care of our kamikaze stallion," Dallie suggested. Cole shrugged, and she smiled. He followed her as she walked from the office back to the kamikaze stallion she'd

17

spoken of. She unhooked his halter from the lead and pulled him into the nearest stall, making sure he had fresh water to suffice. "Alright, let's go," she stated, closing the stall door.

He wasn't sure why Dallie was being so nice to him or why she had taken him under her wing, but he was grateful for the distraction. He followed her to the front of the barn as they walked towards an old beat up '57 Chevy truck. She motioned for him to get in as she slid behind the wheel, the keys already in the ignition, and she attempted to crank it. It took three times before the engine turned and sputtered. Uh oh; it needed some work.

"Hey, Mike," she called out from the open window as they passed the fence. "We're gonna go get Cole here some proper clothes. We'll be back shortly." Mike just waved and nodded.

They rode in companionable silence as they rode up the dirt road, past the house and headed out to the highway. Dallie turned and headed back in the direction of the small town. Cole couldn't hide his anxiety. What if someone in town spotted him? What if the cops already had him down as a suspect? What if...

"Cat got your tongue?" Dallie laughed. He blushed, realizing she'd asked him a question prior to that. *Damn!* She must think he was a certified lunatic!

"Jeez, I'm really sorry. It's been a long day..." he trailed off.

"It's alright," she said with a smile, her bright pearly whites beaming. He couldn't help but smile too. "I asked if you had a last name?"

He glanced nervously at her then and tried to think. He couldn't use his real one. He would just have to make one up.

"Uh, yeah, it's uh—" *Think, dammit, think!* He looked up at the road then shouted, "West," as he saw a sign indicating the highway they were approaching.

Dallie laughed heartily at him. "Ok!" He laughed too, in relief as well as amusement. "So, what brings you to the little town of Abundance, Texas, Mr. West?"

He should have come up with a good alibi—and a back story,

apparently. He wasn't prepared for these types of questions. This felt like having teeth pulled or something.

"Uh, I just needed a change in scenery," Cole began. She eyed him suspiciously then, a perfectly arched eyebrow rose. "I mean, I'm just kinda passin' through is all."

"Oh, so you're a drifter?" Why did that word keep coming up? Apparently, this family was used to "drifters", so he rolled with it.

"Yeah, I guess. Grandma was a hippie, so I reckon I caught the bug, what can I say?" *What...?* "Life is too fast, sometimes you just gotta slow down and take it all in," he rattled out, weaving a web of lies. "I like to come to small towns and be reminded of the good times when people weren't so mean to one another. Things are simpler out here and bad things don't happen as much as they do in big cities." Perhaps that much were true at least. He continued, "I'm working my way to the west coast. I've been through many states and just enjoy traveling and seeing new places." There, that sounded legit... maybe.

"That's kinda cool, I guess, but don't you get tired of not having a place to call home?" She said the word home as if it were the word heaven, and Cole was taken off guard. He looked over at her, her soft features drowning him in emotion. He would love to tell her how he'd been searching for *home* his whole life and when he'd finally thought he'd found it, everything had been ripped from him in a matter of minutes. He looked down then to tear his eyes away from hers.

"I think when I do find *home*, I'll know it." That was the truest thing he'd said since he'd stumbled upon this place. She gave him a weak smile in return.

They rode for a time as a thick silence permeated the old truck. Cole listened to the sound of the road and the engine that needed repairing and suddenly, the stillness was suffocating.

"So, what about you, Miss Kinsen?" Dallie's eyebrows went up in confusion as if she didn't understand the question. "What's your story?" He swallowed as he realized how much he really wanted to know.

"Well, I live on a ranch," she stated the obvious. "Horses have been my passion since I was four years old, and I'm leaving for college in approximately 75 days!" *College?* Wow, she was older than he'd originally thought.

"Which college?" he asked.

"Texas A & M. It's where my father went to school. When I told him, he was as giddy as a school girl." She smiled, her face lighting up like a Christmas tree.

"Wow, that's great. What are you going to study?"

"Veterinary Medicine," she stated proudly.

"Very cool. That makes sense." He nodded. He couldn't help himself as he asked, "How old are you?" Dead silence followed as she looked over at him, humor in her eyes as she blinked from his bold question.

"Eighteen!" she testified then smirked at him, "And how old are you?"

"Twenty-three," he answered. Again, silence followed as the city limit signs came into view. He shifted in the seat. "You have a baby brother..."

Dallie laughed, a full-hearted throaty laugh he suddenly loved. "I do! Needless to say, he was a *big* surprise."

"He's adorable."

"He's a mess!"

"Any other siblings?"

"Yes, I have a thirteen-year-old sister. Savannah. She's at camp this week."

"That's cool. What kinda camp?"

"Music camp. She's practically a prodigy. She plays the piano *and* the violin."

"Cool."

"Yeah. You'll meet her tonight. Mom's gonna go get her later." She looked over at him then. "Do you have siblings?"

He started to say he had no family at all but decided against it. "I did..." He looked down and swallowed. The burning image of Adam lying in a distressing amount of red blood flashed through his mind and tears immediately came to his eyes.

"I'm so sorry," Dallie stated, turning towards him, and he realized they'd parked. "I didn't mean to—"

"No, please don't be sorry," he interrupted. "You didn't know." They looked at one another for a moment before Dallie broke the silence.

"Ok, well, we're here. Let's get you some clothes."

~

*D*etective Art McElroy sighed as he sat down at his desk. It was never easy to have to go inform the wife of a twenty-three-year-old man that he'd been murdered in cold blood, but that was exactly what he'd had to do this morning. Of course she'd cried and appeared destroyed by the news, but there was something about her demeanor that had caused him pause. He'd been in homicide for thirty odd years now and he knew deceit when he saw it. She knew something that she wasn't saying. Then had come the meeting with the parents who truly *were* destroyed by their son's murder. Now, *that* had really been difficult.

It should have been an open and shut case. The patrol car had pulled up to the shop around 7:03 AM that morning and found the dead body of Adam Burns laying in a fairly large amount of blood with a gunshot wound to his head. The gun wasn't far away, but far enough to indicate that it hadn't been a self-inflicted wound. His business partner's car had been in the lot but no business partner. At first, they'd expected another body, assuming there had been a potential break in gone wrong, but when they hadn't found another body or evidence of a break in, they'd assumed foul play between the two partners. So far, a background check of the partner, a Cole Callahan, didn't look good. The guy had a lot of priors, though most were close to a decade old. McElroy wasn't buying it. The partner didn't seem to have a real strong motive to murder Adam; the wife however had piqued his interest.

So far, they'd sent the gun to forensics and the body to the lab, so McElroy would have more to go on once those were analyzed. Until then, he needed Cole Callahan for questioning. The problem was, they couldn't find him. His house was a dead end. No Cole. There was no next of kin listed, just a foster family, who hadn't really spoken to him in years. Another dead end. The evidence was still coming in, but McElroy had put out a local APB for Cole Callahan and would be speaking to Adam's family tomorrow. For now, he continued to look through his paperwork and keep his eyes peeled. All he could do was wait.

～

*D*allie and Cole shopped in a western wear store, picking out shirts, jeans, undershirts and work boots... even a cowboy hat. Despite that Cole was a Texas native, he'd never worn a cowboy hat in his life, and he felt ridiculous in it, but Dallie had insisted that he had to have one. For the sun and the rain, she'd said. She'd put it all on the company account much to Cole's dismay. She had again insisted and told him to consider it an "advance" if he wanted to but to stop arguing. He'd laughed at that, and they headed back to the ranch within the hour. After their return, Dr. Green met them at the stallion's bay, and Cole changed as the horse was examined. He'd then helped Mike with fence repairs and cleaning out the stalls. As his day wore on, Cole realized just how much of a toll Adam's death had taken out of him... then the hay came. To say it was back-breaking work unloading and stacking hay was an understatement. When the sun finally started to fall behind the barn, Cole was drenched to the bone in sweat and covered in dirt and hay. He couldn't wait to stand in a nice, hot shower. That relief came as Jack escorted him down to the basement.

It was a large layout, just like the roomy upstairs, complete with a workout room, a bar and an open game room that included billiard and air hockey tables along with a large three-piece sectional sofa that sat adjacent to a huge television screen mounted to the wall. Towards the back was a storage room and two bedrooms. Jack chose the bigger one of the two and showed him in.

"This will be your quarters while you stay with us," Jack stated.

The bedroom had a queen bed made up with a red quilt for a comforter, a window, a chair, a closet and an adjoining bathroom.

"Mr. Kinsen, this is great. Thank you!" Cole sighed, longing for a hot shower and the bed.

"You're welcome. And call me Jack." He grinned and turned. "Dinner'll be ready around seven. We'll see ya then," Jack called back as he headed out the door.

Cole took a long, hot, relaxing shower, letting the pressure of the water penetrate his already aching back as he washed the day's work from his weary bones. Once his fingers were pruney, he got out, dried off and laid down on the bed just long enough to cool off. He was afraid that if he closed his eyes he wouldn't wake up for two days as tired as he was. He looked around and admired the room that was his for as long as he wanted it. Again, the generosity of this family touched him. They didn't know him at all—didn't know he was running from the law—and yet, they'd been kinder and more giving to him than anyone else ever had...well, except for Adam. Cole tried not to let the emotions overcome him as he remembered all the times Adam had taken up for him when he didn't deserve it, the times he'd invited him to family gatherings and dinners, how he'd just made room in his life for Cole to join anything and every-thing so that he'd felt included. Adam had truly changed Cole's life; he'd gone to college because of Adam, he'd had a career because of Adam. And now he'd let Adam, the best friend he'd ever had, down because he'd been too afraid to stay and talk to the cops. Now, he would miss getting closure with him, miss giving his final goodbye.

He tried to reason with himself on the matter. There was no way he could've stayed and not been accused of his friend's murder. Cole had a record; those officers would know him from high school. It didn't matter that it'd been seven years since his last crime. He'd touched the gun. His fingerprints were on the body. He'd watched enough detective shows to know how it looked; he would be prime suspect number one. Only now, he was the prime suspect and a fugitive. He shook his head. He would run to Canada after a few weeks of working here. It would be enough time to get a little cash saved up but not long enough for the cops to find him. At least, that's what he told himself. Maybe, eventually, they would find the killer, but Cole wouldn't be safe until they did.

At fifteen to seven, he got up from the bed and dressed in a fresh pair of jeans and a shirt that he and Dallie bought earlier that day then he started up the stairs to the main floor of the house as his stomach growled in hunger. He'd truly worked up an appetite. He wasn't sure he'd ever lifted that much or worked so hard in his life until that day, even at the gym he and Adam frequented. He was drawn to the dining room where laughter came in different pitches, deep to trill-like in variation.

He walked in to see baby Jackson covered in a napkin as Dallie, who'd changed, and another girl, he assumed to be her sister, played peek-a-boo with him. When she pulled the napkin away, the baby just laughed and laughed. It was such a wonderful scene that Cole laughed as well. They all turned to look at him.

Cole was struck by yet another beauty in his midst. What kind of water were they drinking in Abundance? The young teen looked up at him with eyes the color of the Caribbean Sea; it was a unique color that he wasn't sure he'd ever seen before, a perfect mix of green and blue. The rose gold glasses she wore only made them pop even brighter. Her hair was the color of maple syrup, again, a color quite unlike any other he'd ever seen. She had an olive complexion like her father and a mouth like her mother. Give her another few years and she would be stunning.

"Cole, this is my sister, Savannah," Dallie introduced. Savannah just smiled shyly up at him and took a seat on the other side of the table, which had already been set for dinner. He smiled back, said a hello, and cooed to the baby as he took a seat on the other side of Dallie, who then put baby Jackson into his high chair.

"I see you've met my other daughter," Jack stated, ambling in and setting a basket of bread down on the table. He took a seat next to Savannah, wrapping an arm around her. "The Kinsen clan." Jack, like Dallie, had cleaned up too and was wearing fresh clothes.

"Dad, that's *so* lame." Savannah blushed and looked down. He ignored that remark.

"Savannah here is quite the artist," Jack began.

"Dad..." she protested.

"She painted that picture there." He motioned to the painting to the right of them. It was an oil on canvas masterpiece of their house, a horse grazing in the front as the sun set in the background. Cole's brows rose in surprise.

"Wow! You painted that?" Cole asked Savannah, who again just blushed, her face red as a tomato. "It's amazing."

"You ought to hear her play the violin," Dallie insisted. "It'll make you gasp!"

Cole could sense that Savannah wasn't a fan of being the center of attention. Their compliments flattered her, but she didn't like being called out. He just smiled over at her.

"Yes, one with musical and artistic talents and the other that talks to animals, what more could two parents want?" Natalie piped in as she placed a glass bowl full of salad on the table. "I won't be surprised if baby Jax here decides to become an astronaut."

Jackson replied with a squealing, "Num-nums." He motioned for the bread. Dallie pulled the bread basket forward and began tearing pieces of bread up and placing them on the baby's plate.

"Jackson say bread," Dallie instructed.

"Mmm, num-nums," he called as he took the pieces she placed before him.

Cole followed Natalie and Jack into the kitchen and helped

25

Natalie bring glasses into the dining room as Jack carried in a giant steaming hot lasagna. Cole's belly grumbled loudly as they took their seats.

"Looks like someone worked up an appetite," Natalie remarked and they all laughed. The blessing was said and the food was passed around.

Once again, Cole admired this family and their familiarity with one another and the peace that came from them as they all ate together. The respect they showed to each other was remarkable. They built one another up. There were no insults or negative remarks. No arguments. It was a change of pace from what Cole was used to. Adam and his family had always ragged on each other. Jeremy and Adam didn't get along well. Jeremy had always been a little jealous of his younger brother. Mostly the Burns dinner talk was easy conversation, but sometimes cuss words flew and occasionally tempers flared, but this evening's exchange was completely different and in a good way. The love the Kinsens shared was obvious in the way they treated one another. Dallie and Savannah spoke eagerly with their parents and each other about their days and in turn, each person reveled in that knowledge. There was hope for humanity after all. These people had something others didn't. With their big home and thriving ranch, they could've been arrogant and selfish, but there was none of that here.

Cole felt welcome on Kinsen ranch, more so than any other home he'd ever graced the doors of. They made sure to involve him in their light banter and conversations, wanting to know more about him. He tried to stick to the story he'd told Dallie in the truck and not give too much information so that when the time came, he would just be another drifter.

After dinner, everyone helped with the dishes which made clean up a quick task. Afterward, they moved to the living room for some board games, at Dallie's insistence, and he got the chance to flirt with her as they played teams which made the atmosphere even more cordial. Finally, he joined the family in the piano room at

Savannah's insistence to hear her play the concerto she'd worked on all week at camp. There wasn't a dry eye in their little audience when she finished. Cole was completely stunned.

"You wrote that?" he asked. Vanna just nodded bashfully.

"Baby, that was utterly glorious," Natalie murmured and wiped at her eyes as she held a sleeping Jackson. Vanna walked to her then and smiled.

"You and Daddy were my inspiration," Savannah remarked under her breath and took her mother's hand as Natalie stood and kissed her daughter's cheek, pulling her in for a hug. Dallie was next to grab her and finally Jack, who gave her an adoring smile and folded her gently into his big arms.

"Do you know how proud of you we are?" Jack whispered softly into her ear. "I love you, bunny, so much."

"I love you, Daddy." She smiled up at him. He kissed her forehead.

Savannah was the first to head upstairs after bidding them all a good night. Then Natalie handed Jackson over to her husband and hugged Dallie to her.

"Good night, Mom. I love you," Dallie said as she returned her mother's embrace.

"I love you, baby. Good night, Cole." Natalie then moved to him, patting his shoulder. "I hope my husband didn't overwork you today."

"Good night, Mrs. K. Thank you for dinner, it was wonderful." He smiled back at her as she walked away.

"Good night, Daddy," Dallie murmured and moved to her father, kissing his cheek then gave Cole a nod and smiled sweetly. "'Night, Cole."

Cole gulped. "Sleep well." He smiled back and his gaze followed her up the stairs. He turned and was now facing a dark-eyed Jack Kinsen. Cole's smile faded immediately as Jack gave him a menacing grin.

"Good night, Cole." Jack waited, holding the baby, who lay slack in his arms.

"Good night, sir," Cole replied and moved toward the basement door.

"Don't take it personal, son, but I'm locking the door behind you."

"None taken, sir. If I had daughters that looked like yours I would do the exact—"

"I'm glad we understand one another," Jack interrupted and shut the door behind him. Cole heard the lock turn as he headed down to his room and gave a crooked smile.

But with the quiet that soon enveloped him in the basement, the humor of the situation suddenly gave way to the sorrow of what had happened that morning. Graphic memories filled his head—of Adam and the gun that had killed him—and Cole struggled to relax as he got ready for bed, his mind racing around to try and grasp the reality of his best friend's death.

Little did he realize that sleep would finally take him, but only after he'd have a horrible nightmare, painted with the blood he'd seen on the ground of the shop—Adam's blood—and he would awaken drenched in sweat, panting, his stomach twisting with revulsion at the persistent sight of his friend's lifeless corpse.

CHAPTER 2

*J*ack Kinsen put his sixteen-month-old son to bed and tucked him in, turned the baby monitor on and joined his wife in their bedroom. She eyed him playfully as he came to his side of the bed and started to undress. He felt her hungry eyes roving him as he unbuttoned his jeans, and he smiled seductively over at her.

"See something you like, Mrs. Kinsen?" He moved slowly as he unzipped his fly and watched her bite on her plump bottom lip. Just like that, he was fully aroused. He laughed internally. After almost fourteen years of marriage, they still desired one another as much as they ever had, which accounted for the baby in the room beside them. Jack could still remember the surprise and delight they'd all felt when Natalie told them she was pregnant. They'd tried for so long to have just one more after Savannah had turned two years old.

"Oh, I certainly do, my sexy cowboy," Nat drawled in that sweet little southern belle accent that she knew he loved. She turned to lay on her side, propping up on her elbow, facing him, giving him her undivided attention. She was wearing nothing but a thin, tight tank top and bikini panties, but it may as well have been the sexiest negligee ever to him. After three children, they had learned to embrace the opportune moments that they were given and with all three of said children currently sleeping, tonight was one of those moments.

Once he was naked, Jack slid in and grabbed his beautiful wife, kissing her passionately and undressing her as slowly as he had himself, his hands moving over her luscious, curvy body with expertise, hitting all her sweet spots. When they were both breathless, he entered her and loved her with a hunger that he'd never been able to fully quench and when they both climaxed in sweet harmony, time stood still as it always had. They simultaneously cried their release, their hands interlacing as they looked into one another's eyes, their breathing and heart rates in sync.

Jack then lay down beside Natalie, pulling her against him. She sighed as he kissed her forehead. He stroked her soft hair, loving the feel of it on his naked chest as they lay in silence for long moments, slowly returning to earth. Finally, Natalie broke it.

"So, what's with this new kid?" she asked.

"I dunno. Quiet one, isn't he?" Jack replied, kissing her face absent-mindedly.

"He sure is."

"I think he's just a young man down on his luck, but he seems nice enough, huh?"

"Yeah. He sure couldn't keep his eyes off of Dallie."

"I saw that too," Jack practically growled.

"Oh, my love. She's eighteen now, give the girl some credit. Her interest in boys has been very minimal over the years."

"I'm sure that'll all change once she leaves the nest."

Jack was glad so far that his ranch hands had given his daughter wide berth without his interference. He really didn't want to have to go to prison for killing one of them. He had two more children left to raise. The one and only hand she'd ever even been interested in hadn't been there long enough for it to matter, much to Jack's relief. Every time he looked at his beautiful blonde daughter, he saw the cherub-faced little angel she'd been when he'd first met her all those years ago; the sweet, innocent doll who'd always looked at him with giant blue saucer eyes as if he'd hung the moon... To know that she would be leaving them before summer's end—even if it was just to go to college—cut deep into him. Dallie'd not only been his little sidekick all these years, but she'd become an integral part of the ranch and her expertise would be greatly missed. But she would have the time of her life at college, he knew. She would learn so much, have life changing experiences and meet new people...and boys. The thought of some degenerate's slimy paws on her, defiling her, made Jack feel murderous. He was just trying to be a protective father. The world could be a scary place, and he wasn't quite ready for Dallie to be all grown up and out on her own. He was ever grateful Vanna was still so shy and not quite into boys yet. He knew it would just be a matter of time though, God help him... He was so grateful their youngest child was a male.

"Darling, did you lock the basement door?" Natalie asked as her hand inched lower down Jack's torso and his breath took.

"What do *you* think, wifey?" he asked, arching his eyebrow at her.

Nat smiled up at him and pulled his face back to hers, kissing him. "I think that perhaps my father should have done the same thing to *your* door."

"Oh, I don't think you would've liked that." He teased and nipped at her bottom lip.

"No?" she asked and giggled.

He pulled her atop him then and began loving her beautiful breasts with his hands and mouth until she was practically putty in his big hands. She took his hard sex then and guided herself down over him, impaling herself slowly. When he was fully engulfed inside her, and he could catch his breath, he laughed on a groan.

"You know it wouldn't have made a difference," he stated, matter-of-factly. She looked down at him erotically as his hands gripped her hips. "I would have torn that door off its hinges to get to you, woman."

31

With that, she began rocking his world all over again.

~

*D*allas Kinsen tried to sleep that night, but couldn't stop herself from thinking about the new ranch hand, Cole West. He was tall, muscular and handsome. He was also quiet. He hadn't given too much of himself away and whether that was because he had something to hide or because he just didn't have much to say, she wasn't sure. What she *was* sure of was that he was attractive, and he made her tingly. That touch in the barn had felt like an electrical current running straight through her when she'd placed her hand beneath his to help brush down the stallion.

Cole, to her, looked a bit like a younger version of her father. His eyes and hair were darker, but there was something about him that indeed resembled Jack Kinsen. Of course they had different cheek-bones and lips, and her father was twenty years older than Cole, but the likeness was there all the same. He was even built somewhat like her father, with a broad chest and shoulders. Perhaps Dallie was just telling herself that because she wanted to find someone that loved her like her father loved her mother, and she had yet to feel that with anyone. Mostly, it was because she hadn't had the time to seek love out, the other reason was that she was afraid she might never find what she sought. She'd always been so busy with school and equestrian jumping competitions and dressage and the ranch. There had never been time for anything else, but now that she was getting older and going to college, she was starting to want it more.

Dallas had looked up to Jack Kinsen since she was four years old. He'd been her protector, her hero and her Superman, and she'd fallen in love with him instantly. He'd made her his daughter and loved her like she was his own child. He loved her mother, built them a home, a business, and made them a family. He'd been her first best friend and he'd helped develop her love of horses and the gift she had into something that she could further her life and future with. He'd been there for every major event in her life, from competitions to rehearsals, ceremonies to graduation; he'd always been there to guide and support her. She would never settle for a man who wasn't all that her father had been to her and more. Whoever she chose to love had very big shoes to fill.

Dallie was looking forward to college, but she also felt guilty leaving the ranch and her family. The ranch had always been such a major part of her life, and she didn't really want to leave it... even if it were to pursue a degree for her to be able to treat and care for the animals she'd always loved. Dallie, her mother and father had all talked about it when she'd been deciding where to go to school, but she knew her dad was going to miss her greatly. She'd always been such a big help to him and her Uncle Nate. Her parents reminded her that she would be back for holidays and summers, but she knew things would never be the same once she left. She was embarking on a wonderful journey, she knew, but it also meant leaving behind something she loved so much that it had become a part of her, and it had been a tough decision to make. Her parents had encouraged her to try new paths, that she might love becoming a vet just as much as life on the ranch, so she'd made her decision. She knew her parents were proud, but she'd also seen the slight disappointment on her father's face and it had upset her to no end. Dallie would always be her Daddy's little girl, no matter how old she got.

She fell asleep dreaming of college and Cole and her father, but awoke feeling more empowered than she had the night before. She still had time at the ranch, and she was going to enjoy every minute she could. After her alarm went off, she showered and dressed and came down the stairs to the usual ruckus in the kitchen. It was still dark outside and her father stood next to the coffee pot talking to her mother. Dallie threw herself into his large frame, stretching her arms as far around his big chest as they would go and tucked her head into his shoulder. He smelled of fabric softener and leather.

"I love you, Daddy," she murmured and felt his sudden intake of breath as his arms immediately came around her. She could almost feel him smile as his deep voice reverberated in her ear.

"Well, good mornin' to me!" He laughed as she looked up at him. "Any particular reason I should know of?" She just beamed and saw him melt as he kissed her forehead.

Dallie then released him and walked over to the fridge to get some juice. She was saving coffee for those finals cram nights in college. She poured herself a glass of OJ and walked over to her mother, who stirred at some eggs in a pan with Dallie's little brother on her hip. Dallie grabbed him as he called out, "Da-wee." She spun him around then kissed her mother's cheek and wished her a good morning. Her mom just smiled at her, her blue eyes tearful.

Her mother had always been sensitive, and she got especially emotional when it came to Dallie and her father. Dallie hadn't understood exactly why until just a few years ago when her mother had taken her aside and had a very long and painful conversation with her regarding Dallie's biological father, Troy Cameron. Dallie didn't remember him at all, so the discussion had been more painful for her mother than it had been for her. Her mom had wanted to come clean, so that if the time ever came that she was confronted by it she would know all the facts, not what her parents had told her to protect her from the truth. Her mom informed her of Troy's crimes, what he'd done to Dallie, his escape from prison and how her Uncle Nate had killed him after he'd tried to murder her mother. Dallie had been both shocked and horrified by what had transpired.

She assumed that time and an abundance of good memories had made her forget all those awful things in her past, which she was eternally grateful for. She'd been aware that Jack had adopted her when she was five after marrying her mother. Her biological grandmother, her Nana, and grandfather had come back into her life when she was six, and her mother had reminded her then that she wasn't Jack's biological daughter just to clear up any confusion that might have caused. Dallie had never known anyone but Jack as her dad though. As far as she was concerned, he *was* her father, he's who she called her father and that would never change no matter what biology said.

Dallie took Jackson into the living room then as her dad continued the conversation he'd been having with her mom before Dallie'd interrupted. She turned on little Jax's favorite cartoon and sat him down on the rug in front of the TV, entertaining him with a couple trucks as her mother got breakfast ready. When she looked up, Cole stood at the basement door. She froze. He looked renewed with a good night's sleep and a shave. He was dressed in one of the new short-sleeved checkered button-down shirts they'd purchased yesterday, jeans and brand new cowboy boots. He gave her a crooked grin and she returned it, feeling her heart do a little flip flop as she did so.

"Good mornin'," he stated, yawning as he approached then grabbed at his back and winced.

"Mornin'," Dallie replied. "Sore?" She asked, knowingly.

He nodded, coming to sit down gingerly on the floor with her and Jackson and picked up a couple trucks from the floor, making noises with them.

"Voom, voom," Jackson mocked, his curly blonde locks bouncing as he crashed the cars together.

Dallie gasped. "Mom, Dad! Jax just learned a new word."

Her dad poked his head in then. "Hopefully it wasn't the F-word."

"Dad," Dallie scolded, and her father laughed as he greeted Cole. "Did you sleep alright down there?" he asked.

"I did, sir, thank you."

"Please don't call me sir, Cole. You make me feel old." Her dad sighed in feigned exasperation. "Or like we're in the army."

"Yes, sir," Cole stated then grimaced. They laughed.

"Coffee?" her dad asked.

"Please?" Cole called back.

"Breakfast is ready, you guys!" Dallie's mom called from the kitchen. Dallie scooped up the baby, and Cole followed as they joined her parents in the kitchen at the breakfast table. Dallie sat

Jackson in his high chair as her dad placed a hot mug of coffee in front of Cole, along with a few painkillers, and patted Cole's back roughly. Cole, in turn, doctored his coffee and popped the pills as her folks brought platters of food to the table. It was a large and plentiful meal of sausage, bacon, biscuits, eggs, gravy and grits. It wasn't their usual breakfast, but her mom always overdid it when they had new guests.

"My goodness, Mrs. K. This is a *feast*," Cole responded at the wealth of food before him.

"A feast fit for a king," her mom replied back and caught her dad's eye. He dragged her into his lap for a smooch.

"You guys!" Dallie scolded. "We have company!" Dallie's eyes widened at them as they looked up, blushing like two teenagers caught necking at the drive-in. "You'll have to excuse them, Cole, they're still newly-weds...thirteen years *after* the fact!" Dallie rolled her eyes in humor.

"Oh, it's totally cool. I honestly don't mind." They all looked at him, frowning. "I mean...it's good to see a couple still in love after that long, you know? I don't know many happily married couples nowadays," he murmured. It was true, but Dallie could tick off a few herself; her mom and dad, Uncle Nate and Aunt Jordan, Luther and Bella...and of course her Grandma and Paw-Paw.

Her father's lips sought out her mother's again, much to Dallie's consternation, before he finally pulled her mother upright and let her sit at the table to join them. Once she was sat, her dad looked around.

"Who wants to say grace?" Her father's eyes fell on Cole. "Cole, would you bless the food?"

Dallie gave her dad a withered look and watched as Cole blushed ten shades of red before responding, "Uh, sure, of course, uh... Our heavenly father..." They all suddenly held hands, bowing their heads, and Cole followed suit. "We want to thank thee for this food before us... uh, bless it and let it nourish us, oh Lord on this day that you have given us... We ask this all in Jesus name, Amen."

"Amen," they all said in unison.

"Cole, that was beautiful," Dallie's mom replied, smiling over at him.

Her dad began passing around the food until they all had dished out a portion of it then they dug in. Jackson squealed, excited to eat.

Suddenly, Cole stopped as if he was remembering something important. "Where's Savannah?"

They all laughed. It was Dallie who was the first to respond. "Oh, Miss Priss doesn't rise before ten in the morning," Dallie stated, stuffing some grits into her mouth.

"Now, now, my darlin', the little prodigy needs to rest her massive brain. It's been writing symphonies through the night," her father retorted, and Dallie belted out a big laugh.

She didn't doubt that was true. They'd all known Savannah was a force to be reckoned with when at the mere age of eight months she was talking, ten months she was walking and by two years old she was playing the piano. She'd written her first song at the age of six and her first concerto by age ten. She began to play the violin at age five and painted her first full landscape when she was seven. She had also gotten into ballet. She was truly an amazing artist and musician with the sky as her limit. She was in the gifted program at middle school and already taking honors classes with ease. She would probably start college within the next two to three years. She might even graduate college before Dallie did.

"Now, don't let her fool you. Dallie's quite the wonder herself," Dallie's mother began, looking over at Cole.

"Mom!" Dallie scolded.

"You are," her dad agreed then looked over to Cole. "Well, you saw a little dose of it yesterday when she rescued you from that stallion." Cole looked over to Dallie, his eyes twinkling. She gulped.

"Her Uncle Nate has always called her the Dr. Dolittle of horses. She's been helping out since she was four years old," her mother insisted, feeding a helping of biscuits and gravy to her little brother.

"Wow! Four?" Cole asked, eyes wide. Dallie blushed.

"It's true," her dad confirmed. "I've seen some unexplainable things in my time, but this girl right here takes the cake when it comes to horses. There's not a one she can't tame. People bring their horses here from all over the country so that Miss Dallas Kinsen can help them. She gets all the tough cases, too! Isn't that right, darlin'? I don't know what I would've done without ya, sweet pea." He smiled lovingly over at her then added, "And, no surprise, but she's musically inclined too. She and her mother both have the voices of angels."

"She got a full ride to Texas A & M thanks to her *own* big brain," her mom exclaimed.

"That's right! Full academic scholarship. We couldn't be prouder." Her dad's eyebrows went up. "Thanks for giving us the opportunity to brag, love." He knew she hadn't given him any such thing.

"You're welcome, Dad," Dallie retorted with a grateful smile and blushed to her toes. "Now can we take the spotlight off of me for a minute? Jackson here learned a new word! Tell them, Jax."

"That's right. Jackson tell Mommy your new word?" Her mother focused on the baby, cooing to him. "What does a truck say?" Jackson looked around at them, amused that he was the center of attention for the time being. He raised his arms and squealed, his chubby cheeks lifting as his little teeth showed in a grin. "Come on, what does it say?"

"Voom voom," he cried in a deep voice. His cackle was too adorable, and they all laughed along with him. Her mother leaned down to kiss his cheek and he squealed again.

Jackson had come along at the most surprising time. It had shocked them all when her mother announced her pregnancy one night to them after dinner. She and Savannah couldn't hide their excitement. They'd both known how much their mother had wanted another baby and as soon as he was born, he'd become the apple of all their eyes. Although, having a little one around was exhausting, she knew, it was also rewarding and amazing to be able to have a sweet little baby to love. Savannah had been a little jealous at first, and Dallie remembered how difficult it had been to share her parents when her sister was born, but Savannah had adjusted easily enough after Jackson's birth. Dallie couldn't believe that he was going on two years old already. Man, how time truly flied.

They finished their breakfast just as the sun was starting to peek over the trees. Her dad stood, rubbed his belly and leaned down to kiss her mom as he always did before he headed out to start the day.

"Da-da," Jackson spoke up as her mother gave him his last bite of grits and grunted, reaching up for his father. "Horsey."

"Aww, Daddy. He wants you to take him riding!" Dallie cried and smiled over at the baby.

Her dad lit up. "You wanna go riding with Daddy this morning?" He moved over to Jackson, who pumped his arms up and down in delight.

"Wow." Cole laughed. "He's *all* excited."

"Oh, he loves anything where he can go 'fas' as he says," Dallie replied.

"Yeah, he's an adrenaline junkie already," her dad piped in and scooped the little toddler up in his arms.

"Fas, fas," Jackson squealed, his little blonde curls bouncing as he jumped up and down in his father's arm.

"Alright, but he needs to be changed first," her mom declared, and her father took him upstairs.

Dallie, Cole and her mom all cleared the table and took care of the dishes, and once her father came back down with Jackson dressed in his cowboy attire, they set off to the barn.

"Nice!" Cole stated and looked over to Jackson, who was tucked into his dad's arm like a football.

"He got his first cowboy hat before he was ever even born," Dallie's mom replied, looking at little Jax, who was decked out in a frill vest and baby cowboy boots. "You can probably guess what he wore for his first Halloween." She laughed.

"Cutest baby cowboy ever," Dallie cooed as she bent to kiss her little brother's chubby cheek. He cried in delight.

Jackson saw the horses and began bouncing up and down. "Horsey," he cried.

Her dad brought the toddler over to his own thoroughbred gelding, Midnight, and the baby began to laugh as her father placed his little hand on the horse's muzzle.

Dallie waved to Mike, Craig and Teddy, but when Todd waved, she ignored him. Todd annoyed her to no end. He had a crush on her, or so she'd surmised. He was constantly trying to get her attention, show her some "amazing" feat he had done or impress her in some sort of way. It was always, "Hey, Dallie, look at this," "Hey, Dallie, watch this," "Hey, Dallie, look what I can do." She didn't know why it bothered her so much, but it just did. She guessed it could always be worse. She'd had a fair share of ranch hands try and hit on her here and there when her dad wasn't around; it was mostly some silly pick up line or a bit of flirting, nothing that bordered on harassment—they were all too afraid of her father for that—so at least Todd wasn't *that* bad. Her mom had gotten it much worse, she'd told her one day when Dallie was complaining, and proceeded to tell her about a hand on her grandfather's ranch, now her Uncle Nate's, who was such a male chauvinist to her mother that her dad had punched him one night. That same hand had later been tried and convicted for attempted murder and assault with a deadly weapon. Her mother had never told Dallie the full story of what had happened, but she knew it involved Bella, the wife of her dad's best friend, Luther.

Todd was a sweet guy and he had a baby face. He'd never insulted Dallie or said anything inappropriate like her mother's pursuer had, but he just seemed so dang immature. She wanted someone she could have a *real* conversation with, share secrets with, laugh with… like her mom and dad did. They'd always just been so in tune with one another, and that's what Dallie wanted for herself.

She watched her parents lovingly look at one another as the baby delighted in the horse. At one time, she'd been a young teen, and their displays of affection had grossed her out, but now, as a growing woman, it made her breath catch. She couldn't help but smile up at them. Cole was right, it was good that they were still so in love after all this time. She volunteered to go saddle up her dad's horse for him, but he declined the offer.

"No, that's alright, thanks hon. I'll do it! Why don't you go for your usual morning ride and take Cole here with ya? Show him how to ride," her dad recommended. They all looked to Cole then who blushed. "You alright with that, son?" her dad asked, seeming slightly amused.

"Uh, of course, sir. I mean Mr... I mean, Jack," Cole stammered. Dallie laughed.

"It's like riding a bicycle," her mom reassured him. "You'll get the hang of it in no time." Her mom patted Cole's shoulder as they all moved toward the barn then in unison, baby Jackson reaching back towards Midnight, who whinnied.

"All right, son, all right! We're gonna ride, just hold your horses," her dad stated to her little brother, who'd started crying as they entered the barn simply because he couldn't see Midnight anymore. Her mom laughed at his pun.

"Jeez, Dad." Dallie chuckled as she approached Ameera's stall and kissed the black beauty's nose. "Your son is already obsessed."

"Takes after his sister if you ask me," her dad muttered as he handed Jackson to her mom and walked over to the gate, clucking to Midnight, who'd already started to approach. He pulled the gate open then led the stallion into the center aisle of the barn.

Dallie laughed and said, "Thank goodness for that."

Mike approached. "We takin' a family ride this morning?"

"Sure, why not?" her mom answered.

"Sweet!" Her father replied a bit too enthusiastically as Dallie opened the Dutch door and entered Ameera's stall, patting her neck.

"Mom, you *know* why he wants you to go riding with him?" Dallie gave her mother a knowing look through the barred window. Her mother feigned ignorance as Dallie motioned for Cole to come into the stall with her. She grabbed the saddle blanket off the side of the stall and threw it over the mare's back then looked over to her parents, who were standing really close to one another, her dad's hand snaking up her mother's arm. "God, you guys should really get a room!"

"A blanket in a field will do *just* fine, I'll have you know," her father muttered, pulling her mom up hard against him, baby Jackson stuck in the midst of their heated passion. Dallie snorted in exasperation, rolled her eyes, and turned toward Cole, shaking her head. He, in turn, blushed brightly.

"Yeah, well. What'll you do with the baby?" Dallie retorted smartly, grabbing for the saddle.

"That's what they made saddle bags for, Dallas," her mom called back.

"Mom!" Dallie's mouth fell open in shock, and everyone was laughing by then, even Cole. Dallie returned to her task, ignoring her overzealous parents as she prepped the horse. After a few moments of cinching the belt, centering the saddle and tightening it down, the color in her cheeks returned to normal and she looked up at Cole. "So, saddle blanket, then saddle... attach the breast collar to the saddle, like so." She showed him where the straps went and tightened the saddle again. "Now, I'm gonna put on her bridle, placing the bit in her mouth." Cole smiled over at her, still amused by her parents' conversation. She just shook her head and tried to focus on getting Ameera ready to ride. "Pay attention because you're tacking up your own horse," she informed him. His eyes went wide. She laughed.

Once she was finished, she led Ameera out of the stall and tied her to a hitching post in front of it. She then moved to Blaze's stall.

She smiled at the beautiful thoroughbred stud she'd had since he was six months old. He was a lovely chestnut color with a white diamond on his forehead.

"Hey, buddy," she cooed to him as she gave the stallion some love then entered his stall. Cole following. "He's my jumping horse," she told him. He seemed confused by that statement. "I won blue ribbons with him in jumping competitions, well Ameera too, but he was trained specifically for that purpose."

"So, does that mean he's gonna jump while I'm riding him?" Cole asked nervously.

Dallie laughed, taking his saddle blanket from the stall and sliding it over the horse's back. "No, not if you don't ask him to." She watched as Cole turned robotically to grab the saddle on the other side of the stall.

"Well, what if I accidentally 'ask' him to?" Cole's green eyes looked semi-panicked as he looked over at her and gulped. Dallie smiled and reassured him as he placed the saddle on Blaze and began cinching and adjusting it.

"Don't worry. It's been a while for him. Besides, you're not his usual rider for that. I wouldn't put you on a horse that would hurt you." She came over beside him and helped him with the saddle belt, making sure it was tight enough and cinched properly. Their fingers touched as they both grabbed for the bridle, and they pulled back in unison, apologizing. They stood frozen for a moment, looking at one another, mere inches separating them. She could almost feel his breath on her face and she gulped, all too aware of the energy sparking between them.

"I trust you," he said barely above a whisper and his eyes softened. She took in the features of his face; assessing the hard line of his jaw, the arch of his eyebrows, the subtle flecks of brown in his green irises.

"Goodness gracious, you almost done over there? I can saddle two horses in the time it takes y'all to saddle one," her dad scoffed.

Dallie blew and turned to grab the bridle then, handing it over to Cole.

"Jeez oh Pete, you're impatient," she called back. She had to help adjust the bridle and place the bit in Blaze's mouth as the stud protested and stepped back. "Besides, I thought you and Mom were going off to play hide the—"

"Dallas Noel!" her mom scolded. Dallie and Cole snickered

beneath their breath and finally, completing their task, stepped out with Blaze in tow.

"Ta-da!" Dallie rose her arms in triumph then gave an exasperated sigh as she saw her mom and dad in their saddles, ready to ride. "Now y'all are just showing off! Give me a little credit here. I got a rookie," she retorted as she brought Blaze forward.

"Da-wee," Jackson called from their father's lap, clapping his little hands together. "Wide."

Dallie gave instructions as she brought Cole to Blaze's side and showed him how to mount the horse using the mane, saddle horn and stirrup. He stumbled a couple times, especially when Blaze decided to move, but he finally got up on the horse. She sighed in relief and handed him the reins then she quickly and gracefully mounted her mare with ease.

"Alright, we're ready, Dad. Lead the way." She looked to her dad. He faked a yawn, then laughed and turned his horse out of the barn. She looked over to Cole, who looked unsteady and like he might puke. "Loosen up on the reins. You don't need a death grip," Dallie instructed. She laughed and showed him how to tap the horse's flanks in order to go forward. "Good, now you go ahead of me. The horse will follow Amadeus, Mom's horse. Just give him a little tap." Cole looked unsure as he did as he'd been instructed. When the horse moved, he jolted. "Just relax. He'll be able to sense your tension. Ease your shoulders and sit up straight." He did so as she said, "Good job."

They headed out at a walk through the gate into the back pasture, taking in the early morning sounds and smells. This was Dallie's favorite part of the day—her morning ride on her fourteen-year-old mare, Ameera. She was a beautiful Arabian, gracefully elegant, and Dallie felt like she was flying when she rode her. Ameera was the horse she'd trained to perform dressage. They were quite a sight in the arena as her black beauty appeared to dance in sequences of perfectly timed steps and prances. And loyal Blaze... oh, how he loved to jump. She was going to miss both her horses, miss these mornings. Dallie felt hot tears spring to her eyes.

They headed east towards the creek, bringing their horses side by side, and Dallie laughed as she heard her brother say, "Fas, fas." She looked over to Cole, who still looked so nervous; he was barely ready for a jog, let alone a lope and definitely not a gallop. She would have to ease him in. She tipped her hat over at her father, signaling him on without embarrassing their rookie. He got the hint.

"Let's race Mommy to the trees," her dad told Jackson, who squealed in glee. He tightened his grip on the little tyke and off they went, dust flying. The sound of heavy hooves echoed in the pasture.

Her mom laughed knowingly as she followed suit, calling out, "Heeyah." Dallie knew who was winning that one!

"Oh my," Cole gazed nervously at them as he took in the speed of their horses in a full gallop.

"I got five bucks says Amadeus wins." Dallie said to Cole and laughed. Her father's gelding, Midnight, was going on nineteen years old. Her mom's horse was barely six.

"Amadeus, huh? Strange name for a horse...I guess." Cole shrugged and looked thoughtfully over at her.

"Yeah, Savannah named him; he's her horse. It's Mozart's middle name," Dallie said, shaking her head.

"Ah." Cole nodded in understanding. Dallie unconsciously signaled Ameera into a trot, Cole's horse followed and he gripped the reigns with all his might.

"My bad," she apologized. "Ameera doesn't really *do* slow. Follow his gait, it's called posting. See how I rise up and down with my horse, jumping when she jumps, now you do the same." Cole followed suit. "Good, good," she called out. "See, you got this. When you're ready, we'll do a canter and finally a gallop. Don't worry," she retorted when he looked over at her with wide eyes. "We won't have them run until you're comfortable with the other gaits."

"Can we just stay like this for a while?" he asked, and she nodded, smiling. Cole seemed to relax some and tried to get himself in sync with the horse, lifting himself up and sitting down in the saddle as she'd instructed with every other beat and watching her for instruction. Soon, they could no longer see the other two horses. "Your dad's actually a pretty funny dude." Cole laughed.

"You didn't think he was?" she asked, a little surprised by his comment.

"Well, he wasn't cracking too many jokes yesterday... He's a bit intimidating. I mean, he's a big guy, you know?"

Dallie shrugged. Yeah, she could see where her dad could seem intimidating. He stood at over six feet two inches, was big chested and broad shouldered and probably weighed a good two hundred and forty pounds...and he *could* look menacing when he wasn't happy.

"He locked me in the basement." Cole frowned.

"Yeah, he's somewhat overprotective." Dallie looked over at him, grimacing apologetically.

"I can see why," Cole retorted, looking her over and blushing. "I'm sure I'm not the first person to tell you that you're beautiful, Dallas."

Dallie blushed too. No, he wasn't the first person to tell her that. Her mom and dad told her all the time, her Uncle Nate and Aunt Jordan, her Grandma and Paw-Paw...and her Nana too. Of course she'd had guys flirt and banter with her before, but Cole—being an older and quite attractive man himself—telling her that she was beautiful...well it made her feel incredibly confident, and she smiled big up at him.

"I mean it!" he stated, matter-of-factly. "And you're not just beautiful on the outside, you are on the inside too. All of you are," he stammered, and she saw what looked like sadness in his eyes as he looked ahead. "Your folks are—"

"Ridiculous! I know. They're worse than some fellow teenagers I know." Dallie giggled.

"No, that wasn't what I was gonna say," he stated, still serious then gave a soft chuckle, "Well, yeah... kind of. But it's great, really!

They love each other very much. It's so obvious. I've never seen quite what they have..." he trailed off.

"I guess I should feel lucky," Dallie spoke, feeling humbled in that moment. She truly had been lucky to have two amazing parents like she did.

"Yeah, you should. Trust a kid who grew up in foster care." He suddenly stopped talking and looked over at her, a panicked look on his face. She frowned.

"You did? But what about your hippie grandmother?" Dallie asked, feeling both sadness and confusion as she gazed into his pained eyes. He was silent as he looked ahead once again, gazing into the grove of trees they were headed toward.

Finally, he spoke quietly, distantly, as if he were talking to himself.

"I actually never even met her. My mother abandoned me when I was just three years old. All I had was my favorite book, a dirty blanket and two labeled photographs; one was of my mother, the other of my grandmother- taken when she was just a teenager." Dallie slowed their horses to a walk then and listened as Cole opened up to her. "I always imagined she was this wild, free spirit who rambled from town to town. I don't know if she's still alive honestly, but I carried this image with me over the years. I guess to inspire me or encourage me—I'm not really sure—but it made being alone a lot easier to think about her out somewhere in the world, just loving life, living this hippie, carefree lifestyle I'd concocted in my head."

Dallie swallowed the large lump that had grown in her throat. She'd never been truly alone, so there was no way for her to understand what it felt like. She'd always been surrounded by a loving family who adored her. She couldn't imagine being abandoned, on her own with no one to talk to, share life with, or love.

She looked over at him. His green eyes had tears in them, and it tore at her heart strings. She reached out her hand to him, an instinctive gesture. He looked down at it then softly took it in his own and gently squeezed. His gaze held hers as they walked for long moments just looking at one another. She could feel the loneliness and anguish emanating from him as she stared into the windows of his battered soul, his green eyes deep pits of longing. It took her breath. This young man, who'd never had familial love, was seeking it so badly by bouncing from place to place in the hopes of filling a void so deep that he'd probably never let anyone close enough to see it.

The horses stopped automatically, and Dallie immediately reacted. She tore her eyes from him as the shade of the trees enveloped them. She looked up to see her father watching them as if they'd sorely misbehaved; Arms crossed over his chest, an eyebrow arched and a scowl on his face, his eyes dropping to their interlocked hands. She released Cole's hand quickly and pulled her own back to her horse's reins.

"Well, we mastered the jog," she nervously stated to her folks, trying to ignore her father's prying eyes.

"Thank God," her father noted sarcastically, looking at his wrist to the watch that wasn't there. Her mom wrapped an arm around his waist then and kissed his shoulder.

"Jack…" Her mom looked up at her dad, giving him "the look". He took it ruefully and wrapped his arm around her as he looked to Dallie and smiled.

"I'm kidding!" he stated, but she knew that wasn't entirely true. He hadn't liked the hand-holding that had taken place, and she knew beyond the shadow of a doubt he'd be discussing that with her later. *Great!* Dallie thought. *I'm legally an adult but can't do adult things.* Well, good! They needed to have this talk anyway… It'd been a long time coming.

"Cole, how do you feel on the horse?" her mom piped in, sensing the tension between Dallie and her father.

"Well, my butt hurts," Cole replied. They all laughed. "But I feel a little more comfortable than I first did for sure."

"Good! You should ride daily. It's good for the horses, and it'll get you used to being around them and vice-versa," her mom insisted. Her dad frowned slightly as he looked down at her mom as if she'd just recommended something preposterous. Her mom ignored him, smiling back up at Cole. "You can ride with Dallie in the mornings." Her dad's frown deepened as he continued to stare at her mother. He ran the hand he wasn't holding her with down his face, looking like he wanted to yell. When he looked back up, he had a forced smile on his face.

"Absolutely! Great idea!" Her father turned then to grab Jackson, who was toddling around in front of them, throwing around old leaves from last fall like they were confetti and giggling, oblivious to them all. "Alright, buddy, let's get back. Daddy has work to do."

Her mom gave her a hard grin as she got back up on her horse and Dallie sighed. All she'd done was hold a boy's hand in comfort and that was only the second hand she'd ever held. Dallie had practically always been a perfect child; she was still a virgin at least.

Her father passed the baby over to her mom while he mounted Midnight then got him back once he was settled atop the horse's back. They all rode in silence back towards the barn until Dallie got a wild hair.

"Race ya, Dad!" she hollered and looked over to him. He cocked his eyebrow in challenge and took off. She laughed and chased him, loving the breeze on her face as she and Ameera became one flying missile across the grassy pasture. She could hear little Jackson squealing in delight. Dallie laughed as she took the hill with great ease and her father's horse tuckered out. She whooped and hollered as she came towards the gate. "I won."

She wasn't sure, but she thought she heard her dad mumble, "Yeah, we'll see about that."

CHAPTER 3

"*D*allie, my office. Now!" Jack muttered to Dallie and passed his son to Natalie as they both dismounted. Dallie gave him a furrowed brow, but he walked away before he blew his fuse. He asked Mike to tend to the horses as he headed into his office. He tried to calm himself as he sat and waited for Dallie to join him. She eyed him wearily as she shut the door behind her. He watched her as she sat in the leather seat adjacent to him, propping his elbows on his desk and leaning his chin down on his knuckles.

"What, Daddy?" she asked innocently as his gaze had the intended effect.

"You tell *me*." He felt his face flood with heat.

"I don't know."

"Yes, you do! You were holding his hand," he stated, accusingly.

"Yeah, so?" She shrugged.

"Dallie," he huffed and rested his forehead on his interlaced hands for a moment before looking back up. "I know that you think your mother and I are overbearing at times and try too hard to keep you safe, but honey…" She needed to know the truth. "You have to know that young men will say *anything*—"

"It wasn't a *line*, Daddy," she said exasperated.

Jack sighed heavily. "That's what you *want* to believe," he stated, matter-of-factly, looking into her sullen face. "Dallas, I've seen the way that boy looks at you. You know, I was young once too, remember? I haven't always been a husband and a father. I understand all too well." He sighed again as she looked away. "Dallie, honey, look at me." She did as he asked. "You have to understand that when I look at you, I still see that innocent little four-year-old in the car seat, it doesn't matter what age you are. You will *always* be my little girl. I just want to keep you and your sister safe. It's my job to protect you, even if you don't like my methods. One day you'll understand why your mother and I have gone to great lengths to safeguard you."

"I *know* why," she started, looking like she might cry.

"Then please try and understand, angel. I love you girls *so* very much," he said and reached his hands out to her then, and she took them. "The thoughts of someone hurting you again," he growled and shook his head in anguish. "After knowing what that animal did to you, to those other two girls, and almost losing your mother because of him..." He sighed and pulled his shaking hands away, the emotions too much for him. He squared his jaw and looked at her with intensity. "I swore to protect you, Dallas Noel, and I don't intend to break that promise, no matter what."

~

*D*allie sulked through most of the day. She tried to stay busy helping Craig with one of the new horses that had been brought in that day. Mike had Cole cleaning stalls, and in the corral doing basic commands with Ladybird, one of the older boarded horses. Teddy and Todd worked on training with another client of her father's. Her dad stayed down in his office most the day on the phone, in meetings and overall kept his distance, much to her relief.

Dallie took a break around lunch time and went into town. She didn't want to see her dad and truthfully, Cole either. She was embarrassed. She had been caught doing something that should have been innocent, but her father had read too much into it. She knew why he was so protective. When Dallie was just three years old, her mother had caught her biological father, Troy Cameron, molesting her. He'd also murdered two people in very vicious ways, and her mother had been completely blindsided by all of it. Her mother's faith in mankind had been shattered, and it had taken her a long time to trust anyone else again; to trust Dallie's dad, Jack.

Her mother hadn't told her any of this until she was around fifteen, when she'd started talking about boys and flirting with one of the ranch hands. After her mom had told her everything that had happened, Dallie understood why her parents had forced her and her sister to learn karate and self-defense and why her father didn't allow the ranch hands to be alone with her. Dallie knew he was only trying to keep her safe, as any good father would.

Dallie pulled into a local drive-thru and ordered some sloppy fast food she didn't need, but she didn't care. She was irritated and wanted to indulge. She headed out to the park to sit by the river and be alone with her thoughts.

She wasn't mad at her dad—not really—she realized, as she sat there watching the ducks and water stream by. She loved him immensely, had always worshipped the ground he walked on, and she was glad he loved her enough to protect her so much from people he thought might hurt her. But he had to know that there would be no way he could continue to protect her when she went away to college. There would be a ton of males there and parties and things she hadn't really been exposed to because her parents had given her a strict curfew and were careful of the people she hung out with. She would probably enjoy some wild nights and kisses and who knew what else. She would be smart and keep her head, but truly she knew college was the place where a lot of people started to live a little, experiment and break out of their shells.

What hurt Dallie was that she felt her dad didn't trust her enough to know she wasn't quite as naïve as he thought. She'd gone her entire high school career without a boyfriend because all the boys were afraid of her dad. She knew that Cole was a drifter. She wasn't going to let herself believe for an instant that he would stick around just for her, and besides, she would be gone in two months, so what did it matter if they indeed happened to have a little fling. He was a handsome, kind young man and she liked him...and maybe he was exactly what she needed before college. Like a warmup before a big competition.

Dallie headed back to the ranch with a new mindset. She was all grown up now. If she wanted to hold someone's hand, she could, and if her father didn't like it, well tough!

~

"*J*ack, your daughter is eighteen years old...she's never even had a boyfriend." Natalie tried to reason with her husband that night when they lay in bed as he pulled her into his arms. He'd been trying to avoid this conversation all day, she knew.

"Well, that doesn't mean she needs one now," Jack argued as he looked down at her. "Come on Nat, that kid is a damn vagrant! We don't know anything about him."

"My love," she said and took his hand, "it was an innocent little—"

"Ha!" He exclaimed and lay on his back, sighing. "We *both* know exactly where those *innocent* little touches lead." He turned back over, facing her. "Baby, I don't like how he looks at her. I know that look *all* too well." He cupped her face and stroked her jaw with his thumb.

"Jack, darling, you've done your job as her father. Now we need to loosen the reins a little and let our daughter make her own mistakes." There, she'd told him the hard truth. "If you aren't careful, you're going to make her rebel against you, like I did with my father," Natalie warned, pulling his face to hers for a kiss. "Dallie deserves to live too. She's passionate like the two of us, and we've held her back because we're afraid. Who are we to decide when she gets to love and who she gets to love?"

"Lust, you mean," he grumbled.

"Did you *not* lust after me, Jackson Edward Kinsen?" she asked, raising her eyebrows.

"It was love from the *very* beginning and you know it," he clarified. Her eyebrows went up. His did too. They laughed. "Fine! She can hold his damn hand...I guess...but if he breaks her heart, I'm going to break his jaw," he stated.

"I would expect no less." Natalie smiled and kissed him again.

∾

*L*ater that night, Cole heard the door unlock and soft footfalls as he was watching TV on the large leather couch in the family room of the basement. He quickly muted the TV and listened.

"Cole?" came a soft whisper.

"Dallie?" he called.

"Hi!" Her curly blonde head popped into view from the stairwell.

"Hi." He smiled.

He hadn't really seen her much that day. She'd worked with Craig for a long time, went to lunch alone and hadn't really spoken at dinner. It had been a little tense compared to the night before, and everyone had parted ways afterward, so he was grateful for her presence now.

She came forward then, and he took in the burnt orange Texas A&M tank top and matching shorts she'd changed into. Her legs were long and muscular, and he swallowed hard seeing them—and her arms—so bare. He smiled up into her big blue eyes as she sat down beside him.

"I came to apologize." She frowned.

"Apologize? What on earth for?"

"For getting us into trouble." She fiddled with her hands. He'd lived in trouble for most of his life. This was nothing new for him, but he wasn't planning on telling her that. "My gesture of comfort to you was misinterpreted by my dad."

"He was pretty mad at you, huh?" Cole asked.

"He's just trying to keep me safe," she countered, defending her father. "Something happened to me when I was little..." she trailed off and looked down. He didn't want to press her for more, not until she was ready.

"Hey, at least he loves you enough to try and protect you from men he doesn't know. You really can't blame him."

"I know. I don't. I just wish he could see that I'm not a baby anymore and that I can take care of myself."

"Maybe it's just hard for him, you know? You're his child."

She just nodded and looked up at the television screen. "Whatcha watchin'?" she asked.

"Some action movie about a rogue FBI agent and a killer."

"Cool! Sounds neat. Care if I hang out with you for a little while?"

"Be my guest," he stated and smiled over at her, turning the sound up to a reasonable volume, so they could hear it.

They began watching the action unfold as a shooting match began and bullets flew as the hero of the movie chased the bad guy through a parking lot. But all the while, Cole was keenly aware of the warmth of the girl beside him. He was aware of her breathing and the shape of her legs stretched out on the coffee table before him. He chanced a glance over at her, and she was looking at him, not the TV. He gulped.

"You like action movies?" she asked.

"Yeah, you?"

"Yeah." She giggled.

"I like scary movies too," Cole added. Dallie shook her head and her eyes widened. "Oh, come on. Those movies are good for cuddling."

"Yeah, if you have someone to cuddle *with*," Dallie murmured, then blushed.

"Hell, I'd cuddle with you!" He frowned suddenly, realizing what he'd just said. She stared at him amused then they both laughed. "I'm sorry, I don't even know why I said that," he tried to recover.

"You'd really cuddle with me?" she asked innocently. He took in her beautiful face then, her blonde eyebrows and eyelashes, her high cheekbones, her perfect lips. His eyes lingered there as he watched her tongue dart across them. He gulped again and glanced back up to her eyes.

"Of course I would! Would you cuddle with *me*?" Cole inquired and instinctively opened his arms to let her into his embrace. She seemed momentarily taken off guard. She worried her lip with her teeth and just when he thought she was going to opt out, she moved closer and settled into his chest, her blonde curls resting on his shoulder. He sighed in contentment as the gentle pressure of her body against him felt more comfortable than anything he'd ever felt before. She was soft and warm and smelled like flowers and leather and something else he couldn't quite put his finger on. He felt her breath on his neck, and her wavy curls spilled softly across his bicep and forearm. She placed her hand on his right pec, and suddenly, his groin began responding uncomfortably. He looked down into her face, and she looked up at him eagerly. His eyes drifted to those sweet plump lips of hers, soft pink rose petals that longed for a drink. He wanted to kiss her so badly in that moment. She was so very beautiful, and he loved how she distracted him from his chaotic life. His hand cupped her jaw, and she sighed then, closing her eyes and tilting her face up to his. Suddenly, a thought came to him, and he began sitting up further and readjusting himself, so she couldn't see what their innocent cuddling was doing to him. She pulled away from him.

"Cole? What's wrong?" Just like that, guilt hit him square in the stomach as he thought about this pure, sweet, innocent girl, and the fact that she'd probably never even been kissed before. Who was he to mark her? He couldn't kiss her! And he certainly couldn't let her see the hard-on she'd inflicted. She wasn't ready for all that. Hell, she'd gotten in trouble just for holding his hand mere hours ago. Her father would *literally* kill him if he knew what was going on right now and in his own house, no less.

"Dallie, I'm sorry. I shouldn't have allowed that to happen," he insisted and took her hand. "Tell me, truthfully, have you ever even been kissed before?"

"What? Of course!" she remarked, haughtily. *Uh oh*, he'd insulted her.

"Of course you have, but...ok, don't take offense, but I'm getting the impression that— I mean, with your father the way he is..." Her eyebrows went up, waiting for him to get the point. "You're a virgin, aren't you?"

The look she gave him made him immediately regret asking. This girl had pride. After all, she was her father's daughter, Cole saw right away.

"What's your point?" she asked, crossing her arms over her chest. *Damn!* She even looked like her father right now. He needed to mend this and quickly.

"Look, it's just...I respect your dad, a lot, and I don't think he would appreciate me getting quite this friendly with his daughter, that's all."

"*Is* that all?" she asked, her eyes looking him over. "Or are you just afraid you might shock me with your boner?" She looked down at his crotch, her eyes taking in the obvious bulge that couldn't be hidden.

He balked, "Dallie!"

"Look, I may remain 'untouched', but don't think for one second, that I'm not aware of how all this works."

With that, she jumped up and darted up the stairs.

∿

*D*allie was all business the next morning as they got the horses ready to ride. Cole needed some assistance as he prepped Blaze, but at least remembered the order and the way she'd taught him yesterday. In no time, they were headed out to the back pasture and into the grey morning. It was an unseasonably cool day for June, and Cole enjoyed the break in humidity. He smiled over at his sassy companion, who was being irregularly nonchalant with him.

Cole knew she'd taken his rejection last night to heart, and he'd felt bad about that, but after witnessing her father's contempt towards his daughter's affiliation with the opposite sex, Cole had gotten the feeling that Dallie had barely even rounded first base and truthfully, he wasn't sure that he wanted to taint her at that moment; not that it wasn't awfully tempting.

Cole didn't deserve something as sweet and pure as Dallas Noel Kinsen. It would be like eating the forbidden fruit. She was like a precious gemstone. She needed to be placed in a glass case and put on a pedestal, not held with dirty hands. Her father was smart to be so defensive when it came to his daughters. Cole knew that Dallie could be easily taken advantage of because of her kind heart and easy nature. And she'd mentioned last night that something happened when she was younger, which had made her father the way he was. It all made perfect sense to Cole. But he had to let her know that his refusal hadn't been for a lack of want.

She instructed him on the canter, and with much reluctance, he led Blaze into a swift movement that he wasn't quite sure he was ready for, but soon, he felt the cool breeze on his face and began laughing as he rode beside Dallie. He even got a smile out of her.

Once they broke the trees, they slowed to a walk and got off the horses to let them drink from the little stream that ran through the grove of trees. That's when he gently gripped Dallie's shoulders. She refused to look up at him to begin with and when she finally did, she swatted at the tears that came to her eyes. Cole sighed, dismayed by her distress.

"Dallie, I swear that I didn't mean to upset you last night," he assured her. She pouted and looked away from him. He softly took her face in his hands and made her look up at him. "Do you have any idea just how much I wanted to kiss you last night?" Her eyes were open pools of sapphire blue as he gazed into them.

"Then why didn't you?" she practically growled.

"Because...you're just—you're so innocent. I was embarrassed by the fact that you turned me on so—"

"Ha! So, you're embarrassed because you got turned on by a *virgin?*" she asked incredulously.

"You didn't let me finish," he countered and placed his arms around her little waist, pulling her straight up against him. Her hands went to his chest then and she gasped at the sudden closeness of their bodies. He slowly sighed, his eyes looking her over. "I only felt bad that my arousal ruined the moment."

"There *was* no moment," she retorted, and he cocked an eyebrow at her.

"Don't even pretend that you didn't feel something last night." He smirked and moved his hand back to her face, stroking her cheek, feeling a slight softening from her. "I need to earn your father's trust before this goes any further." She scoffed at him, and he laughed, leaning down to whisper in her ear, "Then trust me, when I *do* kiss you, I'm gonna take your breath away." With that he pulled back and dropped his lips to her forehead, placing a tender kiss there on her drawn flesh.

She pulled away from him and huffed as she got back on her horse. *Feisty little vixen!* He gave her a crooked smile as he mounted Blaze.

～

"*B*ut Momma, it has *got* to be perfect," Savannah blew out her breath, flustered, adjusting her violin strings as Natalie rocked Jackson to sleep in the rocking chair of the piano room. The sun was sinking low, dinner was in the oven, and Dallie and Jack were both cleaning up after the long day.

Natalie had explained to Savannah over and over how beautiful her piece sounded, but she wasn't having it, and personally, Nat was tired of arguing with her about it. Natalie sighed and pinched her nose, trying to calm her pounding head as Savannah's cat Zara snoozed at her feet.

"Mrs. K, you ok?" Cole poked his head in, smiling at her. He'd changed into clean clothes, his hair still damp from the shower. He reminded Nat so much of her husband. It must be his build and his green eyes, she surmised. No wonder Dallie wanted to hold his hand.

She smiled back at him. "Oh, you know... just the same song and dance. Vanna's not happy with her piece, and I don't know enough about musical notes and pitches to be of much assistance," she trailed off, sighing, tucking Jackson's little fist behind her.

Cole walked over to Savannah then and looked at the sheet of music, smiling.

"Want some help?" he asked. Vanna glanced up at him as if he were crazy. "I can read music too, you know?" He came to sit down at the piano. He played the chorus of a classic piece, and Natalie and Savannah's jaws dropped.

"You can play?" Vanna beamed, and Natalie smiled at her as she ran over to him, violin in hand, and laid the sheet of paper on the music rack of the piano, so that they could both see it. She pointed to the intro, noted the tempo, and suddenly, she counted, "one and two and..."

Suddenly, the house was filled with the beautiful harmony of both piano and violin, and her daughter was in her element as she closed her eyes in passion and swayed with the music. Nat was so enthralled that she didn't notice Jack and Dallie had joined them until her husband came up behind her and lovingly squeezed her shoulders. She looked up at him—a sappy smile on his face—and tears filled her eyes as he watched their daughter play her heart out.

Natalie then glanced over at Dallie, whose eyes were riveted on Cole, his head leaned in, stroking the keys of the piano with ease and grace. She knew that look and it frightened her suddenly, to know that Dallie wasn't a little girl anymore. She was old enough to love and to have feelings for someone. It filled Nat with dread, but yet also a sense of peace. As she'd told her husband just last night, Dallie deserved to know what desire felt like. Didn't everyone?

When the playing ceased, their audience just stared up in awe as Cole and Vanna celebrated, high-fiving.

"That was awesome," he told Savannah with a chuckle. "But let's maybe change this note here to a half note instead." He pointed to the sheet music, and Vanna began erasing a few things and putting in new notes as Cole recommended then they played through that measure again, and Vanna just cried in delight, hugging his neck.

"Yes, that's perfect! Thank you!" She laughed and bounced and turned to Natalie then. "Mom, it's perfect!"

"No, darling, *you're* perfect."

Vanna smiled at that and ran into her arms, and Natalie kissed her cheek, loving her family so much in that moment that it was painful. Nat wiped at her tears and stood, kissed her gorgeous husband and handed the baby over to him, trying not to note the look of shock on Dallie's face, watching as she came over to Cole then. He shrugged and smiled up at Dallie as Nat walked out of the room.

Natalie didn't miss the admiration in her daughter's eyes as Dallie watched Cole over dinner. The realization of her daughter's age, and the fact that Dallie had really and truly entered womanhood was like a hollow ache within her. She always thought she'd be ready when the time came for Dallie to leave the nest, but she'd always thought there'd be more time to get used to the idea of Dallie being all grown up. Natalie had watched Dallie sprout from a little girl into the amazing young woman she'd become and she was so very proud of her daughter. She didn't know why it tore at her so, now of all times, but of course, her sweet little girl couldn't be little forever.

Dallie deserved to fall in love and be married and have children of her own, but her daughter's upcoming departure to college ripped into Natalie like an open wound as the days had slowly started ticking down like a timer in her heart.

Later that evening, as her husband moved to lay on top of her, kissing her face and neck, his big hand cupping her breasts, he paused and looked down into her face, sensing her hesitation.

"Alright, angel, what's the matter?" Jack asked. She just looked away. "Don't even try it. I've watched you all night. What's weighin' on you?" he insisted. He'd always been able to read her so openly.

She caved, the emotions heavy within her. "Oh, Jack!" she cried and began to sob. He pulled her into his arms then and stroked her back. "I'm not ready, yet. I'm not ready for Dallie to grow up. I'm not ready for her to be gone from home." She suddenly realized these thoughts had been plaguing her like a cancer, eating her up inside.

"Oh, my love. Shh, I know," he cooed and stroked her thick hair away from her face, pulling her jaw up to look at him. His beautiful moss green eyes were raw with emotion. "Now you know how I feel. What I was saying... I'm not ready either, but it's here! It snuck up on us. She's all grown up now, and we have to let her be who she is."

"She's too young to go," Natalie protested.

"No, baby, she's not. She's a smart girl. We've raised her in the way that she needs to go. Now, we have to trust that she'll not depart from it."

His words stilled her then even as he lowered his lips to hers, pulling her deeper into his embrace, picking up where he'd left off just moments before. She let his kiss and his hands slowly pull her from reality as he began pulling their clothes off and positioned himself between her legs. He loved her with his big, hard-muscled body, calming her fears and easing her mind into blissful oblivion with each fluid thrust of his hips. When they came together, it was like the heavens opened and rained love down upon them, blessing them with a beautiful ecstasy that went soul deep. Afterwards, she fell asleep in his solid arms, loving the feel of his naked flesh against her own. She felt the cool breeze from the open window and shut her eyes to rest.

She awoke to the startling sound of torment along with Magnus's gruff bark in her ears.

"Jack!" she cried and grabbed for him.

$\sim$

$\mathcal{D}$allie awoke to the sound of screaming, squealing and whinnying as she looked to the open window of her bedroom. It was coming from the barn.

She heard Magnus bark as her mom cried, "Jack!" and she pulled herself out of her covers, stumbling for her shoes in the moonlit darkness.

Suddenly, her door flew open and her shirtless father stood there in the light of the hallway, his big mastiff whining at his heels. They knowingly looked at one another. One of their horses was in trouble!

She shoved her feet into her boots and led the way out the door and down the stairs, gaining speed as she flew to the kitchen. Her fingers fumbled with the alarm buttons, finally getting the numbers in correctly as her dad opened the French doors that led to the back porch. They descended the stairs quickly and both ran toward the barn as fast as they could, Magnus running ahead of them as he barked.

The sounds of fear and torture grew louder as Dallie approached Blaze's stall. She tried to see what had scared him so badly, but looked around and saw no source for the calamity.

"Blaze, baby, you're ok, hush now," she called to her horse even as she opened the bottom half of the door. Her father pulled her back by her shirt.

"No, Dallie. You're gonna have to go over the top," he insisted. She realized he was right as she watched Blaze move from rearing up to bucking with his back legs, hitting the back of the stall with all

64

his might, his fear still as prominent as when it had first started. She looked uncertainly up at him, unsure how she was going to do this. She pulled the bottom half of the Dutch door closed and looked at the top of it, assessing how she was going to climb it and get this right. Suddenly, her dad lifted her from her waist and she steadied her feet on the top of the lower half of the door.

She heard Cole's voice then, "What the hell are you gonna do?" Both Dallie and her father looked over at him.

"I gotta get to where I can touch him," she answered solemnly and looked back at her poor gelding in despair.

"What? No! Are you *insane?*" Cole yelled and tried to take her hand. She swatted him away.

"I don't know, Dallie," her father stammered, looking intently at the crazed horse.

"We have to, Dad! We've got to get him calmed down or he's gonna give himself a heart attack."

"Dammit, I don't like this, honey. Let's reconsider..." he countered.

"No, Daddy! On three." She looked down at her frowning father then and back over to Blaze. "One...two...three!" On the count of three, her father propelled her forward from her hips, and she launched herself at the horse...and thankfully, landed square on his back, astraddle of him. She immediately flattened herself over him, tightening her thighs around him and grabbing his mane to hold herself to him. As soon as she did, she began murmuring and cooing and stroking his shoulders with her free hand, and immediately, he stopped moving. She sighed heavily and came to sit upright on his back, her hands going to his neck and cheek, comforting him. She chanced a look over at her dad and Cole. Cole's hands were cupped around his nose and mouth in shock, and her dad's were on his head.

"Jesus, that was intense!" Cole cried, moving his hands.

"God, I'm so glad your mother didn't see that," her dad stated and sighed, shaking his head in disbelief. Dallie couldn't help but laugh in relief as she tried to slow her racing heart.

"Blaze, buddy, what happened?" The horse snorted and stomped in response. "Shh, you're ok now. Let me look at you." She hopped down and looked him over from the top of his head to his tail and found a little puncture wound on his hind leg. "Dad, he's been bitten by something."

"Do you see anything?"

She looked around the stall, having Blaze move around to check under his feet. "No. I see nothing."

"Damn!" her father swore. "Well, that takes the cake." He turned to check the other horses, making sure they weren't too distressed by Blaze's outtakes.

She continued to comfort the spooked horse, stroking his muzzle and cheek as he whinnied and lay his head on the crook of her shoulder. Finally, she was able to get his breathing and heart rate under control and finally stepped out.

Cole looked at her in awe as she emerged. "Dallie, how did you do that?"

She just shrugged.

Her dad laughed then. "I'm getting too old for this shit!"

~

"So, you can, like, calm them with just your touch?" Cole asked Dallie the next day.

"I guess you could say that." Dallie shrugged.

"Dallie, that's amazing. It's like magic!"

"Yeah, sort of." She remembered the story her mom told her about the horse she calmed at the age of four that was spooked with Vivian atop of it, just by touching him. It was a horse she was unfamiliar with too, which made it all the more fascinating.

"Dude, that's awesome." Cole smiled. "Maybe that's why you're so good on them."

"Yeah?" she asked, amused.

"Yeah, you know, you're a natural. You ride this horse like you're one with her."

She smiled again. "You ain't seen nothin'. Watch this!" Dallie hopped down off Ameera, quickly unhooked the reins and removed the bridle from her horse and threw it on the ground. She mounted her again and using just her legs and position in the saddle, she was able to take Ameera from a walk to a canter, bring her back around for a stop and then motioned her into a piaffe.

"Whoa, that's crazy. How did you do that?"

"She can feel the subtle movements is all. We know each other so well. I can read her body language, and she can read mine. We can actually do it without the saddle too." She leaned down and stroked at her horse's neck and smiled back at the admiration shining in Cole's eyes. "Next time we're in the corral, I'll show you dressage."

Cole nodded. He seemed eager to go into a canter again today. His confidence was growing, but she wanted him to have all the basics down and be truly comfortable in the saddle before she finally taught him to gallop. She looked over to Blaze, who seemed fine this morning, as if nothing had transpired last night even when she was afraid he was going to break one of his legs jumping around like he had. She'd doctored his wound and stretched his legs out before Cole got on him this morning, just in case.

"Alright, ready? We're going to go from one gait to the next." She taught him how to signal, and they were on into a trot. When he felt comfortable, they moved to a canter. They were riding nicely out in the back pasture an hour later, heading back toward the barn when Dallie sensed the change in Blaze. "Cole?" She looked over anxiously.

"Yeah?" he asked, confused at her change in expression.

"Hold on...tight."

Before he could respond, Blaze was jerking back and wildly flipping his head then suddenly he took off, Cole screaming as the horse flew across the pasture.

"Alright, Ameera, this is what we do girl, let's get him." She had her horse in a gallop in seconds, and they charged towards the rogue horse, gaining speed as she yelled to Cole to hold on and stay balanced in the saddle. "Heeyah!" She tapped Ameera's flanks more vigorously as they closed in on Blaze. She grabbed the lasso from the side of the saddle, gripped it with both hands, and raised it above her head. She gave it a spin and launched it at Blaze's head, coming alongside him and reaching for his neck as the lasso took hold. She stopped both horses simultaneously. The big animals breathed heavily, nostrils flaring. Dallie chanced a reach over at Cole, whose hands shook on the reins. She dismounted and came to his side then, holding Blaze's bridle. "Cole? You can come down now." He just gulped and looked down at her, fear in his eyes.

"I want to. I really do…" He looked around. "I just don't know if I can."

"You can. I got hold of him. He's not gonna move." She reassured him. "Just swing your leg around and take my hand." Cole swallowed and stayed frozen in the saddle for a long time. Suddenly, he did as she said and when he took her hand, he put more weight than she'd anticipated, and they both toppled to the ground. He fell atop her, bumping her head with his and they both cried, "Ow" at the same time. She rubbed at her forehead as he pulled back on his arms looking down at her in awe.

"You saved my life." He smiled.

"Yeah, well that makes twice now." She reminded him and shoved him away, laughing. "I guess that makes you my damsel in distress." He landed with his back on the grass and laid there, trying to catch his breath.

"So, I reckon that means I owe you one or two?" They turned then in unison, facing one another as the horses walked away, grazing.

"Yup!" she stated matter-of-factly.

She heard her dad's voice call to them then, "You guys alright?"

She sighed and stood. "Yeah, but we need to call Dr. Green and have him check out Blaze." She extended her arm to Cole, and he took it. She helped him up, and they walked toward the gate where her dad stood. "Blaze bolted, and I had to chase him down." Her father's brows went up, and he looked at Cole, making sure he was ok.

"I've actually already called Dr. Green. We figured out why he was so spooked last night," her dad said.

"Why?" Dallie asked.

"There's a dead bat in his stall."

~

*a*my Burns waltzed into Jeremy Burn's law office that morning, frantic.

"They're onto me, Jer." She strode over to his desk and fell into him.

"What are you talking about?" Jeremy peeled her off him and pushed her away. "I told you, there's nothing to worry about. Would you calm down?"

She sighed. "Stop worrying. No one saw me come in here."

"I guess by *no one*, you mean my secretary?" His eyebrows went up.

"Don't be like that! I miss you." She came back to him and sat on his lap, pouting. He kissed her pout away and again, peeled her off of him.

"Stop it! We can't be seen together. Now you need to leave."

"But that Detective, he keeps asking me questions..."

"So."

"So? I think he *knows*."

He stood then and cupped her mouth shut. "Shut up! He knows nothing. Just as you and I, we know *nothing*! Do you understand?" He pushed her toward the door. "Leave! I will reach out to you when it's safe. Don't come back here."

She nodded and smiled to the secretary once the door was closed and straightened her clothes. She looked around, feeling suspicious and insecure. As she headed down the steps towards the door outside, she thought she heard whispering and increased her steps. She then laughed nervously, her mind must be playing tricks on her.

~

That night, Dallie's Uncle Nate and Aunt Jordan came over for dinner, and the house was loud and bustling as the kitchen became the place to be. Dallie laughed over at her Aunt Jordan who played with her little brother, and her Uncle Nate who had Savannah on his knee telling her a funny story. Her Uncle Nathan had always had a special bond with Savannah since her birth. He'd not been around Dallie until she was almost five, so as much as she loved her uncle and he loved her, they'd not had quite the connection that he and Savannah had. Dallie wasn't jealous by any means; she and her father had their own special connection. Dallie's mother had always said that Savannah's birth had helped bring Nathan back to her. Dallie hadn't really understood that statement until just a few years ago when she'd found out that it'd been her Uncle Nate who'd shot and killed her biological father.

Cole had been standing with her when Dallie ran to open the door to greet her aunt and uncle when they'd arrived, and he'd gaped when he'd met Jordan, saying he was moving to Abundance because there were more beautiful women there than anywhere else in Texas. They'd all laughed then, and her Aunt Jordan had given Dallie a look that indicated they'd be talking about Cole later on.

Dallie looked over to her beautiful red-headed Aunt Jordan. She'd never been able to have any children of her own, so she'd always been fully immersed in their lives, and Dallie was grateful to have her cheering her on all these years. Jordan and her uncle Nathan had been wed when Dallie was seven years old, and she and Savannah, just a toddler herself then, had been their flower girls that beautiful May day. Jordan had become her mother's best friend after they'd moved home from Chicago, and to this day, they still were.

Dallie's Aunt Jordan and Uncle Nate had been a big part of their lives and were actually their godparents too.

Jordan smiled over at Dallie and winked, her eyes darting at Cole discreetly. Dallie mouthed a, "Stop" and looked down embarrassed. Jordan gave her a husky laugh and pulled to her then.

"I can't believe you will be in college this August. Where the hell did time go?" Jordan asked. Dallie shrugged. "We got to take a day and go shopping for your dorm when you and your workhorse of a father decide to take a break." Dallie agreed.

"Ha!" Her father laughed and walked over to the fridge to grab a beer, handing one off to Nathan, Jordan and finally Cole before twisting the top off of his own. "You know as well as I, that ranchers don't get days off. Hell, the last vacation Nat and I had was…what? Our honeymoon?"

Dallie looked over at her mom who looked thoughtful for a moment then nodded.

"Galveston," her mother replied.

"No, Dad." Dallie corrected. "It was when we went to Disney World."

"That's right." Her dad pointed at her and nodded.

"Damn! Y'all need a vacation!" Jordan piped in. "I think we could call David, and see if he could take over for a week or so."

"Well, we're gonna be seeing Dallie off to College Station soon, so that'll be a few days." Her dad's eyes held a certain sadness to them in that moment. It tore into her so that she had to turn away, so she grabbed the baby and began tickling him.

"No, Jack. I mean a *real* vacation. Even Nate and I have taken several since y'all did…" Jordan kept on. Dallie watched her mom shrug.

"Well, it's not been that easy, Jor," her mom confirmed. "The girls have been in every extracurricular thing imaginable, and just when we thought we would go somewhere, this little squirt came along." She grabbed Jackson and kissed his fat cheek as he squealed. Dallie knew that her parents really could care less about a vacation. They'd rather be here on the ranch with their children. Their horse farm and her mother's writing career had been a dream come true for them.

"Honestly," Dallie laughed. "Mom and Dad are *still* on their honeymoon. Just live with them for a few days, you'll understand what I mean." Dallie stated. Her mother turned red as she gave Dallie a withered look, and the guys burst out laughing. Her Uncle Nate piped in then.

"I tend to remember quite well. I had to live with them too, remember?" He pointed over to Dallie, who nodded. "And that was *before* they were married." Cole gave Dallie a confused look, but she appeared not to notice it.

"Nate! You're one to talk, you and Jordan are like a bunch of..." Her mom stopped mid-sentence, remembering the little ears present, and blushed as Dallie, Savannah and Cole's eyes fell on her.

"Speaking of remembering," Her uncle piped in and set Savannah down, moving over to Dallie. "I think someone owes me a rematch of air hockey."

"Nope. Honey, she beat you fair and square," Aunt Jordan piped in, taking a swig of her beer.

"No, no, that last move was illegal!" He chuckled, and Dallie swatted at him as he came up and hugged her.

"Alright, Uncle Nate. You're on!"

With that, the entire party, along with a barking Magnus, moved to the basement where Dallie pulled her sleeves up and plugged in the air hockey table.

Her Uncle Nate moved to the other side and took his hat off, slicked back his black hair and drew his dark brows down in concentration, getting a laugh out of Dallie as she took her paddle and readied herself.

Her uncle was a handsome man in his mid-forties, he favored her mother a lot, save for his deeply tanned skin and his hair, darker than her mom's. His beard and mustache held a few grey hairs, but his eyes were the exact same sapphire blue as hers and her mom's.

Dallie heard the wind whooshing up inside the table as the motor started. Her dad mimicked a referee, placing the red puck in the middle of the air hockey table, and jumped back; the battle was on. She laughed as she took a swing at the puck and propelled it roughly in her uncle's direction. He gasped and hit it back. Dallie came at a sharp angle and whacked the puck into her uncle's goal, cheering in triumph. Her uncle cursed, getting a scolding from her mother. He growled playfully and hit the puck back at Dallie. On and on the puck was sent back and forth as ooh's and aah's came from their audience. Her uncle was answering her score for score, but she continued to be one up on him. Finally, when the scoreboard hit twenty, the table reset, and Dallie jumped up in victory.

"Ha! I got you *again!*" she cried and punched at her uncle playfully.

"Good game. Good game," her uncle scowled then laughed and threw his arm around her.

Everyone gave her a high five as they congratulated her on her win.

Her uncle Nate demanded another rematch, but Dallie shook her head, playfully. She was the champion! He then demanded a new contender, and her dad stepped up to the plate as Dallie laughed and turned around, noticing her aunt Jordan standing with Cole, looking at the wall of pictures that was a timeline of her and her family's life.

"Oh, and here's little Dallie at her mom and dad's wedding. Look how adorable she was in that little dress...and those cheeks, oh," Jordan murmured, pointing to a photo of Dallie and her parents, dressed in their wedding attire. Her parents were blurred out a little, kissing in the background, as Dallie smiled brightly at the camera. God, they had been so very happy that day.

The wall of photographs held an abundance of love in its time-lessness. It was a montage of various pictures featuring Dallie, her mom, her dad, Uncle Nate, Grandma, Paw-Paw, Granddaddy, Nana, Aunt Jordan, Aunt Vivian, Uncle Buck, Savannah and Jackson over the years, at birthday parties, with the horses, with her dog, weddings, competitions, recitals, everything...

She looked ruefully at one of the pictures of her and her Grand-daddy. She'd met him at the age of six and only got a few months with him as he died of cancer not long after their reunion. Her eyes fell on one of her and her Grandma, her holding her baby sister, her and Savannah holding Jackson, her and her dad with a newborn foal... She gazed into the years of memories and smiled as tears came unbidden to her eyes. The emotions were raw within her and although she had nothing to regret, she knew just how much she was going to miss out on in college.

"Oh, baby girl," her Aunt Jordan said and pulled Dallie into her side then, kissing her cheek. Dallie smiled over at her. "This will always be one of my favorites." Her aunt pointed to a picture of her on her Uncle Nate's lap taken up in the hayloft of her grandparents', now her Uncle Nate's, ranch. It was right before Christmas- the year that her and her mother had come home to Abundance. Dallie's laughing face was tilted up, her eyes closed, and her Uncle Nate looked at her, smiling big.

"You only say that because that's your husband and *you* took the picture!" Dallie giggled, and Jordan shrugged.

"Well, I mean it *is* a great picture," Jordan insisted. Dallie and Cole nodded, agreeing. "And it's what I'm good at." She smiled. Her Aunt Jordan was quite a talented photographer, so she had good reason to brag.

"This one's my favorite." Dallie pointed to a photo of her and her dad. It was taken by her Grandma back when her dad was her grandparents' foreman, working at their ranch. Her little blonde head, notoriously topped with a cowboy hat, gazed up in awe at her dad, before he *was* her dad, as he looked down at her with a soft smile on his face. The love literally radiated from the two of them.

"No wonder your mom fell in love with him," Jordan murmured as Dallie just raised her eyebrows in agreement.

"That's one of my favorites too," said her mother as she came over then. "You two were inseparable." She gave Dallie a knowing smile.

The boys yelled loudly amidst their mêlée, Magnus responding equally as exuberant as his tail wagged and he practically bounced off the ground. Her dad suddenly jumped up and down in triumph and shook her uncle's defeated hand before coming over to join the gathering.

"Looking at all our old memories?" he asked as he noted the pictures they were intent on. "It's actually Dallas we have to thank for bringing us together, you know?" her father stated, smiling down at her mom. He kissed her soundly then looked up at Dallie, his soft green eyes appearing watery. Dallie got all teary eyed again, but couldn't stop them from falling this time. She swiped at her wet cheeks as her dad pulled her to him and whispered, "I love you, my little angel," in her ear. She hugged him tightly and kissed his cheek.

Her voice broke as she said, "I love you too, Daddy. You'll always be my Superman."

"Now, dang it, y'all quit cryin'. I'll do better next time," her Uncle Nate joked as he pulled Jackson to his hip. They all laughed, and the girls sniffed and blotted at their eyes.

"Me hit," Jackson said with a paddle in his hand.

"Alright, enough with the tears," Jordan stated, turning from the board. "This is supposed to be a fun evening. Now, let's go eat!" She swiped at her eyes too and grabbed the baby from her husband, leading the way.

It was later after dinner as the guys were down at the barn putting the horses in for the night, and the girls were gathered in the great room that Dallie's Aunt Jordan began to pry.

"So, tell me about this young new stud." She sat braiding Dallie's hair as Dallie's mom and Savannah watched a reality show on television.

"He can play the piano," Savannah didn't skip a beat as she responded, eyes not moving from the TV.

"That's cool," Jordan replied. "So, what's his story?"

Dallie filled her in as best she could on the little she knew about 'drifter' Cole West.

"He's kind of quiet," her mom retorted.

"Hmm, a man of mystery. I love it!" Jordan cooed, getting a laugh out of Dallie. "Has he tried to kiss you yet?" Dallie looked anxiously over at her mom, who's eyebrows went up in curiosity. Dallie blushed all the way to her toes. "Oh, c'mon now, this is a judgment free zone...right, Mom?" Jordan asked and looked over to her mother. Dallie's mom balked for a moment then sighed and nodded. Dallie waited a moment then shook her head. "No? Well, that's surprising... He looks at you like you're a juicy steak." Dallie just laughed at that. "Give it time, he'll kiss you. Trust me. I know what I'm talking about," Jordan assured.

Dallie recalled the way his hard-muscled body had felt against her earlier that day, his hands on her back and his promise that when he kissed her he was going to take her breath away. She gulped in anticipation. She didn't miss the look her mom gave her aunt and frowned.

"Oh, Natalie, she's a grown woman. She's old enough to be kissed," her Aunt Jordan defended and whispered down in Dallie's ear. "Believe me, your mom was younger than you when she was kissed for the first time."

She wouldn't correct her aunt and tell her she'd already been kissed before.

"Yes, I was, but look where it got me," her mother retorted and covered Savannah's ears. "If I had simply waited for a man like your father to come along, instead of going along with the crowd then I would've had no worries, but no, I was young and naïve and..." She stopped, looked down and continued, "What I'm saying is to wait for the right one, that's all! You'll know when he comes along!"

"She has a point, Dallie." Jordan took her face in her hands. "You're a smart girl! Don't go off to college and end up in bed with the first guy who pays you any attention. You let them take you out on dates and work for your attention. Gain their respect first. Don't be like me!" She kissed Dallie's cheek, and Dallie patted her hand and nodded.

They all headed back down to the basement once the boys were back, and her dad let the baby hit some pucks on the air hockey table while her Uncle Nate and Savannah played pool. Dallie and Cole watched a super hero movie and one by one, everyone else finally headed upstairs. They sat several moments in silence before Dallie finally noticed Cole looking at her. She smiled shyly at him again, remembering his words in the field earlier that day.

"I'm a little confused," he started.

"By what?" Dallie asked.

He pointed to the wall of pictures. "You were a little girl when your parents got married?" Dallie just nodded in response. "I didn't really understand what your dad was saying about you being the reason—"

"Yeah, I didn't meet my dad until I was four." Dallie interrupted. Cole frowned, baffled. "Jack isn't my biological father."

CHAPTER 4

*C*ole just stared up at her in surprise, trying to digest her words.

"Jack *isn't* your father?"

"Not by blood," she corrected.

"I'm sorry, I didn't mean to sound... I'm just shocked is all. Your mannerisms are the same. Y'all even favor a little."

"I hear that a lot actually." She smiled, looking flattered, then looked down and became gravely still and quiet for several moments. When she looked back up at him, her eyes were darker somehow. "My biological father was a very bad man. My mother caught him molesting me when I was three. My mother managed to hit him over the head with a lamp, and we fled. She found out later that he'd murdered two people in the time she'd known him. She was a wreck when she came back home, here to Abundance. That's when we met my dad. He *literally* rescued us...in every sense of the word." She smiled at the memory, looking into the distance, her beautiful eyes pools of unshed tears. "I loved him instantly. I don't remember my biological father, not at all really... It's like nothing existed before Jack came into our lives. He became a father figure and my best friend practically overnight. I recall how good he was to me from day one, how he read me bedtime stories and calmed my fears when I had awful nightmares, how eager he was to encourage me in my gift with the horses. It took my mom a little longer to let herself be loved by him, but when she fell, she fell hard." Cole smiled at that. "My biological father escaped prison though...not long after my parents were married, and he came for my mother and tried to kill her." Dallie lowered her head once again and twiddled with her fingers. "She was pregnant at the time and ended up losing the baby. Dad never forgave himself for that. He was almost too late."

"So, what happened to your biological father?" Cole asked, referencing him in the same way she had. Dallie stared up at him, almost as if she'd been in a trance, and Cole's words had brought her out of it.

A dead calm filled her as she responded, "My Uncle Nathan killed him."

Cole's eyebrows went up in surprise. *Holy shit!* Her story was like something out of a horror movie. No wonder her father was so very protective of his family.

Dallie looked up then in alarm. "Oh my! I'm so sorry. I don't know why I told you all that..."

Cole smiled and put his hands up. "Dallie, it's alright!" He took her hands then. "I'm very sorry. I had no idea. I would never have guessed something like that happened to y'all... Your family is so happy...and so *damn* strong. For y'all to go through that and be like you are is—"

"A blessing," she finished, and the look she gave him made him feel warm inside. It was true! It was a gift from God to survive that kind of tragedy and come out on the other side. The love her family had for one another had been earned with literal blood, sweat and tears. He smiled back and much to his dismay, he began telling her more than he'd ever intended to.

"My brother Adam was murdered. It's why I left. Not because I'm seeking freedom or kindness or a hippie's paradise, I just simply couldn't deal with the truth. He's the only person who ever saw the good in me, and now, he's gone...and I feel hopeless without him." Cole stopped, horrified by what he'd told her. He swallowed the lump that had formed in his throat as he looked into her tear-stricken face.

"Oh Cole, I'm so sorry!" She grabbed him and pulled him into her embrace, her arms going around his neck. He sighed and his own arms came around her, hugging her to him. He let himself pull in her warmth and concern, absorb the compassion in her hug, the kindness in her embrace. He closed his eyes and knew he'd never been held this close before. Yes—of course by a woman and in the throes of passion—but never like this, by someone who had given him so much empathy in such a short amount of time. Hugs may be something Dallie and her family were all very familiar with, but the incredible power of a hug had never really been shared with Cole, until now.

They stayed that way for a long time before Dallie finally pulled away, leaving him feeling as bereft as when he'd lost Adam. He gulped, longing to whine like a lonely little puppy, fighting the urge to beg her not to leave him. She smiled up into his eyes and kissed his cheek, sweetly, softly; a gesture of comfort.

"Good night, Cole."

He held her hand until she walked too far away for him to reach then she walked away and up the stairs.

$\sim$

"What the hell do you mean you *can't* find him?" Detective McElroy asked into the phone.

"I mean exactly that, sir. He's vanished into thin air," his fellow detective spurted out. "No one has seen or heard from him since the morning of the murder. His car and phone were left behind in Austin, and there's literally no trail," Detective Trace Cunningham reiterated.

"Well, damn!" McElroy cried.

The prints on the gun had come back with two viable sets. One was Cole Callahan's, the other wasn't found in the database, and neither belonged to Adam. It didn't make sense. It only took one person to pull a trigger.

They'd performed an autopsy of the body and determined the cause of death was a fatal gunshot wound to the head, no surprise there, but Cole's fingerprints were also found on the body along with a long brunette hair fiber. McElroy needed Cole for questioning. If he didn't murder Adam, he had to know who did and things weren't looking good for him right now.

"Alright," McElroy recovered. "Here's what we're gonna do, I'm gonna get a search warrant for his house, and you pin down those employees of his…find out anything and everything. If he's running, I want to know where he's running to. We have to find this kid. He's the key to this whole case."

"I know sir, but he could be heading in *any* direction. We only have a finite amount of resources here, and I've already questioned all the staff and—"

"I don't care! We'll *continue* to question them until we get what we need. Talk to all the surrounding businesses, someone had to see *something!*" With that, Art McElroy slammed the phone down.

~

*D*allie had taken what her mother and aunt had said the night before with great consideration, and they were right. She was too smart to be letting some boy mess with her moral fiber, so she planned to simply do what they'd told her and wait for Mr. Right to come along. The problem was that she wasn't sure she *would* know when that happened as her mother had assured. How would you know Mr. Right from Mr. Wrong until you had met them both?

Dallie considered this dilemma as she rode Blaze that morning.

Her riding partner was busy transporting horses today, so she was on her own. Plus, she was convinced her dad was keeping him as far away as possible, which wouldn't surprise her if that turned out to be true.

Blaze was doing alright, and his wound was healing. Dr. Green had given him another rabies vaccine after they'd found the bat yesterday morning, and she'd kept him in that day for monitoring. This morning, she'd rewashed his wound and bandaged it again and taken him out for a little stroll.

Cole's confession last night had deeply shaken her as well as the fact that she'd practically vomited out her own story to him like he'd been her long-lost best friend. Why had she shared so much with him? And why had Cole seemed so impacted by the hug she'd given him, as if he'd never been hugged before?

"Well, he *is* practically an orphan," she told herself. Maybe she was reading too much into it. After all, he was a male, so maybe he'd simply wanted more than a hug... Well, she wasn't going to let it get to her either way.

From here on out, she wasn't going to worry about boys or Cole or college. She was going to focus on just enjoying her last summer at home, and let things be what they were. If Cole wanted to kiss her then so be it, and if he didn't, then so be it. He was handsome, but she couldn't get too caught up with him. It would be a mistake. Besides, she had too much else to do to let herself get all hot and bothered by him.

She sighed, feeling relieved as she breathed in the fresh morning air. Maybe it was what her mom and aunt had said or maybe it was all the old deep-seated memories that had come flooding back to her last night; the memories of a young child starstruck by a cowboy fourteen years ago. She hadn't realized exactly how much she'd remembered about her father until she'd been reliving it in her reverie to Cole last night. She'd remembered her earliest memories of first coming to her grandparents' ranch, her first ride with her dad, buying Ameera at the state fair, her first real Halloween, seeing her uncle maimed during her first rodeo, getting her puppy, Dash, her sweet border collie who'd passed away year before last, and a million other wonderful memories that filled her head and heart. It was like walking down a hallway of what shaped one's life and made it grand. And Dallie knew that her life—and her mother's life—had seemed to start the day they'd met her dad.

She took Blaze into a canter and let the wind carry them away through the pasture. Suddenly, lightning flashed overhead and thunder crashed. Dallie saw a building storm cloud ahead of her. She turned her horse around and headed back to the barn, the sky splitting just as they entered.

"Whew, that was a close one, huh, boy?" She rubbed his neck as she led him in through the center aisle of the barn, feeling the breeze coming off the rain as the bottom fell out. Blaze just whinnied, and she dismounted and came beside him, stroking his cheek as she murmured to him. He'd never been a fan of storms.

Her dad walked out of his office then searching for her, no doubt. Relief hit him as he saw her. He walked over to her, and she suddenly felt bad for being so moody the other day.

"Man, that came on fast, huh?"

"Very." Her gaze went from him out to the pouring rain.

"Look, Dallas," *Uh Oh!* Her father's tone had turned serious. She frowned and looked back at him. "I realize that I was a little hard on you. It's just…"

"I know, Daddy. You love me and want what's best for me."

He smiled then nodded. "Yeah." She fell into his arms, and he enveloped her. They stayed that way for a time as Blaze nudged her elbow. Finally, she looked up into her father's handsome face. "How about we all go to your favorite restaurant tonight after Savannah's concert?" he suggested.

He'd always been wrapped around her little finger, she knew. She smiled back, nodding.

~

*C*ole was soaked to the bone later that morning while transporting horses from one ranch to another with Craig, Teddy and Todd. The bottom had fallen out on them right smack in the middle of unloading, and they'd returned to Kinsen ranch drenched. They all ran to the barn after pulling in as the rain and wind tore at them.

"Dang! It's comin' a dad-gum gully washer," Craig swore as he unbuttoned his shirt and began squeezing the water out of it. Cole laughed and did the same.

"Dallie, you didn't get wet, huh?" Todd asked, looking over at Dallie, who stepped out of Blaze's stall then.

"Nope," she drawled. "I got back from my ride just in the nick of time," she stated, smiling over at Cole, whose heart did a somersault at seeing her for the first time all day. Her hair was still in the big braid that her aunt had done last night, accentuating her face with its high cheekbones.

"How's Blaze doing today?" Todd asked, again trying to get Dallie's attention.

"He's doing fine. Thank you," Dallie replied as she walked over to Ameera.

"Are all the horses in, Dallie?" Craig asked.

"Yeah, Dad and Mike pulled them in earlier."

About that time, Mike stepped out of Jack's office and sighed.

"Well, looks like we're in for rain all day... You boys want a day off?" Mike asked.

"Hell yeah," Teddy responded. Todd just nodded and Craig shouted a, "For sure!"

Mike dispersed their paychecks and sent them on their way. They waved goodbye to everyone and took off. Mike himself wasn't far behind. Cole walked over to Dallie then.

"These cowboy hats make great umbrellas, ya know?" he said and elbowed her gently as she loved on Ameera's nose.

"Not with rain like that! It would seem you found that out the hard way." She motioned down to the shirt in his hand that he was still attempting to wring out. She gave a throaty laugh then as he looked up at her with a defeated expression. "You know my mom can wash those for you." She motioned to his wet clothes. He shrugged. "Nice tat by the way." She pointed to his right arm.

Cole looked over at his bare upper-bicep, where two black-inked wrenches formed a cross on his skin.

"Thanks. I got another one here on my back." He showed her his other tattoo; a three-dimensional musical note on his right shoulder blade. She just smiled, seeming impressed by his ink. "So, not much can be done here in the rain, huh?"

"No...and the horses are already fed and have been tended to, so they get to hang out in here today, but I can tell Ameera's not too happy." Dallie sighed. "We'll ride tomorrow, girl. I promise. Rain or shine." Ameera whinnied and flipped her head.

"You know, it wouldn't be a bad day for a movie," Cole began. "That one Savannah was talking about last night..."

"Oh yeah, that funny new superhero movie?" Dallie smiled.

"Cole?" Jack called and motioned for him to come into his office. He heard Dallie whisper, "Good luck," as he turned and followed. He turned to shut the door, but Jack shook his head, indicating that it wasn't necessary, so Cole came forward and took a seat. "I was gonna give you your first paycheck."

Cole relaxed a little as he took the envelope extended to him. "Thank you, Mr. K."

"*Finally*, it's only taken you five days to stop calling me sir." Jack joked.

Cole took a look at the see-through envelope. "Sir, this is cash."

"Damn, nix that!" Jack rebutted, laughing. "Yes, it is," he said.

"You're payin' me off the books?" Cole asked, surprised.

"I figured, as a drifter, you knew how difficult it could be to get a check cashed without a bank account, so I thought I'd save you the hassle and just pay you in cash."

"Well, thank you. I really appreciate that." Cole smiled up at his new boss.

"No problem. So, you kids gonna go catch a movie?" Jack asked. "There's not a theater in Abundance, but Denton's not too far. Y'all could hit the mall." Cole blinked several times, not sure how to respond.

Dallie came to the rescue then. "You don't mind, do you, Daddy?" She poked her head into the door frame.

"Of course not! Go enjoy yourselves. It's summertime. It's Saturday! Just make sure you're back by 4:30. We've got to leave for your sister's concert not much after," Jack said and busied himself with some papers on his desk. Cole just stared at him, wondering why he was all the sudden okay with this.

"Cole, let's go." Dallie pulled at him.

"Uh, thanks, Mr. Kinsen."

Jack just gave them a crooked smile. "Have fun...and be safe."

Cole turned then and let Dallie drag him out of the office.

~

*J*ack came back to the house for lunch, the rain still coming down in droves. He sure hoped Dallie was driving safe in this mess. He was also hoping he hadn't made the granddaddy of all mistakes, basically giving this vagabond kid permission to go out with his daughter. At least Savannah was going along which would prevent them from getting too friendly with one another...and if they did, Vanna would tell on them.

Jack remembered being eighteen- Young and stupid and reckless. Actually, he hadn't been too reckless until *after* college, after his parents had passed away, and he'd gone into the rodeo circuit after his girlfriend had cheated on him. Yeah, that's when he'd been reckless, to say the least, it had been in his twenties...not too far from Cole's age. Damn.

He came through the French doors of the back porch, the smell of something hearty hitting his nose. He looked over to see a big pot on the stove and looked into the baby-gated great room to see his son toddling around carrying a giant stuffed horse. It reminded him of the pink horse Dallie used to carry around as a little girl.

"Whatcha doin', son?" he asked and watched as Jackson stopped and looked up at him, his big blue eyes full of wonder.

"Whoa," his little tyke responded, pulling on the plastic reins of the stuffed pony he was astraddle of.

"Nice! Takin' a rainy-day ride, huh?" Jack grabbed his son up and kissed one of his chubby cheeks as he looked around for his wife. It didn't take long before he found her in the laundry room. When she stood suddenly with a basket on her hip, she froze, startled by him. He gave her a cock-eyed grin.

She looked so beautiful standing there in her typical lounge day attire. White tank top and those stretchy pants that hugged her butt and thighs in all the right places, a long thin tan sweater covering her shoulders, and her dark hair up in a bun on her head with a few untamed tendrils that fell down in various spots, one particular wave of hair curling under her chin. If he hadn't had his son in his arms, he would have taken her right there against the wall with wild abandon. That's what her presence had always done to him. It over-powered him. It tore through his defenses. It unleashed a longing in him so intense that he was utterly helpless to resist it. And for as long as he'd known her, there had been no remedy for it because satiating his appetite had never been enough, it had simply made the hunger even more ravenous.

"Hi," she cooed to him, and he knew she was feeling the same emotions he was in that instant.

"God, how I wish you were naked right this second." He craved.

"And if I were? What would you do with *him*?" Her eyebrows went up in question.

"I'm sure that we have some of those saddlebags around here somewhere!" he remedied.

Her laugh was deep and throaty and sexy and only made his desire for her even worse. She moved forward and countered, "He has a nap coming up soon, so try and contain yourself, at least until then." She kissed his nose, winked and sauntered by. He practically whimpered in unsatisfied longing.

He followed as she set the basket on the breakfast table and moved to stir the soup, Jackson pulling at the hat on Jack's head. Natalie moved to the fridge then, and Jack grabbed a toy from the top of the curio cabinet and set the baby down with it as he moved to embrace his wife while she fixed sandwiches. He hugged her from behind, pressing his aching pelvis into her bottom, his big arms wrapping around her small waist, his lips touching the pulse point in her neck. The smell of her perfume took him back to their first night together, and he moaned aloud.

"So, you let the kids go to the movies in Denton?" Nat asked, randomly.

"What else can they do on a nasty day like this?" He sighed. "I know what *I* plan to do..." he insinuated. His wife laughed and kissed his jawline.

"I appreciate you trusting them and letting them go." Her eyebrows went up.

"Yeah, yeah! I'm trying to soften myself because I've been told that I'm too strict, yadda, yadda," he replied. "Plus, I wanted to get them out of the house, so I could get *you* into bed." He nibbled at that sweet, sensitive spot that his tongue loved to torture on her neck as he rubbed his erection against her and squeezed her breast. She moaned too, and he felt heat rush through him.

"Don't you have some phone calls this afternoon?" she murmured into his ear even as her head fell on his shoulder and she arched her back, pressing her breast further into his hand.

"I forwarded all the phones to my cell," his voice trembled as his body responded to her wanton need. "Don't worry, wifey. I can take a break...or two." His laugh was muffled as he turned her in his arms and planted a hot, hungry kiss on her soft lips.

∾

*C*ole had been a little nervous about going into a bigger town. He was afraid he would be easily spotted, but it was an awfully rainy day, and they would be in a big mall with lots of people then in a dark theatre, so he tried to ease his mind. Dallie had asked him immediately when they'd gotten in the truck if he were planning on joining them for Savannah's concert that night to which Savannah replied, "Cole, you have to go!" How could he say no? But he hesitated, telling Dallie he didn't have anything to wear, to which she laughed and told him that they were going to the mall after all.

They'd arrived in Denton in record time and ran to a clothing shop Dallie knew well before heading off to the food court for some lunch then got to the movie just in time.

The outfits weren't really his style; he wasn't used to tight jeans and embellished button-down shirts. His usual wear was baggy cargo pants and cotton logo shirts, but he *was* on the run, so what better way to disguise himself than dressing out of character?

He'd felt like a model when Dallie asked his size as they'd walked down the aisles and grabbed article after article of clothes, handing them off to him and shoving him towards the fitting rooms.

"Come out and let me see them when you're ready, doll." She'd laughed, and he'd shaken his head in amusement.

He'd undressed and donned the attire she'd picked, stepping out of the stall like he was on a runway as Dallie and Savannah oohed and aahed over him, and he couldn't remember the last time he'd felt so alive. When he'd come out wearing something they liked, they'd clapped in thunderous applause, and Dallie'd given out a cat call, at which point, Cole'd been afraid they were gonna get kicked out. He'd narrowed it down to two outfits. After all, he didn't want to spend *all* his money in one shot. But Dallie had once again insisted on putting it on the company card, and he couldn't convince her otherwise as she handed the cashier the clothes, throwing in the other shirts she'd liked back into the mix.

He'd bickered with her about it on the way to the food court, and she just shook her head.

"Would you relax? Clothes aren't cheap, and they can be written off on our taxes." She was just trying to make him feel better. He knew *these* clothes couldn't be, then again, what did he know about taxes.

"Fine, but I'm getting the movie," he demanded.

They'd sampled various food items amid the vast array of vendors, and he and Dallie settled on a sandwich place while Savannah had chosen Asian cuisine. They filled their hungry bellies, laughing and talking about movies, music and Shakespeare, video games, cars and ice cream, and Cole really relaxed for the first time since Adam's death. When they were full, Dallie checked her watch, and they'd had to run to the opposite side of the mall to make it to the theater.

They were seated in the center row just as the last movie preview started to play. Although they'd just ate, Savannah couldn't go to the movies without popcorn and a soda, she'd explained. Cole hadn't minded if they were late; he was just enjoying their company.

They were both good-hearted, highly intelligent and polite young ladies who put others before themselves. They hadn't come from a broken home, like he had, without adequate affection, attention or care. The love their parents had for one another had laid an unfaltering foundation for the love that beamed out of their daughters. The girls had a rock-solid moral fiber and Christian upbringing with a light that shone from within them that was brighter than other people seemed to have. No wonder Jack put his family up on a pedestal, that was exactly where they belonged, Cole saw.

As the movie played, Cole looked over at Dallie, who sat between him and Savannah. She shared Vanna's popcorn and looked over to him, giving him a bright smile. He felt his heart do a queer jerk. He gulped and forced himself to look back at the screen. All through the movie—a funny and action-filled celebration of one of his all-time favorite comic book superheroes—he fought within himself not to take her hand. About three quarters of the way through it, he failed.

They got tickled at the scene and turned to laugh at one another and that's when he made his slick move. It was subtle but effective, his hand falling over her arm rest, as if on accident, to the hand that rested on her jeaned thigh, his fingers interlocking in her soft hand. She looked up at him then, a seriousness taking hold of her face. She quickly recovered with a soft smile and squeezed his hand, looking back up at the big screen. His heart swelled and took off then on a blanket of bliss as his whole body became aware of the amazing girl who was slowly driving him wonderfully insane. If his life never got any better from that moment, he would always remember this day and how he felt in that instant of simply holding her hand and connecting with her.

Too soon it was over, and they were leaving, his hand feeling bereft as they exited. Savannah and Dallie were excited as they relived the big scenes of the movie. All three of them laughed and strolled together toward the other side of the mall.

Suddenly, Dallie stopped dead in her tracks with an, "Oh, no." She looked forward to a group of three guys a good-ways in front of them, and Cole prayed he didn't have to get into a fight. For if he did, it would be his undoing, but he knew in that moment that if these two girls were threatened, he would fight to the ends of the earth to protect them.

～

*D*allie's heart hammered uncomfortably in her chest when she saw the boy from high school, the one who'd always made her uncomfortable, as they walked toward the mall exit. He'd constantly hit on her and said some inappropriately provocative things to her over her senior year, and she, unfortunately, hadn't forgotten them. She'd been able to use Nick—the former ranch hand she'd been dating at the time—as an excuse for why she couldn't go out with him, but now she didn't have one. Damn! Unfortunately, there was no way around him, he was blocking the way out.

She looked at Landon Russell approaching her with two other guys she couldn't quite place, but thought their names might be Chris and James, and she froze.

"Well…hey there, Dallas," Landon said, delighted as his eyes roved over her in unhidden admiration. "I didn't expect to see you any time soon."

She tried to calm her racing heart and come up with something smart to say to him, but simply said, "Hi," in the most uninterested voice she could muster.

"How's your summer goin'?" His eyebrows rose, making her feel like he wanted to know more about her "summer" than she wanted to tell. He was closer now, too close for comfort, and he reached out his hand towards hers. "You know, I was gonna see if you wanted to —", he was suddenly cut off as Cole stepped to her side and slightly in front of her, extending his hand.

"Hi, I'm Cole West. Dallie's boyfriend. I don't think we've met." Cole's presence was both commanding and formidable as the shorter and less stocky Landon just looked up at him in both shock and disappointment. Landon took his hand and shook it mechanically, the disdain in his eyes unmistakable.

"Landon," he faltered.

Cole pulled his hand away and looked down at Dallie with a big smile then. "Well darlin', your mom's waitin' on us. We ought to head back, huh?" His hand came to her waist, and he propelled her forward as the three boys made a hole for them to pass. She just gave Cole a nod and Landon a weak smile and let Cole escort her out.

Savannah was the first to speak as they headed back down the road, Cole driving her truck.

"You ok?" she asked, her small hand going to Dallie's forearm.

Suddenly, Dallie was back to reality. She smiled big at her beautiful little sister and took her hand.

"Yeah, I'm fine," she reassured her then chanced a look at Cole, whose hands gripped the wheel. "Thank you. You didn't have to do that, you know?"

He gave her a forced smile, and she could see he was still trying to reign in his anger.

"Just tell me that punk never touched you?" he asked, practically growling.

"No!" She declared. "He's just..." She looked over at Savannah, who'd leaned her maple head on her shoulder. Dallie's arm went around her then, embracing her and letting Savannah's head rest on her breast. Dallie's voice lowered, "He's said some things to me that he shouldn't have is all... He just makes me incredibly uncomfortable."

Cole seemed to be calmer when he finally replied, "That was *immediately* evident."

Wow! Dallie hadn't realized she was as open as a book when it came to her emotions. She would have to work on that. Dallie absent-mindedly stroked Vanna's thick hair as they all rode in silence, the rain still coming down in buckets. Finally, Cole's grip on the steering wheel appeared to relax, and he dropped his right hand down to take hers. The look he gave her stilled her heart as he brought his lips to her knuckles.

"I was afraid I was gonna have to knock his lights out." He looked back up at the road only for a moment. "And I would have too, if he'd touched you." His hazel eyes burned into hers then, and she felt an intensity overtake her that she'd never felt before. It was both thrilling and frightening. She gulped.

They rode in silence as the rain lulled them into a peaceful tranquility and the miles flew on. Cole's hand stayed interlocked with hers and his thumb stroked hers as they entered her hometown. She had to direct Cole from there, and once they pulled into the driveway, Dallie spoke.

"Let's not tell Mom and Dad about this, ok?" She was mostly speaking to Vanna, who always told their parents everything. Vanna nodded, and Dallie relaxed. "Ok, who's gonna blow this concert out of the park?"

～

ole actually laughed when he saw the minivan, and Jack's big frame squeezing into the driver's side.

"Not a word, West! Not one word." Jack glowered at him in the rear-view mirror as Cole moved into the back row with Dallie. Cole reluctantly stopped laughing.

They were all more formally dressed and heading down the road when Dallie giggled over at him and replied, "Daddy's not real fond of this vehicle, as you can tell." She gave her father a knowing look.

Dallas was stunning tonight in a flowy black one-shouldered dress, her porcelain skin glowing. She'd applied more makeup than he'd ever seen her with and her blue eyes were accented in smoky hues. Cole had changed into khaki dress slacks and a dressy short-sleeved collared shirt.

"Da-da, mewsic," Jackson called as he kicked his little legs; he'd been changed into a dress shirt and khaki shorts.

"Cole, you'll have to forgive me," Jack apologized and turned up the volume in the car.

Their ears were bombarded by children's tunes and Savannah cried, "Oh, Daddy, you're such a sucker." To which Jack shrugged, and they all laughed.

The torture ended as the car was parked and shut off, much to Cole's relief. They entered the music hall and headed into the auditorium, taking their seats next to Nathan and Jordan as Savannah headed backstage. Cole was introduced to Dallie's grandparents, David and Corrine Butler, and liked them immediately. Natalie's parents were as warm as the rest of the family, and he felt a peace within their presence.

Savannah was as amazing on stage as she'd been in the comfort of her own home; dressed in a shimmering brown gown that complimented her unique hair color and sea green eyes as she played her solo like a master violinist. They all clapped and cheered as the spotlight shone down on her, and her eyes closed as she expressed

SHANNA SWENSON

herself in the melody of the music. Cole knew that feeling. He too, loved music. It was one of the many likenesses he and Adam had shared together. Adam had been a piano player and taught Cole, and Cole, in turn, had become a self-taught guitarist.

When the concert was over, they all went to Dallie's favorite Tex-Mex restaurant and ate. It was an enjoyable meal with this incredible family he was starting to really take pleasure in getting to know, next to the girl he was starting to feel things for that he couldn't push away. She was young, too young for him. She was beautiful and smart and funny and...

He couldn't let himself fall for her! He was on the run. No matter how much he wanted to, he couldn't stay here. He couldn't allow this wonderful family to be damaged by his recklessness, like Adam had been. He'd made a huge mistake in coming here and taking this job, but for the life of him, the thought of walking away now was completely unthinkable. He'd spent less than a week with them, and already, he was all too aware of their impact on his life. They literally defined "family" in every sense of the word.

Oh, God! What have I done?

"...And Cole helped me. He plays the piano." Cole heard Savannah say. He smiled over at her, mid-bite of his chimichanga.

"Oh, you play piano?" Dallie's grandmother asked. "I do too!"

"Yes, ma'am. Actually, I play more electric guitar than piano. I just happened to learn on a piano." All eyes were on him then, eyes of surprise and admiration. He wasn't sure if he'd ever had anyone really admire him, and it made him feel good in that moment. He blushed. Dallie suddenly elbowed him, and the look she gave him took his breath.

"Wow, you're just full of surprises aren't you, Mr. West?" she asked. He gulped, momentarily cringing at that fake ass last name he'd given himself. Those beautiful sapphire eyes that glimmered back at him made him tingle all over. It was Dallie's dad who broke the look, giving Cole a familiar scowl.

"Well, hell, I think we should start a band. Nate, you play drums.

96

I'll play the tambourine," Jack stated to Nathan and Dallie's grandfather. They all clinked their margarita glasses together, laughing.

Savannah began eagerly telling everyone about the movie they'd watched earlier that day, and they'd finished their dinner and headed back to Kinsen Ranch.

Cole retired downstairs later that night after agreeing to accompany them to church the next morning at Dallie's pleading.

At church the following morning, he'd gotten to hear Natalie and Dallie's angelic voices praising their Lord, and he found himself falling irrevocably in love with the gorgeous blonde who smiled over at him, his throat tightening with emotion. What was happening to him? It couldn't be...but it was. He had come here to hide from his past, his sins, his cowardice, and he'd found a family who'd taken him in without hesitation and with open arms. He'd felt led to them, almost like it'd been a sign. But falling in love had never been part of the plan, and it jeopardized his escape in so many ways. He knew he was only doing more harm than good by falling for Dallas Kinsen, but God help him, he couldn't resist the magnetism he felt in her presence.

He listened intently as the preacher spoke of love and charity and God's leading those on a path. He felt as if the man was speaking directly to him and found himself tearing up before the sermon was over.

Afterwards, he and the Kinsens went to a big lunch and he, Dallie and Jack changed and went down to the barn to care for the horses after they returned home. It had started drizzling again before they were done, and Jack called him into his office. Dallie was nowhere in sight, perhaps she'd already headed back to the house.

As Cole stepped into his office, Jack motioned for him to close the door and when Cole turned, the eyes that burned into his were unflinching.

That was the first time Cole really and truly feared Jack Kinsen.

CHAPTER 5

*J*ack broke the stare he had on young Cole momentarily as he turned to the hidden liquor cabinet and opened a twenty-year-old bottle of scotch. He poured a couple ounces into two highball glasses and set them down, one in front of Cole, one in front of himself then he took his seat.

He looked at Cole intensely, trying to assess him further. He seemed a nice enough kid and his daughter appeared to be smitten with him. The problem was that this conversation needed to be had before it was too late.

"Drink it!" he commanded as he looked down at the untouched glass in front of Cole. "I wouldn't have poured it if I didn't intend for you to drink it." Cole gulped and picked the glass up, bringing it hesitantly to his lips. Jack followed, swallowing the entire contents in one gulp. He needed another hit, so he grabbed the bottle and poured more into his glass. He looked up again at a terrified Cole. Jack knew he was intimidating the hell out of this kid, but dammit, he simply had to let him know where he stood. "Alright, look! Man to man," Jack began. "I don't like the way you look at my daughter." Cole started to respond, but Jack brought his hand up, silencing him.

"Don't!" he stated sharply. "I'm a man, ok? I get it." He tried to remain calm. "My daughter, as you've probably already noticed, is incredibly innocent and by no fault of her own, as you can, again, probably notice." Cole said nothing, just stared back at him. "Her mother and I have done our best to protect her and for good reason. *Nothing* is more important to me than the safety of my family, but I'm not an idiot. Just like *every* father, I know the day will come when my daughter—" He sighed heavily and looked away. "Loses her innocence," he ground out the words. "It's how I got here, it's how you got here," he rambled. "I don't need to know about the specifics, I don't *want* to know and I don't need to know when it happens," Jack said and leaned forward.

"Mr. Kinsen, trust me. I have *no* intentions of defiling your daughter." Cole's hands came up, palms to Jack. Jack flinched at the word 'defiling' and practically growled. He reached down to his gun safe, spun the dial and pulled the revolver out, holding it carefully in his hand. He looked back over to Cole, who'd immediately paled, then released the cylinder, giving it a rough, quick spin with his index finger as he watched it rotate. He looked back up, his eyes boring holes into the young man before him.

"When the time comes..." Jack paused. "My daughter's purity needs to be handled with *great* care." Jack's eyes penetrated Cole's with daggers, forcing him to understand exactly what he meant. "She will *not* be forced into anything she's not comfortable doing." He replaced the cylinder and popped it back in, cocking the gun. "Do you understand?" Cole just gulped and nodded. "So help me," Jack laughed humorlessly, "if you hurt my daughter, I will not—for one second—hesitate in killing you," he said his words slowly, deliberately, watching as Cole attempted to pull air deeply into his lungs while staring at the gun. *Good! He knows I'm dead serious.* "Do I make myself crystal clear?" he enunciated the last two words with a grave voice, devoid of emotion, so much so that it didn't sound human.

Cole just nodded, somberly, probably too afraid to do anything else. Jack held the glare for a moment longer then sighed. "Good!"

He smiled, replaced the gun and shut the cabinet. "I'm glad we had this little talk." He stood and downed the contents of his glass, Cole anxiously watched him as he moved to do the same then sat his glass down. He watched Jack for a few moments before Jack walked over, patted him roughly on the back and they walked out of the office together.

~

*C*ole was stewing that night down in the basement after everyone had parted ways by nine o'clock. He wasn't angry, not really, just incredibly despondent over his predicament.

Jack Kinsen was a no-nonsense kind of man. When he said something, he meant it. Dallie was his little girl, and he would do anything in his power to keep her protected, even if that meant threatening someone with physical harm, as he'd done to Cole.

Cole remembered walking out of the office, his legs feeling like jelly and his stomach, a rolling coil of bile rising to his throat. Once he'd gotten to the house, he'd ran to the bathroom and puked. Cole had seen firsthand what a gun could do to a person...and he'd been scared to death for a few minutes that the man might *actually* kill him—to say that he hadn't would be an outright lie—but Cole also respected the hell out of Jack Kinsen and took his words for what they were.

Had anyone in Cole's short life ever cared enough about him to threaten someone else? No. Not even Adam. He'd loved Cole like a brother, but would he have hurt someone else to protect him? Cole wasn't so sure. Looking over at Dallie that night at supper had been a difficult thing to do with her father watching on, but Cole had smiled because he couldn't help himself and he didn't want Dallie thinking something was amiss. In that moment, he'd risked a glance over at her father and noticed that Jack's scowl was no longer there, much to his relief. Dallie would be horrified by what Jack had done, but Cole would never mention it. One day, if he was lucky enough to have a daughter of his own, Cole knew he would understand how difficult that had been, even for a tough guy like Jack. After what Dallie had told him about their past, Cole understood all too well how tragedy changed people and made life more precious.

Cole was battling these emotions when Dallie popped her head through the stairwell.

"Boo!" she cried then laughed over at him, and his joy at seeing her couldn't be suppressed. "I'm sneaking down here."

"Well, you've done a piss poor job of it, Miss Kinsen; you're supposed to actually *be* sneaky, like a burglar," he scolded playfully and shook his head in amusement.

"Ok, well, teach me your tricks, Mr. Larceny." She tip-toed over, laughing quietly.

"Oh, you're much too pure to learn the tricks of breaking and entering, young lady," he countered and tickled at her as she approached him.

"Try me!" she cried in indignation. "Besides, what would you know about it, anyway?" She laughed at the question, but he grew quiet, feeling suddenly uneasy because he unfortunately *did* know a good deal about it. "Cole?" She gave him a confused look, and her soft eyes were his undoing.

"I've actually been arrested for it a few times...more than a few." He looked away because the accusation in her eyes was too much for him to bear.

"What?" She gave a nervous laugh. "You? Arrested?"

Well, now, she knew he wasn't the sweet guy she thought he was. He didn't know why he was telling her this, but under her scrutinous gaze, he couldn't seem to help himself.

"Being the kid that nobody wanted wasn't always easy, you know? I stayed in trouble through most of my high school career. I was well on my way to becoming a criminal. I broke into houses and took things that weren't mine. I defaced public property. I had no conscience about it. I didn't care." He looked far away, seeing his past and the regret he felt for it. "I don't know how I didn't stay out of juvie for some of the things that I did! I was arrested a lot." He looked back up at her, and the look she gave him was of pure compassion. It warmed him. She touched his face then; a soft, sweet gesture, her palm melding to his cheek. He interlocked fingers with the hand that cupped his face and closed his eyes against the tears that threatened to come. In all his life, he'd never met anyone like Dallie and now he'd wished he'd have met her sooner.

He looked back up into her caring, perfect face, made even more beautiful by the radiant soul hidden beneath, as an unbidden tear streamed down his cheek. She kissed his tear and pulled him into her arms, embracing him, caring for him despite all that he'd done. All his prior sins and flaws and discrepancies forgotten. He let himself absorb the tenderness she offered him for long moments before she finally pulled back.

"Hey! I have an idea. Let's play a game." She beamed.

The game, for the most part, wasn't really a "game". It consisted of telling each other things about the other. Favorite colors, movies, songs, flavors, places, pastimes, goals, etc. Then it became more of a 'Would you rather?' questionnaire then finally a list of difficult questions to answer—like worst day of your life, most painful experience, etc.

He learned that Dallie's favorite color was pink, her favorite movies were romantic comedies, and her favorite flavor was vanilla. Dallie's worst day had come when her mother had been attacked by Dallie's biological father, killing the unborn child in her womb, and breaking multiple bones. Natalie had to be hospitalized for a couple days following the assault and Dallie remembered how scared she'd been for her mother. She'd also included the day her grandfather had passed away from cancer. Sweet Dallie, always thinking of others before herself. Cole's had been more difficult to answer because he couldn't tell her all the pain and details of the day Adam had died. She wouldn't speak to him ever again if she knew he was running from the law…

"Ok, most embarrassing moment!" Dallie cried gleefully as she lay on the couch, one elbow propping her head up as she looked down at him. He'd ended up sprawled out on a blanket on the carpet below her. He laid his head back in thought.

"Easy. The day I got off the bus in middle school with a raging boner in front of a bunch of high school girls. Ha! Now that was something that you can never un-see. I was completely mortified." He blushed even now, remembering how much they'd laughed at him then looked up to Dallie, who'd gotten quiet all the sudden. "I'm sorry! I think maybe that was *your* most embarrassing moment." He tried to joke, but she grimaced. "Dallie?" He reached his hand up to take hers. She gave a soft laugh then eased a little bit. "Ok, tell me, honestly, have you ever been turned on, like really badly?" She blushed, but he persisted. "Come on, we've told quite a *lot* of things about ourselves. This is no time to get quiet."

She smiled sweetly down at him. "You're gonna think I'm a weirdo."

"You? Never! Tell me. Is this leading to your most embarrassing moment?" he asked. She pulled her lips in and nodded. "Ok, good. Give me the juicy details."

It took her a few moments, but then she said, "Well, so...being a typical young teen at fourteen with racing hormones, me and my friends decided we wanted to know more about the...well, you know." When he looked intentionally oblivious, she balked. "Sex!" she cried, exasperated, and he stifled a snicker under his breath as she went on. "So, we went to my friend Anna's house and got online and started watching porn."

"Ooh, you naughty girl." He laughed, liking where this was going, but when she suddenly looked away, he frowned.

"It wasn't exactly what I was expecting," she confessed. Her brows drew and she gulped. Dallie sat up then and pulled her knees into her chest, taking the hand he extended to her as he too sat up. She stared off into space. "It was...violent...and forceful...and...*terrifying*." She flinched at each word, and he imagined this precious gullible girl who'd never witnessed anything but the warm love she'd seen from her parents and grandparents taking in this vivid, explicit picture. She looked painfully down into his grim face, and he smiled ruefully at her priceless inexperience. "I lied. I told them I was bored and wanted to go outside and play... basketball, baseball, *anything*... but be forced to watch that disgusting—" She sighed. "It really traumatized me," Dallie laughed humorlessly. "So, I made a point, as difficult as it was going to be for me, to talk to my mother about it. Now, here's the embarrassing part you wanted. You're gonna think I'm a freak." She covered her face with her hands.

"Ha, *please*, Dallie," he scoffed, "you've got nothing on *me*. You could never do anything that would make me think that of you." He patted gently in comfort at the hands across her face. Finally, she relented.

"We'll see," she stated sarcastically and looked back up, far into the distance. "So, there I was—it was probably close to midnight— and I'm walking down the stairs. I could hear my parents whispering down there. It was dim. The only light on was the lamp in the corner and it shadowed me from them. Suddenly, I crouched down because they were kissing." She paused and worried her bottom lip. "French kissing, their mouths opened, fully involved. The sounds that came from them were frantic and hungry." She gulped, struggling to select the right words. "Mom's back was to me. My dad had one hand on her face, the other on her waist and he angled her face to his as if he were sipping the very essence from her, as if he couldn't get enough." Dallie pulled her hand from his and fiddled with her fingers, her cheeks blushing brightly as she looked down in embarrassment. "They were fully clothed. I couldn't see anything except my mom's thighs that weren't covered by her dress. My dad laid her back onto the couch and grabbed her hips."

Cole shivered; he knew where this was going.

"In one smooth easy motion, he thrust his hips against hers. It was gentle, not like the poking and prodding I'd seen on that video, and her head flew back and the way that she moaned..." Dallie swallowed and looked into his eyes, her own eyes brimming with tears.

"It turned me on." She looked down again. "It was the most pleasurable sound I'd ever heard, and I realized that I wanted to know that kind of passion when I made love for the first time. Not the horrible animal-like sounds I'd heard from the video." She looked back out into the distance. "I continued to watch them for a couple minutes more, unable to tear my eyes away from the ecstasy that emanated from their love-making. It was beautiful and passionate, and I wanted to know what it felt like to feel what they were feeling, to know what brought about those sounds they made. When my dad's hands began to move up my mom's dress, it was too much, and I turned away, feeling horrified at what I'd allowed myself to see. I'd been spying on their sacred moment, and I was completely embarrassed and ashamed that it had aroused me." Cole expelled his breath in a smile and took Dallie's hand. "You think I'm disgusting, don't you?"

"Are you kidding?" Cole smirked. "Absolutely not! What's the difference in being turned on by your parents as opposed to someone else's parents?" Dallie's brows drew in confusion. "You think people who work in the porn industry aren't someone's parents?" She looked away thoughtfully. "Besides, it would worry me more if you had witnessed two people in the throes of passion and it *didn't* turn you on. I'm honestly shocked that that's the only time you've ever walked in on your parent's going at it." He laughed. "As touchy feely as they are, I would have expected it to be much more often than once."

"With three kids, I guess they got good at being discreet," she countered.

Cole laughed again. "I don't doubt that!" She continued to look down in shame until he pulled her chin up with his finger and sat down beside her. "Dallie, seriously, don't feel bad. Your parents are attractive people. Seeing them in that moment cleared your conscience about sex and what you'd seen in some over-exaggerated video that hadn't been your expectation of it. In an instant of chance, you were *shown* that sex doesn't have to be frightening." He took her hand. "You don't have any reason to feel bad about what you accidentally stumbled upon and how your body reacted to it." At that, she looked up at him shyly. "Us guys, we get turned on from a bumpy bus ride or just seein' some half-naked babe on TV; it sucks because when it happens, there's no way to hide it."

"Like the night *I* turned you on?" she asked innocently enough, but he didn't like the way her voice sounded. He gulped.

"You seem surprised by that," he stated.

"I guess I kinda was."

"Dallie, you touched me. You were laying against me. It was a normal reaction," he explained, defending himself. She gave a slow smile. "I think you're happy about it!" He chucked her chin.

"Maybe."

"Why? I'm sure I'm not the first guy you've turned on." His mind went in a different direction. "Wait. Do I turn *you* on?"

"I dunno, you've never let me close enough to see." It could've been a total line, but he wouldn't dare do anything to turn her on now, not after the confrontation with her father earlier that evening. He remembered that gun all too well. "Cole." Dallie pulled his face up to look at her then, and he froze as she asked, "You've had sex before, right?"

After several awkward moments of looking into her dazzling blue eyes, he replied, "Yes."

"How many times?"

His eyebrows went up. He honestly wasn't sure how many times. It wasn't exactly like he'd been counting.

"Well, I've been with three girls. I'm sure that was your next question...but I really don't know how *many* times. If I had to guess..." He shrugged. "Maybe a dozen." Dallie's eyes widened in surprise, and he couldn't help but laugh.

"I guess you think I'm silly." She looked down, dropping her hands.

"Dallie, of course not, why would I think that?"

"Well, naïve then, at the very least."

"No, I don't. Dallas, you're absolutely perfect." He took her face in his hands. "If I had my time to do over again, I would give anything to wipe that slate clean and have my first time be with you." The impact of his own words hit him then, and he gasped as she leaned into him, her lips brushing his. Before he could protest, she was kissing him.

～

allie leaned into Cole, closing her eyes and pressing her lips softly to his as the meaning of his words filled her heart and mind. She could feel his intake of breath as she did so and wasn't even really aware of what she was doing until she felt the hands on her face pulling her further into the kiss as her own hands naturally moved to his chest, bracing herself. His lips were soft and pliant and felt good against her own. He smelled like fresh laundry and peppermint and an earthy yet sweet cologne that gave her a heady feeling. She pressed her mouth firmer to his, his lips softening as they molded to hers. He moaned, and she was hit with a barrage of new tingling feelings that started in her core and flared out throughout her entire body. Her mind soared as her body yielded to the feel of his solid warm frame against her. Cole angled his head, moving his plump lips in gentle, eager, puckered strokes across hers. His hands moved as her tongue slowly slid into his open mouth. She moaned then and felt his hand cup her throat as his tongue caressed hers over and over and delved deeper into her mouth. His other hand went to her waist as she angled her head, but suddenly, he withdrew his tongue and closed his mouth, his lips pulling lightly on hers then as he dampened down the fieriness of the kiss. He hesitantly pulled back, sighing and looked into her eyes. She realized she was gripping his shirt in her fists. She, too, pulled away.

"I thought I was supposed to be the one taking *your* breath away, not the other way around." He smiled. Dallie realized her heart was pounding and tried to slow her breathing.

"I'm sorry. Was that wrong?"

He stifled a laugh and cupped her cheek. "Did that feel wrong to you?" he asked. She blushed. "Dallie, I could just *keep* kissing you."

"But you stopped," she countered. She waited as he frowned and looked away. She could almost see the wheels turning in his head as he chose his words.

"I just don't want to get too carried away is all."

His green eyes burned into hers and being so close to him, she noted the tiny specks of brown and gold in them that looked like sunburst radiating from his cornea out. She looked at his moist lips, her body still craving the feel of them, and gulped.

"Is sex like that?" she asked curiously.

"Well, Dallie, sex is very different than kissing is." Cole gave a surprised little laugh.

"Duh!" she huffed. "I *know* that."

"Are you asking me if sex takes your breath away?" he asked, finally understanding what she'd meant. She only nodded, feeling her cheeks flame up again. "Well, sex is…" He scowled, drawing his eyebrows. "Just like kissing, sex feels good—*really* good—but there's so much more to it than just the physical part."

Dallie huffed again, looking away. "Now you sound like my mom!"

"Well, it's true," he explained, taking her hands in his. "You want me to tell you what sex feels like?" he asked, in earnest.

"Yes," she said exasperated, "I do!"

He gave her a sweet, amused smile then and drew her further onto the couch with him. He swiped a piece of hair away from her face. "You seem to be in such a hurry to find out. I remember that I was the same way." She looked at him, surprised to hear that. "Yes, Dallie, believe it or not, I, too, was once a virgin. Shocker, I know." He laughed and she shoved him. Now he was mocking her—*Jerk!* "Oh, come on. You appear to be super intimidated by your virginity."

"I am *not*," she replied, indignantly. She wasn't intimidated by it, but she *was* curious, dang it. She waited for him to tell her what she'd been wanting to know for a while now—What did sex *feel* like?

He sighed and leaned his head back against the couch, pulling his hands behind his head, looking thoughtful. "Dallie, you know that sex is different for men than for women." When she looked up at him in exasperation, he recovered, "Obviously! What they *don't* tell you in sex Ed or what you don't see in porn is that…well, it's kinda hard to describe. It's an overwhelming feeling of losing yourself. You're overcome with desire and passion and then when you reach your climax, it's the most satisfyingly amazing thing that you've ever felt and you feel like you're flying through space and time and—" He stopped suddenly, looking at her as if he'd said something he shouldn't have.

This was everything she'd ever expected and more and now it was confirmed.

She'd read many romance novels and watched movies and like any dreamer, she longed to know what it felt like to be overcome with passion like that. It sounded wonderful, and she couldn't wait to know what it felt like. She was in love with the idea of love, and Cole was telling her that it did exist—out there in the scary world that she'd always been hidden away from. She couldn't hide the glorifying feeling she felt in that moment, but Cole was frowning at her. It seemed he'd regretted telling her this.

"But what they *don't* tell you," he continued, "is that there are emotions that come with the act that you aren't prepared for."

"Like what?" Dallie was intrigued.

"Like…"

"Love?" she asked eagerly. He scowled.

"Can I be honest here for a second?" She just nodded, eager to hear more. "Dallie, I never *loved* any of the girls that I was with." *What?* Wasn't that the reason to even have sex in the first place? "Dallie, it's true what they say. Guys will give love to get sex, girls will give sex to get love."

Dallie swallowed that pill hard. Her parents had basically said this without actually saying it. They'd warned her. And they'd been right all along. "But you just told me about the desire and the passion and…" She grasped at hope.

"I never said anything about *love*," Cole countered, shaking his head.

Dallie gulped. She couldn't hide the disappointment she felt; tears brimmed her eyes. She tried to force them away. This was the most anyone had ever actually told her about sex, and she wanted to know more, but the truth was eating away at her optimism.

Cole sighed. He could see that she'd not been ready to hear all this, now she understood his original hesitation. "Dallie, sweetie, do you want to know about my first time?" She wasn't sure that she did now, but she nodded and crossed her arms over her chest, feeling cold as her heart drowned in disenchantment. "I was sixteen when I lost my virginity. It was to an older girl. She was eighteen; her name was Brittany. Adam and I went to a co-ed teen bible camp that summer. She had been flirting with me all week, practically throwing herself at me, and I was putty in her hands. An older girl wanted *me*." He grinned and put his hand to his chest for emphasis.

"Finally, it was nearing the end of our week together, and we had church that night, but she and I snuck out, and she took me back to her bunkhouse. She showed me all kinds of things I had never known about sex. Things your buddies talk about but don't really know what they're talking about. Things you are eager to do but have no experience with. She was very knowledgeable and shared the wealth of knowledge with me. I was in a teenage boy's dream." He smiled again, and Dallie looked down, too shy to ask him exactly what kind of things.

Then Cole's voice dropped, regret took the place of the joviality his voice had just seconds prior. "But then I found out *why*… Dallie, she used me." His eyebrows went up in remorse as Dallie looked up at his face in surprise. "That's what she did. She had a bet that summer with her friends to see how many virgins she could 'deflower'. She had a clear advantage. She was older, more experienced, and we were none the wiser. And honestly, it hurt like hell. I really liked her, would have wanted more, but she'd had no intentions of making me more than a mere mark on her belt. She had taken five other guys' virginities that week alone. I meant nothing to her." Dallie couldn't hide her surprise. That must have been an awful thing to feel. "Everything she'd told me, everything she'd shown me, was all part of her master plan to 'corrupt' me. And see, my virginity had been no big deal to me. I didn't cherish it like I should have, like Adam did. I wanted it gone as soon as possible, but that wasn't an easy way to have it taken from me. Because you see, Dallie." He took her face in his palm, looking deep into her eyes. "Once it's gone, you can't get it back." Dallie worried her lip then. "So, you have to choose wisely about who you decide to give it to. Don't be giving it to guys like that—what was his name? Landon? Make sure you mean something to the person who takes it from you and make sure, by God, that he means something to you too."

So, her mom hadn't been feeding her a load of "hog wash" when she'd emphasized the importance of losing one's virginity. She was hearing it from a guy now too.

She swallowed and only nodded because she didn't know what else to do. Cole sighed and stroked her hair.

"I'm sorry if what I've told you isn't what you wanted to hear. Just know that sex should be something you do *after* you love someone, not before. At least, that's what I wish I would've done." He looked down, and she could see that he was truthful. He finally looked back up at her and searched her face, seeing how she'd digested all that he'd said. When he seemed satisfied that she wasn't too distraught, he smiled. "Who came up with the name Dallas for you?"

"My biological father," she murmured. His eyes widened in surprise. "I asked my mom several years ago, and she told me that it was his favorite team growing up, and he'd always wanted to play for them, but he got drafted to Chicago instead." When Cole's brows drew in confusion, she explained, "Troy Cameron was a professional wide receiver in the NFL then he had a career-ending knee injury and became a sports broadcaster."

"No shit!" Cole exclaimed.

"Fame has its price though. My mom lost her virginity to him at fifteen. I know she wishes that it had been *anyone* else."

"No way…if it had been with anyone else there would be no *you!*" He gave her a crooked grin that stilled her line of thinking, and she gazed off wistfully. He could see that her heart was heavy, so he said, "Dallie, it's getting late. We both need to get up early. Wanna call it a night?" She just nodded and he leaned into her, giving her a gentle peck on the lips. She took it then pulled away and solemnly walked up the stairs, her heartstrings pulling tight as her heart dropped.

∾

*D*allie had tried to hide the disappointment she'd felt after her awkward conversation with Cole for days and days now. Her heart literally hurt as she evaluated all that they'd talked about. It lingered, tucked away in the recesses of her mind, while she worked and dreamed and pondered about boys, sex, and college… Even after she'd told herself she wasn't gonna let it all distract her from her last summer at home. She was completely overwhelmed.

Dallie realized that she might just be too sensitive for this world and too unprepared. She didn't really know why she felt so distraught or had been so surprised by what Cole had told her. What had she expected? To hear that everyone had the love that her parents had? She knew that wasn't true! Her friend's parents weren't like that; even her friends weren't like that. They all just wanted to party and hook up as of late.

She'd gone to see her grandmother that next day, to help ease her anxiety, after she'd tended her horses, taking Ameera further into Butler land than usual.

Her grandfather had originally inherited five hundred acres of land from his uncle August back when he was a young man and he and her grandmother were just starting out. David Butler had founded Starlight Valley Stables almost fifty years ago and thus had begun their legacy. Her grandfather had given her father a hundred acres back fourteen years ago to form his own ranch. A hundred acres had been sold to try and pay her grandfather's debts before that, but had since been returned to them, and was now her father's.

Dallie's uncle Nate now ran the other three hundred acres of Starlight Valley. Kinsen Ranch and Starlight Valley were really one and the same, extensions of the other. No one kept up with where one lot ended and the other began; it wasn't as if there were a line there, there never had been and never would be.

As she'd rode up to the small log house that had been built for her grandparents in the back of their property several years earlier, Dallie smiled at her grandmother. Corrine Butler had been kneeling on a little pillow, tending her flower garden on that hot June day.

Her dark mahogany hair—kept that way thanks to her hair-dresser—was shaded by a big floppy hat, and she'd turned to wave at her granddaughter.

"It's about time you came to see me, child," Corrine had stated and smiled.

"Hey, Grandma." Dallie dismounted then and tied Ameera to a nearby hitching post set up out front of the home.

Dallie had pulled her grandmother into her arms in a fierce hug, loving the strength and certainty the older woman possessed. She and her grandmother had always had a powerful bond. Dallie would come to her when she needed to talk, and Corrine would always listen with the patience of a saint. Dallie's mind had started to ease some as they trimmed down roses, watered and weeded the flower beds together, and she'd conversed with her wise grandmother about weather, life and the future.

"How'd you know Paw-Paw was the one, Grandma?" Dallie had asked as they'd moved into the cool house and her grandmother filled some glasses with cold sweet tea.

Corrine had laughed then and her bright blue eyes had sparkled at the memory. "Well, after I ran headlong into your grandfather, I knew my life wouldn't be the same."

She'd proceeded to tell Dallie about how she'd literally crashed into Dallie's grandfather in the hallway at school and how handsome he'd looked in his cowboy hat and jeans. They both had laughed as Corrine recalled how David had gotten her into trouble with a note he passed and they'd ended up having to spend the afternoon in detention together.

"I loved his passion for horses, the cowboy way, and life in general. He was so vivacious and had a thirst that I didn't realize that I, too, possessed until I was with him. He made me feel alive where before I hadn't." Dallie had smiled at her grandmother's reminiscing as they sat on the couch. "Dallas Kinsen," her grandmother's tone changed, sounding solemn. "What's buggin' you, sweet angel? This doesn't have anything to do with that handsome new ranch hand of your daddy's, does it?"

Dallie admitted that it did, explained to her grandmother how upset her dad had been when he'd caught them holding hands, and even divulged a little about her curiosity of the opposite sex and love in general, leaving out the awkward conversation she and Cole had had in the basement...and the kiss she'd given him.

"Oh, sweet girl," her grandmother cooed and stroked her hair as stinging tears bit at her eyes. "There ain't a thing wrong with being curious. I can't speak for most because your grandfather and I have only ever known each other, but I remember how curious and ready I myself was the first time." Dallie's eyebrows went up in surprise at that. Corrine had laughed then. "Oh, don't look so shocked! Your mom and dad aren't the only ones with a passion for one another." She'd winked as Dallie smirked. "Just don't be so eager to give yourself to someone before you're truly ready, alright?" Her grandmother had cautioned.

Now, Dallie tried to shake herself from her all-encompassing thoughts about love and sex. So, she'd been told by a decent number of people as of late not to be so generous with whom she took to bed for the first time; it was just a precaution after all. Besides, it wasn't like she was on the verge of doing it any time soon anyway.

She let that fact propel her to enjoy her day as she helped her dad with a hot horse and her uncle with a gelding that didn't want to back up for a new client and rode her beautiful mare that afternoon, watching Teddy mow the grass. She loved the smell of fresh cut grass. It was one of summer's signature fragrances. She rode Ameera around the back pasture for a good long while before heading back into the arena. She cleared the area and had Mike turn on her CD mix of classical and Celtic pieces Savannah had put together for their dressage freestyle. Ameera knew exactly what Dallie wanted her to do the minute she heard the music. Her horse was as free-spirited as Dallie and loved a challenge. They started with an extended trot into an easy passage then into a fluid half-pass and finally a soft pirouette before Dallie noticed she'd drawn an audience. The moves were seamless and made the mare appear to float across the enclosure, Dallie knew, as she looked out at the hands, Cole, and her father. She gave them a big grin as she went down with Ameera into a well-rehearsed bow as they clapped for the two of them.

"Holy crap! I didn't know horses could dance." Cole laughed amicably.

"Magnificent as always, my girl," her dad stated proudly.

"Thank you, guys." Dallie blushed. "If I didn't know any better, I would think she missed this more than I did." She laughed and dismounted, pulling Ameera's bridle off her head. The happy mare quickly flicked her head back and nuzzled Dallie. "Yeah, yeah, you're welcome, you brat!" Dallie giggled as she rubbed her forehead and cheek. "You're a show off, you know?" She rested her head against Ameera's cheek and began stroking her neck and shoulder. "I'm gonna miss you so much, girl." Tears came to her eyes then and the beautiful raven mare leaned her head into Dallie's as if she understood. Dallie kissed her and wrapped her arms around her neck, petting her throat latch, just absorbing the emotions she felt in that moment.

She'd had Ameera since she was a yearling, been training her the day after they'd gotten her, and she'd started fully riding her when Ameera was four years old and Dallie was almost nine, which had been perfect timing because Dallie had begun to explore the world of dressage not long after racing. She and Ameera had grown up together; she'd ridden her almost every single day, religiously, for the last decade.

"I reckon I'm gonna have to have your mom take the reins while you're gone." Dallie heard her dad say as he approached her. She wiped her eyes and spun around to face him. He gave Ameera some love then too and elbowed Dallie playfully in the process. "You aren't getting all sappy on me now are ya, darlin'?" She wanted to throw herself into his big, capable arms and just cry like a baby, but she held her ground. She felt so out of sorts at the moment. Why was she so unsure of her future and afraid to go out into the "real world" as her mom called it? Before she could decide what she was going to do about her feelings, her dad squeezed the hand that rested on Ameera's neck. "Hang in there, pumpkin doodle," he said and winked before turning to walk away as Cole came up.

"That was super cool, just so you know," he stated.

"Well thanks. It took a lot of work!" she clarified.

"I bet." He looked at Ameera and warily patted at her forehead. "So, I wondered if you might wanna get out of the house for a little while tomorrow night?" he asked, nonchalantly.

"Umm, like, go out on a date?" Dallie's eye rose in surprise.

"Exactly like a date." He gave her a crooked grin as his eyes met hers. "I've got a little more money than I did before coming here, and I heard the guys talking about this cool pizza place that opened in town a few weeks ago...and I asked your dad, and he said I could take you out!"

Dallie almost choked on air as she sputtered, "He *did*?"

"Boy scout's honor." Cole held his hand up and placed his thumb in his palm. *Wow!* She wasn't sure if she was more shocked by the fact that her dad had said yes or the fact that Cole had gotten the guts to ask. "So... is that a yes?" he asked, shuffling his boots.

"Sure. I would like that," Dallie stated, smiling.

"Alright then, it's a date." He nodded his hat to her, and she laughed. It was a gesture he'd copied from the hands, and although he did it correctly, she knew it was an unnatural motion for him.

Mike called Cole over then, and he ambled away, but she didn't miss the sparkle in his eyes as he left. She smiled to herself and cooed to her horse, "He likes me, you know?" Ameera gave a little whinny. It was their normal banter, her and Ameera. Every now and again Dallie knew Ameera understood her and responded, and Dallie did the same.

Once Dallie got over the initial shock of being asked out on a date by the good-looking new hand that she'd kissed merely four days ago, she got a little nervous and giddy about it. She led her mare to her stall and began the process of removing her gear and grooming her. She began to get really happy and started humming to a new hip-hop song she'd heard on the radio the other day when they'd all went to lunch.

She kissed Ameera's nose and led her out to the back pasture to graze for the evening and headed up to the house. She came in through the back French doors and all was quiet. Her mom must be working on her writing piece for her article, which was usually what she did in the afternoons when Jackson took his long nap. Dallie headed upstairs to shower and change. She thought about what she was going to wear for her date tomorrow and smiled as she went through her closet in her head. The thought of being out alone with Cole put butterflies in her tummy and made her heart flutter. She couldn't wait to tell her mom...and her Aunt Jordan! And her friend Shannon! She took a quick shower, dried off, and ran a comb through her hair. She smeared some gel through her long tendrils and left her head wet since she was now burning up after the hot shower. She dressed in a pair of comfy shorts and an old Texas A &

M t-shirt that was now too small for her dad, but a little big on her, and headed downstairs to tell her mom about her date.

The kitchen was the place to be as Savannah sat painting in the breakfast nook with earphones in her ears, her long-haired Turkish Angora cat, Zara, at her feet. Jackson was corralled in his playpen fence banging on a musical baby keyboard and laughing at their mom, who stood at the stove singing along loudly to an 80's rock ballad. Dallie laughed and joined in with air guitar as her mom came up to her side with a wooden spoon "mic" and they sung their hearts out and laughed and danced. Jackson jumped up and down happily, and Savannah huffed off—her focus clearly disturbed—as she took her canvas, cat, and easel to the basement. They laughed at Savannah's annoyance, and Dallie grabbed up little Jax and spun him around as she danced, his blonde curls bouncing and his little fists pumping in glee.

Jackson was obviously a fan of 80's hair bands as Dallie and her mother had been doing this very same performance frequently during her mom's pregnancy with him. The song changed to one of their favorite Journey songs, "Faithfully", and she heard her dad's voice pipe in as he entered the kitchen, his hair damp from his shower. He wrapped his arms around her mom's waist as she stirred a pot of noodles. He kissed her neck and spun her around, serenading her and dipping her as Dallie and Jackson laughed. He spun her out and Dallie imitated the same with Jackson, who cackled his cute baby laugh. Her dad grabbed his son up then and held him high as Jax's hands grabbed at him, laughing. Dallie grabbed her mom's waist, and they cried the chorus out as the guitar riff came on. She was in the middle of air guitar again when she turned to see Cole, wide-mouthed, staring at them all. His expression was so intense that they were momentarily thwarted. They froze; her mid air guitar, her mom mid stir of the spaghetti sauce and her dad mid throw of the baby. Cole gulped and gave them a weak smile, but her mom couldn't let the look pass.

"Cole, sweetheart, are you ok?" Dallie's mom had, in the last week and a half, taken a more maternal interest in their latest ranch hand, whom she said had a "profound sadness" about him.

He tried to recover as if he wasn't touched by their familial antics. "Oh, I'm great, ma'am. It's just—well, it's not every day I get a live performance before dinner, is all."

They all laughed.

"Oh, you ain't seen nothin'," her dad enlightened him. "Nat, put on Bon Jovi!" He motioned over to her mom as he began lifting Jax up again. Her mom swiped at her iPod and selected a classic. Dallie smiled over at Cole, who blushed, and she grabbed him and pulled him in for a dance.

That evening, they all sat down to homemade meatballs and spaghetti, garlic bread and salad. Savannah had recovered from her irritation by then, and her mom fed the baby, who literally had sauce from the top of his head to the bottom of his feet—her mom hadn't fared much better. Her dad laughed as Jackson slurped some noodles into his little mouth and a piece shot right onto her mom's cheek. Her sweet, patient mother just shook her head, wiping her face.

"So, Cole, you're not used to a crazy family, huh?" her mom pried.

"Oh, yes ma'am. I've seen all kinds of crazy, but that isn't a word I would use lightly. Now, a *fun* family? No, I haven't been around many fun families," he said, almost regretfully.

They all looked over at him then as he solemnly looked down and continued eating. Her mom sighed and caught her eye, and Dallie felt the need to lighten the mood.

"Well, I'm glad we're considered in with the fun, not crazy, category," she stated in relief. They all laughed.

After dinner, Dallie helped her mom in the kitchen with the dishes as Savannah, little Picasso, worked on a brilliant masterpiece in the den, and her dad took the baby upstairs for a bath.

"I'm going to head to your Aunt Jordan's for our girls' cocktail hour if you want to come with me," her mother stated. Dallie had never been invited to their girl's cocktail time as she'd always been too young for the conversations they'd had and the booze as well. To say that she was surprised by the invitation was an understatement. Dallie just gave her mom an incredulous look as she dried the pan she was holding. "I've noticed you've been a little out of sorts lately and thought you could use some 'girl' talk," her mom added.

"Yeah, ok. Sure. Why not?" Dallie laughed and bumped her mom's hip as they finished up with the dishes.

They were in the car heading to Starlight Valley when her mom explained why Dallie'd been invited to her girls' hour, "Your dad told me Cole asked if he could take you out on a date." This was more of a question than a statement, really. Dallie smiled shyly over at her mom. "I want you to know that I'm thrilled," she added before Dallie could respond.

Who is this alien creature beside me? Dallie thought. "Mom? Really?" Dallie's brows drew.

"Yes, believe it or not. I'm accepting that my daughter is a young woman now who needs to get out there and enjoy herself. Honey, you're such a social person, and I think it's great that you're hanging out with someone your own age. I've noticed how melancholy you've been lately." Her mom took her hand and squeezed it lovingly. "I was young once too, remember? I left home to explore the world as well. I was terrified and believe me, I had a lot to fear then. But now I'm so glad that I did. I got to enjoy what I loved to do, and I got you as a consolation prize." Her mom looked over at her and gave her a big smile. "Dallie, I used to have all these regrets about leaving home and 'abandoning' my roots. But now, I know that despite what you and I went through all those years ago, and despite the horror of it all, and the fact that I jettisoned…you and I, we healed! We came back home and we found the path that we were meant to be on, and we're so much better for it. And I'm so glad because life is too darn short, honey." Dallie had tears glistening in her eyes as they pulled into her aunt and uncle's carport.

"Thanks Mom," Dallie said as her mom leaned over and hugged her. "I needed to hear that."

"Now, keep in mind, I'm happy about the 'date' part of it because that's what you should be doing at this age, understand?" Her mom's brows raised in all seriousness. "Your friends don't really *get* that concept, I know, but don't be in such a hurry to rush things, ok? Learn from my mistakes." Dallie just nodded and smiled then they got out of the car, walked up the old steps, and knocked on her Aunt Jordan's door.

Dallie's Aunt Jordan opened the door after the third knock and greeted them, martini in hand. Dallie could tell from the way that her aunt sauntered and smiled at them that she'd already had one or two before they'd arrived.

"Margarita time!" she called then lifted her eyebrows at Dallie. "Oh, we have a newcomer! Welcome, love." She hauled Dallie in and hugged her to her. "We must have a girl emergency here." Her aunt mocked the sound of a siren and laughed as she showed them in.

"Not an emergency, per say," Dallie corrected. "Just some much needed girl time."

"Dallie has a date tomorrow," her mom cooed as they walked into the kitchen where her aunt began pouring some liquor into a metal shaker.

"Well, butter my butt and call me a biscuit, Dallas Kinsen! It ain't with that good-lookin' new hand of yours, is it?" She glanced over at Dallie, who laughed and sat herself down at the breakfast table. She couldn't stop herself from blushing up at her gorgeous aunt, who was dolled to the nines in a sleeveless cotton dress the color of cappuccino that accented her copper red hair and whiskey-colored eyes. "Girl? Yes. I'm so happy for you. He's a stud muffin! You know he reminds me of a young—"

"Don't you dare say it, Jor," Dallie's mom scolded even as she grinned and took the martini glass Jordan handed to her.

"Natalie Kinsen, you know exactly what I'm thinkin' because you're thinkin' it too," Jordan rebuked and clinked her own glass with Dallie's mom's. She then walked over to Dallie and handed her a glass, clinking it as well. "Let's go out on the porch, so I can smoke.

We need to talk," her Aunt Jordan beckoned, and they all walked out the kitchen door.

Dallie took in her aunt and uncle's home. It had originally been her grandparent's home; her mother and uncle's childhood home, and even Dallie and her father's temporary home for a time before her dad had their own home built. Her grandparents now had their little cabin not far away, but this home, save for different pictures on the walls and some updated furniture, had remained much the same as it had been when Dallie was a child. The old wood floors still creaked in all the same places, and it still smelled the same as she could remember from the thousands of memories she had growing up.

They sat on the rocking chairs out on the back porch over-looking the barn and land as they watched the sun winking its last hooray to the sky, painting it in beautiful unreplicable variations of color.

"So, you think Cole looks like Daddy?" Dallie asked Jordan as she sipped on the pseudo-cosmopolitan—straight cranberry juice—that her aunt had made her.

"Son-ov-a— See, she thinks so too! It ain't just me." Jordan elbowed her mom, who laughed unreadably.

"Ok, maybe he favors him a *little* bit," her mom began, "but he *ain't* no Jack Kinsen. Sorry baby, but, it's true. Your father could smile the skirt off of a—"

"Mom!" Dallie looked over at her mother in shock, blushing.

"Now, little lady, this here is girl time," her aunt scolded, lighting up a cigarette. "We get to talk like that here. It's a safe zone." She took a deep drag and slowly blew it out. "Besides, your mom ain't just whistling 'Dixie' on that one! Your father is like a damn Greek god." With that, her aunt and her mother burst into a fit of laughter so long and hard that Dallie couldn't help but join in. When they all finally caught their breath, Jordan coughed and said, "Lord, but remember that? Holy crap! Who even knew then what a great thing you two would have?"

"Oh, I knew." Her mom threw her drink back and swallowed it. Jordan snatched it away to go grab another, snuffing out her spent cigarette. "Practically from the minute I saw that man," her mom said and swooshed her breath out.

"You did?" Dallie asked, curiously looking over at her mom as Jordan headed back into the house to refill her mother's drink. Her mom smiled reminiscently, her beautiful face looking so poignant, as if she were in a dream.

"Well, I fought what I felt. Hard. But after he kissed me the first time in that barn." She pointed to the old red barn in the distance. "I knew that I'd never felt that much intensity in all my life and after our first time…" She glanced over at Dallie uneasy with how much she was sharing, but Dallie was intent on hearing what her mother was saying and nodded for her to go on. "When he made love to me, I knew I would never want another man ever again." Dallie's eyebrows shot up in surprise. *Wow!* That was some powerful stuff! Dallie blushed, remembering what she'd seen those years ago of their unbridled passion on the couch, and her mother sensed that she was upset. She reached out for Dallie's hand and took it in her own. "Dallie?" she asked softly. "What is it?"

Dallie felt her cheeks flame, embarrassed once again at being witness to something so intimate between her mom and dad. She heard the screen door bang and her aunt came out the back door as she said, "I saw you two 'together' once. Years ago. Y'all were downstairs on the couch," Dallie spoke in short, broken words. Jordan and her mom just looked at her in silence and she gulped as she went on, "I was coming down the stairs. Y'all were still in your dress clothes, and I saw you kissing…and then Daddy leaned you back and—" She stopped. She couldn't look up at her mother. Her eyes teared up, afraid that her mom would be upset with her.

It stayed quiet but a moment longer, and her mother sighed. "Baby, I'm sorry. I guess we should have been more careful," her mother winced and squeezed her hand.

"I wasn't," Dallie stated and finally looked up into her mother's astonished face.

"Ha!" Jordan laughed as she handed her mom her drink. "I wasn't sorry either all the times I walked in on my folks goin' at it." Dallie looked over, surprised to hear her aunt's revelation. "It's probably why I wanted to do it so badly the first time. I thought it sounded fun as *hell*," she stated. They both just stared at Jordan and couldn't help but laugh at her conviction.

Dallie smiled back over at her mom, sheepishly and her mom returned it and said, "I'm just glad it didn't, like, traumatize you or anything. I was lucky enough not to have ever been one to walk in on my parents." Her mom cringed then laughed.

"I'm sure it's better than watching some of that nastiness they videotape and label as fetishes." Dallie scoffed and took another sip of her mock cocktail.

"Preach, baby girl!" Jordan exclaimed.

"Dallie! You've watched p—p—" Her mom struggled with the word.

"Well, I did once. When I was younger, under peer pressure, and it freaked me out. So, I'm actually glad I saw what happened between you and Daddy, and it wasn't anything close to that," Dallie said. "But I felt guilty for walking in on such an intimate moment between the two of you."

"Oh, honey. Don't feel bad. I'm glad that at least your mind was put at ease." Her mom smiled, and they all sat in companionable silence for a while just listening to the forthcoming night. Dallie felt good about opening up to her mom and aunt. It felt somewhat soothing.

"Dallie, baby, you should be *so* thankful you're still a virgin," her aunt divulged. "In many ways. Take it from a woman who knows what she's talkin' about." Jordan looked over at Dallie, a seriousness came over her that Dallie wasn't used to seeing in her aunt. "You're too young to remember the type of reputation your ol' aunt here had back in the day. Your mom can attest that what I'm saying is true. Sex is better when you both have a little experience under your belt."

"Jordan!" Dallie's mom exclaimed.

"What I mean to say is, it's better when *he* has some experience under his belt."

"Not any better." Dallie's mom shook her head, frowning over at her aunt Jordan, getting a giggle out of Dallie.

"Sex is more fun when you're older!" Jordan proclaimed. "Because teen boys don't know what the *fuck* they're doin'." With that, Dallie's mom huffed, uncomfortable with the direction this conversation was leading, Dallie could tell, and threw her drink back again, handing it over to Jordan for a refill. "Truth is, Dallie, there's a difference between being poked at by a teenager and having a man *love* you with his whole body." Jordan winked and drained her own drink.

"JOR-DAN," her mother cried, exasperated.

"Nat, come on. Better for her to know that *now* than to do what we did." Dallie nodded, agreeing with her aunt. "See!" Jordan exclaimed and pointed to Dallie. "She already knows exactly what I'm talking about because she saw it with her own two eyes with you and Jack that night. There's a straight up difference. You know it, I know it and she knows it. Which is probably why she hasn't given herself to anyone yet, ain't that right, baby girl?" Jordan asked, standing to go refill the drinks again.

That's when Dallie realized it was true, and she was glad she had waited and was going to continue to wait. She might be okay with making mistakes, but that didn't mean she had to be reckless with herself or her body. With all the personal experiences she'd heard recently, she felt like the heavens themselves were trying to tell her to just be happy and let love come to her. She felt at peace for the first time in a while with her inexperience, and she smiled.

"Is that how you knew, Aunt Jordan, that Uncle Nate was the one for you?" Dallie asked when Jordan came back out with the drink refills.

Jordan sat down, looking out into the darkness of the night in deep thought. She lit another cigarette and took a drag, pulling it in deep. She finally blew it out and answered her niece, "Dallie, it's hard to explain. All I can tell you is that love burns hotter than simple desire ever did and when that man is the one, then you just know."

CHAPTER 6

Cole Callahan smiled as he heard Dallie laughing that morning in the corral. He was excited to get to be alone with her that evening. She looked as lovely as always in a lavender button down and well-worn denim, her ever present cowboy hat on her head, as he watched her coaxing a pony around the circular corral.

Cole couldn't believe he'd gotten up the nerve to ask Jack Kinsen for a date with his daughter. He'd watched as his words during their awkward conversation in the basement not even a week ago had hit Dallie hard, and felt bad that he'd given away so much information.

He'd realized then just how innocent and unaware she really was when it came to guys and sex. So, he'd made sure to give her some space and time to digest all that he'd told her, sensing he'd frightened her, despite that her kiss still burned hot on his lips. She'd been so down and despondent these last few days that Cole had to do something, and once he heard the hands discussing a new place to eat, the idea popped into his head that he needed to get her off the ranch and out for some fun. That's when he'd gone to his boss and asked him for a date with his daughter.

Despite the fact that Jack had practically promised to kill Cole if he touched his daughter, the man had been very amicable lately and seemed to be warming up to Cole. Jack knew good and well that Cole had gotten his message- loud and clear. If he hadn't of, he would have been a fool! So, perhaps Jack was starting to trust him… or he was going to make good on his promise, either way, it hadn't been an easy thing to ask and when Jack looked up at him with a smile on his face, Cole nearly fell out in shock.

"You know what, son? That's a great idea! Dallie needs to go out and enjoy herself. By all means!" Jack had said. At first, Cole wasn't sure if he was being a smart ass or not, but then he proceeded to ask details and pretty soon they were laughing. Cole was still astounded.

Cole was also glad they weren't heading back to Denton. Downtown Abundance suited him just fine. It was quiet, small and easier to hide in, he felt. There would be less attention on him here than in a larger city. He could actually enjoy himself without looking over his shoulder, waiting to be taken into custody. Not that that couldn't still happen, but no one knew that he was here in Abundance. That fact had begun to ease his mind some. He was starting to feel comfortable here, at home with this wonderful family who'd welcomed him with open arms.

He'd woken that morning to hear loud music blaring, and he'd come out of his room to find Dallie running on the treadmill in the workout room of the basement alongside her father, who was lifting a heavy barbell over his bare chest in a bench press. Cole wasn't sure what surprised him more, seeing Dallie clad in only a sports bra and tight yoga capris or seeing her father easily lifting well over 250 lbs. with little difficulty. On both accounts, he'd gulped, waved at a smiling Dallie, and wished them a good morning as he headed off to shower for his early morning chores.

He glanced back over at Dallie through the barred window of the stall he was now cleaning, she caught his eye and blushed. He grinned at her all crooked and felt himself melt a little. He couldn't wait to feel those full lips of hers on his again and let her kiss him as she had that night, so sweet and responsively.

It had been an intense kiss despite how short it was, and he wasn't sure any girl had ever taken her time feeling him out as Dallie had. She was fresh and new and reveled in the experience of it, and it had taken his breath away.

She was an easy distraction from what he was running from, and he just wanted to enjoy the little time he had to be with her before it was time to run again. It wouldn't be long before that time would come, and he would have to leave. The thought upset him more than he wanted to admit. To disappoint her was disheartening, to hurt her was unfathomable, and to leave her was going to be the hardest thing he'd ever do. For now, he tried to just focus on the here and now. After all, that's all he could do. He made a point to stop thinking about the uncertainties of the future. For now, this beautiful angel was his date for the night. He smiled and got back to work.

~

y husband is up to something, Natalie surmised when Jack came in at lunch to eat and had given her that sultry, knowing smile she was all too familiar with. She couldn't help but blush as his eyes licked at her through her shirt. He'd said nothing telling but had given her a passionate kiss before heading off back to the barn. She'd just finished her usual chores and played with Jackson, teaching him some colors and numbers before he took his nap and she worked on her column.

Before too long, he was crying, and she was coming to soothe him. Then, Dallie was coming in to shower for the date that Natalie knew she was super excited for. They'd picked out a lovely coral sundress that came to her knees with spaghetti straps and a thin cardigan to cover her shoulders. Nat had laid it on her bed after ironing it this morning. She was glad Dallie was going out to have some fun. She hadn't been out of the house with people her own age in quite some time and despite Jack's misgivings, Nat knew that it was what she needed to be doing.

"Momma, can I go spend the night with Kelsey?" Savannah asked and ran to her then as Natalie cut vegetables for dinner in the kitchen. Savannah held the cordless phone in her hand and looked up at Natalie with the sweetest, most eager look on her beautiful little face.

"Sweetie, I don't mind at all... just make sure your father's ok with it, alright?" Nat stated and smiled at her daughter.

"Daddy already said yes, and she's on her way," Vanna called and turned, heading out of the kitchen, squealing into the phone.

Nat shook her head, amused. Yup, her husband had a plan! She felt her body tingle eagerly, knowing Jack was purposefully getting the girls out of the house so they could have a night together, alone. She smiled over at her son, who was corralled in his playpen, throwing a little football around and giggling.

She'd gotten the chicken marinated, vegetables cut and a salad thrown together when Jack came through the back door. The eagerness in his eyes was unmistakable as she met his gaze and gulped visibly. She'd seen that look at least a thousand times before, but it never failed to stop her dead in her tracks as the sheer sexuality of it blasted her with heat. He said nothing as he approached but came to a stop in front of her, leaning in for a sexy kiss and gripping her bottom with one hand.

When he pulled back she asked, "Kelsey's coming to get Vanna?" He just answered her with his eyebrows, and she laughed as he walked away to shower, noting his hard-muscled arms covered in dirt.

Dallie came down then, looking lovely in the dress they'd picked out as she searched impatiently for something downstairs and ran back upstairs. Vanna called for Natalie then, and she ran upstairs to help her pack her overnight bag. By the time she did that, and helped Dallie with her makeup, she was running to the answer the door, but before she could, Jack was pulling it open and greeting their guests.

"Luth," Jack stated happily grabbing his best friend and pulling him in for a half hug. "How the hell are you ol' friend?"

"Jack, I'm well. It's been too long, buddy!" Luther patted Jack's back with a smile as Kelsey pushed forward, annoyed at her dad, who was obviously in her way.

Kelsey Jean Boyd was Luth and Bella's oldest child. Not yet thirteen, she was tall and skinny with a beautiful set of chocolate brown eyes and golden blonde hair—like her mother.

"Hi, Aunt Nat," Kelsey said and looked up at Natalie, who was still standing at the bottom of the stairs. "Where's Vanna?"

Natalie smiled at her goddaughter and pulled her small frame in for a tight hug. "She's in her room, sweetie. You can go hurry her along if you'd like. You know how long it takes her to pack." Nat trailed off as Kelsey ran up to Savannah's room, huffing. Nat smiled, amused, as she moved forward to greet Luther.

"Natalie Butler Kinsen." Luth pulled her in for a big hug. "My first love." He laughed even as she swatted at him.

"Luther, I swear you say that every time I see you." She gave him a big kiss on his scruffy cheek. "I'm sure Bella enjoys the reminder." She playfully cut her eyes at him as they all moved into the kitchen, Luther grabbing the baby as little Jackson reached up for him.

"Aw hell, Nat," Luther laughed. "My wife isn't threatened in the least. She might like it if I'd give her weary body a rest." Nat scoffed at him even as she knew that they had three children and one on the way. For a woman who'd been brutally attacked and was a walking miracle, it was astonishing to say the least that Kelsey had ever even been born, let alone two more.

"How is she?" Nat asked, returning to her preparations as Jack pulled two highball glasses from the cabinet and poured a bit of scotch into them.

"She's about ready to pop," Luther answered, clinking Jack's glass with the one that was handed to him.

"Bless her," Natalie replied. "Summer time is the worst time to be pregnant."

"Thanks for letting Vanna stay the night," Jack stated, taking a seat next to Luther at the island bar across from where Natalie worked. Jackson grabbed at his Uncle Luther's hat, and Luther tickled him.

"Not a problem in the least. Kels has been begging for her to come over, and I figured with Levi's party tonight and all those dang wild ass boys around, she'd appreciate having another girl to hang out with."

"How the hell are you gonna manage a house with that many kids?" Jack asked, brows drawn.

"With the help of my friend, Johnny Walker, here." Luth held his glass up and downed it as Nat and Jack laughed.

"Yeah, I'd probably have to do the same," Jack replied and grabbed Luth's glass for a refill, walking back over to the wet bar.

"Dang, that girl still packin'?" Luth asked, looking over at the clock on the wall.

"Oh, yes!" Jack laughed, pouring another shot of scotch. "Give it a minute, this is like clockwork." Jack handed the glass back to Luth and checked his watch, looking knowingly at Natalie, who nodded.

Jack's finger went up at the exact time that Savannah called, "Momma?"

"Yes, my love," Natalie sang and tried not to laugh at Luther's stunned expression.

"Where's my blue shirt?"

"It's down here in the laundry room, washed and folded and ready to go into your bag."

"Damn, that was creepy." Luth looked wide-eyed at the baby, who laughed at his expression.

"She's got to have every little thing in order, my sweet little Einstein." Natalie sighed and began coating her vegetables in olive oil and spices.

"Yeah, I gotta say, I like it when she comes over because I know

she'll get Kelsey's room in some kinda order. That girl is a slob."
Luth picked Jackson up over his head, getting another giggle out
of him.

"Oh, no. Savannah can't deal with that. She'll get a literal
headache," Jack smirked.

About that time, the doorbell rang again, and Natalie's brows
drew, wondering who on earth that could be. Jack just gave her that
big, sexy smile she loved and headed towards the door. Natalie just
cocked a brow at him in amusement.

"Where's my little angel baby?" Natalie heard Jordan's husky
voice as she approached then. Jackson saw Jordan and immediately
began grabbing for her, grunting.

Jordan had been in the hospital with her and Jack when Natalie
had given birth to Jackson, and from that moment on, there had
been an inseparable bond between Jordan and baby Jax. Natalie was
thrilled, knowing that her best-friend/sister-in-law had been denied
that right and ability, and she was all too happy to have an extra
cheerleader there for herself.

Jordan took him from Luth and began greeting everyone, kissing
their cheeks and then she grabbed Nat.

"So, apparently your husband wants to rock your world tonight,
or so I've led myself to ascertain," Jordan whispered into her ear
while tickling the baby. Nat just blushed brightly, and Jordan
elbowed her and winked. "Luther, how's your wife?" Jordan asked,
turning to Luth.

"Woman, she's ready to beat my head in," Luth replied and
drained his glass again. Jordan grabbed it and took it to the wet bar,
filling it back up for him.

"Hell, don't you know what causes that *shit?*" Jordan laughed and
handed it back over to him. "Where's Kels?" she asked. They all
pointed to the upstairs. "Ha, well good, since there aren't little ears
around here..."

"Uh, little ears." Nat pointed to the baby in Jordan's arms.

"Fine, I'll improvise. Y'all remember that camping trip we took to the lake the summer between freshman and sophomore year?" Nat and Luth nodded.

Then Luther asked, "Hell, which one?"

"You know, the very *first* one. When Buck got hammered and Troy—" Jordan stopped mid-sentence, realizing she'd brought up Troy, but Natalie just nodded at her to go on with her story. Nat knew that unfortunately he was part of the crew back then, therefore, he was part of their history together. "What you said about Bella beating your head in reminded me... that's what Buck told you that he was gonna do to you that night, remember, Luth?" Jordan asked as the memory of the scene took her.

Luther started laughing big then. "Oh Lord! Yes. I've never seen him so fired up." They all smiled as he went on, "Damn, we were all only...what? Fifteen at the time? God, that was so long ago. It's because we were raggin' him about getting thrown off that bull. That's how he got the nickname Buck." He elbowed Jack, enlightening him.

"That's right. He told you to shut your freakin' mouth or he was gonna beat your head in." Jordan laughed and nodded, then gave Jackson some smooches. "And he and I were already stoned out of our gourd."

"Yup, that's also the night that Natalie made out with me," Luth reminisced.

"What?" Jordan laughed as if Luther were being ridiculous then she turned toward Nat, her smile fading when she saw that Nat was blushing. "When?"

Natalie gulped. All eyes were on her, including her husband's, who looked both surprised and uncomfortable by this revelation. She laughed uneasily then looked at Luther, who carried on as if she weren't giving him the death look.

"Troy was being a dick and made her cry," Luth answered.

"Shocker there," Jordan muttered, placing the baby on her hip.

"I was out by the campfire still, everyone else was out like a light. She came over and sat down, and I couldn't help but go to her and comfort her as she cried. Next thing I know, we're making out!" Luther looked down as he stopped talking. He quickly looked up at Natalie, and she swallowed hard at the sadness in his eyes. "I never should've let you go back into that tent with him."

Natalie's heart hammered in her chest, remembering that night all too well as the sudden memory flooded through her. "Luth, you —?" she stammered, confused. *How could he have known?*

"Yes. I heard," he confessed.

"Guys, what am I missing here?" Jordan asked, grabbing Nat's arm, frowning.

"Natalie lost her virginity that night." Luth's eyes were full of mirrored pain as Natalie looked back at him. She turned her head suddenly, both embarrassed and upset as she recalled Troy's heavy body on top of her; the smell of his drunken breath, the feel of his rough hands on her.

"Nat, baby?" Jack's deep voice asked. "Is he sayin' that—" his steady tone wavered as he frowned at her, "Troy *forced* himself on you?" His obvious discomfort tore through her and tears filled her eyes.

"Troy never did *anything* gently," she answered him and watched the recognition hit his mossy green eyes as he clenched his fist on the bar then looked down, anger overtaking him. "Y'all know that." She looked to Luth and Jordan as a tear fell down her cheek. "But it was a long time ago, and it doesn't matter now." Natalie recovered, trying to push the painful recollection away.

"I should've come in there and tore him off of you." Luther's lip quivered, and he shook his head.

"Luth, please?" Natalie begged.

Jack sighed heavily and unfolded his big frame from the stool he sat on. Nat wearily watched her husband's shaky hands as he turned, grabbed for the door knob and walked out the French doors. She closed her eyes, hating that he was hurting so much over something that happened to her such a long time ago.

"Nat, I'm really sorry," Luth began.

"It's ok, Luth. You have nothing to be sorry for." She took his hands. "I was head over heels for Troy Cameron back then, so it wouldn't have mattered what you did." She sniffed and wiped at her nose, giving him a smile. She then turned to see Jordan staring at the doorframe at a tearful Dallie.

~

*J*ack stood outside on the back porch for what seemed to be an eternity as he tried to calm himself down. For the life of him, he couldn't keep his anger at bay, and wanted to destroy a punching bag with the rage building inside him at the long dead Troy Cameron. Jack tried to tell himself that the injustice to Natalie had been done over twenty-five years ago, he hadn't even known his wife then, but that didn't change the fact that his blood boiled after finding out just how much that man had truly hurt her; how much he'd continued to hurt her...until he'd been killed. When Jack finally felt he could return inside without bursting at the seams, all the kids were downstairs, and Dallie was throwing herself into his arms. His anger seemed to dissipate somewhat, if only momentarily. At least *one* good thing had come from Natalie's union with Troy- Dallie.

"I love you, Daddy," she whispered up to him.

"I love you, sweet pea. Now you and Cole enjoy yourselves tonight, alright?" Jack stated and tipped his hat at Cole, who gave him a weak smile. "Oh, here." He dug into his pocket and fished out the keys to his truck, tossing them over to Cole. "Take the duelie."

Jack knew for a fact that Cole wouldn't be enjoying himself quite as much as he would like to as Jack recalled their conversation in his office. But Jack respected that the kid had recovered and had the balls to ask him if he could take his daughter out on a date. Jack had been both surprised and happy about it all because he knew that Cole wouldn't *dare* touch her now. Not if he wanted to live.

Savannah and Kelsey flew to him then, hugging him and telling him bye, and he kissed both their foreheads. Luther grabbed him next, apologizing for bringing up such a tender subject. Jack just patted his back and told him not to worry and bid the three of them farewell.

Jordan was grabbing the diaper bag then, and Jack picked up the playpen. He carried it out to her car as she walked out with Jackson in tow, and Natalie waved goodbye to their baby boy. Jackson wouldn't be gone too long, just long enough to be out like a light when Jack picked him up in a few hours.

"Have fun tonight," Jordan said as she buckled Jackson into the secondary car seat she had installed, and Jack leaned down to kiss his son on the cheek. "And Jack." Jordan grabbed his shirt. "I'm sorry. I didn't know about all that...but Nat's ok. It's done and over now. No sense in crying over spilt milk, huh?" she stated and patted his arm, looking into his eyes. He sighed and nodded, knowing it was true, but couldn't shake the hate he'd always felt for the man who'd been the bane of his wife's complete existence.

When Jack came inside the house, he leaned against the closed door and took a deep breath in. He did it again to try and relax before finally walking back into the kitchen to his wife, who had her back to him. He wanted to apologize to her for the wrong that had been done to her all those years ago, but instead, he let his gaze fall down her plump backside and suddenly, his body had other ideas.

He came up behind her and gently pressed himself into her frame, his pelvis against her bottom, his chest against her back. His arms came around her waist, and his mouth went to the crook of her neck, his lips lingering there. The audible gasp and sigh of sexual yearning she emitted evaporated all the anger from him, and he let his body absorb the eagerness he felt in that moment to take her. His hands moved over her breasts, and he pulled her tighter into his embrace as his mouth kissed and sucked at her neck. She moaned, and he was suddenly fully aroused.

"You pawned our children off," she said as her hands went to his.

"I did," he confirmed, pulling back for just a moment. "I had this incredibly naughty dream about you the other night, and I just couldn't *wait* any longer to act it out."

She turned in his arms then and gave him a sultry smile as her eyebrow cocked at him. "Oh? Pray tell!" Her excitement amused him, and he laughed.

"Well, your wardrobe is upstairs on the bed...but I'm not sure I want to have you be so naughty now." He looked down, sadness filling him. "It seems I have something to make up for."

"No, Jack." She pulled his face up to look at her and kissed his jawline. "Trust me when I tell you that making love with you, each and every time, has *more* than made up for that night all those years ago." The look she gave him seemed to confirm that, and he gave her a weak smile and squeezed her arms, comfortingly. "Now, tonight, I'm going to be your *naughty* wife and don't you forget that." Nat leaned up and kissed him, wrapping her arms around his neck, and he forgot what he was going to say as her tongue plunged into his mouth. Jack moaned aloud and pulled her into him again, bringing her leg up to his hip and gripping her bottom as he backed her into the counter. She gasped as his mouth left hers and began kissing her neck again, sucking at her sensitive flesh there as her head fell back. His eager hands went to her breasts and squeezed them in his hands, loving the sounds that came from her as he did. Just as she was untucking his shirt—his hands grasping at hers—she stopped and pulled back. He looked up questioningly. "Not so fast there, cowboy. I need to don the correct costume for this occasion." She pulled away, taking his hand to follow her and sashayed up the stairs. He just smiled in amusement and let her lead him to their private place of pleasure.

When they got to the bedroom, Natalie looked down at her black cowboy hat, red high heels and the black G-string that he had placed on the bed.

Jack wedged himself in the doorframe, propping his hip there. He crossed his arms over his chest and watched her eye him. She licked her lips and his cock jumped in response. He nodded his head and gazed longing at her as she turned to face him and slowly began to undress. She did so shyly and achingly unhurried, so that when she finally donned the hat and pulled the thin piece of lace up her thighs, his mouth was dry, and his sex was pulsing with eager anticipation. She stood proudly before him, looking every bit the fantasy he'd imagined with her dark wavy hair framing her face, the hat atop her head, her body naked save for the thin sliver of silk between her thighs and the red heels on her feet. His eyes licked down over her beauty, falling over her breasts, her slender torso and down her muscular legs. She gripped her hat with her thumb and index finger and swayed her hips towards him.

"Just a moment there, darlin'," he said, stroking his chin thoughtfully. "We're missin' something." He looked down at her full perky breasts and back up into those blue eyes that burned with desire for him. Jack walked over to his jewelry box, grabbed a turquoise bolo tie, and came back to her. He removed her hat, placed the necklace around her neck and replaced the hat then he smiled and nodded. "There we go! Just like the dream," he mumbled, his voice thick with want.

Nat grabbed at the bolo tie and smiled. "Nice touch," she added and leaned into him then, "but I don't believe you're dressed for *your* part, my love." With that, she began unbuttoning his shirt and left it hanging open, adjusted his hat and unsnapped his jeans, unzipping him a little then stepped back, pleased with herself. "Now. That's more like it," she stated and bit at her lip as she looked up at him all sultry.

He practically growled as he pulled her into his embrace, knocking his own hat off in the process, and began loving her flesh with his mouth and hands. He kissed her deeply as his big palms kneaded her bare breasts then moved down to squeeze her muscular bottom, pulling her into his raging erection as her hands caressed his naked chest. His head dipped, taking her hard nipple into his mouth as her hands went to his fly. He groaned as she pulled it down, freeing him, and her hands cupped him through his boxers. His tongue struck her nipple with a rhythmic flicking and she cried out, "Oh, Jack." He moved his mouth to the other breast and teased that nipple into a pulsing peak as his hands gripped her bottom, and she whimpered and slipped her hand into his boxers. Jack gasped and sighed as her hands worked his cock into a rock-hard missile and his mouth and fingers moved back to continue their torment of her breasts. Suddenly, Natalie pulled away and went down to her knees, pulling his sex to her lips. He nearly came undone as her tongue struck him, and she took him deeply into her silky, hot mouth. She began to lick and stroke and suck until he had to step back, afraid this would be over far too soon. She just looked up at him, a knowing smile on her face.

"As much as I love having your exquisite mouth on that part of me, I must insist that we stick to the script, sweetheart," he said and pulled her to her feet, taking her mouth again and plunging his tongue in to stroke hers as his hands moved hungrily over her body.

"Then take me how you want me, you sexy renegade," Nat teased and giggled, placing her hat on his head. Jack guided her to the bed and they fell together, grabbing for one another as his mouth found hers once again. He couldn't get enough of her beautiful body that ached for him as she moaned, one hand stroking her breast and the other pulling her thigh against his as he kissed her breathlessly. Suddenly, he turned her over on all fours and came up behind her. "Ooh, *you're* the naughty one now, husband." She moaned and grabbed a pillow to prop herself on as she pushed her bottom into his hardness. He freed his hips from his jeans as he centered himself and guided his steel-hard member slowly into the delicious heat that was hers alone.

"Oh, my sweet angel," he shivered as he felt her silky wetness close in around him. He nearly exploded when she gasped and arched her back, pulling him further in.

"I'm all yours, cowboy," Natalie purred longingly when he was fully engulfed inside her. Jack groaned as he withdrew then thrust, again and again, gripping her hips and driving into her as she pushed herself back against him, their movements syncing together in a steady rhythm. His hands moved then and came beneath her, cupping her breasts, squeezing with each thrust as his thumbs and index fingers pinched her nipples lightly. She whimpered and moaned, and his appetite increased as his rhythm became faster, more urgent. Soon, she was getting close, he could feel it. He moved one hand between her thighs and stroked the tender, wet folds of flesh there, arching his hips as his other hand gripped her upper thigh. Suddenly, she was crying out as her center quickened around him, and her body spasmed, her bottom hitting hard against his thighs. He moaned as he tried to hold himself back from his own orgasm, feeling her tightness contracting around him. She writhed and gasped as she rode her sexual high, and he gritted his teeth in bittersweet agony.

Quickly, Jack pulled out and flipped her over to face him. Natalie's eyes widened in both surprise and desire as he pulled her back to him, tilting her hips up at a sharp angle to his, and plunged inside her once again. Her head flew back in pleasure as he lunged and his hands slid beneath her to grip her tight little rear-end in his palms. He drove hard and fast, his need blinding him, and he felt himself slowly slipping into oblivion as her hand fell between her thighs to stroke herself. He smiled in triumph as her eyes met his, and she came again, crying his name, her legs wrapping tightly around him.

Jack felt the grip of pleasure take him as her incredible tightness possessively squeezed around his cock and his grasp returned to her hips as he cried, "Oh, Natalie, baby." He let his body go and his mind soar as his head flew back in climax and he thundered his release with a powerful plunge as his seed gushed into her. He held her against him as his body shuttered and his breathing slowly returned to normal. After several moments had passed, he let her legs down and came to lay beside her, pulling her to him. Her skin and cheeks were hot as he cupped them in his hands and kissed her softly.

"Jack, that was super sexy," she said as she settled her small frame in his arms.

"I thought so too, wifey." He stroked her back as her breathing steadied against his chest.

"I really like naughty Natalie," she confessed, looking up at him, cocking her eyebrow.

"I won't disagree with that." He gave her a crooked grin and kissed her soft lips once more. He leaned his head back then and sighed. "You wore me out, cowgirl."

She smiled up at him. "Oh, I haven't even *begun* to wear you out," she corrected him and pulled the hat from his head, placing it on her own. "It's *my* turn to ride." With that, she straddled him, and he gasped as her hands fell on him.

~

"*L*J, I ain't tellin' you again, boy. Get off that tractor!" Bella exclaimed as Luther ambled up the front porch stairs of their ranch-style home, five pizza boxes in hand. Kelsey and Savannah shot ahead of him into the house, giggling.

He smiled over at his beautiful wife, clad in a thin yellow cotton dress, fanning herself with a *People* magazine. She looked every bit the southern belle she was with her lightly tanned skin, long blonde hair and deep brown eyes. Her big pregnant belly pulling the short dress up a bit higher on her sexy thighs as she shifted to make room for him on the porch swing. He wanted to hike that dress up and take her right then and there, despite all the children playing not far away in the front yard.

He leaned in to kiss her before turning around as his eldest son, eleven-year-old, Luther James Jr. or LJ as they called him, smarted off at Bella.

"You sass your momma like that again, son, and I'll bust your ass in front of your friends," Luther yelled. He then placed the pizzas on the small table to the side of the door and planted his butt down beside his wife, throwing his arm around her as she scooted in closer to him. "Damn, I can't wait to get you outta that dress, woman." He practically growled in her ear as his mouth found her damp neck and nibbled there.

Bella giggled and her hands flirted with his belt-line. He moaned as his mouth found hers and he sipped at her lips, his tongue swiftly stroking hers.

"Behave, husband," she scolded, pulling away, even as her hand cupped at his aroused sex. "There are children present."

"Like that's ever stopped you before, Mrs. Boyd." He cupped at the breast bumping his chest.

Bella giggled again. "You always come home horny after being around Natalie. Should I be worried?" She was teasing he knew.

"Absolutely not! Natalie Butler was my first love. You, Bella Boyd, are my *last*."

"Is that why you keep knocking me up?" Her mouth moved to his neck, and he groaned again, swearing.

"Daddy!" He heard as he looked up to see Kelsey and Savannah coming out the screen door. He and Bella immediately moved their heads and hands, and Luther crossed his leg over the other to hide his raging boner.

"Yes, pumpkin?" he asked as he watched Kelsey come forward, a VHS tape in her hands.

"Can we watch *Dirty Dancin'*?"

"Uh…"

"Vanna says she ain't never seen it."

Luth looked to his wife, who shrugged, then up to his daughter as she waited patiently for his answer. "Well, baby doll, I dunno if Savannah's mom and dad would want her watching that. It's probably not appropriate."

"Daddy." Kelsey huffed and rolled her eyes, looking so much like her momma in that instant.

"I tell you what? Why don't y'all watch *Harry Potter* instead?"

"Cuz we seen it like a million times already."

"Alright, Kels. That's fine. But fast-forward through those certain parts, alright? You know which ones I'm talkin' about," Bella stated, eyeing Kelsey with intent and dismissed the girls, who ran back into the house squealing.

"*Dirty Dancin'*?"

"Aww, it's fine, honey. We watched it when we were younger 'an them." Bella reassured as her head rested on his shoulder. He sat content with her in his arms for a few moments, listening to the kids in the background laughing and running, and he took in her smell as he buried his nose in her silky, damp hair. She smelled of earth and sweat and lilies, and he flashed back to when he almost lost her all those years ago. She'd come so close to dying that night in his arms. There had been so much blood, so much *red*, it had covered them both as he'd raced to save her life. After she'd healed, he'd begged her never to wear the color red, for that's all he saw in the days that had followed. He held so much rage in his heart for Dan Wilson—still to this day—fourteen years after the fact. He cringed as he thought the name that plagued his nightmares. Dan was still in prison, still alive. And at times, Luther Boyd had wished Dan was dead for what he'd done to Annabella Smith. But as Luth looked over into Bella's brown eyes, he sighed. God how he loved her. He hadn't realized then that the night she almost died, their lives were only just beginning. They'd been married just a year or so shorter than Jack and Natalie, but their love for one another was just as strong. He smiled as he took her hand in his and kissed the back of it. Bella Smith Boyd had once taken so much from him, but in the last thirteen plus years had given it all back and then some.

"You know how very much I love you, my baby Bella?"

"As much as I love you?"

"Even more." His eyes held hers as hers filled with grateful tears, and she leaned in to kiss him. He savored her lips once more before Levi's whining voice came up the porch stairs.

"Eww, Dad!" Levi, Luther's now—as it was his birthday—seven-year-old son, scoffed and panted, attempting to catch his breath. "Can we eat now? I'm starved."

"You can be all grossed out if you want to, my boy. But one day, you'll enjoy kissing a beautiful woman like your momma as much or more than you like pizza. Trust me when I tell you."

Luth laughed as his sons and their friends smirked at that. One day they would understand love themselves, he prayed, and they would be blessed to know it by name.

CHAPTER 7

*D*allie smiled over at Cole as he cranked the big diesel truck. She couldn't tell if he was more nervous about the date itself or driving her dad's truck as they buckled up.

Dallie tried not to dwell on what she'd overheard regarding her mom and biological father. She'd walked in to hear her dad ask if Troy had forced himself on her mother, and she'd been taken aback as her mother practically admitted that he had.

Apparently, her Uncle Luther felt guilty about not stopping it. Dallie had missed the earlier talk on how he knew all this or what all had happened, but her mother had explained that she'd loved Troy back then, and obviously, didn't regret it as much as Luther did. Still, Dallie's dad had gotten so upset that he'd had to walk away after hearing this news, and her Aunt Jordan looked like she'd been slapped. It was disturbing, to say the least. But her mom had seen Dallie's reaction and grabbed her, reassuring her. It didn't take the shock of it all away though; her biological father had taken her mother's innocence and violently according to what she'd overheard her uncle say.

That atrocious act Troy had committed against her mother had simply been the prelude to the onslaught of evil he would later unearth.

"You *do* like pizza, right?" Cole asked, looking over at her as they rode down the two-lane road toward downtown Abundance.

Dallie laughed. "Of course."

"Ok. Good. This place is supposed to have wood-fire grilled pizza. I've never had pizza like that."

"Me either," she said. "I've always wanted to try it though!"

He smiled over at her then, and she felt his eyes rake over her. "You look beautiful," he stated.

"Thanks, Cole." Dallie blushed.

"I especially like the boots." He pointed down at her bedazzled new cowboy boots. They were black and sparkly with rhinestones, unlike the real ones she wore daily.

Dallie giggled, almost feeling naked without her hat to accompany them. She looked over at her "date" then and took in his jeans and green polo shirt. His hair was lightly spiked, and she liked the look on him.

"You like Daddy's truck?" she asked, motioning to the leather interior with wood accents; a Christmas gift she and her mom had picked out for him.

"Yeah," he said and gripped the steering wheel a little tighter. "It rides real smooth, but *damn*, it's big."

Dallie laughed. "Yes, it is."

"What's that place?" Cole pointed to the giant dilapidated neon sign of a cowboy boot with a flashing red spur. "The...Rusty...Spur." He read as they passed sight of the old bar. "Hmm... Sounds like a cool place to go."

Dallie balked at that. "Ha! If you knew what I do about that bar, you'll steer clear of it. That place is nothin' but trouble." She laughed again, recalling the stories her aunt had recently told her regarding her mother, father, aunt and uncle...and The Spur.

"Let's see what's on the radio," Cole said then and turned up the volume on the stereo of the truck. An old country song belted out in a deep twang, and Dallie wrinkled her nose and shook her head. She leaned forward and spun the dial to seek out a good tune for the ride. She stopped when she heard the chords of an electric guitar as The Eagles played "Hotel California" and nodded her head to the rhythm as she looked over at Cole.

"Cool," he said. "I didn't know you liked The Eagles."

"What's not to like? Besides, there's a lot you don't know about me." Dallie grinned slyly. Cole's eyebrows shot up at. She began riffling through the large console between them, looking for her dad's CD case. "Let me surprise you even further." She pulled out the large black case of her dad's CDs that had music from light jazz to heavy metal and began flipping through the pages. She chose one and pulled it out, popping it into the CD player. She selected the track she wanted and waited for it to play. Cole's eyes widened as he recognized the song as Metallica's "Fuel".

"Holy crap, Dallie! You like heavy metal?"

"Love it! Daddy too, believe it or not." She laughed as he gaped.

He recovered with, "Well, I shoulda known that when I heard y'all listening to it this morning during your workout."

"Yeah, Daddy says heavy metal pumps him up more than any other music, so that's what we work out to. I guess it does kinda help..." she trailed off, sensing his discomfort at talking about her father. She smiled then. "Jack really intimidates you, huh?" she asked. She didn't refer to her dad by his first name very often, but Cole now knew that her father didn't actually share her DNA, so it wasn't such a big deal.

"Well, yeah!" he declared as if the reason were completely evident. "He's super protective and he's freakin' huge. I mean, do you not notice how big he is when y'all are working out? He could leave me in a *world* of hurt. He's like the Duke on steroids." His cheeks flushed in embarrassment as she giggled. "Yeah, of course you don't get it, you're his little precious," he stated, scowling.

Dallie belted out a big laugh then. No, she knew what a bad-ass her dad was. She didn't need reminding. Poor Cole. He was truly terrified of her dad. "I'm sorry. I don't mean to laugh at you! It's just...when you said that, it reminded me... I used to tell my dad that he was Superman." She looked off, reminiscing.

"Yeah!" Cole retorted. "I can understand why." With that, they both laughed.

She took his hand then, and they sang along loudly to the song. She took in Cole's handsome face as her mother and aunt's words filled her head. *Holy shit!* she thought. *He really does favor Daddy.* Was it his green eyes, his light brown hair or his square jaw? She wasn't sure exactly what it was, but she truly felt once again like she was looking at a younger version of her father. Maybe that's why she was attracted to him... Didn't girls subconsciously seek men like their fathers? Dallie wasn't sure if she should be concerned by this thought or comforted by it, after all, hadn't she already come to the conclusion that she was going to find a man like her father to love?

She suddenly didn't care either way as a handsome Cole West beamed over at her—pearly whites shining—and arched a perfectly defined brow at her as he mimicked the guitar chords oozing out of the stereo system. She admired his muscular arms as they extended toward the steering wheel. No, they weren't quite as large as her father's, but they were still as impressive in their own right. His hands were big and capable. His fingers, long and straight, perfect "piano fingers" Savannah would conclude.

"I can play that whole riff on guitar, you know?" That beautifully arched brow shot up again, and Dallie couldn't help but smile back at him.

"Is that so?" she asked. "I would like to see you play guitar. I can see it in my head. I bet you're good."

"Well," he faltered. "Not as good as you are on a horse, but I'm not too shabby." He elbowed her, playfully, as he winked.

"You're being modest, I'm sure," she countered.

"Maybe you'll find out," he proposed. "Just gotta find a guitar lying around somewhere..." He looked around. Dallie laughed.

When they rolled into town, the streetlights were just starting to come on, and Dallie admired the strip of parallel brick buildings on either side of Main Street, the scattered elm trees and the old white marble courthouse that made up historic downtown Abundance. It might not be much, but to her it was home. They noted the light crowd on this early Saturday evening. Town wasn't usually so quiet at this time of night, even on the weekends, Dallie knew. But it was summer after all, and most people were on vacation. Aside from the few eateries in town—save for cruising around and hanging out in the Ingles parking lot—there wasn't much else for young adults to do.

The new pizza joint wasn't but a couple buildings down from an old Mexican restaurant that her family always went to. Cole ended up parking the big duelie behind the newly labeled Vinny's Pizzeria, it was just too big to fit into a standard sized space, and they walked up together, hand in hand. She smiled up at Cole as he opened the door for her and she walked in ahead of him. His hand came to the small of her back as he came in behind her and they waited at the line ahead of them. Dallie's nostrils were immediately hit with the smell of charred wood burning and savory meats as her eyes took in the quaintly lit and decorated vintage style pizzeria. The walls were a deep red brick, save for the white subway tiles that lined the kitchen located in the center of the joint, which was mostly open with a large wide mouthed oven, alight with orange and red flames. To their right, sat the hostess stand and mirrored bar beyond with a concrete countertop and to the left, a row of booths with black vinyl upholstery. Tables filled the remaining spaces and the ceiling was black and vaulted with exposed air conditioning ducts, giving the place a modern, industrial feel.

Dallie immediately loved its uniqueness and was pleased with the crowd that had gathered to try Abundance's newest restaurant. She smiled and waved over at Peggy Freeman, slightly cringing internally, as she felt Cole's hand go to her waist. Peggy waved back and gave Dallie a big Cheshire cat grin, looking at Cole like she had some secret she wanted to tell.

Great! she thought. *I'll be part of the next rumor spreading around town now.*

Peggy was a fellow member of the Abundance First Baptist Church, Dallie's church, and had known Dallie's family for a long time. She was in her mid-fifties, her children long gone and out of the house now, and she simply had nothing better to do than to create drama in her life where there was none.

Dallie silently begged the young hostess not to sit her anywhere near the town gossip and sighed in relief as the short brunette escorted them to the row of booths, hopefully far from the prying eyes of nosey Peggy. She smiled up at the young girl, who couldn't be more than fifteen, as they sat opposite one another and the girl handed Cole and Dallie their menus, looking a little longer at Cole than Dallie would've liked. He seemed completely oblivious though as he smiled over at Dallie and the girl walked away.

Dallie tried hard to focus on the menu but felt the laser like eyes of her fellow community member and turned her gaze in time to watch Peggy, who stared back at her, whisper into Betty Steven's ear. Dallie rolled her eyes and sighed heavily, bringing the menu up to block her view.

"Dallie?" she heard Cole's voice call out. His finger pulled the menu back down, and she felt her cheeks flush as she looked into his deep emerald eyes. "What's the matter?"

"Oh nothing!" Dallie exclaimed and darted her eyes over, motioning to Peggy. "We're just suddenly an item now because I'm pregnant with your illegitimate baby."

Cole's mouth widened and his brows crinkled as he asked, "Say what?"

Dallie couldn't help but laugh at his expression and said, "That lady over there is the local town gossip, and she saw us come in together, so guess what? We will be the new talk of the town. Get ready!"

"Oh," Cole said, relieved. "Is that all?" He waved his hand, dismissively. "I was afraid you didn't like the place or something."

"No, I love it! It's darling." Dallie looked around then back to the menu. "That pizza smells wonderful. I'm starved. I can't wait to taste it." She perused the items on the menu. Everything sounded so delicious. They had antipasto, fresh mozzarella and homemade meatballs. She wanted some of each!

"So, you wanna split a pizza? They're pretty huge, after all." Cole pointed to a hot, steamy, cheesy pizza as it passed by them on the way to the table to Dallie's left. It *was* huge. "What kind do you like?"

"Well, all kinds really. My favorite is magherita, but I love Italian sausage and theirs is made in house."

"Then sausage it is," Cole stated and gave her a crooked grin. She felt butterflies fill her stomach as she noted his intent gaze on her. Was this the look her father had said he didn't like? It didn't look like lust, not that she would know; his eyes appeared to twinkle. "Those salads look great too. Want one?" He pointed over to a large tossed salad with lots of cheese, drawing Dallie's gaze from his. She smiled and nodded.

When their waiter arrived, they ordered some Cokes and their food and waited patiently, Cole reaching out to take Dallie's hand. She shook her head and declined.

"Not until Ms. Vulture over there leaves." She tilted her head over at Peggy.

"Oh, Dallie. C'mon! You don't mean to tell me that you're gonna let some snoop get the best of you on your first date with me, are ya?"

"You don't know how she is," Dallie insisted. "I'm serious. When I tell you that the next thing you'll hear coming through the grapevine is that Dallas Kinsen is pregnant, and Peggy saw her at the—what's this place called again?" She paused, thoughtfully.

"Vinny's," Cole added and laughed.

"...*Vinny's* with the bum ranch hand who knocked her up, don't say I didn't warn you," Dallie finished and crossed her arms over her chest.

"Ok, first of all, I may be a wanderer, but I am *no* bum!" His brows went up in amusement. "And second, who really cares what she says?"

"Half the town! And they *believe* her. That's the problem."

"Ok, ok... You *do* realize that me holding your hand isn't going to get you pregnant?" Again, with that sexy, crooked smile of his; she was tingling on the inside. Suddenly, his smile faded and a solemn expression took hold of him. "I'm getting the feeling like maybe she spread a rumor about you before."

"Well, *yeah*," Dallie replied and noted Cole's grim expression. "She was the one to throw me to the wolves when—" She stopped suddenly. She didn't want to talk about her private life here, not with Peggy within potential ear shot. "We'll talk about it later," she told him as the waiter sat their salad down in front of them along with two plates and some silverware.

"Fair enough," Cole said and began tossing the generous bowl of salad. He scooped her up some first then himself, and they toasted glasses as he cheered, "To new beginnings."

"To new beginnings," she concurred.

They enjoyed their salad and talked about their work on the ranch, Cole's improving progress with horseback riding and the comfort and confidence he was garnering among the horses. It wasn't long before their giant pizza came out, and they admired it with hungry eyes.

"Wow, look at that fresh mozzarella." Dallie pointed out.

"Yeah, this looks awesome."

"Dallas, honey, how are ya? Who's this strapping young gentleman you're with tonight?" Dallie flinched as she recognized Peggy's chipper voice before actually seeing her standing before them. Peggy was somewhat heavyset with brown eyes and hair. Tonight, she wore her usual short-sleeved floral sun dress, her short, permed hair forming a big brown mushroom atop her head.

Dallie tried to recover as she cleared her throat and coughed. "Oh, umm... Peggy, this is Cole West. He's our newest ranch hand. Cole, meet Peggy."

"Peggy Freeman." She reached her hand out to shake Cole's. He obliged. "I saw you join the Kinsens at church Sunday last. Will we be seeing more of you then?"

Cole took her hand and plastered on his beautiful smile and nodded. "Yes, ma'am. I'll be there."

"That was quite a sermon, didn't you think?"

"It was. I enjoyed it thoroughly." Cole just beamed up at her.

"I see you've taken to Dallie real quick like," she muttered, and Dallie almost choked on her drink she was sipping.

"The Kinsens have welcomed me with open arms. They're such a beautiful family, don't you agree?" Cole didn't miss a beat as he continued to shake Peggy's hand.

Peggy practically harrumphed and replied with, "It's good to see new faces in town. See you on Sunday." She pulled her hand away, gave Dallie a suspicious glare, and left as quickly as she had come.

"I think that went rather well, don't you?" Cole's cheeks flamed slightly in anger as he turned back to Dallie. It was an emotion Dallie hadn't seen on him before, but she was too busy being mortified, wanting to slink down beneath the booth they sat at.

"You didn't help with that comment on open arms. You may as well have said open legs for all she—" Dallie shut her eyes tightly. "I can only imagine what's going through her head right now."

"Yeah, well, fuck her," Cole exclaimed, and Dallie's eyes shot open in surprise. "Don't give her the satisfaction of seeing you so upset. You're not doin' anything wrong being here with me, and I'll be damned if I let her ruin our night."

With that, Dallie watched Cole walk over to their waiter, pull out the wallet from his back pocket, hand the man some money and walk back with a pizza box in his hand.

"Come on, we're going to go enjoy our dinner in privacy."

~

*C*ole looked over at Dallie as she bit into a slice of pizza. A long string of cheese followed as she pulled it away from her perfect lips. Cole laughed as she tried to wrangle the stray line into her mouth.

They sat on the lowered tailgate of her dad's truck overlooking a streaming river, in the park. Dallie had pulled out a horse blanket from the truck bed tool box—which had come in handy as it had a slew of useful items inside, including the paper towel that Dallie was using to wipe the grease from her fingers with. It was a nice night, not too hot despite that it was early summer, a nearby street lamp provided the perfect amount of light for them to see while they ate without being too bright.

Cole had gotten angry when Peggy made Dallie feel so cheap at the restaurant. Cole was all too familiar with people and their judgment. Where did this woman come off making Dallas feel guilty when she was doing something as harmless as going out to dinner with a member of the opposite sex? As if Jack's protective nature wasn't enough to deal with, now Dallie couldn't even been seen out on a simple date without the whole town thinking she was up to something scandalous? *What the hell?*

"So, now's a great time to tell me about this Peggy lady," Cole began.

Dallie sighed and swallowed her bite before she said, "Yeah, I guess it is huh? So, she assumed that Nick and I..." She paused when Cole gave her a confused look. "Nick is my ex, and a former ranch hand of my dad's. He and I dated for a few months last year. Anyway, she assumed that he'd knocked me up and took off."

"Are you freakin' kiddin' me?" Cole asked, interrupting her story.

"Nope. So, that's why I hesitated in holding your hand at the table earlier."

"Wait!" Cole felt his anger flair up again. "That's one *hell* of an assumption for someone to make about you. Did she have a reason to even jump to that conclusion?"

"Are you gonna let me tell the story or not?" Dallie grinned up at him, amused.

"Not 'til you answer the question," he retorted and elbowed her side, playfully.

"No, she had no reason to assume that Nick and I had even slept together. She just came to that conclusion on her own. She's 'old school', my mom said. She didn't like the fact that he was staying on the ranch and figured that we were sleeping together."

"Jeez," Cole grumbled and looked out over the river into the night.

"His sudden departure and absence, and my melancholy mood over the following weeks only tended to encourage her thinking. At one point, my dad heard the rumor about my being pregnant..."

"Oh boy!" Cole grimaced. "I can only guess how *that* went. She should be glad she's not a man."

Dallie laughed. "Yeah, he was quick to pull her aside and put her in her place. It wasn't pretty, and she avoided us like the plague for months after that. Not everyone believed the gossip, especially those who really know us, but it was an ugly stain that was hard to wash away."

"My God, small towns really are Satan's playground," he stated and shook his head. "That's utterly ridiculous." Cole looked back over at her and smiled, ruefully. "I'm sorry that happened. People can be cruel sometimes, but you, of all people, to have that kind of rumor circulating about you is *completely* unfounded. Anybody can take one look at you and see that."

"My dad told Peggy the same thing." Dallie sighed. "I was an honors student, president of my class, constantly absorbed in my dressage and at the ranch. Not like that would prevent me from being sexually active, I mean, truthfully, teen pregnancy is a real issue."

Cole shrugged and responded, "Still. Who is she to spread something like that without considering your reputation?"

Dallie went on, explaining herself. "It's not like I had a ton of time on my hands and under my parents' watchful eyes to boot. I mean, I could have done it with him if I'd *really* wanted to. He *was* my first kiss though, and I enjoyed our time together. He just didn't stick around; he was a drifter...like you." Her eyes were deep and sorrowful as they looked up at him, the word "you" said so softly, as if she were telling a sad story.

"Dallie..." Cole sighed.

"No, it's ok!" She laughed. "I seem to have a knack for attracting guys who are rampant with wanderlust. Maybe it's my forte in life." With that, Cole belted out a big laugh. Dallie followed.

They ate in companionable silence for a while, enjoying the delicious, albeit slightly cold, handmade pizza with its San Marzano crushed tomatoes, big chunks of sage sausage and crunchy crust. After a couple slices each, they covered the rest with the cardboard lid and lay back on the blanket that they spread out in the back of the truck bed and just stretched out to enjoy the stars.

"So, are you excited about starting college?" Cole asked as he looked over at Dallie, whose curly locks lay framing her face.

"Yes...and no." She laughed and turned to face him. "I'm anxious too. I'm eager to meet new people and start classes and learn and all but..." She looked down, and he waited for her to find the courage to continue. "I just, I'm gonna miss this place. I know that sounds so petty, but it's true. It's all I've ever known. And despite what he says and how great of a trainer he is, Daddy's gonna really have a hard time without me here."

Although Cole was very aware of Dallie's rare gift with the horses she loved, he doubted that Jack was going to struggle too much without her; he would no doubt miss her, but he was more than capable of holding his own, Cole had seen. Dallie was just afraid of the unknown and knowing she had never really been far out of her small town, he assumed her fear had started to outweigh her curiosity. Cole was all too familiar with fear... and new places and families.

"It's ok to be scared, but you shouldn't worry." He took her face in his palm then and raked his thumb across her flawless cheekbone. She gasped at his touch, and he felt his body tingle as he turned to face her. He gulped as she moved closer to him. "You're going out to make your mark on the world, and I know that you're going to do great. You're smart and you're driven, and you know what you want out of life, which is awesome. With most of us, that's half the battle. You're a good person, you're passionate about life and that's important."

"What do you know about my passions?" she teased as she reached her hand up to his hair. The look she gave him made him super eager to find out *exactly* what they were, but the image of that spinning gun in her father's hands was a memory he wouldn't soon forget, and he warned himself not to be overzealous.

"I've *seen* your passions. You're a little transparent, you know?" He laughed even as she gaped and shoved at him.

"And you're too damn cocky for your own good," she scolded as he grabbed at her pushing hands and pulled her into his chest.

"That doesn't mean that you aren't still mesmerizing, Dallas."

She stopped struggling then and succumbed to the warmth of their bodies lightly pressed together and the hand that cupped her cheek as he smiled at her. He watched her face as she gazed at him, her eyes falling to his lips, her own bottom lip worried by her teeth, and he gulped.

"You think I'm mesmerizing?"

"You're beautiful and amazing." His other hand came to her forearm, stroking her where the thin cardigan didn't cover.

"Are those lines?" she asked, so unaware. He threw his head back and laughed. She gave an uneasy smile, waiting for the answer.

"If I were sixteen again? Yeah, maybe. But no, Dallie, I wasn't feeding you a line. I truly mean what I say," he reassured her. She sighed in apparent relief. "But you're wise to be cautious. You'll be getting many lines like that when you get to college." Suddenly, the thought of her lying like this with another guy gave him a tightness in his gut that he didn't like, and he gritted his teeth as the unwelcome vision filled his head.

She must have sensed his discomfort because she asked, "Did I say something wrong?"

He tried to recover and grinned. "No, but it sure was a shocker to hear that nasty cuss word come from those sexy lips of yours." The minute he said it, he regretted it.

The sultry look she gave him was unmistakable as she arched a flawlessly lined eyebrow at him. "I can cuss if I want to, I'm a big girl, you know?"

"Don't I know it!" he confirmed as he looked down at her chest, playfully. "But that don't mean I'm over the shock of it."

"Well, get used to me shocking you then." She leaned into him, her lips puckered.

"Whoa there." He pulled back. "Don't you know you aren't supposed to kiss on the first date?" He was stalling, and they both damn well knew it.

Dallie scoffed, "We've kissed before!" When Cole didn't acquiesce, she smirked, "You just said that I had sexy lips."

"You do," he agreed. Her eyebrows went up as if to say, "And?"

Cole sighed and tried to think of what to say to make her understand his hesitation, but just the look on her face squelched any ideas he might have. "Look." He pulled her chin up when she looked down. "Let's take this slow, ok? There's no rush."

"I didn't realize a simple kiss was considered 'rushing'. I was just going with the moment." Now she was embarrassed. *Damn!* he thought. He was screwing this up, royally.

"It's not," he said. "I'm just more worried about where a *simple* kiss will lead." It wasn't a lie. She was so sweet, and it would be easy for him to lose himself to her kiss. Plus, he was fairly certain her father was keeping an eye on his watch back home with a large baseball bat in his hand.

"I'm sorry if I'm coming off as easy," Dallie stated, regretfully.

"You are no such thing, Dallas Kinsen. I wasn't trying to make you feel bad, you know?"

Too late for that, he thought. She just shrugged. "It's fine, I'm sure there'll be *many* guys in college that wouldn't have any qualms about rounding second base with me." Her eyebrows went up in challenge.

Cole frowned. "Hey! No fair. You're failing to see that I *want* to round second base with you...just not on the first date."

Dallie rolled her eyes. "What's the taboo thing about a first date anyway?"

"Give me some credit here. I'm being a nice guy trying not to take advantage of you. I deserve some *serious* points."

She laughed at that. At least now she was smiling, if only momentarily. "Ha! You're just intimidated by my lack of experience. You're afraid you'll 'corrupt' me." She laughed again and shoved his shoulder, playfully.

"Yeah, maybe."

"Uh," she scoffed and frowned. "God, you're insufferable."

"But handsome," he added with a sly smile.

When she finally seemed content with the fact that he indeed wasn't going to kiss her, at least not yet, he relaxed a little, and they bantered playfully about college life and what classes she would be starting out with. He missed his college days even if he hadn't gone to a big school. He'd gone to a technical college in Austin and he'd done a lot of hands-on work in automotive repair and technology after his pre-requisite classes to become a master mechanic. He loved the challenge and skill it required. He loved rebuilding an engine and watching it purr to life. He wanted to tell her how much fun he'd had with all his classmates and about his shop, but he didn't want to divulge too much. When the time came for him to leave, the less she knew about him the better.

They placed the blanket back into the truck tool box and went for ice cream at a local shop that made homemade custard. Cole ordered cookies and cream and Dallie went with strawberry both in freshly made waffle cones. They headed out to a clearing to sit back on the tailgate and gaze up at the stars over the big Texas sky. Being out here in the "boonies" away from the lights of the city, the stars seemed bigger and brighter than they had in Austin.

"So, you really *aren't* gonna kiss me, huh?" Dallie sighed in exasperation as she looked over at him.

He just gave her a disappointed look without answering her, and she crossed her arms over her chest as if she suddenly felt a chill.

"I get it. You won't be around long enough for it to matter anyway." Her voice sounded so despondent that he almost lost all his inhibitions. He was two seconds from grabbing her and planting one on her when she jumped down off the tailgate.

The ride home was awkward to say the least, but Cole tried his damnedest to stick to his guns and listen to reason. As much as he wanted to lose himself to Dallas Kinsen, the reality was that he was a fugitive running from the law. At any moment, he was going to have to up and leave. And in a hurry. She was an incredible young woman with a big, bright future ahead of her and he was a man who, at no fault of his own, had eternally lost his. The two of them just weren't meant to be. But looking at her sitting so quiet, so innocent and gorgeous as the moon cast shadows over her, his heart lurched. Some way, some *how*, he was going to have to let her go. And God help him, he knew that it wasn't going to be easy!

~

*N*atalie looked over at her husband as they rode together to get their baby for the night. The few hours they'd spent at home alone was well-needed and well-deserved. They'd made love several times and eaten a hearty dinner while watching a movie they'd been wanting to for months now. It was a long overdue date night that had been worth every second. But now Natalie was ready to have her son back in her arms. As much as she enjoyed her husband, and his love-making, being without her children for too long made her feel incomplete somehow. Jack must have felt the same way. They'd been cuddled up together on the couch merely ten minutes ago when he'd asked if she were ready to go retrieve their toddler. She'd only nodded, and they'd taken off.

They pulled up to the carport and parked behind Nate's new Ford F-250. Jack came to her side as she got out and took her hand, bringing it to his full lips for a light kiss as they walked up the stairs to her brother's house. This home held so many memories. It was the home Natalie and Jack had fallen in love in, the home where they'd been married, where she'd met his family for the first time... where she'd lost their first baby.

The sting of it had never truly left her and never would as long as she lived. It was an open wound that had never completely healed over. She wondered now what he would look like; she'd always felt it had been a boy. She tried not to contemplate the what-ifs in her mind or focus on the would-haves, although at times it over-whelmed her. But they'd been lucky and gotten their baby boy after all. And he was beautiful and precious, and Natalie couldn't be happier. Her husband had a male heir, and she thanked God that he was healthy and happy.

Nathan greeted them at the door as Jack draped his arm around Natalie and kissed the top of her head, and they entered the foyer.

"Good evenin'," Nate whispered as he pulled Nat in for a hug then pumped Jack's hand with his own and patted his shoulder.

"My boy must be sleepin'," Jack assumed as Nathan led them into the living room.

"He's been out for a good thirty minutes now." Nate motioned over to the couch where Jordan lay with Jackson, who was sprawled out on Jordan's ample chest, out like a light.

His sweet baby cheeks were squished on Jordan's tan skin and his long, dark eyelashes rested on them. His pert little nose and cupid bow lips looked as if they'd been painted on and Natalie smiled lovingly at the little angel that God had sent to them. Jackson favored Dallie so much with his curly blonde locks.

"I'm surprised you let him share," Jack stated and pointed.

Nate laughed. "He knows those are mine. He's just admiring the goods."

"Takes after his dad and uncle if you ask me," Jordan insisted. "He definitely likes the boobs. Nate couldn't get him to calm down. I laid him right on me and in a couple minutes he was out."

Jack just shrugged, and Nate laughed again. "Yeah, I didn't have the proper equipment, apparently," Nate added. "I would ask how your evening was, but by the look of it, I would say y'all enjoyed yourselves." When Natalie looked at her brother in confusion, he pointed to her shorts.

Nat immediately flushed as she realized they were on inside out; the pockets sticking out like donkey ears. Jack and Nate burst out laughing then, and Natalie looked down in sheer embarrassment. She ran to the bathroom and took them off, flipped them outside in and put them back on before returning to the living room. Her husband gave her a crooked grin and arched an eyebrow, pleased with himself. She just shook her head and blinked her eyes. At least Dallie and Cole hadn't seen her that way.

"Is Dallie back from her date yet?" Jordan asked, as if reading Nat's thoughts.

"I'm really shocked that you let her go out with him, Jack," Nate said.

"He's starting to come around," Natalie offered. Her husband just gave her a withered look.

"He's harmless," Jack added. "But that doesn't mean I like it."

"Hell, Jack. The girl is eighteen. Let her live a little," Jordan stated. Jack glared over at her then his look softened as he sighed.

"I know, I'm overbearing, pig-headed, selfish..."

"She's still your little girl, we understand. I don't really like it either, but what can we do?" Nate replied, looking over at them.

"We can't keep her in the nest forever," Natalie told Nate. "She's got to spread her wings at some point, and unless her father wants to camp out and follow her around campus," she scolded, "then we need to cut the puppet strings here before she leaves." Jack just glowered. He knew it was true. They'd already talked about this; each trying to convince and reassure the other. No one had told them it would be this difficult.

"Aww, I'm sorry guys," Jordan said as she pulled up to a sitting position, bringing baby Jax to her shoulder and cradling his head as she rocked. She would have made a wonderful mother, Natalie knew. Too bad a biological child of her own had never been in the cards.

Nat recalled when Jordan had told her that she would need the hysterectomy some thirteen years ago. She'd been smiling, but Natalie remembered the glimmer of sadness in Jordan's whiskey eyes. Deep down, she'd been devastated. And why wouldn't she be? She wasn't yet thirty when it had happened.

"It sucks," Jordan said. "We know this hasn't been easy for y'all." She stood and brought Natalie the baby, kissing her cheek as she turned him and placed him in Nat's arms.

Natalie just smiled up into her best friend's eyes. "Thanks, Jor. For everything."

"Of course! We all deserve mind-blowing sex every now and again." She winked. "I'll be getting mine here soon enough." She ambled over to Natalie's brother and kissed his lips seductively.

Nate smiled so happily that Nat felt tears come to her eyes. "Tell me again what exactly we did to deserve these two knock-outs?" Nate asked Jack.

Jack wrapped his arm around Natalie's waist, looking down into her upturned face. He gave her a sly grin. God, her husband was so handsome. "I'm still trying to figure that out myself."

They were headed home not much after, Jackson still cradled in Nat's arms. They hadn't bothered with the car seat; they only lived literally three minutes from Jordan and Nate. Her husband looked over at her, a seriousness on his face.

"I've been hard on Dallie, haven't I?" he asked.

"No, Jack, you haven't."

"I have. I know I have." He hung his head a little as they pulled into the garage.

"You only did what you thought was best in order to keep her safe and for that I'm ever grateful." The look he gave her then wiped all sadness away, and she smiled. "You coming into our lives was the most wonderful thing that ever happened to Dallie and I." He pulled her and the baby into his arms then and gave her a passionate kiss.

～

*D*allas was miffed as Cole pulled the big duelie up behind the garage. She noted her dad sitting on the porch, whiskey in hand with Magnus not far from his side.

Damn! she thought. *He's literally trying to ruin my life.*

Cole looked anxious as he watched her father leave the porch and go inside. Dallie sighed, relieved that he was giving them some privacy and smiled over at Cole, who gulped.

"Well, looks like we are on the clock. Better head inside." He turned the ignition off and opened the driver side door.

"Uh," Dallie huffed. "Seriously?"

"What?"

"You're seriously *that* afraid of my dad?" She looked at him incredulously. "I don't believe it!" She felt the anger ignite within her and turned to open her door.

This guy really was preposterous. What did he honestly think her dad was gonna do? Hadn't he been the very one to tell them it was okay to go out on a date in the first place?

Dallie rounded the back of the truck and was coming up beside the driver's side door, planning to side swipe him, when Cole grabbed her arm and slammed his door shut.

"Dallie?"

"No! Don't. I didn't realize you were such a *pansy!*" she cried, feeling angry tears in her eyes as she pulled her hand away from his grasp, turning from him.

Next thing she knew, she was jerked back and turned around so quickly that she gasped. Suddenly, her back was against the side of the truck and she was being pulled roughly into Cole's chest. She felt an arm around her waist and a hand at the back of her neck as his head lowered.

His lips were firm as they crushed against hers. Her protests died all at once. His head moved and he deepened the kiss as her mouth opened to him. His tongue plunged in and stroked at hers as he pulled her even tighter against him. She moaned as his mouth moved over hers, making her melt into his embrace. Their kiss was passionate and unabashed and— erotic. She felt her center tingle and throb with newfound desire as her hands moved and her fists grasped his shirt. Cole moaned as her tongue caressed his, the rough sound of his pleasure encouraging her on.

When they were breathless, he pulled back, planting soft sweet kisses on her lips, hesitant to release her. Her chest heaved as she tried to calm her breathing. When she dared to glance up into his eyes, the look he gave her startled her. The want in those sparkling green eyes was unmistakable.

"Damn!" Cole swore. "I forgot just how sweet you taste." Dallie gulped, his words eliciting a deep stirring in some primal part of her. "See," he reprimanded as he pulled back a little and looked at her lips in misery, "here's what happens with a *simple* kiss."

She didn't reply, just pulled at her bottom lip with her teeth, and suddenly his lips were on hers once again, and she was moaning, her arms moving up his chest and wrapping around his neck. He deepened the kiss and his hand dropped from her hair, down her shoulder, running the length of her arm. Large hands covered the span of her back as his tongue tormented hers until she was panting and pulling back for a breath. His mouth moved to her jawline then to her neck, and he nibbled there, the feeling so exquisite that she cried his name. He groaned and pulled away suddenly.

"Fuck," he swore again. "Sorry, I didn't mean..." he trailed off and looked at her lips again then finally up to her face as he tried to catch his breath. That look of desire had intensified, and she gulped again. Now she understood what he'd meant about taking things slow. "Your dad may end up shooting me with that gun after all."

"Huh?" Dallie asked.

"Nothing!" Cole recovered and laughed half-heartedly. He turned away and ran his hands through his hair, his gaze focused in the distance. Dallie readjusted her thin sweater and smoothed her dress and looked at herself in the side view mirror, making sure her hair wasn't all over her head. When she was satisfied that her parents couldn't tell she'd been making out, she turned to Cole, whose hands were shoved into his jeans pockets. He gave her a weak smile.

They walked silently hand-in-hand into the house. It was quiet, no one was around, and Dallie expelled the breath she'd been holding. *Thank God!*

Cole seemed just as relieved as he looked down at her and smiled.

She was about to ask him if he wanted to watch a movie when he took her hand and kissed the back of it gently.

"Goodnight, Dallie. I had a wonderful time with you tonight."

She gulped again as she looked into his eyes. "I did too. Thank you."

He sighed as he dropped her hand and slowly turned to go to the basement.

CHAPTER 8

*D*allie woke the next morning and came down for breakfast after her shower as usual. If her dad had any inclination that Cole had kissed her last night, he made no comment about it. In fact, he seemed completely oblivious…either that or he was putting on a good show. He came up to her mother while they were talking about last night.

Of course she'd told her mom about the amazing kiss that had knocked her socks off. She'd always told her mom practically everything. Her mom was just another best friend now that Dallie was older.

"So, how'd it go last night?" her mom had asked after Dallie came into the kitchen. Dallie had looked around, making sure her father was nowhere in sight then blushed to her toes and immediately, her mom had picked up on it. "Ah, he kissed you?" Her mom had sounded surprised. As if her dad hadn't kissed her mom on *their* first date. Well, maybe he hadn't.

Her mom grabbed her then and grinned, needing the gritty details. Dallie had caved after a moment's hesitation and told her mom what had been said, leaving out several details—including the fact that Dallie had practically thrown herself at Cole first before he'd finally gotten the guts to act on his impulses. "Well, of course he was hesitant, he's afraid of your father, Dallie," her mom had said knowingly as she turned to stir the grits. "He has every right to be. Jack is his boss! But I'm glad you finally know what it's like to be kissed."

Dallie looked at her as if she'd gone insane. Why on earth would she be glad for that? "Mom, I've been kissed before." Dallie shuffled her feet.

"Not like *that* you haven't," her mom concluded and lifted an eyebrow at her.

It was true. When she'd described her first kiss to her mom, it hadn't been toe-curling and passionate, and she hadn't felt like she had last night. She hadn't been overcome with desire. Her mom could tell. She knew the difference.

Dallie'd started to ask her mom why she was glad that her daughter had been ravaged by a random drifter when her dad came in and she'd walked over to the bar to sit shyly, avoiding his prying eyes. But he wasn't even looking at her.

"Mmm, there you are." Her dad grabbed her mom around the waist from behind and turned her into his arms. Her mom gasped and laughed even as his lips came down on hers. Dallie watched them, blushing, knowing now what that felt like. She looked down, giving them some privacy until he finally pulled back, keeping her mom close as he sighed and kissed her forehead. He finally looked over to Dallie, and she gave him a weak smile, waiting for the blow to come. He just gave her a crooked grin back and said, "Mornin', baby. Did you have fun last night?"

Dallie perked up then, seeing no reason for dread, as he released her mom and walked to the fridge, acting no different than any other morning. "It was fun... well, before Peggy Freeman spotted me." Dallie recalled.

"What? No," her mom asked, huffing.

"Yup."

"Damn! Well, I'm sure that made for an interesting dinner." Her dad scowled as he poured himself a cup of coffee.

"Well, actually, Cole decided to get our pizza to-go after she came to our table and insulted me."

"She insulted you?" Her mom stilled in flipping the French toast she was browning.

"Well, kinda," Dallie stammered, not wanting to make a mountain out of a mole hill. "She just made the statement that Cole had 'taken' to me real quick."

"That bitch!" her mom exclaimed and looked over to her dad.

"Unbelievable." Her dad shook his head and poured the creamer he'd retrieved from the fridge into his mug, his jaw ticking. Dallie knew what that meant. "I reckon I'm gonna have to have another little talk..."

"No, Dad. Please, don't. It'll just make it worse," Dallie pleaded. Her dad looked up to her then and grimaced.

"Dallas, no hypocritical, self-righteous—" he paused and clenched his fist on the countertop. "She has no right to make you feel the way she has, and I'm *damn* sick of her making our family look bad when she's just jealous."

"And that's all it is," her mom concluded and looked over at Dallie. She moved from the stove and approached Dallie's dad, her hand coming to rest on his big bicep. She looked into his eyes, stilling his anger. "Jack, let me handle this one, ok?" His brows drew for but an instant as her mom gazed intently up at him. Finally, his facial features softened and he grinned.

"Alright," he agreed and smiled over at Dallie. "I have a feeling that we won't be hearing anything else about another bastard grandchild of mine on that note."

With that, Dallie laughed. She knew that even as protective as her father was of his family and how he went to bat for them no matter what, her mom had her own way of handling things—not with brute strength or a deep voice—but with words. She was a writer, after all.

Her mom had grown up in this same small hometown and had

known most of the people in it her whole life, despite that she'd lived in Chicago for almost ten years. Her mom must have some juicy detailed leverage to hang over Peggy's head, Dallie surmised.

"So, are we looking at a potential *second* date?" Dallie's dad piped in after taking a long sip of his coffee. He'd moved to the edge of the kitchen island and had propped his hips there, gazing intently at her. Dallie's anxiousness returned suddenly and she gulped, looking over at her mom who just grinned and nodded. Dallie gulped again before looking back at her dad. His handsome face and emerald green eyes gave nothing away as he just stared back at her.

She shrugged. "Nothing was said about a second date." She tried to sound nonchalant about it, so her dad couldn't see right through her. Her mom came to her rescue then.

"Oh, there will be another one, trust me when I tell you…" her mom trailed off as her dad's frown returned, his menacing gaze now focused on her mom this time. Dallie almost laughed. "Relax husband, I simply mean they had a good time and they like each other, so there will be more dates," her mom reassured, her eyebrows popping up at him, stymying any response he might've had.

Her dad truly relaxed then, and even when Cole came walking into the kitchen and Dallie's cheeks burned crimson and she looked over at him, her father didn't seem the least bit put off. Not that she really noticed; she was too entranced by Cole and those lips that had both taken and given so much last night.

"Mornin'," he said as he smiled over at her and walked over to the coffee pot.

"Good mornin'," Dallie responded and tried to calm her hammering heart as she took in his still damp brown hair, his blue button-down shirt and the jeans that hugged his butt just right. The kitchen grew quiet, save for Jackson goo-ing and gah-ing in his playpen, the sound of his little hands banging on a musical toy. Dallie's mom smiled knowingly over at her and Dallie's eyes widened as if to say, "Stop it!" She didn't dare chance a look at her father for fear of her eyes giving away her secrets. She need not worry.

"We got that rescue coming in this morning, Mr. Kinsen?" Cole asked and came over to stand beside her dad, who shook his head at Cole once again addressing him as Mr. Kinsen. "I'm sorry," Cole said. "Jack." Her dad laughed at that.

"Yeah, got a rescue, a couple new clients and some that need boarding... Dallas has a busy morning." Her dad looked over at her, smiling.

Dallie scoffed, "Thanks Dad. What are you gonna do when I'm gone, huh?" Her eyes burned into him, and he laughed.

"You'll be surprised at what I can do! After all, my daughter is a whisperer, I've been taking notes." He winked. She laughed back. "Besides, maybe I'm just trying to keep you busy and distracted while I work my magic behind your back."

Dallie's eyebrows went up at that. "Magic, huh? Ok, Dumbledore," she bantered.

"Dallie, don't seem so surprised," her mom added. "Your dad's a very talented man. I should know." Her mom's eyes gave her father the once over and she grinned slyly at him.

"Oh lord, here we go," Dallie rolled her eyes, getting a laugh out of all of them.

When they finished breakfast and headed out to work, Dallie tried hard to focus on the horses and not at Cole's eyes as they seemed to scorch her. Her mind couldn't help going back to the incredible kisses she'd shared with him last night. His hands on her waist, her back, her face. It had been unlike anything she'd ever felt before, and she couldn't wait to feel it again. The thought of his solid chest against hers, his breath sweet and hot on her skin, the smell of his manly, woodsy cologne in her nostrils.

"Dallie! Whoa!" Mike called as the new horse on her lead almost plunged headlong into him as he approached her.

"Oh, Jeez. I'm so sorry!" Dallie grimaced and apologized. She hadn't even been paying attention as she longed the mare in a canter around the corral robotically. She blushed, embarrassed by her thoughts.

"Your dad wants to talk to you," Mike stated, looking annoyed as he took the longe line from her.

She smiled weakly at him and headed toward the barn and into her dad's office. He was on the phone and smiled at her as she came in and grabbed some water. Thirsty, she gulped two down cups and sat in the chair opposite him as he said, "Ok, great! Thanks so much. See you tomorrow," and hung the phone up.

Dallie noted the twinkle in his eyes and cocked an eyebrow at him in question.

He smiled again and began, "I'm hiring a new trainer to replace you."

Dallie never would've expected the hit those words would take to her gut. She gulped.

"C'mon, baby. Don't look so shocked." He extended his big hand to her, and she took it, tears coming to her eyes. "I'm not trying to upset you." Dallie just nodded in response. "Replace isn't the right word, and you know that! There's no replacement for your abilities, none whatsoever. We're just getting so busy lately, and I need more hands, especially with you leaving. Looks like I'm gonna be doing less managing and more working." He gave a quick laugh but then frowned. "Dallas, sweetheart, please don't cry."

Dallie hadn't even realized that she *was* crying until she sniffled and felt the tears running down her face. She was ugly crying now, she knew, and brought her hands to her face.

"Jesus, babe. I'm sorry. I never knew you would take it this hard." She heard her father stand and come around his desk, his boots scuffing on the concrete floor. She was pulled into his big arms as he cradled her head to his shoulder. "You know how much I'll miss workin' with you," he murmured and stroked at her hair as she continued to squall.

Her emotions overtook her then. The knowledge that her time here was coming to an end had her all tore up inside. Her memories bombarded her at that moment; this ranch that was also her home and all these horses that were her passion; this man who'd been her rock, her father, her boss, her co-worker, but mostly her best friend and mentor for the last fourteen years of her life. This felt like good-bye, and she didn't like it one bit.

"Darlin', you know that you'll always have a place here." It was as if Jack could read her thoughts. "I just want you to enjoy your last two months, ok? I don't want you having to feel the pressure of working, you know? That's all," he soothed and pulled her chin up to look at him. His deep green eyes reassured her as she sniffled. He smiled. "Sweetie, this isn't goodbye. Not in the least."

She hugged him tightly then, pulling herself against his massive, solid chest as her arms went around his waist and she closed her eyes against the flood of tears that spilled forth again. His big hands rubbed her back, and he sighed heavily. Finally, Dallie's outburst of overflowing emotions had taken their course, and she pulled back and wiped at her eyes and nose. She looked up at her dad, who smiled lovingly at her and kissed her forehead.

"You know how proud of you I am, right?" he asked. She just nodded. "You're my first child, Dallas, and this has been hard on me and your mother as I know it has been for you too…but, you're gonna be just fine. We all are. Your time has come, my daughter."

It took her long moments to pull away and when she did, she helped herself to the tissues that sat on her father's desk and sat down reluctantly across from her father as he, too, took a seat. He looked at her expectantly, waiting for her to break the silence first.

She finally spoke. "I'm sorry, Daddy."

He shook his head. "There's nothing for you to apologize for, baby."

She nodded but still felt apologetic for her waterworks and poor timing. She looked down and continued to blot at her nose, finally she was able to look back up at him.

"I don't know why I've been so emotional lately."

"Growing up is hard to do," her dad answered.

"Yeah it is!" she huffed, blotting again at the tears that stung her eyes. "But why? I should be relieved. I mean all of my friends are just *ecstatic* to leave home and the overreaching grasp of their parents. They're overjoyed for their freedom, but me...I guess there's something wrong with me. The idea scares me, and I don't understand why." Dallie felt another tear leak from her eye and groaned, frustrated with herself and her unstable emotions.

"It can be overwhelming at first...a new place, a new home, new people. It's all unknown to you. Of course it's scary, but trust me, there's nothing *wrong* with you, darlin'," her dad reassured. "You have every reason to be anxious. I guess your mom and I shouldn't have held on so tightly." He frowned.

"No, I'm glad that you did." He just gave her a confused look in response, and she faltered. "I mean, *freedom* isn't all it's cracked up to be, right? When you're an adult, you got bills and responsibilities and..." she paused as her dad gave a big hearty laugh.

"You're an old soul, Dallie."

"Maybe." She dropped her head then. "Can I ask you something personal, Daddy?"

He looked at her hesitantly but said, "Dallie, you can ask me anything."

She wasn't so sure about that as she asked, "How did you know that Mom was the *one*?"

She wasn't even sure why she was asking him this. She'd known the story of her parents and how they met—Hell, she'd literally been there—but she'd discussed this with her Aunt Jordan, her mom, and her grandmother. Now she wanted her dad's take on love. His opinion mattered more to her than almost anyone else's.

Instead of seeming surprised by her question, which was what she expected, he actually grinned. "Well, Dallie, when I first met your mother, I immediately fell in love with her. I didn't recognize it right away though." He laughed. "It was your grandfather who pointed it out, in fact." His expression become solemn as he said, "Obviously, Nat had a lot of issues to work through before her and I could be together as you now know." Dallie just nodded. "Love is a very unique feeling, and I knew that what I felt for your mom was unlike anything I'd ever felt with anyone before. I wasn't whole without her. I *had* to be with her. We were pulled together like two magnets; there was simply no fighting it. It was just meant to be. And to this day, she never fails to take my breath away." He was now looking past her into the open space between them as he spoke, and when he looked back at her, he actually blushed. "Wait...why do you ask? Do you think you may be in love?" he asked, cautiously.

Dallie immediately scoffed and shook her head vigorously, and her father breathed a sigh of relief.

He was all business again as he said, "I want you to be here to interview the new trainer with me tomorrow. His name is Wyatt Montgomery. He comes highly recommended by your Uncle Nathan." Dallie nodded, ashamed of her jealously at the mention of the trainer's name. "Dallie, I want your professional opinion of him when you see his work." Again, she nodded. "Now, go enjoy your day. If you want to work today, fine. If not, go. Enjoy your summer," he stated and smiled. "I love you, sweetheart." He took her hand again, and she smiled, half-heartedly.

"I love you too, Daddy," was all she could say as the tears came to her eyes once again. She squeezed his hand tightly then reluctantly pulled back. She stood and exited his office, needing to get away.

Dallie was almost to the house when she burst out in tears again. She couldn't contain them as she climbed the stairs up to the back porch, her eyes blinded by the salty rivulets. When she got to the French doors, she hesitated but for a moment. A part of her was ashamed for her mother to see her this way and a part of her wanted to run into her mother's arms and be comforted like a child, but she wasn't a child any longer, she knew. That didn't stop her from whimpering as she came inside, looking down at baby Jackson lying on a blanket in his playpen yard fast asleep. She was going to miss his sweet little voice and their daily games together. She tip-toed past him, careful not to make a sound.

The house was silent. She looked over to the stovetop clock and saw that it wasn't yet ten in the morning. Her mom would be in her study, writing. She was heading out of the kitchen when her mom popped in from her office.

"Dallie?" The sound of her name coming from her mother's mouth brought her lips to quivering again. When her mom looked up at her, Dallie gave way to the emotions that took hold. "Oh, baby," was all her mom said and she ran to her and gathered a sobbing Dallas into her arms. Dallie was as tall as her mom now, maybe even a few centimeters taller if the truth be told, but she lay her head on her mother's shoulder and let her soothe her and rub her back as her mom held her and stroked her wet hair from her face. "Goodness, love. You knew this was coming, didn't you?"

It was a rhetorical question, Dallie knew, but that didn't take the sting of the truth of it away. *Yes!* She knew that she would need to be "replaced," but she'd wanted more time. She needed more time. But here it was, as her dad had put it, 'your time has come'.

She was a blathering mess as her mom drew her into the living room and down to the sofa as she grabbed some tissues from the coffee table and brought them to Dallie's face.

"Alright now, look," her mom commanded gently. "We can't have this, ok?" Her mom pulled her chin up, and Dallie's blurry eyes met hers. They were sapphire blue orbs of comfort and reason that shot through her. "Dallas, we still have two months left, honey. If you start this now then the two of us will be babbling fools the entire time until the day comes. Hmm?" Her mom's composure faltered but for a moment as she pulled her lips in, quenching her own tears.

Dallie knew it was true. It was too early for these tears. She nodded and tried to calm herself. She took some deep breaths, accepting two more tissues her mom offered her, and within minutes, she was collected enough to speak.

"I'm sorry. I don't know what's come over me," Dallie began.

"Oh, sweetie. Don't apologize. It's alright. You just needed your momma," her mom reasoned and smiled. Dallie nodded and leaned into her mom again, hugging her to her. "No one is ever too old to need some comforting words and the voice of reason from her mother. I still need that from my mom too every now and again, believe it or not." Her mom stroked her hair again, down her back and Dallie just sighed, letting herself enjoy being held for the moment. "We all want to grow up so fast, that soon enough we forget how good we had it when we were young." She motioned over to the baby; they could see his sleeping face through the slats in the play fence. "He hasn't a care in the world. He has nowhere to be, no one to answer to, no one to take care of... No worries over anything. He's got it made and he has no idea." Dallie just nodded in response. It was true.

Her mom held her and stroked her hair for a long time as the tears continued to slowly flow like gentle, persistent rain down her cheeks until finally her mom pulled back and smiled down at her.

"What say we go shopping and out to lunch together for a girl's day?" her mom recommended.

Dallie perked up a little. "Yeah, I would like that."

Dallie frowned suddenly, looking over at Jackson. "What about the baby?" she asked.

"Oh, I'm sure your grandmother would love to watch him."

Dallie knew her mom probably had at least a dozen things on her to-do list, but she and her mom had little time left before Dallie would be absorbed in college and she was grateful that her mom was interrupting their usual routine to accommodate a girl's day.

"Go wash your face and change, and I'll go talk to your dad, ok?"

Dallie nodded and went upstairs to attend to her red face. When she came back down about fifteen minutes later, her dad was in the kitchen, whispering with her mom. They both stopped talking as they saw her and turned to face her as she approached. Her dad took in a deep breath and just gave her a look that made her want to start crying again, so she moved her gaze to her mom, who just gave a weak smile.

"Are you ready?" her mom asked and cleared her throat. Dallie just gulped and nodded, afraid that if she spoke she'd be back in the same boat.

Jeez, she thought. *What is my deal? It's not even that time of the month.*

Her mom kissed her dad deeply and then turned to escort her out. She just waved at her dad, and he gave her a weak smile back.

Once they were in the car, heading north, her mom took her hand and took a deep breath in as if she were preparing her for something awful.

"You *do* know that your father wants you working with him until you leave for college, right?"

"Of course! I never thought he was kickin' me to the curb." Dallie insisted. "I—"

"Ok, good. I just wanted to make sure you understood that." Her mom sighed. "Your father feels horrible for hurting your feelings." She put her hand up when Dallie brought her hand up, starting to protest. "I know. I explained to him that you didn't think that, but he just wanted to make sure that you knew." She laughed then. "He adores you, baby girl. He always has and trust me when I tell you that this is killing him as much as it's killing you."

Dallie sighed. "I know, Momma. I'm sorry that I overreacted. It's a good business decision, and he should have done it before now. I know I'm the reason he's hesitated."

"Oh, sweetie. He hesitated only to save your feelings. It was me who insisted that he go ahead and hire this man *before* you leave and not after."

"Why?" Dallie asked.

"Well, honestly, your father wants your opinion on the man's abilities. He values your input… more than you know. He trusts you, Dallie."

"Ok? But he's been in this business a *lot* longer than me. You both have *all* the capability in the world to see who's a good fit for the ranch, probably even more so than me." Dallie confirmed.

"Well, you see, your father didn't tell you the whole truth."

"What do you mean?" Dallie felt butterflies fill her stomach at the anticipation of hearing her mom's answer.

"Wyatt Montgomery isn't just a horse *trainer*."

"O—K—?" Dallie scowled. "*What* is he?"

"He's a horse whisperer."

~

*W*yatt Montgomery didn't look at all like what Dallas had pictured in her head. He was lean and tan; His messy platinum blonde locks were pulled into a man bun beneath his worn leather cowboy hat—which curved up dramatically on either side—and the underside of his head was shaved and black as night, a stark contrast to the blonde. He had a Van Dyke type goatee with a thin mustache. His arms were sleeved in various tattoos ranging from stallions to tombstones and his left ear lobe adorned a dangling silver cross. His smile was big and lit up his whole face as he took her hand in his.

"And you must be the famous Dallas Kinsen!" Wyatt drawled in exuberance.

"Ha," Dallie laughed big. "I wouldn't go *that* far!"

"Are you kiddin' me? I would! Don't you know I heard talk 'o you and your dad as far north as Big Sky, Montana and as far east as Natchez, Mississippi?"

Dallie's eyebrows went up in shock at that as Wyatt's big brown eyes gazed into hers.

"Yup," he continued. "Sure as the world! When I got that phone call from *Jack Kinsen* of all people…hell, I nearly fell off a' my horse."

Dallie laughed again at Wyatt's deep southern drawl and his excitement of meeting her and her father.

She hadn't been upset by her mom's confession in the car yesterday, not in the least bit. In fact, she'd actually been relieved to hear that her dad was hiring on a horse whisperer. It made her feel better about leaving. She'd visibly relaxed and enjoyed the day as she and her mom shopped for her dorm room. They even picked out some clothes for fall semester and dined at a modern sushi joint afterward. She'd been her happy-go-lucky self once they'd gotten home and eased her dad's worry with a big hug and a laugh. Dinner had been light and conversational, and she and Cole had sat on the back porch chatting for a long time about everything and nothing at the same time. She'd filled him in on what had happened that day, and he'd turned to her in surprise at the mention of the words, "horse whisperer".

"So, now what *is* that precisely?" he'd asked, grinning at her as if it were a private joke.

"It's strictly what it states!" she'd clarified. "It's someone with a gift for communicating with horses when no one else can reach them."

"So, there's a 'title' for what you do?"

Dallie had laughed at that. "Not exactly. As far as I know, there's only me that can do what *I* do...but essentially, yes, there's a 'title' for people who are sensitive to animals. We're called whisperers."

"That's pretty neat. Have you *met* many 'whisperers'?"

"Surprisingly, no. We've traveled all over the west, even up to the Dakotas, to many a horse show, event, rodeo and auction over the years. We've been introduced to those that claimed to be 'whisperers', but much to mine and my dad's disappointment, they always turned out to be frauds." Dallie had frowned.

"So, what makes this dude any different then?" he'd asked.

"Well, Uncle Nate met him when he was just a kid and has known his family for years. Turns out, Wyatt's in the business of planting some roots down here in Texas and has been lookin' for a place in need of skills like his." Dallie had smiled then eager to meet the man.

Now, here that man was, in front of her, seemingly bedazzled by her presence. Time to see if he could put his money where his mouth was.

After Wyatt gave her hand back, he sidled up next to her as the two of them, along with her dad, her grandfather, and her uncle Nate, walked out of the barn and into the long arena next to it.

"Dallas Kinsen," he said her name again like some star-struck fan. Dallie couldn't help laughing again. "What an outright pleasure!" Wyatt exclaimed, grinning crookedly at her then looked over to her dad. "Jack, I bet you gotta put blinders on these boys around here."

Her dad scowled big and nodded, glancing over at Cole, who had a big frown on his face as he watched them from the back pasture. "Yeah, pretty much."

Dallie couldn't fight the bashful giggle at her throat.

Wyatt had an even bigger reaction when her dad introduced her mom, who'd come down to the fence to see his magic; having another 'whisperer' on their property was a big deal.

"Good lord, Jack! You just got a house *full* of beauties. You sure are one lucky S.O.B." Wyatt had kissed the back of her mom's hand as he introduced himself. Her dad just smiled knowingly over at her mom, who'd blushed.

Teddy brought in a fresh new stallion; he'd been giving them a handful of issues over the last couple days. Dallie had yet to touch him as she'd been tied up working with three other steeds up to that point, but already she could see he was hot and uncooperative as Teddy attempted to guide the lovely paint into the arena.

"Whoo," Wyatt exclaimed and grinned. "He sure don't like you, boy. Be careful there," he cautioned as the stallion planted his hooves and flicked his head at the lead that tugged him.

Teddy froze and looked to her dad who nodded at him to stop.

Her Uncle Nate and her dad moved to the fence—where her mom was draped—as Dallie and Wyatt approached the horse that Dallie suddenly remembered had the ironic name, Lightning. Wyatt took the lead gingerly and murmured to the big stallion, whose black and white coat appeared to be randomly and marvelously "painted" on. The muscular, lilac-eyed horse nervously whinnied at him. Dallie grinned, knowing what that meant.

"Alright, alright," Wyatt grumbled and stepped closer. The stallion stepped back. "I see this one's gonna give me a run for my money, huh? D' y'all set me up with this bully on purpose?" Wyatt spoke softly over at Dallie and winked.

"Hey, I had nothin' to do with this," Dallie insisted and crossed her arms over her chest, giving him a crooked grin in return.

"Figures," Wyatt mumbled and attempted another approach.

This time he stepped to the side. Another head flick. Dallie laughed under her breath.

"You see what you're doing here, big fella? You're making me look bad in front of the ladies. Cut it out." Wyatt's voice was low and slow as he playfully scolded the horse. He was right next to the stallion and gently his hand went up to the horse's cheek.

Lightning's tail rose then as Wyatt murmured to him and let his other hand come up to the paint's muzzle. Wyatt stroked him and cooed to him, but the stallion's demeanor showed his anxiety was still hanging there, Dallie could feel it.

"Easy, boy." Wyatt's hands moved to the horse's throat latch and neck then, and Dallie watched Lightning's eyes in apprehension. She could feel his building unease as Wyatt's touch and words only tended to make it worse, not better. The horse was on the verge of bolting, Dallie knew and just as she stepped forward, Wyatt muttered under his breath, "Dallas, a little help here, please?"

With that, Dallie took two strides and rested her hands on the bridge of the stallion's nose, stroking gently and gazing deeply into his big eye. She began humming, easily, just a soft, slow tune; a church hymn she knew well. She felt Lightning relax even as Wyatt continued to pet him.

"Wow, you really are somethin' alright," Wyatt whispered excitedly, looking over at her, mesmerized. "Man, that could've been bad." Dallie just smiled in response. "Thanks for not letting him make an ass of me in front of your dad." Wyatt winked.

"No, problem," Dallie said as she winked back. She'd seen that Lightning wasn't a stallion Wyatt couldn't have handled had she not been there, but she'd wanted to spare him the embarrassment and the fence the damage that the horse would have more than likely caused if she'd simply stood by and done nothing; especially when she'd known she could help.

But Wyatt was there for an interview after all, so after several moments of cooing and singing to the uneasy stallion as Wyatt continued to feel him out, she decided it was time to see how accurate her Uncle Nate was on Wyatt's abilities. She easily stepped away, still facing the horse as she backed up to stand between her dad and her Paw-Paw. Wyatt just frowned over at her and mouthed, "Traitor." She giggled gently as she crossed her arms over her chest again and waited.

It took Wyatt several attempts to ease the horse into following him and even longer for him to get the horse to properly longe, but when he finally did, it was with grace and pride and Dallie smiled, knowing that he'd proven himself to them all. When Wyatt stopped and drew the horse in to him, Lightning obeyed his command and Dallie grinned up at her dad in triumph. He just beamed right back at her; sheer happiness lining his face.

She headed back over to Wyatt then and began asking him questions, things that only people who talked to horses could understand: How he connected with them? What challenges he'd faced over the years? What he loved most about it? How had he come to know he was gifted?

He answered them all while he led Lightning around the arena, Dallie keeping pace with him. Then he had many questions of his own to ask her.

"How in God's name do you *know*?"

"It's amazed my family for as long as I can remember," Dallie recalled. "At the age of four, I could sense their emotions, read their moods...feel what they were feeling."

Wyatt stared back at her in awe and grinned. "I heard that at your mere touch, a feral stallion running straight at you instantly calmed." His eyebrows went up in question.

"That's one hundred percent true," Dallie admitted.

"Wow, I bet that was a sight to see!"

"I also stopped a bucking horse with a rider not long after."

"Yup, I heard that one too- Vivian Alexander." Wyatt shook his head in amazement. "That's quite an amazing gift, Miss Kinsen. You are *truly* one of a kind, believe me when I tell you." Dallie just blushed and nodded. "You're gonna make one fine veterinarian."

With his interview concluded, Dallie's dad shook his hand and invited Wyatt back for dinner and to all their surprise, he acquiesced.

~

*C*ole scowled as Dallie's beautiful face tilted back once again to laugh at their comical guest, Wyatt Montgomery. They'd dined on juicy grilled chicken breasts that Jack had barbecued outside on the grill along with fresh green beans from the garden, roasted potatoes and salad. All the while, Cole felt an abysmal void grow deeper inside his heart.

Wyatt had taken to the Kinsen and Butler families as easily as flowers took to soft summer rain on a hot day. Even Savannah was more bubbly than usual in his presence.

It wasn't that Cole didn't like the guy, after all, he was funny as hell. It was just that, once again, Cole felt alone in the world. He couldn't compete with Wyatt—nor his and Dallie's shared gifts with the horses—and he couldn't fully understand or encompass the ranch life, even though he truly wanted to.

Oh well, he thought, *I don't really belong here anyway.*

But be that as it may, it didn't stop the pain from ripping through him as Dallie flirted and talked with the only other single man at the table. Once dinner was over, Cole took off downstairs, pretending that the day had just been long and tough and that he was tired. It wasn't far from the truth, but not in the way that he'd portrayed to Mrs. K.

He found himself pouting as he entered the silent basement, a grim reminder of his isolation. *I'd better get used to this*, he thought, for isolation would be his future; whether that be behind bars wasting away in a cell or wandering aimlessly seeking refuge from his uncommitted crimes. That was going to his life...whether he wanted it to be or not.

So, Dallie had found a good man she could laugh with and one who understood her better than Cole ever hoped to. Good for her! As happy as that should make him, it didn't. Cole wanted Dallas Noel Kinsen. He wanted her with a yearning he'd never felt before. To him, Dallie was like a shining beacon in a raging storm; a radiant angel opening her arms before him as the very flames of Hell licked at his feet. He wanted her laughs and her passion, and he wanted to tell her his sins and get her absolution. But he could never soil her innocent ears with his transgressions. She didn't deserve that! She deserved so much more than Cole Callahan could ever dream of giving her. She could have any man she wanted. Not only was she gorgeous and funny and sweet, if the fame Wyatt mentioned was any indication, she was also gonna be rich as hell. Rich enough to ensure that her future was as gleaming as her personality.

Cole let his mind drift in this way to the point that when he finally undressed, showered and changed into his pajama pants and t-shirt, he was spent, both mentally and physically. He sighed as he plopped down on the big, comfy sectional, propping his head on his arm and stretching his legs out. He turned the TV on and flipped to the news. He'd been watching it each and every night, trying to see what he could gather on Adam's murder investigation. Since they got Denton's local news and not Austin's, he'd been thoroughly relieved to see that there hadn't been anything mentioned regarding himself.

However, tonight was different. He'd patiently listened absent-mindedly, letting his eyes drift closed as his thoughts drifted back to Dallie. That was, until he heard the name of his shop. "...where Adam Burns, a well-liked community member in Austin," the news anchor stated, "was found murdered in cold blood last month. The investigation has taken a stalemate as police are looking for his fellow business partner, one, Cole Callahan for questioning in this tragic death. He was last seen in Austin on…" Cole heard the door to the basement open and quickly flipped the channel, mentally trying to relax as he reminded himself to get on the computer later and find out exactly what the media knew about him.

Dallas's frame stopped mid-way down the stairs to gaze at him. He couldn't help but smile.

"Were you sleepin'?" she asked quietly.

Cole just shook his head, afraid his voice would crack.

"Good. I wanted to come and see you."

"To what do I owe the pleasure?" He finally asked jovially as she approached.

"Well, I missed you up there." She sat, pointed to the upstairs and grinned down at him shyly.

He felt his cheeks flush as he looked back up at her. "Yeah, I—"

"Was jealous? Yeah, I saw," Dallie called him out and arched an eyebrow at him.

He gulped. It wouldn't do for him to lie. She already had his number. "Yeah, maybe…"

Dallie belted out a rich, sexy laugh and suddenly and unexpectedly, Cole was fully aroused. He grabbed her and pulled her down next to him. She gasped as his arms wrapped tightly around her. His hand gripped her thigh and pulled it around his own as he moved his body slightly atop of hers, his mouth coming down hard over hers. The moan that escaped those soft full lips only spurred him on as his tongue plunged into her open mouth. He answered it with a growl of his own as he angled his head to deepen the kiss. Her hands moved to his back and up to grasp his shoulders as she pulled herself into him. His hand moved to grip her firm bottom as he arched his hips against hers and he thought he would die from the sheer pleasure he felt in that moment of having her sweet body pressed so closely to his. His head flew back as he tore his lips from hers and he cried out, "Oh God."

His other hand moved from her back to her torso and he looked down at her breast as he gently squeezed the plump, shapely mound in his hand. It was Dallie's head that flew back then and she looked up at him, her blue eyes shining with desire. His head dipped to tease her soft neck with feather-light kisses and she whimpered and cried his name. He growled again as his mouth opened to suck the sweetness from her tender skin and his hand continued to knead at her breast, his thumb teasing the puckered nipple that poked up at him. Dallie panted as his tongue licked a trail down her neck to her collarbone then his lips flirted with the apex of her V-neck t-shirt.

"Cole," her suddenly sultry, raspy voice ground out to him and he paused and pulled back a little, looking down at her beautiful form beneath him. Her hand moved from his back to his hips to the hem of his pants. He gazed into her face, at those beautiful lips, blue eyes and high cheekbones, the hair that spilled out in curly platinum ringlets around her head. God, how he wanted to take her, right there, right then. Sex would no doubt feel as incredible as everything else with her had felt thus far, but he simply couldn't do it. He suddenly stilled the soft hand at his groin and shook his head. Her brows drew in a frown, and he sighed heavily.

"Too fast, too soon," he stated. "I'm sorry. I shouldn't have started this." He removed his hand from her breast, and it suddenly felt so empty. He lowered his head, feeling his sex hard against her, and tried to pull away. Her hips held him still.

"But this feels so good," Dallie protested, her hands going to his chest.

Cole's breath faltered as he practically smirked. "You're damn right it does."

"Then what's the problem?" she countered.

Indeed! Ah, he could name at least a dozen of them, but declined as he pulled her legs from around his hips, leaned back down to kiss her, and finally, came to her side.

She sighed but said nothing. She cupped his jaw and turned her body towards his, aligning their chests and thighs. She kissed him, melding her tongue to his, gently exploring his mouth. The kiss became softer, less hurried, but no less steamy as Cole tried to slow his pounding heart. He willed his body to enjoy simply making out with this amazing, blonde-headed beauty even though his sex painfully protested against her thigh.

After a time, he pulled away and just stared at her mouth, red and ravished from his kisses. He smiled weakly at her, and she begrudgingly returned it. He watched her beautiful face gazing at him for a time before he finally spoke.

"Dallie, Wyatt is a cool guy..." Cole blushed.

"He is," Dallie agreed with a smile.

"You guys would make a great couple."

Dallie laughed. When Cole frowned, she said, "Cole! He's married with two kids. Besides, I'm crushing on *you*. Obviously! And Wyatt... Well, he's not my type anyway." She stroked his cheek with her finger then and ran it down the length of his jaw.

He gulped. "Y'all have a lot in common."

"Be that as it may, that doesn't mean I want to *be* with him," she protested.

She had a point, but she had been flirting like crazy. Of course that could have just been his jealous mind making assumptions. He decided to just drop it. In a short period of time it wouldn't matter anyway. He wouldn't be here...and well, neither would she for that matter.

"I'm personally thrilled that my father found him. He's really gonna be good for this place." That seemed true enough. Although, Cole couldn't tell either way, Dallie knew what she was talking about on the matter. He just nodded. "Cole?" Dallie asked, frowning. "Are you ok? Something seems off?" Those beautiful sapphire blue eyes shone into his, making him want to confess, but he just lowered his head. "Cole. I promise I don't like Wyatt," she reassured.

"No, I know." He gave her another weak smile.

"Did I do something wrong?"

"Absolutely not. You are *utterly* perfect, Dallie. In every way possible." He cupped her sweet face in his palm and kissed her gently again, angling her face up to his for the taking. His tongue plunged into her gracious mouth again as he attempted to make her forget this whole conversation; the embarrassment of his jealousy and that there had ever been anything but this amazing passion raging between them. He simply wanted to enjoy their time together before the day came when he would have no other choice but to leave her.

They made out again for a time, and he tried very hard to keep his hands only on her waist and back. As much as he wanted to take it further, he wouldn't. Not for anything. To claim her would be unforgivable. She wasn't his to take. If the circumstances had been different, there would be hope for them, but as it were, it just wasn't meant to be. Perhaps, if he'd only met her *before* Adam was killed… but life was like that, he surmised. He could curse his fate all he wanted to, but that wouldn't change the fact that he truly was a man on the run and now his name was on the news and the police were going to find him if he didn't run… and even if he ran, he could still be caught. His future was entirely grim; as grim as hers was luminous. Dallie deserved better, and he knew it.

Cole pulled away suddenly as this realization, although not a new one, struck him hard. He pretended to simply be tired instead of being aloof to their hot, melting kisses. He decided to flatter her, so she couldn't see right through him.

"You're a really good kisser, Dallie."

"I am?" she asked so innocently, as if she were surprised.

"Well yeah! Can't you tell?" He looked down at his still full-throttle erection and she blushed.

"I'm sorry," she began.

"I'm not," Cole clarified with a laugh. She just gave him a sly smile, unsure how to respond to that. "I wanna take you out again soon. That is, if you want to go?"

"Yeah. I do," she responded, matter-of-factly.

He smiled and pulled her into his arms, tucking her head against his chest. He kissed the top of her head, right on her flowing locks.

They smelled of lilies and sweet peas; sweet and fresh and fragrant. He lost track of time then as he held her warm, soft body against his and breathed in her captivating scent and stroked her smooth back. Soon enough, his eyelids became heavy as he listened to her soft breathing and felt its warmth fall across him.

CHAPTER 9

*C*ole woke to the sound of a whispered voice calling Dallie's name insistently. He groaned and his hips instinctively thrust at the softness gently pressed against his morning erection. He cleared his throat and his eyelids fluttered open to fall on Mrs. K, who hovered over him. He frowned, not understanding what was happening until he felt the warmth and movement of Dallie's back and bottom pressed intimately against his chest and thighs. They were spooning! And her mom was scolding them! He realized all this with a start.

"Dallas Noel!" Natalie called out, shaking Dallie's shoulder vigorously.

Dallie grunted and whined, still groggy from sleep. "Mom, what?" she protested.

"Hurry! Get up before your father *sees* you! He'll be down here any minute for his workout. Dallie. Get! Up!" Mrs. K was practically shouting now.

"Huh?" Dallie came to then and turned her head back to look at Cole. She breathed in deeply, trying to gain her bearings, and took her mom's outstretched hand, sitting up.

Cole immediately drew his knees in so that they wouldn't see his protruding hard-on, but that seemed to be the least of Dallie's mother's worries. "Cole," she insisted, "go to your room. Now! Quickly! Before Jack gets downstairs."

He looked to Dallie apologetically as he moved to sit up, and the girls moved away towards the stairs. He ran to his room and shut the door, waiting for the shit to hit the fan. After several long, nerve-wracking minutes of silence, Cole finally decided to shower. If Jack came at him, he wouldn't have an advantage either way, so he figured he'd just begin his day like any other normal day, all the while, praying that Dallie's father didn't decide to kill him.

Cole literally held his breath as he came out of his bedroom door and walked past the workout room that lay adjacent to the basement door. He saluted his boss, who nodded at him from the treadmill he was running on, then looked anxiously at Mrs. K, who winked at him from behind a set of free weights she was lifting in a standing chest fly. Cole visibly relaxed and proceeded out the back basement door to head to the barn. Mrs. K had covered for him and Dallie, thank goodness. Perhaps, she wouldn't have been so supportive though if she'd seen how they'd behaved on that same couch the night prior. Cole had to start watching himself around Dallas Kinsen. Hell, he was already a man on the run...he didn't need any other reasons to draw attention to himself.

~

*I*t had been exactly two weeks to the day that Detective Art McElroy had been called to investigate the murder of Adam Burns. In that short but incredibly long period of time, the body had been buried, the family had given statements, and the investigation was at a standstill. The fate of McElroy's case hung in the balance of finding this mysterious and evasive, Cole Callahan. He'd fled and to parts unknown, much to McElroy's dismay. No one knew where he was, no one knew where he might have gone, and no one could tell McElroy why on earth Cole would want to kill Adam. There was much more to this case than McElroy had originally predicted.

Art had gotten the search warrant for Callahan's house and vehicle last week, and his team had searched every inch of both, and to no avail. There was no suspicious evidence found in either location; nothing in the car, no questionable phone calls in or out of Callahan's cell phone. In fact, the evidence pointed to a happy and fulfilling friendship between Cole and Adam, and Adam's family had confirmed it. There were loads of pictures of them together at work, at home, on vacations, at Adam's wedding... The pictures were on Cole's phone, in his office, his home, even on Cole's fridge. According to the Burns' family, Adam had been like a brother to Cole. But all too often, McElroy found that even the closest relationships had their dark secrets.

Perhaps, Cole had been jealous of Adam; envious of his life, his wife, or even desperate for money, but Adam's family insisted that that wasn't the case with Cole and Adam. Besides, the insurance policy had Mrs. Amy Burns, Adam's widow, as the beneficiary, not Cole. So, what exactly could have been his motive to kill his best friend? Had the two gotten into an argument that had, unfortunately, ended in tragedy? Had Adam walked in on something he shouldn't have and Cole shot him? Or vice versa? McElroy wouldn't know until Cole Callahan was questioned. And it didn't look like they were going to be finding him any time soon.

Cole's employees said he had no family, no one to run to. None of the nearby businesses had seen or heard anything, of course. The outside video surveillance camera showed both Cole and Adam coming in, both at separate times, but no one else, and it never showed anyone leaving. The inside video tape was missing, presumably taken by the killer.

McElroy sat back and scratched his head. It was hard to be a super sleuth when there was literally no trail to follow. McElroy sipped his coffee and began outlining his case, trying to tie in connections, phone calls, encounters, even clients of the shop in the weeks leading up to Adam's death. There *was* a connection, he just had to find it. He sighed after two hours of staring at papers and leaned back, shoving the heels of his palms into his aching eye sockets. He stood and proceeded to the break room for yet more coffee.

Until Callahan was found, Art was virtually useless.

~

*A*nother two weeks passed in a short span of time. Cole got into a routine at Kinsen Ranch. He woke, worked out with his favorite cowgirl, showered, dressed, dined each meal with the wonderful Kinsen family and sought to hide among them as he worked his hands and back to the bone on a daily basis. Since starting at the ranch one month prior, he'd gained the confidence of horse-back riding, fence mending, shoveling horse manure or "apple picking" as Jack and Dallie called it, hay bale stacking (yes, there was a science to it) and even mowing. He and Dallie had gone out on multiple dates, went to church each Sunday and hung out as much as possible when they weren't working.

Wyatt had just begun his first workday the day prior and it had come as a shock to Cole that even though Montgomery was an experienced "whisperer" and trainer, Dallie had many things to show him. Cole had seen Dallie in her element many times, up close and personal in fact, but seeing her with Wyatt made her gift all the more awe-inspiring as she seemed to be in perfect sync with each horse she touched, whether she was riding or training. It was as if she were inside the horses' heads and even though Wyatt had an impressive gift himself, he couldn't come close to doing what Dallie could do with them. Of course, all that could just be Cole's bias. After all, as he'd told Dallie all those nights ago, she was perfect in his eyes.

Cole had been doing some research on a desktop computer that sat in a little alcove in the basement, one of many computers in the house, for any and all articles he could find on the murder in Austin, but only after he was alone downstairs; he didn't want them seeing what he was looking at. He was even extra cautious to delete the browser history, afraid that all his searching might give him away. The police were looking for him, but according to what he'd read, they were no closer to finding Cole than they were to finding Adam's killer. The case was at a standstill apparently as they hunted for him. He'd felt tangible relief then knowing that he was somewhat safe...at least for a little while. The outside cameras hadn't caught him leaving and no one had seen anything. Thank goodness! Although, that didn't help Adam's case...at least Cole had some time before he was found, he surmised. He'd started wearing his cowboy hat on a regular basis and had gotten the brilliant idea to grow a goatee to act as a sort of disguise while he hid out. He still couldn't fathom why anyone would want to kill his best friend; Adam had been such a wonderful person and had no enemies that Cole ever knew of.

"How's a good rack of ribs sound for dinner?" Cole asked Dallas as he ambled over to the side of the fence where she stood. She was taking a break at the fence of the corral that she was working in.

"Delicious," she responded, breathless from her hard labor. She licked her lips at him, enticingly, and he groaned in blissful agony.

Cole watched her wink and walk away from him, and he smiled. He didn't miss Wyatt's eyebrows raise in surprise; he'd heard Cole ask Dallie out for a date.

They'd done a lot of dating lately and well, kissing too—out of everyone's view of course—and although they'd made out many times now, things hadn't gotten as out of control as that one night they'd fallen to sleep in each other's arms. Cole had been ever grateful to Mrs. K for covering for them. If Jack had been aware of their misbehaviors he'd said and done nothing, much to Cole's relief. But be that as it may, Cole had no intentions of getting that hot and heavy again, no matter that Dallie's lips and hands had gotten ever braver since then.

Cole just grinned at Wyatt's unspoken response. Wyatt gave him a thumbs up and mouthed, "You go boy."

It was getting hotter as the days progressed into the dead of summer. It was especially hot on this July day. Cole rounded the outside of the corral and walked into the barn. He was looking forward to getting Dallie to himself once again. Each time they went out together he was struck with how wonderful Dallas Kinsen really was. She was one of the most giving, loving and selfless people he'd ever met. She was always thinking of others and always laughing, finding humor in almost everything, and she was incredibly determined. If she set her mind to something, she did it and with perfection. Cole was smiling to himself, thinking about last night's discussion at the dinner table and Dallie's take on recycling and saving planet Earth from consumerism, when he heard Jack's loud voice booming into his cell phone.

"Three *weeks*?! Andrew, I can't wait three weeks... No," Jack turned then to look at Cole and frowned. "Alright. Well thanks for tryin', buddy." He pulled the phone from his ear and scowled as Cole approached him. "I wanted to try and get Dallie a new engine put in that damn truck before she heads off to school. I offered to buy her a brand-new vehicle, but I'll be damned... she refuses to part with that old clunker. Our mechanic, Drew, just said he can't even get to it for at *least* another three weeks and didn't know when or if he could get it done by the time she has to leave for college."

"I can do it." Cole said before he even thought. Jack's eyebrows went up in surprise. Cole laughed, trying to cover for himself. "I mean, I have a lot of experience with building engines." *Fuck! Even worse,* he thought. "Me and a friend of mine used to work on cars back in the day..." He left it at that. Let Jack come to whatever conclusion he wanted to.

"Alright, well how 'bout you take a look then," Jack said as he hopped up. They headed out of the office and toward the front of the barn. "Dabbled in mechanics, huh?" Jack asked as he looked over at him.

Cole just blushed. He hadn't wanted them to know too much about him... oh well. There was no going back now.

When they reached the old '57 Chevy truck with its peeling paint, Jack popped the hood and Cole glanced down at the ancient engine. He instantly knew that he had his work cut out for him as the engine below resembled the brittle bones of a senior citizen. Not that he hadn't noticed the clanging and choking on his first ride in it, but this was much worse than he'd anticipated. Frankly, he was shocked that the old girl could still turn over.

"Wow," Cole remarked. "Original engine, huh?"

"Yup," Jack murmured. "Two hundred thousand miles and counting."

Cole looked thoughtful then. He would need an engine stand, a decent number of tools and a lot of time.

As if reading his mind, Jack reached into his back pocket and pulled out his wallet. He handed him a credit card and said, "Here. Go buy what you need. Take the time you need. Make sure my daughter is safe on the road."

In response, Cole just gave Jack a nod and took the keys from him. He took the old truck into town and bought what he could get; the rest he'd have to order online and have shipped. He then took the truck to Nathan's shop. Dallie's uncle had been dabbling in mechanics for the last several years and had some of the equipment Cole would need for the rebuild and the proper location for disassembly.

Cole began at once. He jacked up the vehicle, disconnected the engine from the tranny, as well as the motor mounts, and put Nathan's cherry picker to work pulling the engine out of the truck. Once placed on the engine stand, he began the tough part, and after the valve covers were off, he started evaluating the damage.

Cole spent the next several hours tearing the engine apart and mentally listing all the parts that needed to be either replaced or rebuilt. He was in the zone and when he was there, nothing else existed; not Adam's murder, not the fact that he was a fugitive, nothing but Dallie... *Oh, crap! Dallie!*

He checked his watch and saw that it wasn't quite as late as he'd originally assumed. He still had an hour before they were supposed to leave for dinner, but then he realized that he had no way to get back to the ranch. After all, the truck was engineless now. He looked down at his sticky, black hands, grabbing one of Nate's shop rags and wiping what he could off of them.

He headed to the house then and rang the doorbell, hoping either Nathan or Jordan, if not both of them, were home. Otherwise he'd have to walk and it wasn't far but...

He sighed in tangible relief as Dallie's Aunt Jordan whipped the door open and gave him a crooked grin. Her curly red hair was half up and half down and she wore a form-fitted sundress.

"Well, well... How'd it go, master mechanic?" Jordan asked as she motioned for him to come in.

Cole gulped, a sense of panic seizing him as he wondered how she knew. At her laugh, he realized that she was only kidding and gave a breathy laugh in relief.

He walked into the foyer and let Jordan lead him into the kitchen where she grabbed a glass from the cabinet and began filling it with ice and water. She motioned toward the sink, signaling him to wash his hands. He obliged.

"So," she began, "You can rebuild an engine, huh?" She looked back over at him and just gave him a knowing smile as she sat the glass in front of him. "You're just full of surprises, aren't ya, Cole?"

Cole just gave her a weak smile, wishing the statement were anything but true.

Jordan just stared at him, assessing him. He felt a little like he was being held under a microscope beneath those honey whiskey eyes of hers.

Cole wondered again for the dozenth time, if he'd somehow died and gone to Heaven since coming to Abundance, Texas. He had truly been surrounded by some of God's most beautiful angels; angels with blonde, red and dark hair and eyes of various captivating colors.

Jordan finally cleared her throat and sighed, giving him a sense of reprieve that her evaluation of him was sufficient.

"So, you and Dallie seem to be hitting it off pretty well?"

"Yes ma'am," Cole agreed and sipped thirstily at his water.

"That's great." Jordan smiled. "She's a good girl- Dallas."

"She is," Cole again agreed, watching Jordan prop her hips against the island.

"She's a bit naïve when it comes to the world."

Uh, oh. She was fishing and he knew it.

"She's got a fragile heart, but she's strong," Cole admitted. Jordan just smiled big at his words. He continued, "She's a beautiful woman both inside *and* out."

A gruff laugh chimed in then, and Cole turned to see Nathan standing at the doorframe.

"Sounds to me like someone might be in love," Nate stated inquisitively and ambled over to his wife. He wrapped a deeply tanned arm around her slender waist as he came up behind her and gave Cole the once over. Cole gulped into Nathan Butler's icy blue stare, not sure how to respond to that statement.

Jordan broke the tension then and gave a husky laugh. "Now, now. Don't be throwing the L word around like that, babe. Cole and Dallie have just started dating, besides they're too young for all that mushy stuff."

Jordan turned in Nate's arms and patted his chest, looking up at him. Nathan just gazed down into her face and that smoldering look in his eyes was all too familiar. Cole ached to have Dallie look at him that way; the way that all the couples in her family tended to look at their significant others. Again, maybe it was the water here in Abundance. Appropriate name for the small town.

Cole gulped again when they looked back over at him. After an awkward silence, he finally spoke. "Love is a powerful word...and one that's used all too often if you ask me, or lot of times, not enough," he grumbled that last part as he looked over out the window then, swamped with emotion in that moment as he realized the last person to tell him they loved him was... Adam.

Jordan laughed humorlessly and agreed, "You're right about that one! But on a lighter note, we need to get you back to Miss Dallas or I'll catch hell for it. As I hear, y'all got a date tonight." Jordan winked at him and tilted her head toward the door. Cole gratefully followed as he nodded at Nathan and thanked him for the use of his garage and tools.

Nathan just smiled and told him he'd see him tomorrow.

Thankfully, Nathan had the shop and most of the necessary equipment for what Cole had needed to do his work on Dallie's truck. He wasn't quite sure what he would've done otherwise.

Cole followed Jordan to her red SUV, a brand-new Nissan X-Terra, and hopped into the passenger seat as she cranked the car.

"I'm sorry if my husband took you off guard back there," Jordan stated as she peeled out of the gravel drive. "He's mostly joshing you, you know?"

"It's ok, Mrs. Butler."

"Jordan. Please? Mrs. Butler is my mother-in-law," she protested. "I'm not quite old enough yet to be called that...but thanks, kid. You're polite." She elbowed him as he blushed. "So, where y'all goin' tonight?" she asked.

"To this barbecue place that Teddy told me about- The Smokin' Hot Hawg," Cole answered.

"Yeah, that place is great. I hope y'all have fun." She eyed him again and he felt a little uneasy. "I know you and Dallie have been hanging out a lot lately, and I think it's cool and all but, just...be careful," she warned. "Even as sweet as you are, you go breakin' that girl's heart and you're gonna get on Jack Kinsen's bad side. Trust me when I tell you, that's not a place you *ever* wanna be." Her eyebrows went up.

"I would never do anything to hurt Dallie," he insisted.

"I certainly hope so and deep down, I feel like that's a true statement, but…well, you've already seen how protective Jack and Nat are of their girls."

"And for good reason," Cole stated.

"I think it's really nice what you're doing for Dallie. Redoing that truck is a mighty kind gesture."

"Thank you. It's the least I can do after all that family has done for me."

"You seem to be pretty genuine, kid. I just hope you're honestly doing this for Dallie and not to try and get her dad's approval." At that, Cole's head came up and he frowned. Jordan's smile didn't quite meet her eyes. "Well, here we are." She pulled the SUV up to driveway and cut the engine.

~

*D*allie smiled as Cole's scruffy face came down to hers. They lay on a blanket beneath the bright stars of a clear Texas night. The pop of a log bursting from the heat of the campfire was overheard in the process of her pulling his larger frame into hers. Their lips connected, and she kissed him eagerly as his arms went around her. She enjoyed these moments of passion between them and craved them frequently. She loved losing herself to his touch and his lips. Cole was generous with his kisses and her feelings for him were starting to grow. He was giving and kind to her, and they shared a lot of laughs and easy conversations. Cole was funny and witty and despite their different upbringings, they had a lot in common.

She'd gotten him a guitar just a few days ago and when she'd given it to him, he'd played a beautiful melody that she'd never heard before then much to her surprise, he'd serenaded her. His voice was gruff and raspy, and she'd loved hearing it. She'd gotten all warm inside and cried tears of happiness. Cole was incredibly talented and special. It was hard to believe that any foster family hadn't taken one look at him and fallen in love. She could talk to him like one of her best friends, and he really listened to her. She was genuinely going to miss him when she went away to college.

But for now, she let his soft full lips kiss hers as her hands gripped at his shirt and her body arched against him. He pressed his pelvis intimately against hers, and her head flew back as his mouth descended to her neck. Goosebumps broke out on her entire body, and she started to tingle and hum inside.

"Oh, Cole," she cried breathlessly and grabbed at his hand, placing it over her left breast.

He groaned and squeezed the firm flesh that filled his big palm. Her hands lowered from his chest to his bottom, and she gripped his muscular butt cheeks as she rubbed her aching center against his rock hard erection.

"Son-of-a—" he swore and took her mouth again, angling his head. His tongue plunged in and caressed at hers, and she answered it back stroke for stroke. When they were both breathless, Cole pulled back slightly to look at her. "Damn, Dallie. You're something else, you know that?" She just smiled and arched her eyebrow at him. "Girl, you're getting *super* hard to resist," he murmured as his mouth returned to her neck. She gasped and he groaned again. "See... That!" He pulled back again and gave a heavy sigh. He just stared at her for a moment.

"What would happen next?" she asked, innocently blushing.

"What do you mean?"

"You *know* what I mean. If we were to do it." She blushed as she said the word "it".

"Have sex?" he asked. She just nodded. "Well, we aren't *goin'* to, so it doesn't matter," he began.

"But if we *did*," she exclaimed.

Cole sighed. He didn't like talking about this stuff. Making out was one thing, but sex was something else. They'd practically had this discussion before, Dallie knew, but that didn't stop her curiosity. He knew this too, which was why he was so patient with her right now. She should feel lucky; most guys would have ripped her clothes off and taken her already. Cole was different than most guys though. He was patient and logical...and he was also absolutely terrified of Jack Kinsen.

"Well, if we *were* going to have sex right now...which we *aren't*," he frowned then continued, "I would begin by taking off your shirt and start..." He paused, blushing. She nodded for him to go on. "At your breasts." He gently squeezed the breast still in his hand and looked down at it, uncomfortably. She gulped and imagined what his big rough hands would feel like beneath the fabric of her shirt and bra, on her sensitive bare flesh, and shivered. He continued, "I would touch you and kiss you there."

Dallie's intake of breath was enough to make him pull his hand away, but she didn't budge as she looked into his face. "Go on," she boldly said.

"Dallie... Your friends are coming to join us soon. We don't need to be all hot and bothered when they get here," he reasoned.

"Shannon and Ian are *constantly* hot and bothered." Dallie laughed.

Cole scowled again, but after a few moments, went on. "After that, I would unbutton your jeans."

"And where would *my* hands be at this time?" She was flirting with a thin line and she damn well knew it, but she couldn't stop herself from asking. This was the closest she had ever been to a member of the opposite sex and aside from her little brother's, who didn't count as far as she was concerned, she had never seen a penis up close and personal.

Cole cocked his head and gave her a withered look.

"Cole, come on," Dallie insisted.

"Really? What do *you* think?"

"They would be touching you. Here." She tried to move her hands towards the front of his jeans, but he stopped her.

"What are you doing?" he glowered.

"Just—Let me touch you," Dallie scoffed even as his hands gripped her wrists. "Cole, I just want to see what it *feels* like."

"Jesus!" Cole swore as he disentangled himself from her and stood. "Are you *trying* to kill me, Dallas?" he huffed and planted his hands on his hips, looking menacingly down at her even as his raging boner jutted out at her defiantly.

"No!" she countered and sat upright on the blanket, hugging her knees to her chest dejectedly. "Why are you so damn self-righteous, anyway? Who nominated *you* to be the one who gets to decide the fate of my sexual downfall?"

"Ha! Now you're being a bit dramatic, don't you think?" he asked incredulously.

"*Me?*" Dallie popped up from the blanket. "You're the dramatic one! You've been warning me of the 'dangers of sex' since we first met."

"And for damn good reason. You have no clue what you're doing!"

"Yes, I continually get reminded of that...*constantly*! You know what?" Dallie sulked, feeling the tears of anger hit her eyes. "Just forget it!" She started to stalk back to the truck then only to be grabbed by Cole. He turned her around in his arms and pulled her face up to look at his.

"Dallie, baby, I swear I'm only trying to protect you."

"Well, stop it! You aren't my dad."

She'd wounded him with that statement. She could see it in his eyes as he gulped.

He sighed before saying, "I'm not trying to hurt your feelings or prevent you from doing things that you want to do. It's just that," he paused and shook his head. "You deserve better than me." She just frowned and looked at him like he was nuts. "No, really. I'm serious! You do. But please know that I want you, Dallie. I do...so very much."

With that, he pulled her hand down to his crotch. Her palm was suddenly filled with his hard, bulging, denim-covered flesh, and she gasped and looked up into his eyes; eyes that darkened with desire as she delicately let her hand envelope the thickness and length of him.

She pulled back slightly to look down at the hard-on he bore, the confined protrusion that jutted out at her. He shuttered and groaned, closing his eyes as she squeezed and tested the firmness of his magnificent erection. Suddenly, his hand pulled hers away. "Ok," he expelled his breath. "There. Now you know what it feels like," his voice was thick with restraint, and Dallie immediately realized how difficult this must be for him. She felt bad, but was still in awe, as he walked back over to the blanket, readjusting his jeans and grimacing.

Dallie tried to collect herself before going to sit down beside him. He sat with his legs bent, arms covering his knees, looking forlorn. Dallie sighed. She didn't realize the turmoil she'd put him in and furthermore didn't entirely understand it. But then again, she was new to all this stuff.

"Cole," she began but stopped as he looked over at her and took her hand in his.

"Dallie, you're *so* precious. So sweet. So wonderful. Being with you would be sheer heaven and I know that...but as a sinner, I fear I'm not worthy of taking your innocence from you."

"It's tempting though, right?" Dallie tried to laugh, tried to lighten the sexual tension suffocating them in that moment.

His face was a torrent of emotion as his eyes glistened up at her in the light of the fire. "You truly have *no* idea."

Before she even had the chance to respond, he moved and pulled her face up to his, an arm going around her waist as his lips crushed against hers. His passion was unlike anything she'd ever felt before; as if he'd been holding back on her and had suddenly unleashed it all at once.

His hands were everywhere; in her hair, on her waist, on her bottom pulling her down to the blanket and into the impressive erection she'd just felt firsthand. She moaned as she returned his fervor with an unbridled yearning of her own, and her body responded to his in a tempo as old as Eve and Adam. She bucked her hips against his hard flesh as one of his hand's gripped her upper thigh and the other went to her breast, cupping and kneading it, bringing her center to a painful, pulsing ache. His tongue stroked at hers the way his thumbs darted across her peaked nipples and she cried out. His body moved atop of hers and he settled himself between her legs. She reached for the button of his jeans then, longing to see his curious manhood bare in her hands, his going to the hem of her shirt.

That's when lights blinded them, and they both gasped as the roar of a loud engine killed their moment. They breathlessly moved to sit up and straighten their clothes just as a giggling Shannon and Ian approached them.

"Damn, dude. Sorry to interrupt." Ian laughed and gave Cole a fist pump.

"Dallie! You should've texted me. We could have given y'all another fifteen minutes." Shannon laughed and as Dallie stood, pulled her in for a hug then whispered into her ear, "Girl, he is *fine!*"

Shannon looped her arm through Dallie's as Ian and Cole got acquainted. Dallie gratefully let Shannon lead her to the side of Ian's Jeep, her legs feeling like Jell-O as her mind continued to race, her breathing and heart rate finally starting to slow.

"OMG!" Shannon giggled and took Dallie's hands in her own. "If I didn't know any better, I would think he was going for gold back there."

Dallie blushed. "I'm so sorry. It happened so fast." She regretfully frowned at her gorgeous brunette friend.

"Girl, don't be. It's *all* good. Trust me. I know." And Shannon would. She and Ian had been together all of their high school career, and they'd done it for the first time back when they were juniors. Sex wasn't something new for her. "So, I see this is the first time y'all been—well, like *that*, huh?" Dallie just nodded, too embarrassed to do anything more. "I really *am* sorry," Shannon apologized.

"*I* should be sorry."

"No. Not in the least," Shannon grinned and readjusted Dallie's shirt. "He's gorgeous. You got nothin' to be sorry for. If he was mine,

I wouldn't be able to keep my hands off him either." She laughed again. "Ok, ready to go introduce me to him?"

Dallie took a deep breath in and nodded, finally composing herself. She felt mortified. Neither Shannon nor Ian had ever seen her behave that way; it wasn't how she wanted to be seen by *anyone*...but at least these were her friends.

Shannon smoothed Dallie's hair down and wiped the gloss from her chin as she gave her the once over. "Good for you, by the way." Shannon winked and took Dallie's arm again as they walked back over to the boys.

Dallie finally got the guts to look up at Cole and when she did, she noted that the reservation and sternness had returned. "Cole, this is my best friend, Shannon. Shannon, this is Cole," Dallie introduced the two as she playfully shoved a laughing Ian who called her, "Dilly Dallie."

It was one of several nicknames Ian had for her. Dallie was grateful he hadn't called her something much worse. She was especially glad they'd not caught her and Cole with their pants down.

"Ian, shove it!" Dallie cried as he poked at her ribs and pulled her in for a hug.

They all sat down then, dispersing to the logs that sat serving as benches around the campfire that Dallie's dad had built long ago. It was where they all hung out occasionally when there was nothing better to do.

"So, what else do you do besides mess around with your boss's daughter?" Ian asked, taking a swig from the beer bottle that Dallie suddenly realized he had.

Cole looked angrily over at him. Dallie looped her arm through his and took his hand, shaking her head when he looked sharply at her, trying to indicate to him that Ian was only kidding.

"You mean besides knock out smart-asses like *you*?" Cole countered then laughed, getting a laugh out of Ian as well. Dallie guessed that he wasn't entirely kidding as Cole squeezed her hand protectively in his. "I work and I play guitar. You?"

"Well, I'm headed off to college next month." Ian threw back his beer and offered one to Cole, who took it.

"Where?" Cole asked and twisted the cap of the beer, taking a swig.

"A & M. Same as Miss Dallie here." Ian motioned over at Dallie, who grinned shyly at him.

"Oh, is that right?" Cole asked and glanced back at her, looking perturbed by this newfound knowledge. She frowned into his accusing eyes, feeling as if he were overreacting.

"Yup, me and Miss Kinsen here will be seeing a *lot* of one another in the coming weeks. We'll have Algebra and Psychology together."

"Oh?" Cole's eyes darted back to a grinning Ian then to Dallie, who suddenly blushed at Cole's raised eyebrows.

"Yup," Ian said again. "I'll be playing baseball. Short stop."

"That's cool," Cole stated and seemed to be trying to relax a little as he took another swig of beer.

"So, Dallie," Shannon piped in then, "I heard your mom and Peggy Freeman had a little talk just last week."

Dallie's cheeks flamed red as she looked over at Shannon, whose back rested against Ian's chest. "Oh yeah?" she questioned, wanting to know what was running through the grapevine now.

"Yeah, she told Barbara Cox that your mom told her to, and I quote, 'watch herself," Shannon said with a laugh. "Damn girl, what the hell happened?"

"Ouch!" Ian exclaimed, "Dallie, your mom is a total MILF!"

Dallie ignored Ian and answered Shannon with, "She saw Cole and I out at Vinny's one night and came over and just made us feel totally uncomfortable with her questions and stuff. You know how she is... I told Cole not to be surprised if she started another pregnancy rumor."

"God, she's such a cunt!" Shannon grumbled and leaned into Ian as he wrapped both his arms around her.

"The worst," Dallie agreed. "When I told Mom and Dad about it, of course Dad said he was gonna say something, but then Mom said that she would 'handle it'. I can only imagine what she said. Mom must have somethin' on her."

"Your mom can be as intimidating as your dad," Shannon agreed.

"That's so fuckin' *hot*," Ian stated.

"Oh, shut up, Ian. We are all *very* aware of how you feel about Natalie Kinsen."

They all laughed at that. Her mom had interviewed Ian for her column several months ago when he was accepted to A&M for his baseball talents. He'd been smitten ever since.

Dallie and Shannon chatted more about college and the upcoming school year as the guys continued to sip their beers. Shannon was going to beauty school and was super excited. She had a real talent with hair and makeup and was always hooking people up around prom and for weddings. Dallie knew she was going to be a real wizard with a brush, plus she had a knack for gossip. She couldn't stop talking about being accepted into one of the top beauty schools in Denton.

Cole added more logs onto the fire, and he and Ian walked over to Ian's Jeep to grab more beers from the cooler that Ian had brought along.

"So, you finally gonna have sex with this hottie or what?" Shannon asked when the guys were out of earshot. "I see the way y'all look at one another."

"Oh c'mon, Shannon." Dallie elbowed her friend. "I don't know. I mean if it happens fine, if not..." She shrugged.

"If not then there will be many college boys that, I'm certain, will be *happy* to oblige you," Shannon said with a laugh.

Dallie wasn't so eager with the way this discussion had progressed. After all, she was still uncertain about losing her virginity. Following the talks she'd had recently with all the influencing adults in her life, she felt compelled to hold onto it just a little longer. The passion that had overcome her prior to Ian and Shannon's arrival had both thrilled and terrified her. Feeling the ferocity of Cole's intense desire for her, sharp in her palm—and shoving aggressively against her—had been a bit of an eye opener.

Sure, she enjoyed the kisses and touches, but was she really ready for the rest of it? She wasn't so sure. She was aware that the first time would be painful and once the act was committed, she would have to worry about pregnancy...and STDs...and— *Oh lord!* Now she was starting to sound like her parents!

Shannon just continued to stare at her, waiting patiently for an answer then laughed and pulled her in for a hug.

"Oh, Dallie," she murmured into her ear. "You're so innocent."

It was true and Dallie knew it. After all, Cole continued to tell her the same thing.

Ian and Cole walked back toward them then. Ian staggered a little but righted himself as he sat on the log opposite them and looked over at the two of them as they pulled back from one another.

"You girls making out over there?" Ian asked, chuckling, then took another swig of his beer.

"No, you dumb ass! We're talking," Shannon retorted.

"Well, I wouldn't mind seeing a little girl-on-girl action."

"Well, sorry to disappoint you, but we aren't auditioning for a Jenna Jamison video over here, dickhead," Shannon trailed off and rolled her eyes.

"Hey, Dallie, wasn't your dad a serial killer?" Ian asked, randomly.

Dallie froze and Shannon hissed at Ian to shut up. She gulped and looked up to see Cole, who was almost to where they sat, stop dead in his tracks to look over at Ian. She replied with, "My *dad* is Jack Kinsen."

"No, dude. I mean your *real* dad."

"Ian, what the fuck?" Shannon scolded and turned to face Ian.

"Didn't he, like, molest you or something?"

With that, Cole launched himself at Ian, pushed him backwards and jerked him up by the collar of his shirt. Shannon and Dallie ran over to them, and Dallie's arm went to Cole's shoulder, trying to get him to ease his grip on Ian. Ian's hands went up in defense as Cole's voice growled out, "Apologize!"

Ian stammered, "Dude, I didn't mean to start shit."

"Well you did. The first time you opened that damn smart mouth of yours. Now, apologize to Dallas, or I'm gonna beat the hell out of you! You stupid. Arrogant. Egotistical *motherfucker*."

"Ian!" Shannon beckoned.

"Dude!" Ian said with a gruff half-laugh. "Take it easy." When Cole shook his collar roughly, Ian finally succumbed. "Alright, alright. I'm sorry, Dallie."

"Her name is *Dallas*. Not Dilly Dallie or anything else. Dallas."

"Ok...Dallas, I'm sorry. Now get this roughneck off me." Ian was angry now as well.

"Cole, please?" Dallie begged and finally, Cole's grip eased.

"Fuck, man, you really need to chill." Ian grumbled as he backed away from Cole.

"It's time for you to leave," Cole stated and ambled off in the direction of the truck as Dallie turned to follow.

She took a look back at Shannon who mouthed, "I'm sorry."

Dallie just nodded and walked to the blanket, grabbing it off the ground and shaking it as she watched Ian and Shannon take their leave. Cole poured a bucket of water over the campfire, and he and Dallie worked in silence as they got their gear and packed up to leave. She watched Ian's lights peel out of the clearing and opened the passenger door of her dad's duelie.

Cole's hands were shaking on the steering wheel and his head was bowed.

Dallie said nothing as she climbed in and shut the door.

They sat in silence for long moments before Cole lifted his head and said, "I'm sorry, but I absolutely *hate* bullies." He then turned to her and asked, "Are you okay?"

That's when Dallie burst into tears.

CHAPTER 10

*J*ack Kinsen sat on the front porch, sipping a whiskey on the rocks and petting the massive head of his mastiff, Magnus. Nat was rocking their son to sleep, and Savannah was upstairs quietly painting the next masterpiece to be displayed in the Louvre. Life was good!

If only his mind would stop wandering to Cole and his eldest daughter and what on earth they might be doing, he would be alright.

Dallie was well of age, he knew, but that didn't stop the father in him from worrying about her safety and well-being. He was in for many nights of worry in the coming months as she went off to college and away from his protective net to do as she pleased. Drink. Smoke. Have sex; all the things he himself had done in college. People said one paid for their raising. Well, Jack hoped that he wouldn't have to pay too harshly through his child.

Dallie was smart, level-headed and a fine Christian any father would be proud to say he'd raised. She would do well in her studies and make them even prouder than she already had, he knew for a fact. But Dallie was still so incredibly naïve to the evils of the world, so trusting of others and always saw the good in everyone. That wasn't so much a weakness as it was simply her loving nature, but Jack feared it all the same.

All he could do was pray for God to guide her safely through life and that she wouldn't live to find out the hard way—like he and Natalie had—that true evil lived, well-veiled, among them. Jack had seen it firsthand; he'd stared into its very eyes.

He'd tried—so very hard—to forget that day when he'd come face to face with evil incarnate all those years ago. Even now, Troy Cameron's maniacal laugh and black eyes still haunted Jack's dreams. Jack *still* felt the utter panic of seeing his wife's lifeless body as he cradled her in his arms; he *still* saw the crimson blood that covered her. He smelled the acrid smoke of the gunpowder waft through the air and still heard the heavy thud of Troy's dead body fall onto the wood of the foyer. He still wondered about the child that had been murdered that day. And still wished he could have arrived just a little sooner.

Jack's thoughts were interrupted by the lights and diesel engine roar of his Chevy duelie. He smiled to himself, his baby girl was home. And safe. He thanked God.

As they approached, he saw Dallie wipe her eyes and his blood stilled. The truck pulled into the driveway, and Cole looked over at him, a regretful look on his face. Jack sat his drink down and stood, motioning for Magnus to stay put.

He watched as Cole and Dallie got out of the truck, his eyes never leaving his daughter's red, splotchy face. She stopped as she saw him looking at her and immediately, Jack's gaze flew to Cole. Jack contemplated two things as he walked toward them: One, Cole was a dead man, and two, Jack was going to prison for murder.

Jack was over halfway there when Dallie ran at him.

"Daddy!" she cried and fell into his arms. Jack immediately embraced her and felt his blood boil in rage. What had this son of a bitch done to her? He sighed heavily, his eyes narrowing, as he looked into Cole's guilty face.

Before he extricated himself from Dallie to destroy the enemy, Dallie looked up, sniffling. Her sparkling blue eyes took in his murderous ones and then her gaze flew to Cole. She immediately saw what was happening.

"Go inside, Dallie," Jack stated, deathly calm as he moved her away from him.

"No... Daddy." Dallie grabbed for his arm, but she wasn't strong enough to stop him- not by any means.

Jack took two strides forward, and Cole slunk back— snake that he was.

"Daddy!" Dallie yelled.

Two seconds before he lunged, Dallie came between him and Cole, and Jack stopped, the flames of anger seizing his face.

"Move," he told her.

"Dad! Cole didn't *do* anything."

Jack had the audacity to laugh, for perhaps this would be his last as a free man. "The hell you say, you're crying!" he stated the obvious.

"*He's* not why I'm crying. It was Ian." Dallie pushed at Jack's chest then, and his head came back down to look at her. He assessed her face to see if she was lying. "Cole took up for me. He made Ian leave."

Jack felt the anger leave him as quickly as it had come and he stepped back.

"Oh?" he said. "Well, in that case, thanks, Cole." Jack extended his hand, and Cole flinched before realizing Jack had no intentions of hitting him. Cole looked down to Jack's hand then back up and gulped, gingerly grabbing his hand and pumping it.

"You're welcome, sir," Cole said, suddenly relieved.

"I probably don't want to know what he said, do I?" Jack asked, his face still drawn in a stern frown.

Dallie shook her head then added, "He brought up Troy Cameron."

"Are you—?" Jack blurted out and attempted to rein in his anger. He held his breath and counted to ten then gave them both a tight smile. "I assume that Cole took care of it?" Cole and Dallie both nodded. "Alright, well, y'all enjoy the rest of your night. Magnus and I are going in." He whistled to Magnus as he turned to head back up the porch stairs, then he suddenly turned back to face them and tipped his hat to them as he opened the door. "Don't stay up too late. Tomorrow comes early," he stated as he closed the door behind him and mentally cursed Ian Myer to Hell and back.

Jack had never been a fan of Ian's in the first place. The boy was arrogant, self-centered and rude. Jack had simply put up with him when his daughter and Shannon hung out. Maybe Dallie wouldn't see too much of the punk in college despite that they would have a couple classes together; it was a big campus after all.

Hopefully, Cole had put Ian in his place. Perhaps he'd laid a nice punch or two to that jerk's ugly face. How dare that smug prick bring up Troy Cameron as if Dallie hadn't been through enough already.

Suddenly, Jack was ever grateful that Dallie didn't seem to remember those dark days in her past.

As he entered the door frame of his bedroom, he glanced over at his wife and all thought faded from his mind. He was suddenly wrapped up in the sweet floral scent of her perfume and the beauty of her flawless face and body as she lay on the bed reading in a sexy little white nightgown.

He would never forget the day he had first seen her on that old two-lane road. Come to think of it that road's name was—

"What on earth was all the yelling about? I was afraid y'all were gonna wake up the whole—" She stopped when she saw the frown return to his face. "Jack?" She moved to sit from her reclining position on the bed.

He shook his head, smiling and putting his hand up. She stilled. "It's ok, my love. Just a misunderstanding."

Nat's eyebrows went up. "A misunderstanding?"

If he thought she was gonna leave it at that, he was sorely

mistaken. She was a journalist; it was in her nature to question everything.

"Dallie was crying when they pulled in. I assumed that Cole made her cry, but it wasn't him. It was Ian. He apparently brought up Troy."

Natalie huffed, "That little shit!"

"Right?" Jack stated and patted Magnus's big head as he came around the bed. He removed his hat, tossing it on the hat rack in the corner and turned to his wife while he undressed.

"God, I can't stand him," Nat said. "What did that S.O.B. say to her?"

Jack pulled his shirt off, threw it into the nearby hamper, and unsnapped his jeans as he shook his head. "I didn't ask." He sighed as he pulled his jeans down and threw them into the hamper as well.

Magnus whined as he settled down on the floor at Natalie's side of the bed, his usual spot.

"It's probably for the best," Nat added then sighed, "You were gonna kill him, weren't you?"

Jack just looked back into the shimmering blue orbs that held him captive in that moment. Suddenly, he grabbed his wife and effortlessly pulled her curvy frame against him as his mouth sought hers. He kissed her breathless before finally pulling back, stroking her arm and cupping her cheek in his big palm.

"Do you have any idea how very much I love you?" he asked and kissed the tip of her nose.

She smiled then, her hands absent-mindedly stroking his chest. The feel of her touch on his bare flesh made him shiver as her hands lowered and her fingertips traced the indention of his abdominal muscles.

"I'm sure I have *some* idea, but you can feel free to tell me all you like," her sultry voice cooed to him.

He groaned and sighed easily as he kissed her again, loving the feel of her lips on his.

He gave her a crooked grin and said, "I think I'd rather *show* you."

His mouth fell to her neck as his hands gripped the bottom of her gown.

"Oh," she purred as her hands slid into his boxers, "even better." She giggled as he moved atop of her.

～

"Getting close, huh?" Jordan asked as Nate and Cole came through the door.

"Yup!" Nate replied and smiled at his gorgeous wife, who was clad in a tight little red dress beneath her apron. He couldn't wait to tear it right off of her! His eyes loomed over the ample breasts that threatened to spill out of the lacy top of it and his sex hardened.

He and Cole were completely covered in grease and had he not been, Nate would have pulled her tight against him, so she could feel just what she'd done to him with that sexy ensemble of hers. She gave him a knowing smile as he walked by and cocked her eyebrows as if to say, "I'm jumping your ass later, cowboy."

Their sex life had been completely fulfilling over the last twelve years, especially once Jordan had her hysterectomy. After she was fully healed up, they had been like teenagers again in their urgency to satisfy their desires and the passion that raged between them. At times, it had been almost difficult to keep up with her physical demands. Nate only assumed it was partly because she finally felt no pain once the endometriosis was gone, and sex had officially become what it had been meant to be for a woman with the sexual prowess of Jordan Tate. Whatever the case, her insatiable need for him sizzled on, and he wouldn't begrudge her one iota. No one would find Nathan Butler complaining, not one bit. His drop-dead gorgeous wife could use him *all* she wanted to satisfy her womanly needs.

Their love for one another had been soul-quenching and selfless in the beginning and time had only sweetened it like age to a fine wine. Jordan Tate Butler was his best friend, his companion, his everything. He'd never loved anything more than he loved his wife. She'd truly rescued him from the darkness that had consumed his life after he'd killed Troy in self-defense; a true monster who'd come close to destroying his entire family. Nate was so grateful that Jordan had come into his life and patiently brought him back from the dead.

"We'll probably be done within the week," Cole interceded, seeming to be oblivious to the sexual charge between Nathan and his wife. Either that or he was easing an awkward moment, Nate couldn't tell.

"Wow, that's incredible. I can't wait to see it. I know Dallie's gonna be thrilled," Jordan replied and closed the front door behind them as they came through the foyer. "You boys go get cleaned up; supper's almost ready." She leaned in to kiss Nate's cheek, lingering as her breasts brushed his chest. He could have practically growled with desire. It was hard to believe they'd tore the sheets up just this morning; his sex pulsing with unquenched want.

She pulled away as Cole turned and regretfully said, "Well, I forgot to bring fresh clothes."

"I reckon Nate has some extra ones you can borrow; y'all must be fairly close to the same size." Jordan's sultry eyes told Nate that she knew they weren't the same "size" and it took him a moment to respond as he imagined pulling that infernal dress to her waist, yanking down those lacy thongs of hers and pushing himself deep inside her.

"Uh, yeah, sure. I've got some clothes you can wear," Nate mumbled finally after Jordan's hands went up in question, breaking his fantasy.

"See, it's settled then. Go take a shower. I'll bring the clothes down to you." Jordan steered Cole in the direction of the lower bedroom as Nate took the stairs.

It wasn't long before Nate was all soapy and scrubbed free of most of the sticky grease covering his hands and arms. He half expected for his wife to join him in the shower as she was known to sporadically do, but Nate figured that since they had company, she would be hesitant to be her usual carefree sex kitten self. At least until Cole was gone.

Nate dried off and dressed quickly. He headed downstairs and heard the oven timer go off as he came into the kitchen. He looked around for Cole, but realized they were alone. Nathan took that moment to come up behind his wife as she bent forward to grab a dish from the oven and gripped her hips, pressing his perpetually erect cock against her bottom.

"Nathan David Butler, you bad boy!" She scolded playfully as she came upright and sat the dish down on the stove. She bent back down to grab the oven door to close it, and Nate pumped softly against her plump bottom and groaned as his body reacted to the stimulus. When Jordan came back up this time, she turned in his arms, facing him, her finger thrust in his face, and he grinned his Cheshire cat grin at her. "You," she began even as his eyes and hands moved over her, "could have been a gentleman and offered to get that dish out of the oven for me, you jerk, but I see you were blinded with lust."

Nate just responded with an, "uh, huh," as he lowered his face and his lips sought hers. Her arms went around him, and she immediately deepened the kiss, thrusting her tongue punishingly into his mouth. He moaned aloud and squeezed her big breast in his hand. It didn't take long before she was melting in his arms, his pelvis thrusting against her as she gripped at his shirt and rubbed herself back against him, like a cat against its master's leg. She was breathless and came up for air as his lips went to her neck. She whimpered as his fingers pinched at her nipple and his mouth found that sweet spot on her neck that he knew made her wet for him. She moaned as he replied, "If you wanted a gentleman, you shouldn't have worn that porn star dress again... I warned you." His tongue licked the sweetness right off her damp skin, and he mumbled against her ear as his hand moved up her thigh, "Perhaps I should spank you for your insolence." She giggled then moaned as he nibbled at her tender skin with his teeth. "You love it when the bad boy comes out to play." She whimpered again as his fingers softly brushed the lace between her thighs, and he got to feel for himself just how true that statement was. "Oh baby," he growled and took her mouth again as another onslaught of aching lust filled his blood.

Suddenly, they heard footsteps and pulled away from each other as if struck by lightning. Nate moved behind the island to hide his massive erection, and Jordan opened the fridge, readjusting her apron and dress subtly.

"Well, those fit just fine, don't they?" His wife smiled at the younger man as she peeked over the fridge door. Nate just grinned at their clandestine secret as she handed him a beer and took one for herself, offering Cole one as well before she closed the fridge door as if nothing had transpired.

"Yes, ma'am," Cole replied and thanked her.

It was Nate who responded then, feeling his hard-on start to wane. "Ah, it's no problem." Nate raised his bottle to Cole and congratulated him on a job well done. "We've worked our asses off over the last two weeks. Here's to getting that beautiful Chevy of mine back to her former glory." Nate smiled.

Jordan cried, "Here, here," as she raised her bottle in turn, but Cole gave Nathan a funny look as his bottle lowered and he swallowed a sip of beer.

"What's the matter, Cole?" Nate asked.

"Well, sir, you said *your* Chevy," Cole replied.

"Yeah."

"Don't you mean Dallie's?"

Jordan laughed and approached Cole then. "Of course, but you know, that truck was once Nathan's before he gave it to Dallie for her eighteenth birthday, right?"

Cole just shook his head, embarrassed.

"I reckon she just didn't get around to telling you the story, is all," Nate began. "It was actually my parent's truck before it was mine."

"And your grandfather's before that, right, hon?" Jordan asked.

"Yup." He nodded to his wife then turned to Cole. "I inherited it years ago, back when I was a teenager myself, not too long before my bull riding days."

"You were a bull rider?" Cole asked, surprised.

"Oh, yeah. For a good decade. Until a horn got me."

"Wow! That's insane," Cole remarked, and Nate raised his shirt to show the kid his scar. The one where Big Gus about did him in that fateful day in November some fourteen years ago. "Holy shit!" Cole's beer almost spurted out his mouth as his eyes fell on the raised flesh that marked Nate's russet skin just at the bottom of his ribcage. "That's intense!"

"I was lucky. I guess it just wasn't my time," Nate responded.

"You still had a redhead left to tame." Jordan smirked and winked at him, mouthing an, "I love you."

Riding bulls hadn't been nearly as adrenaline pumping as falling in love with that beautiful wife of his had been. He just smiled back at her.

"So, why did you give the truck to Dallie?" Cole asked.

"Well, I had bought a duelie for haulin' the horses a few years back, and it was starting to get pretty neglected just sittin' in the carport day in and day out. Dallie always loved that truck, and one day last year she dropped the hint that she wouldn't mind to take it off my hands, so Jordan and I came up with this elaborate plan to give it to her on her birthday. We had wanted to fix it up for her before then, but she wouldn't have it. Said she wanted it exactly the way it was."

"Yeah, well, she'll be glad you did," Jordan stated as Cole paled at Nate's words. "Don't you worry about that. She's gonna love it. Y'all hungry?"

Nate grabbed the casserole dish with pot holders and moved toward the dining room table that was set for the three of them. Jordan and Cole followed.

Jordan scooped out a heaping portion of shepherd's pie for both them and a smaller portion for herself before remembering she'd forgotten the bread. Nate smiled at her red cheeks as she hurried to the kitchen to retrieve it. He'd distracted her, he knew. She soon returned with butter and freshly sliced French bread.

They ate heartily, filling their hungry bellies as they told Jordan about all the work they'd done on the engine and what more needed to be done before it was finally finished. They were going to paint it a beautiful turquoise color too before giving it to Dallie on the day of the mayor's birthday next week.

The mayor's birthday had become a big celebration in their hometown over the years. It had all started when the town council members had found out that the mayor's birthday coincided with the date that Abundance was officially founded. What had started as a simple party had now become a literal tourist attraction, complete with a parade, festival, a street dance, and fireworks. It had become almost as big as a national holiday for their small town, and everyone showed up to join in the festivities.

"I'm ever grateful for Nathan's help with this rebuild. It has saved me a lot of time and effort having an extra set of hands," Nate heard Cole chime in.

"Nate always enjoys tinkering with cars," Jordan stated proudly.

"I do. It's a fun hobby outside of horse training... although, I have to say, I'm exhausted." Nate said, stretching out his stiff arms as the weight of all the hard work they'd done the last two weeks started to hit him. "I love my niece though and would do it again to see her happy." He smiled, looking over at his wife, whose whiskey eyes suddenly pooled in unshed tears.

"Those kiddos mean everything to us," she stated wistfully and looked down.

"How come y'all don't have any kids of your own?" Cole asked, mid-bite. He stilled suddenly as he realized how silent the room had become at his question.

Nate felt the familiar tug within his chest at the mention of children and the pain that that simple question always seemed to elicit no matter the dozens of times it had been asked. He sighed heavily.

"We're unable to have children," Nate replied gravely, his eyes focused on his empty plate.

"Jeez, I feel like such a heel… I'm so sorry. I don't even know why I asked."

"It's alright, Cole," Jordan responded, voice as steady as a steel bridge. Nate looked over at her; his amazing wife and her iron mask. "You have no reason to apologize. I had to have surgery years ago, and Nate and I just never got around to adopting. We got into a routine and our lives were fulfilled with the Kinsen babies. We never needed anything else." Her eyes met Nate's, and he swallowed the suffering that her words churned up inside him.

For the first time in years, the blaring silence of an empty house reverberated in his ears, and he needed to escape it. He looked over to Cole whose plate was empty now too and gave a weak smile.

"Well, you about ready to go see your girl?" he asked. "I'm sure she's missin' you somethin' fierce by now." Nate cleared his throat and stood, scooting his chair in. He didn't look to his wife, for he knew if he did, he would crumble and he needed to keep some semblance of order here.

Nathan walked back into the kitchen and grabbed his keys from the rack, ambling out the door as Cole followed solemnly.

It wasn't before they were halfway to Jack and Natalie's that Cole spoke.

"I'm real sorry for upsetting you back there, Mr. Butler. I didn't mean to bring up a sore subject, honest."

"Ah, hell, kid. Don't be sorry. You can't do nothing about the stars, the moon or the planetary alignment, can you?" When Cole looked at him with stark bewilderment, Nathan laughed. "It's just the way things are. It's hard to miss somethin' you never had, you know?" Cole just nodded in response. Nate went on, "Jordan and I weren't meant to be parents. I know that. I accepted it long ago. We've lived through these amazing children of my sister's. Being an aunt and uncle has been a true blessing to us. Savannah and Dallie were our pride and joy, then Jackson came along and now we have him to help raise. We appreciate them so much more because we don't have any of our own." And it had always been enough, their lives had been focused on one another and their relationship had flourished. Their lives had been complete, even without children to fill them.

They pulled into the quiet, dark driveway of his sister and brother-in-law's, and Cole moved to exit Nate's truck.

"Chin up, young man. No regrets! Life's too short for that." Cole just nodded and hopped out.

When Nate got back to the house, the kitchen was cleaned up and dark, and he moved upstairs to go console his wife. He knew she would be as stoic as a warrior on the outside, but Cole's words would have greatly affected her, and Nate's reaction to them would have been just as shattering.

As he came through the doorframe, the soft light from the bedside lamp hit him first then the look of utter agony on her face assaulted him next. She moved nothing but her eyes, the red-rimmed honey whiskey orbs gazing up at him beneath the black framed glasses that sat on her nose. She was tucked into the covers reading her latest epic fantasy novel wearing one of her tank tops and probably a thin pair of cotton PJ pants underneath, he assumed. Anyone else would have just assumed she'd been reading the whole time he'd been gone, but not Nathan. He knew his wife; he knew Jordan Butler all too well!

He took in a deep breath as he approached the bed, kicking off his boots and unsnapping his jeans.

"I was rather hoping I'd get to take that dress off of you myself," Nate began and gave a little pout. Trying to feel her out and decide exactly how best to approach this.

"Well, I'm not much in the mood anymore," she retorted, looking back to the book she was doing her best to pretend to read. He might not be a genius like his nieces, but he could tell she'd been crying; her eyes and cheeks were red.

His hand stilled on his fly. "You? Not in the mood? That'll be the day!" he smirked and waited for a sassy retort, but none was forthcoming. "Perhaps, I can change your mind," he exclaimed as he slowly pulled the zipper down. Her eyes shot back to his, and the look of annoyance gave him more answers than any reply she might have.

So... He needed a new approach. She just watched him and waited, her eyes a dead giveaway. She gave him that same look often, when he'd say something stupid or was interrupting her reading, which he'd been known to do many times over the years. How was he supposed to know when there was a climatic event or major catastrophe happening on those wordy pages of hers? Besides, at this moment, they both knew she wasn't reading at all.

He sighed again and plopped down on the bed on his belly, fully dressed, ready for the confrontation.

It didn't take long before she started. "Why didn't you ever tell me that our lives weren't enough for you?"

"Whoa! I never said that."

"You didn't have to."

"Jordan, my love, you are everything I've ever needed."

"But you were a fool to marry a woman who couldn't give you children or a future."

"Don't call me a fool, gingerbread."

"Well, you are! What kind of moron marries a barren wasteland?"

"First of all, you're a *gorgeous* barren wasteland and a sex crazed banshee at that, and I'm the kind of moron who worships the ground you walk on! I wouldn't change a *thing* about our lives."

That's when the tears started and he moved swiftly, scooping her up and into his arms.

"Oh, sweetheart."

"I'm so sorry! I just never want you to regret anything and I could tell you were feeling some tonight after what I said."

"Jordan..."

"Don't even *try* to deny it." Her teary whiskey eyes looked up into his, tearing at his heart strings. "I saw your face! You should have married someone else, Nate. Someone who could have given you a beautiful raven-headed baby."

"Do you honestly think I could have been happier with anyone else? I love you so very much. You make me complete. Without you, I couldn't live and I wouldn't want to. Yeah, so there are moments when the silence is profound, I know you feel it too..."

She was quiet for several moments before responding, "I do."

"But that doesn't mean that we're angry or upset or regretful about it, it just means that we're human. It's in our nature to wonder about the unknown. We love to travel, and we love our hobbies, and we love the quiet sometimes, even if it can be deafening."

Jordan nodded. "But...I love having that baby's head on my breast. He's such an angel."

"But you also love having my mouth there too." He laughed as she swatted at him. "Sweetie, you would have made a wonderful mother, and I'm sorry that you never got that chance. That choice was taken from you, but you haven't ever had any more pain like you were having and look at it this way," he cooed and brought her chin up, "we are so blessed to have a nephew and two nieces that we adore as much as they adore us. We can babysit them and hang out with them and then send them home when they get on our nerves."

"You're not making me feel better, Nathan." She sighed. "Swear to me that you honestly don't regret that we didn't try to adopt?" she pleaded, taking his hand.

"I swear! You are all I need to make me happy. And if we had kids here all the time then I couldn't have you all to myself like I do now."

With that, his face descended to hers, and he sipped at her pouting lips, his mouth melding to hers until her tears turned into moans. Only then did he pull her top over her head and jerk her beneath him. He had her bare-legged and panting and ready for him within minutes. His mouth and tongue moved over her curvy body with an expert skill he'd mastered over the years. He knew all her secret, sensitive spots and she, in turn, knew all of his. His hard-on was full throttle, and she was dripping wet when he eagerly thrust himself into her hot silkiness.

"Oh, yeah," he cried as he drove deep inside her. "I love you so much, my sweet gingerbread. Feel it, feel my love for you." His hand moved from her thigh to her belly then to her breast.

"Oh, Nate." She moaned as she arched her back up to meet his lunge. It didn't take long for his need and pace to increase, and suddenly they were both reaching and climbing and coming apart to the stroking of each other's body. Jordan came first, her sex milking his in the most amazing way possible as she whimpered and screamed his name.

Nathan groaned. "Jordan, oh baby," he cried, as he climaxed and sailed away into a blissful spray of starlight and pleasure. His hips plunged, his hands squeezed and his lungs grabbed for air as he came down from the wonderful high of carnal paradise.

After long moments, he slid slowly out of her and came to lay beside her, kissing her teary cheeks and stroking her damp hair. He smiled as he looked into her eyes. "*There's* yet another perk to not having children."

She looked at him as if she couldn't possibly fathom what the hell it could be.

"Being alone in this house, I can make you scream to the top of your lungs like I just did." She just gave him a withered look in response. "Come to think of it, I believe someone is overdue for a spanking, if I remember correctly."

She smiled, ruefully. "You aren't worn out yet, old man?" she teased, playfully.

"That's it! I'm throwin' in a thorough tongue lashin' too since you wanna get all smart-mouthed on me, you fiery ginger, you. That sweet lil' bottom's about to be as red as that beautiful head of yours," he warned, even as his hand curved around that sweet, plump lil' bottom of hers he'd just mentioned. His cock jumped in response, aroused once again.

She moaned then replied, "Is that so?" Her nose touched his, and she smirked, "Well, you'll just have to catch me first, cowboy!"

With that, she turned, jumped off the bed and giggled as she ran out of the room.

Nate sighed, a man in sheer bliss. God, he loved his wife... and her spontaneity.

~

*C*ole was super nervous. The day had come to reveal the work that he and Nathan had done to Dallie's '57 Chevy truck. They'd fully rebuilt the engine, put in a new transmission and painted it a beautiful shade of turquoise blue, getting it as close to its former glory as they could.

It had taken them almost three weeks, and Dallie had no idea. Well, she had an idea that *something* was going on, but she thought her truck had been at Drew's shop the whole time and didn't know that her uncle and Cole had been the ones to do all the work. She'd assumed her father was simply keeping Cole as far away from her as possible or at least, that's what he'd led her to believe anyway. A little white lie didn't count if it meant giving her this big surprise. Besides, what was one more lie in the culmination of lies Cole had told since he'd come to Kinsen Ranch.

Cole once again felt a pang of guilt and regret fill him as he thought about Dallie and the rest of the Kinsens. They'd become like family to him this past month and a half, even Jack had started to warm up to him.

It isn't fair, Cole thought. He'd never really felt as if he'd belonged *anywhere*, and now, when he was on the run and needing to escape, he felt more at home than he ever had. Life was unpredictable like that and just when a person thought they were on the right path, it veered off in an entirely different direction.

Cole sighed heavily. He couldn't think about all that now. This was a good day, a happy day, and he was looking forward to seeing Dallie's face when he pulled in with her spiffy new pickup. He was also looking forward to taking her to a dance and enjoying the festivities of the small-town celebration for the mayor's birthday.

Jack and Natalie had told him how enjoyable and big this gala was every year; how it had started out as just a big birthday party that happened to include most of the town one year to now five years later, a big blow out that brought people from all over the state. That was one thing that Cole wasn't looking forward to; being surrounded by all those people—people that might recognize him—but then again, he reminded himself that the police still weren't any closer to finding him. He was a literal needle in a haystack. Although that gave him some ease, in the back of his mind he had a nagging suspicion that he was getting too comfortable here, and soon it would be time to move on.

He spotted Jack and baby Jackson playing out on the front lawn with Magnus and waved as he pulled the truck into the driveway.

Jack approached with the toddler in his arms and whistled as Cole stepped out.

"Ooh-wee, man…ain't that a beauty!"

"Oooh, eee," Jax mimicked and reached toward it, grunting. "Mmm tuck."

"Yeah, well maybe by the time you're old enough to drive it, your sister will be willing to part with it," Jack responded to his son and laughed, shaking his hand as Cole approached the two of them. "You did a fine job, Cole. Dallie's gonna be amazed! I can't wait to see her face."

"Me too." Cole stepped back to admire the beautiful, smooth lines of the vintage truck and couldn't help but feel a sense of pride; it purred like a kitten. "She's gonna be the envy of the entire campus."

"Who's gonna be the en—?"

Jack and Cole both looked to the porch stairs at an awestruck

Dallie, whose eyes were riveted on the beautiful turquoise blue pickup truck sitting in the driveway.

She gasped, "Oh my God! It's gorgeous." She came forward and looked to Cole, who held the keys out to her. "You?"

"Yup! Well, me…and your uncle Nate, but it was your dad's idea. And *his* money."

Her eyes sought her father's, sending appreciation his way before she turned back to Cole. "But…" She frowned then smiled, confused.

"He and your Uncle Nate rebuilt the engine and transmission and painted it for you," Natalie called from behind her on the porch, smiling. Dallie turned to acknowledge her but instead responded to Cole.

"Cole, I—I don't even know what to say." Dallie's eyes bounced between him and the truck. "I…Wow! How did you…?"

Cole just smiled back into her beautiful face and gawking eyes as she reached out to touch the truck. That's when she began to cry.

He immediately stepped forward and pulled her into his arms. Her arms instinctively went around his neck and her head fell to his shoulder. He sighed. He hadn't expected this, and by the looks of her folks, they hadn't either. They both stepped forward, Jack begrudgingly as he eyed the familiarity of intimacy between the two of them and Natalie, anxiously as her concerned eyes looked from Dallie to Jack.

Dallie composed herself after a few moments and pulled back slightly, covering her mouth and wiping at her eyes. She apologized, and they all shook their heads at her.

"I don't know what came over me," she began, looking ruefully among them.

Her mom reached out and cupped her arm, rubbing it comfortingly as a tender look crossed her face. "Oh, baby," Natalie murmured to her.

"I'll take that as a sign you like the work Cole did?" Jack asked, arching an eyebrow at her; his attempt to lighten the mood.

With that, she laughed and nodded, looking back to Cole, who blushed in return.

"It's unbelievable! Really. I can't believe this is actually *my* truck!" She looked at the truck again, as if she were seeing it for the first time.

Jackson piped in then, his silence ended for the moment being, "Dawee." The toddler reached out to her, and she took him from her father, hugging his little body to her then she kissed his plump cheek and smiled. "Sad?"

"No sad," Dallie stated, shaking her head. "Dallie's happy now, sweet boy. Look at my truck! Isn't it pretty?"

"Pwetty," Jackson concurred and patted at the chrome side view mirror. "Me wide?"

Dallie laughed and her head flew back, her mouth wide in a gorgeous smile, her flowing platinum ringlets falling down her back.

It was then that a sharp, profound awareness came over Cole; an awareness so intense, so vibrant, so unwavering in its clarity that he knew right away he was head over heels in love. The knowledge was shocking, amazing, and horrifying as all the terrible consequences of it came flooding into him. Being able to know what love finally felt like was magnificent yet powerfully agonizing, and he wasn't sure if he was going to cry, faint or be sick... or all three at once. The all-encompassing feeling that shot through his heart and brought a tingle throughout his entire body, he suddenly realized regretfully, would have to be completely contained, quarantined and never allowed to see the light of day. Dallie must be kept in the dark about this and not permitted to see or know in any way, shape or form; this was to be Cole's eternal secret. He was a fugitive of the law after all, and his love for her would only serve him, not her; it would do nothing but hurt her. And he would never do anything to hurt the woman he loved...ever.

He gulped and frowned as the pain this knowledge brought him overtook him completely. The irony was that he'd never felt love before in his life, not from anyone—save for a brother's love with

Adam—and now that he did, he couldn't even fully embrace it. True love had been just within his grasp, and yet so far out of reach at the same time. But then, no one had ever said life was fair.

"...right, Cole?" Dallie called to him from the driver's seat, and his painfully exquisite reverie came to a screeching halt as the woman of his heart looked over at him.

He coughed and tried to come up with some reason why he wasn't listening. "Sorry, I was distracted by that beautifully humming engine of yours," he retorted in perfect sync with the purr of the motor she'd turned over just seconds before.

She laughed again, and the divine sound of it ripped his soul in two. She was blissfully unaware, and that's how she would remain. He smiled into her angelic face and tried to calm his beating heart as he came around the other side of the truck and hopped in next to her.

"Good ol' Betsy sounds like a fine-tuned machine," Dallie cooed to him.

"Don't you know it!" Cole exclaimed.

"Are there any more tricks you have hidden up your sleeve?" she asked, pulling the cuff of his navy polo shirt up, so she could look at his arm.

Cole laughed big and loud. "Ha! A magician never reveals his secrets." He winked.

"Kids, be careful and have fun," Jack stated as he popped his head into the open driver's window. "Be home by eleven." He patted the door and looked intently at Dallie then nodded at Cole, a gesture of admiration and gratitude. Cole sighed happily, glad to receive the approval from a man with the commanding presence of Jack Kinsen.

Dallie waved at the baby in her mother's arms as she backed out of the driveway then looked over at Cole with the same admiration and gratitude he'd seen in her father's eyes. How was it even possible that the two of them weren't blood-related?

Once she and Cole were well down the road, Dallie asked, "So, this is what you've been up to these past few weeks, huh?"

"Yes, early mornings and late evenings, and with the help of your uncle."

"Dad said you were having to go back and forth to Tyler, hauling horses and helping Eli Coleman, which is why you haven't been on the ranch much lately. I just figured Mom had finally told him about finding us on the couch that morning and perhaps, this was his way of keeping us apart."

It had been increasingly difficult over the past few weeks being away from Dallie as much as he'd had to be, in addition to keeping the work a secret. He'd missed many dinners with the Kinsens, had short breakfasts with them, and returned well after dark, exhausted, coming into the basement through the back door, showering and heading to bed. He'd worked on his days off even and one day, when they had been about halfway through, Jack insisted that Cole had to take a break as Dallie was starting to get suspicious. That's when they'd both come up with the plan to lie about where Cole was and what he was doing. Eli Coleman was a fellow ranch owner and friend of the Kinsens, and Jack had said to use him as an excuse for Cole's absence. Even still, Dallie had questioned why Cole, of all the ranch hands, had been made to go help out another ranch when he was such a "green horn", so she'd come to her own conclusion that this was her dad's way of punishing them. It had worked out perfectly. She'd had no idea.

"I had no clue you could work on cars," she said, taking his hand.

"It's one of the few things I'm really good at," Cole stated, bashfully.

"That's not true. You can play guitar and you have a great voice."

"Well, thanks." He laughed.

Suddenly, Dallie was pulling off the road and into an old abandoned gas station. She cut the engine and looked over at him, a crooked grin on her face and awe in her eyes. Before Cole could respond, she was straddling him and his hands gripped her bare thighs beneath the aquamarine dress she wore. Her mouth swiftly covered his and his hesitance faltered as his lips softened to kiss hers. He expected the passion to accelerate and her hands to go to his beltline, where they were known to go as of late, but she surprised him by not deepening the kiss and pulling back to look in his eyes just as he'd started to feel the stirrings of desire hit his sex. He sighed heavily as he looked at her. Perhaps it was his newfound knowledge of love, but she looked more gorgeous tonight than she ever had. She was clad in a silky, figure-flattering, knee-length aquamarine dress with her tan cowboy boots and matching Stetson. He himself was clad in a navy polo shirt, jeans and a tan cowboy hat of his own.

Dallie smiled as her clear, sapphire blue eyes searched his and she tilted her head as she spoke.

"How can I ever thank you for all your hard work on my truck?" By the look in her eyes, Cole got the impression that she had several ideas for how she could. He gulped. "Is this your way of trying to impress me, Mr. West?" Cole almost balked at that fake ass surname he'd given himself. "If so, I must tell you - I'm *incredibly* impressed." Her eyes darkened, and Cole couldn't stop his body from responding to the lust that he found there. It would be so easy to lose himself to her sweetness, so easy in this quiet lot to pull her down beneath him, part her slender thighs and truly love her with an absolute tenderness unlike any he'd ever known. Loving her would be the easiest, most wonderful thing he would ever do in his life, but losing her was going to literally tear him apart. As uplifting as these flashbacks of Dallas Kinsen would be in his future when he was all alone in the world again and had nothing else to keep him grounded, to keep him hopeful, he couldn't stand the pain that those visions would also bring into his heart.

"I didn't do it to impress you," he blurted out.

"Oh?"

I did it because I'm hopelessly in love with you, was what he wanted to say. But instead remarked, "I did it to get your dad off my back."

With that, Dallie threw her beautiful head back and belted out a sexy, throaty laugh. Cole joined in, easing some of his misgivings for a moment or so.

"It kinda worked a little, don't you think?" Cole asked, dropping his hands from her enticing thighs.

Dallie just shook her head at him and lowered her face to his, kissing him tenderly and cupping his hairy jaw.

"You're such a ham, Cole West."

"If not a funny one, at least."

"You're afraid to show the world just how wonderful you are, aren't you?"

"Well, it's hard to share the limelight with the famous Dallas Kinsen."

Her eyes changed, and she frowned, studying him, trying to determine if he was telling the truth or not. She must have come to her own conclusion because she moved off him then and sat, crossing her arms over her chest.

"Well, I know you didn't do it to get into my pants because you could've done so already."

They rode in deafening silence all the way into town after that, with only the beautiful rumble of the engine that Cole had rebuilt and the sexual tension hovering between them.

Town was a jumble of people. There were road blocks all over the place, so they had to be rerouted a few times before finally ending up in a makeshift gravel lot behind the courthouse annex.

Dallie parked quickly, opened the door, and was out of it before he could even call out, "Dallie!"

He exited the passenger side and had to run to catch up to her. When he spun her around, he pulled her into his chest, but she was shoving at him, fighting his embrace.

"Don't touch me," she cried and pushed his arms away, hands going to her hips. "You've had your chances over and over again and you keep rejecting me. Why?"

Cole looked around quickly to see if they were drawing a crowd, but to his utter shock and amazement, they were completely alone.

It wasn't too much longer 'til dusk, the sky was starting to darken, the heat wasn't as suffocating as it had been earlier in the day.

He calmly tried to think of any excuse he could make, but none was forthcoming.

As if reading his thoughts, she said, "And don't give me none of that shit about the fact that I should guard my body under lock and key and how unprepared I am to have sex. I mean you're such a damn saint that you make me feel dirty." A saint! If she only knew what she was even talking about. He was a man running from the law, nothing even close to a saint. She continued, "I don't understand you at all, Cole. Obviously, you care about me or you wouldn't have done all this work on my truck. Most guys would have jumped on me the second I showed the least bit of interest, but you..."

"I'm not *most* guys, Dallie, in case you haven't figured that out by now. I'm sorry that I'm as eager to *postpone* taking your virginity as you are to give it away."

"I'm not just *giving* it away!"

"Aren't you? You barely know me." She swallowed hard at that and lowered her head. It was true, and she damn well knew it. She looked embarrassed as her suddenly teary eyes came back to his. Before he could let her grovel, he took her back into his arms. "You know how much I want you, angel," he whispered into her ear. "I've shown you. I've let you feel it for yourself. Let that be enough for now. Please?" His lips came to her wet cheek, and he stroked her back. "Being with you is the best thing that's ever happened to me. I'm so lucky to even *know* you, let alone be able to kiss your beautiful lips, to hold your beautiful body against me." He pulled back just enough, so she could look into his eyes and see the truth that beamed out of them. "You're the most amazing woman I've ever met. Forgive me if I feel unworthy of you." He dropped his arms in defeat then.

His words might seem like a complete line to most people, but his statement wasn't entirely untrue. As much as he wanted to take her and claim her for his own, the action was unthinkable, especially in the predicament he'd found himself in. Making love to her would be selfish and cruel, knowing that their relationship was only here and now with no hope for a future ahead. At some point, very soon, he would have to leave her...and to be subjected once again to the rumors that had plagued her not so long ago. He refused to be that man. He had enough red in his ledger as it was.

He pulled her against him tightly, smothering her in a smoldering kiss, willing her to feel his love for her without asking him for more than his breaking heart could give, and when he pulled back, he saw that she got the picture, even if she didn't fully understand. Maybe one day she would. And she would thank God that he'd not acquiesced to her sexual demands. She would be grateful that he'd saved her from more heartache, saved her from more regret than what she would already feel at his betrayal, the regret of being so intimate with a convict such as himself.

When they'd both calmed down, he took her hand and walked her toward where all the commotion was on Main Street, where a large elevated platform was raised for a stage in front of the courthouse and two giant subwoofers sat leeching out a familiar country rock tune. They were surrounded by crowds of people meandering around seeking a spot to stand. The many shops and restaurants were alight with dazzling twinkle lights and balloons and the streets were lined with confetti from the earlier parade. A band was taking the stage as Dallie was elbowed by a bystander, and Cole put his arm around her, bringing her closer to him and out of the reach of strangers. For now, more than ever, the thought of others touching her made him crazy mad.

The country rock band was a local one that played several catchy tunes, and Dallie's mood seemed to lighten as she danced with him. They laughed and kept the beat and when a slow melody began to play, Cole pulled her tighter against him. She came so easily into his arms, her soft curls tickling his beard-covered cheek as his forehead rested against hers. He absorbed this amazing moment with her and let it plant itself deep in his memory. The look of her eyes, the feel of her breasts against his chest, the touch of her fingers on his neck, the sweet floral scent of her perfume, the ripple of her skin as she breathed longingly beneath his palms.

It wasn't long before the mayor, Brad Carter, was announced, and the band and crowd together sang "Happy Birthday" to him. He graciously thanked them all for coming out to celebrate his 59th birthday on this beautiful night, spoke of what an honor it was to serve in a community as involved and giving as Abundance, and talked a little about upcoming projects and events. The mayor was a stout man in a linen shirt and khakis, looking younger than his 59 years with little grey in his hair and a set of keen brown eyes. When he was done with his speech, they all applauded him and the band took a break. Dallie and Cole took it upon themselves to worm through the crowd for some food then. They filed in line for the food trucks that were lined on the east side of the stage and settled for Caribbean fare with a twist, Cole choosing coconut shrimp tacos and Dallie getting a jerk chicken gyro.

As they waited for their food at the window, Dallie spoke to various passersby; Darla from church, Sonia from school, Taren from horse jumping events. She never failed to introduce Cole, and he just tipped his cowboy hat at them, trying to be as inconspicuous as possible. He didn't want to be remembered by these people in any way when the time came to become scarce.

They ate their food at one of the many picnic tables lining the street then grabbed a funnel cake. After spotting Dallie's parents and siblings, they ran over to greet them and hung out for a little while then they met up with Shannon and a scowling Ian. There was more dancing, a cake cutting and finally, fireworks, and by the end of the night, they were both sweaty and exhausted.

They were headed back to the truck when Dallie came to a stop next to it. She looked up at Cole regretfully and took his hand.

"I'm sorry for my earlier behavior," she began.

"Don't be. Honestly. It's really alright."

"I have no right to badger you about being a perfect gentleman, Cole."

It was true, but it didn't matter. He just shook his head at her, indicating that he wasn't upset. "You want to know what it's all about. I get it."

"I do, but that doesn't mean I'm hell-bent on throwing it out the window like it means nothing because honestly, it means a lot."

"As it should!"

"It's just—" She pulled on her bottom lip as she drew him into her like one of her horses and intertwined their fingers. "I really want my first time to be with you, Cole." Her sparkling baby blues took all the thoughts from his mind and stilled his breath as they glittered in the light of the streetlamp behind them. "I don't know why and I don't know your intentions and maybe I'm completely stupid because you don't owe me anything. I don't even know that you'll stick around long, but I want it to be *you* that shows me what it's like to become a woman."

CHAPTER 11

C ole had trouble sleeping that night as Dallie's words echoed through his brain. How could he have let this get as out of hand as it had, as quickly as it had? He was in deep shit and he knew it.

He'd just stared at her as the impact of her words hit him like a brick to the face. She gazed back into his eyes, gauging his reaction, until she'd finally said, "Say something!" She might as well have shouted at him for he'd flinched. He'd started to tell her what a mistake she was making in choosing him, of all people, but for the life of him, the words wouldn't come.

She'd then explained why she wanted it to be him. "Cole, I know what you're thinking." As if she *could*! "I'm naïve and immature and don't know what I'm doing or talking about or taking on... I know." Did she? "But you've been so good with me and so gentle and so patient. You're perfect." "Perfect for *this*," she might as well have said and definitely didn't say "perfect for *me*."

He'd tried not to let the sentence hurt him, but it had. She spoke of him taking her virginity as if it were as easy as breaking a horse to her, like it was something as simple as putting a check mark in a box. Apparently, for her, this was just another obstacle to tackle like horse jumping or dressage, not love, prompting her to ask him. It wasn't personal as sex should be. If he had any hope that she loved him back, that statement had cemented it for him. He was to be used! And this should make him glad, for she wasn't looking for a future with him, and he wouldn't be breaking her heart when he left. But it only served to deepen his misery. As much as he loved her, she felt nothing for him. Nothing! He was just a means to an end. That's all he meant to her. Even if she hadn't meant it that way, and he'd heard her wrong, the doubt was now there in his mind.

He'd never fit in anywhere, why would this place be any different? He'd never been accepted, he'd never been loved, so why had he expected his perfect Dallas—of all people—to love him? He'd truly lost all hope now. He should just take his leave from this place immediately and cut his losses. Then the pain would be over. He could rip off the band-aid quickly and then it would be done and over with. But he knew that was far from the truth. Pain would be as much a part of his future as isolation would be; the pain of losing Dallas Kinsen, the pain of loving her…for falling in love with her had been the final nail in his coffin.

He sighed as he rolled over and stared into the moonlight that came through the window. He wanted to kick and scream, cry and shout, beg and pray. Why was his life so meaningless? Why did Adam have to die? And why couldn't a beautiful soul like Dallas Kinsen just love him and want him for who he was? Was he really such a bad guy; was he really so undeserving of love? Was this to be his punishment for all the wrong he'd done in his life?

Anger filled Cole's veins. He had a mind to march right up to Jack Kinsen and tell him what his daughter was plotting behind his back. Her parents would be horrified to learn of her plan to use Cole like he was a breeding stud and they would be appalled at how careless Dallie was being with her precious virginity. This knowledge would be the push Jack wanted to lock his daughter up and throw away the key. Her recklessness with her body was proof that her father's protectiveness had back-fired on him.

A weaker man would have driven her to a quiet place somewhere, hiked her dress up and given her exactly what she'd wanted. But that wasn't Cole. He would never take advantage of her. He wanted her with a painful ache, but as much as he wanted to claim her virginity, he wanted her love even more.

Thus, he'd kissed her with a heavy heart and nodded, promising nothing and faking indifference, as they'd climbed into the truck and headed home. She'd probably assumed he was just digesting her words, but all along he was doing his best not to brood. She was none the wiser when he'd sighed and went on downstairs after bidding her a goodnight. She'd hesitated as she pulled away from him though, searching his eyes for something—he wasn't sure what —before she left him and with a scowl went upstairs. If she was expecting him to take her then and there, he'd disappointed her but, dammit, let her be disappointed. She was going to have to give him time to figure out exactly what he was going to do about what she'd told him. She was a spoiled brat, he reckoned, pissed because he hadn't just bowed to her will and given in to her every whim. Well, now she could get a small feel for what his whole life had consisted of because he wasn't aimed at destroying her virtue right away, no matter *what* she wanted. She was used to getting her way, but this was too significant of a decision to be hasty about. She needed time to reconsider it, although, he knew she'd made her mind up. Maybe he should tell her that he wasn't the guy for the "job" or maybe he should call her bluff.

~

*A*my Burns sat by the phone that night, biting her nails into the quick and scanning the news. She couldn't keep from fighting the nagging suspicion that the police were onto her and Jeremy. It had been Jeremy's idea to kill Adam, but it had been Amy who'd done the deed herself. Now, Jeremy was avoiding her like the plague, and she was forced to live with the repercussions of the crime she had set in motion.

It had been two months now since Adam's murder, and not a day had gone by where she hadn't lived to regret it. She and Jeremy should be in Mexico right now, squandering away the life insurance policy that she would be getting soon, but as of yet, he hadn't contacted her. Many months ago, he'd professed his undying love for her and told her how they had to get rid of Adam as he was in the way of their life together. Thus, began the idea to frame Cole for Adam's murder. It had come to fruition, but now it seemed things were so screwed up. No one could find Cole, and the case was up in the air. The cops had come to question her a couple times and didn't seem to be none the wiser to her actions, but that meant nothing if Cole wasn't found. He had to be caught and arrested in order for this to work.

She tried to reason with her own uneasy mind—ticking off a number of reasons why Jeremy might be avoiding her. He was simply trying to protect her, trying to keep the heat off of her while they waited for Cole to be found and arrested, trying to keep their affair on the down-low until the case was closed. But as much as she tried to convince herself, there was a part of her that doubted his true intentions. He had been so hateful to her that day in the office, so dismissive. He knew how insecure she was, knew how needy she could be, but he apparently wasn't thinking about that; that, or he didn't really love her. As much as she didn't want to believe it, there was the possibility that he had tricked her.

She and Adam had been together since they were in high school. Their love had been sweet and innocent and—in the end—boring. Loving Adam had been easy, too easy. He was just too damn perfect. Amy had needed a change, something exciting, a bad boy—and there Jeremy was. It didn't matter that he was her husband's brother, when he'd approached her that day at the family barbecue and seduced her with his words and his hands, she'd been overcome with desire and awareness—awareness that her life needed some spice and chaos. The affair had been hot and heavy and continued on and on even though Amy knew they were going to get caught, it didn't matter because the thrill of it excited her more than the fear had. Jeremy had been a smooth talker, a charmer down to the very end, and Amy had complied with anything and everything he'd asked of her. That, perhaps, would be her downfall.

She glanced at the television screen again. There was still no news on Cole's whereabouts. She sighed and threw the remote down and screamed in frustration. She couldn't keep sitting around like this. She was going nuts! Where the hell had Cole gone? He had nowhere to go. That's why he'd been the perfect scapegoat. He had no life outside of Adam. No family. No loved ones. He was alone in the world. Where would he run to? And for what reason? He was innocent. Why would an innocent person run?

Sitting around like this made her think too much, made her miss Adam and his funny laugh and his sweet cuddles. She had to find something to do besides think about him. She needed to get away for a little while. Amy picked the phone up and called her sister, Alyssa. She made plans to go down to her place and spend a little time on Padre Island. The sand and salt would do good to cleanse her and perhaps, give her some clarity. She then phoned her work and told them she wouldn't be in until the following week; they'd been so good to give her all this time off to grieve.

Little did they know, she needed to do more than to grieve; she needed to come to terms with her sin, needed to find her backbone. Otherwise, she was going to ease her conscience, and Jeremy Burns would just be shit out of luck!

∾

*N*atalie heard Savannah huff as she walked from the kitchen into the living room, Jackson in tow. It had been well after 10:30 AM when her daughter came groggily down the stairs, yawning. She'd quietly ate her breakfast of eggs and toasts, as usual, then moved into her customary spot in the dining room with its "perfect" lighting to begin painting.

Savannah wasn't much for morning conversations and today was no exception, Nat knew. But despite that Vanna wasn't a morning person, she wasn't usually moody or ill-tempered. Nat could see that today something was off.

"What is it, angel?" Nat asked, cautiously, once she'd placed Jackson down in front of the TV and moved back into the open door frame of the dining room. She wanted to ask if her junior Einstein was lacking inspiration today but held her tongue.

Savannah huffed again and brushed at the sleep in her eyes with the back of her index fingers. When she looked up at her mother, the circles beneath her eyes were dark. Nat immediately felt apprehensive.

"I didn't sleep well," she grumbled.

Nat knew that wasn't unusual for her and asked, "How come?"

"I was having bad dreams."

Nat tried not to tense at her words, after all, both her kids had nightmares often, but the look on Savannah's face was similar to one she'd seen before.

Natalie had to go to her school in the middle of the day one day to pick her up when Vanna was about seven years old. Her eyes had been red from crying, and she was completely hysterical. Once they got to the car, Nat pulled her sobbing child into her arms and soothed her, begging her to explain what had happened.

"Peter said that Dallie wasn't my *real* sister."

"Oh, honey, of course Dallie's your real sister," Nat admonished as she'd stroked her daughter's beautiful maple hair.

Savannah had shaken her head then. "He said that Daddy wasn't her daddy." With that, another wail escaped her lips. Natalie scowled, angry with the situation.

She'd known the day would come when she and Jack would have to explain things to Savannah about Dallie, but Nat had hoped that would be long into the future. And not from the mouth of a cruel kid like Peter Sullivan.

"Oh, baby," Nat had cooed and wiped at the tears on her daughter's face, "Look at me." When Savannah obliged, Nat softly told her. "Savannah, Dallie…" How to break this to her? Savannah wasn't like other kids. When Nat told her that Jack wasn't Dallie's father it was going to break her heart even further than it already was. "Your sister doesn't share *all* of your blood, but you know what? That doesn't even matter. What matters is how much you two love each other, how much Mommy and Daddy love each other, and how very much we love you both. Dallie has always belonged to your father; from the very beginning. The minute your sister and I met Jack, she was his, fully and completely…and well, so was I for that matter. I just didn't know it at the time." She trailed off, trying to get back to the point of the conversation as Savannah hung to her every word, her tears starting to wane. "The point is, baby, your daddy is as much Dallie's father as he is yours. In his heart, and hers, that's *all* that counts. Dallie *is* your sister, she's your family, and Peter Sullivan is just jealous."

Savannah had been content with that, so Nat had thrown out a joke, getting a laugh out of her then they'd gone into town and washed their cares away with ice cream and art gallery shopping, bringing home a vintage replica of Van Gogh's "Starry Night" to make things all better.

The look Vanna gave her now mimicked that look on her face all those years ago, and Nat realized with startling clarity that she'd never told Vanna the full story about Dallie's biological father. Maybe she could get away with it for a little while longer, she prayed. Savannah's heart was as delicate as Dallie's, and she would be truly shattered when she found out what her sister and mother had gone through.

"What kind of bad dreams?" Nat came up to her then and stroked her daughter's wavy locks.

"I was having nightmares...about Dallie." Nat's hand stilled on her daughter's head and she gasped out loud.

She couldn't stop the fear that seized her heart at that moment. She flashed back to that fateful day thirteen years ago when Troy came back to kill her.

"Mom? What's the matter?" Savannah grabbed for her hand then.

"What did you dream about your sister?" Natalie tried to rein in the panic she felt.

"I dunno. It was just a feeling of danger and fear. It was disturbing."

Nat gulped and tried to tell herself that it was only a dream. Troy was dead. He could never hurt either of them again, but her heart wasn't listening as its hammering beat intensified.

Suddenly, the phone rang and the tension seemed to ease from her. She smiled down at Savannah and ran to answer the living room phone.

"Hello?" Nat asked and squealed when a familiar voice greeted her. "Vivian! Oh my goodness. It's so good to hear your voice." She listened as Vivian asked if she could come stay with them. "Oh, of course. The kids will be thrilled... When?"

It was then that she forgot all about Savannah's dream and the fear it had brought her.

~

Dallie sighed again as she worked alongside Wyatt with an exceptionally stubborn mare from Tulsa. Her mood wasn't helping things she knew, but dang it, she really needed to get Cole to herself just long enough to apologize...explain herself...do whatever was needed to fix this wretched silence and aloofness that emanated from him since she'd told him she wanted *him* to be the one to take her virginity. He'd not even responded to her at all that night after she'd made that ridiculous and mentally unsound statement of hers. Where had that boost of confidence even come from in the first place?

She'd been overtaken and frightened by his unleashed passion that night in the field last month and they'd barely seen each other over the last three weeks as he worked on her truck then boom, suddenly, she had thrown herself at him and gotten mad when he hadn't consented. Instead of thanking him, she'd practically belittled him for not being a typical red-blooded sex-crazed male. Was she going nuts? Perhaps! That's all she could figure. Growing up and moving on—and facing her out-of-control hormones—was starting to make her lose her mind. Maybe it was because she only had a month left before she would be heading out to College Station and the fear was causing her to do things she never would've done otherwise. The time, or lack thereof, was eating away at her as the minutes had started to tick off the clock with an insistently loud banging inside her heart.

For two days now, Cole had made himself scarce, and Dallie was perplexed. He didn't appear angry, just disappointed, upset, and aloof. She couldn't quite place the exact vibe she was picking up from him, but she was definitely starting to see what her mother had meant when she'd said that Cole exuded a 'profound sadness'. Dallie had never picked up on it before or perhaps it was just stronger now that she'd put him on the spot and made him feel like he was being used.

She again felt guilty for her erratic behavior. She had never acted this way before with anyone else, and she wasn't sure why she'd acted that way with Cole. His kisses made her soar and his touch made her tingle. So, why wasn't that enough? Why had she continued to push him into something that he obviously wasn't comfortable doing with her? He was a drifter after all. Maybe this was his way of trying to protect her from the inevitable, but instead of being grateful, she'd acted like a child having a temper tantrum. He had every right to shun her.

She frowned again as the big mare flicked her head back in defiance at her command. The mare was picking up on Dallie's bad mood, and it was making the horse incredibly uneasy. Before Dallie could try and touch her to soothe her bristling spine, Wyatt pulled at the mare's lead, taking her in the opposite direction. Dallie turned, head lowered, frustrated that now her mood was disturbing her work with the horses she loved. She was just gonna have to—

"Dallie, watch out!" She heard a deep voice call out to her and felt something slam into her body from her right side. The jolt of it shocked her more than the pain as she realized suddenly that she'd been tackled. She landed hard onto her left hip and felt her elbow scrape the ground as a heavy body covered her. She was jerked upright as her eyes opened and she felt strong arms lift her as she was cradled into a chest and rushed into the barn. Still reeling from the surprise of the attack, she tried to look around and figure out what had happened and struggled to ease out of the grip she was in. She pushed against a hard chest and started to get panicky when she couldn't get loose.

"Put me down, dammit!" she cried and arched her back.

That's when her legs were dropped, and she saw that it was Cole who was holding her.

His breathing was labored as his chest brushed hers, his face startled. Before she could ask him what the hell he was thinking, his hands went to her face and he looked her over with such concern in his eyes that she stood transfixed.

"Are you okay? Did she get you? Turn around and let me see." He spun her around, and Dallie scoffed. What was he talking about? Did who do what?

Suddenly, her ears focused on the struggle in the corral she'd been in just moments before, and Dallie realized the horse was kicking and bucking.

"Wyatt!" she cried as she flew towards the barn door, where her father stood just inside the frame.

His right arm shot out, stopping her, and she bumped into the back of his tricep and shoulder with an expulsion of breath. "Wait," he stated as he signaled her to watch Wyatt. "Let's see if he can handle it on his own."

Dallie huffed but held fast as she and her dad looked to Wyatt, attempting to control the spooked mare.

At first, he seemed helpless as he fumbled with the lead, drawing the horse's head down as she kicked and snorted, which only served to infuriate her all the more, then they watched as his demeanor changed and he stepped to the side, loosening his grip on the lead rope. He took in a deep breath and appeared to close his eyes. He stood still for but a moment then softly called out to the mare. Her ears went up and her legs stilled. Her head flicked, but she didn't move away as Wyatt's hand came to her cheek, and he murmured to her. Both Dallie and her father blew out the breath they'd been holding and his arm fell from in front of her. Her father turned towards her and gripped her shoulders gently, looking her over.

"Are you alright?" he asked. When she nodded, he pulled her into his big chest for a brief hug and kissed her lightly on the head. "You almost got kicked, baby. And hard too. If it hadn't been for Cole, you would have been seriously injured," he said as he pulled back, frowning. He grabbed her arm up then, noting the cut on her elbow. "You're bleeding. Damn. I'm sorry."

The look of regret on his face was palpable. Jack Kinsen wasn't one for drama, but he also didn't like it when people got hurt on his watch. Dallie started to tell him that a little scrape sure wasn't going to kill her, but her dismissal of the harm inflicted on her was stymied as Cole stepped up to them.

She turned her head to look at him and any response she might have had died on her lips.

The worry that was deeply etched on Cole's face shook Dallie to her core as he gazed down at her bloody elbow then back to her face. He sighed heavily as his eyes flew up to her father's.

"I'm so sorry, sir," Cole began.

"Sorry? You prevented her from needing a trip to the hospital," her dad retorted, matter-of-factly.

"But I'm the reason for *that*." Cole motioned to the gash that was suddenly starting to sting like fire.

"Jeez, Cole. I guess I'm just gonna have to fire you then." Dallie couldn't help but laugh at her dad's sarcasm. "Well, could you at least go bandage up our wounded warrior here first before I go and get baby Jackson to escort you off the property. I need to go check on Wyatt and make sure we don't have a heart attack victim on our hands."

With that, her dad patted her arm and moved in the direction of the corral. Dallie just snickered under her breath as Cole robotically and gently took her injured arm in his hand and escorted her to her father's office.

"Yeah, yeah, he's really funny when he's not intimidating the hell out of me," Cole remarked glumly as he sat Dallie down in her dad's high-backed chair then scrounged up the first aid kit from the top of the bookshelf.

She gave him a knowing grin and just patiently waited for him to patch her up.

"Why are you smiling?" he asked as he took some hydrogen peroxide and held a cotton ball over the open bottle he inverted. "He'd fire me in an *instant* if he knew all the parts of you I've had my hands on lately." Dallie scowled, as much from his words as from the sting of the liquid to her scraped elbow. When she didn't respond, he continued, "He'd hide you away in a tower somewhere if he knew what you'd asked me to do the other night."

Dallie glared at him. "Yeah, well, he'll get over it! I'm a grown woman now and I can do as I please. I don't need his permission. Besides, I'm not doing anything *he* wasn't doing at my age."

She wasn't exactly sure *what* her dad had been doing at her age, but she was pretty sure it wasn't far from the same. Cole just frowned, not pleased with her answer. When he'd gotten the blood cleaned off and the hydrogen peroxide had stopped bubbling, he took some antibiotic ointment and smeared it on with a Q-tip.

"Am I supposed to apologize for what I said? Because I'm *not* sorry, Cole. I meant every word! I really thought you'd be happy about it."

He sighed heavily as he ripped open a packet of gauze. "Dallie, I care about you."

"And I care about *you*."

"Do you?" He just stared her down, holding the gauze in his hand.

"Yes! Why would you think anything different?" He looked down and gulped, returning to his task. She stopped him then. "Wait! That's it! That's why you've been so distant with me lately. I wounded your pride, didn't I?" He said nothing as he placed the gauze on her elbow. "Ow." She recoiled as the gauze pad, although not made of rough material, felt like sandpaper against her raw skin.

"I'm sorry," he murmured and gently replaced the gauze, looking into her eyes. She saw swirling green torrents of emotion there and felt bad about being snippy and selfish.

She sighed. "No, *I'm* sorry. I didn't mean for it to sound so..."

"Impersonal."

Had it sounded *impersonal* when she'd said it? She hadn't remembered that. She'd just thought he'd be jumping for joy at the fact that she told him that it was to be him that won the gift of her "treasured" virginity. That hadn't seemed impersonal to her.

"You listed off all these things, but you didn't say..." He paused, searching for the right words.

"I said you were gentle and sweet and patient," she offered.

"But you never said anything about..."

Dallie thought for a minute, then blurted out, "Love?" At the words, his eyebrows came up. Dallie balked, "Cole, aren't you the very one who told me that you didn't love *any* of the girls you'd slept with? When did love become a part of this?"

"And I also told you that you *should* love the person you give yourself to. I'm surprised you wouldn't want that! I warned you not to be like me," he grumbled and grabbed at the medical tape. "You should not only love the man who claims you, he should love you back." Dallie just rolled her eyes. "This isn't just some *job* that a guy signs up for, you know?"

"Job? What are you talking about?"

"I'm not gonna be just another mark on someone's belt, Dallas."

Dallie gulped and frowned at his words. She felt the tightness of the tape go across the skin of her elbow as Cole secured the gauze and stepped back, crossing his arms over his chest.

Is that how she'd made him feel? She tried to think back, but couldn't for the life of her pinpoint what she'd said that had offended him so. She just stared at him, trying to understand.

"You said I was perfect for the job."

"No..." *Had she said that?*

"Ok, well you might as well have. You didn't exactly say I was perfect for *you*! I'm not a horse, Dallie."

"Of course you're not!"

"I have feelings too and maybe I don't wanna just have sex with you so that I can *prime* you for college life."

"That's not why I wanted it to be you."

"Ok, I'm waiting. Why did you want to lose your virginity to *me*?"

The phone on the desk rang loudly, startling them both, and they jumped. Dallie looked at the caller ID; it was the house calling. She picked it up.

Her mom's voice greeted her, jovially. "Hey babe, you need to come up to the house. I got a big surprise for you."

Dallie tried to answer happily with, "Ok, I'll be right up." She hung up and had to rush to catch Cole before he walked out of the office. She shoved at his chest with her palms, stopping him from going forward. He just huffed, his jaw set in a hard line.

She looked his handsome face over; his brown beard and hair, his green eyes, his plump lips, his muscular build. She couldn't stop herself from smiling at how attractive he was to her.

"Cole, look... I'm sorry. I never meant for my words to upset you. I apparently screwed this up really badly and I offended you. I would never do or say anything to make you feel like you don't mean more to me than just a roll in the hay. I'm sorry if it came off that way. I really like you and I enjoy being with you. I want you to know that." She stared up at him, willing him to believe her, to know that she would never use him as the girl had done in his past.

The corner of his mouth ticked in a half frown, he looked down then back up to her.

"Maybe I just want to be loved this next time."

"And maybe you will be." She launched herself into him, her arms going around his neck as she planted her lips on his. He moaned as he absorbed her kiss and opened his mouth to her tongue as it delved in. His arms went around her waist and he pulled her tighter against him with a desperation that startled her. He returned her kiss with equal fervor as his hands moved up her back and he gripped her shirt in his fists. His tongue stroked hers and he angled his face to deepen their kiss even further. Dallie melted against him as the joining of their mouths became hot and steamy. Her hands moved into his hair. They were breathless all too soon, and Dallie heard a throat clear just before Cole pulled back. She felt his frame stiffen and turned to see her dad standing there, arms crossed with a cocked eyebrow, along with a frowning Todd.

~

*D*allie felt her heart literally leap into her throat as her dad's eyes narrowed, and he glowered at her. She gulped, looked back at Cole and immediately pulled herself away from him, feeling her cheeks flame in embarrassment.

"Todd," her dad began, peeling his eyes from Dallie's just long enough to glance at Todd, "give us a minute, would you?"

Todd scowled at both Dallie and Cole as if they'd been caught eating the forbidden fruit and turned on his heel in the opposite direction.

Her dad cleared his throat and motioned with his eyes for them to head back into his office.

Dallie felt the blood rush to her ears and her spirit weaken as she turned around and headed towards the desk. She dared not look at Cole as she sat herself in one of the chairs adjacent to her father's. She heard the door close behind her, heard the scuff of his boots as he came around, and it took her a minute to get the guts to look back into those accusing green eyes of Jack Kinsen's. He'd flipped out on her just for holding Cole's hand. She could only imagine the tirade that was about to ensue. She took a deep breath and faced the firing squad.

Her dad sat there, leaned back in his high-backed dark leather chair—his tan Stetson atop his head, eyes shaded, mouth firm, jaw set, elbows on the chair arms, his fingers intertwined. He was ready to chew her up one side and spit her out the other as he sighed and leaned forward. Dallie held her breath and tried to still her jangled nerves.

"I'm just gonna ask that you guys keep the PDAs to a minimum, if you would," he said easily.

"Wait...huh?" Dallie asked, incredulously.

"Yeah. I just don't want your sister or brother seeing you like that. And especially not the guys. I don't want them getting the wrong impression about you."

"So, let me get this straight..." Dallie looked intensely at her father, trying to see if he was actually being serious. "You're not *mad*?"

"Should I be?"

"Umm..." Dallie looked over to Cole, who had a deer-caught-in-the-headlights look as he stared ahead. He would be no help in this matter. "Is that a *trick* question?"

"Just—you know, next time shut the door or head off to one of those clandestine make-out spots you kids go to or whatever. Just keep it discreet," he added. "And don't even try and say that your mom and I aren't. Dammit, we've been married almost fourteen years, we're allowed to do that kinda stuff!"

Dallie only stared at her dad in shock. Was he for real? "Oh

—kaayy…"

"Ok, good. Thank you."

"So, you're really *not* mad?"

"No," her dad gave a weak smile, his voice softening even more than it already was. "I'm not mad. But you do know that I have a reputation to keep around here, especially since Todd saw you two. So, here's what I want you to do, I want you to barge out of here. Be a bit dramatic, slam the door pretty hard and yell something clever."

Dallie gaped at her father as if he had truly lost his mind.

"Alright," he insisted. "Go. Cole and I will be up to the house in a few minutes." When Dallie just sat there staring, he added, "No… it's not a joke. C'mon, Dallas. Sell it!" He gave her a big grin then, and Dallie popped up and just shook her head in disbelief at him, wondering why on earth he wasn't screaming his lungs out at her. When his brows went up, she huffed and yelled as loud as she could.

"Fine!" She stomped toward the door and threw it open as she blew. She turned and saw her dad wink and give her a thumbs up as she cried, "You know *what*? You are RUINING my life!"

~

"**S**omebody get that girl an Emmy!" Jack chuckled as Dallie slammed his office door closed and he looked at Cole.

Cole couldn't return his enthusiasm. He was simply waiting for Jack to shoot out from the desk and beat him to a bloody pulp. When the man just tucked his arms behind his head, Cole gulped. So, it was going to be a slow death then.

"Damn, Cole. You look as if you've seen a ghost." When Cole didn't respond, he continued. "Ah, hell, I can't really be mad about two youngsters enjoying a passionate kiss, now can I?"

Maybe Dallie was onto something. This *had* to be a trick… *Right?*

"I'm just glad your hands stayed above Dallie's waist, that's all. Now, if I'd have caught you copping a feel of my little girl… then I would have hurt you." Cole wouldn't dare even *think* of all the feeling

261

he'd been doing of Jack's "little girl". He gulped visibly and looked down to the safe, the same one that held the gun Jack had threatened him with not long ago. This brought a boom of laughter from Jack's throat. "No, Cole. I'm not gonna shoot you. At least not today, that is." As if that did anything to ease Cole's mind. He just dared a glance back at the older man. "Ah, don't ask. I don't even know *myself* why I'm taking this as easily as I am. Maybe I'm just in a good mood today. I reckon y'all are two consenting adults. So long as my daughter is ok with your advances," Jack added for good measure.

That's when Cole's voice finally took hold. "Of course, sir."

"I thought I'd told you *not* to call me that," Jack grumbled, but there was no conviction behind it. "Well, I guess we can head on up to the house too then. Make sure you still have that same look on your face and keep your head down. Don't talk until we get back to the house. Got it?"

Cole just nodded, and they both stood in unison. Jack opened the door and motioned for Cole to go on out, setting his face in a stern scowl.

"And I don't want to see that shit anymore! Is that clear, Cole?"

"Absolutely, sir!" Cole responded, lowering his head.

With that, they passed a still frowning Todd as they exited the front of the barn and headed in the direction of the house. Jack waved at Wyatt, told him he'd be back down later on, and they walked in silence to the back porch. Cole did as instructed, being sure to keep his head down and maintain the sullen look on his face.

When they entered the French doors, chatter filled the air, and Cole smiled as he heard Dallie laughing. Jack patted his back and escorted him into the living room, saying, "Nice job, kid." Then Cole's eyes fell on the gorgeous blonde that sat on the leather couch.

He gasped as he recognized the face he'd seen in at least a dozen movies.

Holy shit! He was looking at the incredibly beautiful—and famous—Vivian Alexander!

CHAPTER 12

*N*atalie laughed again as she looked over at Vivian, who bounced baby Jackson on her lap. She was decked out in a beautiful eggplant-colored silk blouse, grey trousers, and a pair of open-toed zip up booties with big tortoiseshell sunglasses mounted in her mass of wavy blonde hair. Even though they'd developed a bond that had persisted over the years and seen each other as recently as eight months ago, Natalie suddenly remembered exactly how Vivian had looked that day at Starlight Valley so long ago. She remembered just how envious she'd been of the younger woman's youthful bliss. It had literally bounced off of her, as it still did now. Vivian was just as beautiful as ever with her high cheekbones, perfect lips and chocolate brown eyes; her flawless, lightly tan complexion hadn't changed one bit. Of course, she was a little older and wiser now, but she still exuded that amazing determination she'd had back then.

Vivian looked up as she saw Jack and Cole walk into the room, and Nat took the baby from her.

"Jack!" Vivian jumped off of the couch to embrace Jack as he approached her. "I swear you just get better looking as you age, cowboy." She pulled back and smiled up at him.

"Likewise, Viv. Does time simply stop in Hollywood?" He held her shoulders and looked her over as he smiled that gorgeous smile that stopped most all women in their tracks. Natalie remembered just how jealous she'd been when he'd been training Vivian that October thirteen years ago. How silly that had been of her! Even now, she saw, as her husband held one of the most beautiful women Nat had ever seen, he'd never looked at any other woman the way he looked at Natalie. Pride swelled in her heart at that realization.

"Ha," Vivian balked and swatted at him as his arms fell. "I wish!" She then looked over at Cole, whose startled face took her in as if he'd just witnessed an alien landing. "And who's this?"

"This is Cole." Dallie jumped up and placed her arm around Vivian's waist as she introduced the two of them. "Cole, this is—"

"Vivian Alexander," Cole breathed out. He just gazed at her as if he wasn't believing what his eyes were seeing. "You *know* Vivian Alexander?" He looked to Dallie.

Dallie laughed big and squeezed Vivian with affection. Viv returned her embrace and kissed Dallie on the forehead. They were the same height now, both right at five foot seven inches tall.

"We're practically family, honestly. The Kinsens and I have been close for many years now. It's nice to meet you, Cole." Vivian extended her hand, and Cole gingerly took it, gulping.

"Hell, if you think that's somethin', wait 'til you see who *else* we invited for dinner tonight!" Jack boomed as he came to sit down next to his wife. He leaned in and kissed her, and Nat smiled as he grabbed his baby boy and held him high, burying his face in the toddler's belly and imitated biting him. Jackson squealed, and Vivian turned, coming back to the couch.

"Who?" Cole asked timidly as he and Dallie took the adjacent couch.

"Well, if you're a fan of football then you might just fall out on us."

Nat didn't miss the look of repulsion that suddenly passed on Vivian's face as she looked back to Natalie then covered it with a smile. "Nat, he's so gorgeous!" Vivian exclaimed as she looked at baby Jackson, who Jack had now moved into the crook of his arm as he played with the new light-up train Vivian had brought him. "I mean all of your children are, of course," she added, "But he looks so much like Dallie when she was little. It makes me want to cry." Vivian pouted over at her.

"I know, he does!"

"He's precious…" She grabbed the baby's little hand and held it as he beamed up at her. "I still hate that I missed Savannah's birth." Vivian frowned and looked over at Savannah, who came to sit on her lap then.

"It's ok, Aunt Viv. You had to work," Savannah reckoned.

"Well, work isn't always what's important, sweet girl," Vivian said. "Family is." Vivian looked around, and Nat didn't miss the tight smile she put on for them. Something was going on with her. Perhaps this was what had prompted this spontaneous visit of hers. Nat would get to the bottom of it later when they were having their customary night caps out on the porch after the kids were asleep.

"I missed you, Aunt Viv." Vanna turned in her arms and hugged her, and Vivian squeezed her with all her might, her head falling on Vanna's little shoulder.

"Oh, baby girl. I missed *you*."

"Hey," Vanna pulled back and smiled exuberantly at Vivian, "wanna hear my latest concerto?"

"Do I? Absolutely!" Vivian answered, wiping at her eyes. She stood and let Savannah lead her into the piano room.

Nat smiled at her husband, who gazed at her, those gorgeous green eyes burning into hers, the look making her insides tingle with such promised intent. Jackson grabbed for her and kissed her cheek.

"Aw, such a sweet boy," Jack said. "Does he love his Mommy?"

Jackson turned and nodded at his proud papa. "Wuv Mama." He squeezed her neck again, and Nat's heart simply melted. The love she had for her family could never be compared to anything else in the world. She'd truly been blessed beyond measure, and she knew it.

"What about Da-da?" Jack asked, and Jackson squeezed Nat even tighter. "Hey, c'mon now, son." Jack's voice dropped lower and he leaned in as he whispered, "You wouldn't even *be* here if it wasn't for me. I worked *hard* on that." His brows went up as he looked into Nat's face and her breath took. She was eager to again be naked beneath that big, sculpted body of his. But for now, she would have to wait.

"Get him, Jax." Natalie grinned as the baby launched himself at his father, "tackling" him, their latest rowdy game as father and son. Jack made a big deal out of being "defeated" and tickled Jackson's little tummy, getting a slew of baby cackles out of their son.

Natalie laughed and looked over to see her eldest daughter holding Cole's hand. She smiled to herself and heard the beautiful rapid tinkling of the piano in the background.

"Oh, I've known Vivian since I was four. That spooked horse I told you about with the rider on it? Yeah, that was Vivian." Nat heard Dallie softly telling Cole.

"That's *so* cool!" he answered.

"Yeah, that's when Mom and Dad were training her for a movie at my grandfather's ranch. I got to hang out with her a lot then and we've all been close ever since."

"Man, that's super neat to be B.F.F.s with a star."

"She's not the only 'star' Mom and Dad are B.F.F.s with."

"You're not gonna tell me who it is, are you?"

"Nope," Dallie said and giggled. "You'll just have to be surprised."

Natalie smiled again, thinking how "cool" it really was that she knew and had befriended two wonderful celebrities who'd become a big part of their lives. She'd known Bobby "Buck" Jenkins since she was in grade school, long before he'd become a legendary defensive end in the NFL. He'd been one of her best friends before she'd met Jack. They'd still remained friends even after Nat and Jack had gotten married, but they weren't as close as they'd once been back when Nat had been married to Troy, but then again, Troy'd been in the NFL himself and there had been not only games, but all those galas, events, and charity benefits they'd attended too.

Life had simply carried on, as it tended to do, after Nat and Jack had gotten married; she and Jack had a ranch to run and children to raise, and Buck had been busy with football and the organization he'd started since retiring from the NFL just a year ago. But they'd definitely been seeing more of Buck lately since he'd come home to Abundance just months ago, what with his mom being diagnosed with terminal cancer and all.

Vivian and Savannah returned to the living room then talking about concerts and how Vivian wanted to take her to see the Phil-harmonic orchestra. Nat smiled as Savannah came to sit next to her. She stroked her daughter's beautiful maple-colored hair, looking over at Magnus who lay napping near the hearth, oblivious to the humans.

Jack spoke up then, "Hey, Dallie. Would you and Cole mind runnin' to the store for your mom?"

"Of course not, Dad." Dallie smiled and shot up, pulling her hand from Cole's. Natalie knew that Dallie was more than likely just looking for any excuse to be alone with the young man she was starting to really crush on. Nat looked in surprise over at her husband then, amazed that he seemed to be encouraging them.

"My list is on the counter. I appreciate it," Nat added as Dallie ran off to do as she was asked.

Once they were gone and Savannah went upstairs to work on her newest piece, the adults moved into the kitchen, and Jack placed their son in his play fence along with his most recent toy. He moved over to the fridge and pulled out two beers, handing one to Vivian, who smiled knowingly over at Nat and Jack as she sat on one of the stools at the island.

"Dallie's really liking that young ranch hand of yours, Jack."

"Oh, lord! Tell me about it." Her husband groaned as he moved over to the wine rack to pour Natalie's favorite red; he knew she wasn't a fan of beer. "You'll never guess what I saw them doing in my office earlier." He turned to look at Natalie then and handed her the half-filled wine glass.

"No?" Nat exclaimed, her hand stilling as she took the glass from him.

"Yup." He sighed heavily. "They were engaged in a pretty intense kiss."

Natalie's eyes widened and she gaped at him, feeling the sudden need to chug the full glass of wine and ask for another. "And Cole is still *alive* to tell about this?" Her hand went to his bulky bicep, gripping it. "And you just sent them off together...*alone*? My love, are you feeling alright?"

"I was just about to ask the exact same thing," Vivian added and took a swig of her beer.

"I know, I know," her husband mumbled. "Maybe I'm getting softer in my old age." Jack shrugged. "I don't know, I just couldn't work up a good mad about it. Dallie's eighteen now, after all. She's a responsible girl. I trust her." His eyes gazed into his wife's, searching.

Natalie and Vivian just continued to stare at him as if he were out of his mind.

"Oh, don't worry! I threatened to kill him several weeks ago if he hurt my baby girl. It's all good." He took a swig of his beer.

Natalie snorted at him and Vivian laughed and said, "I'm so glad you handled that rationally, Jack."

"No problem." He raised his beer and winked at Viv.

"My dad wasn't quite as protective of me as you are of her. I would have never gotten out of the house if that was the case."

"Well, Dallie's just so innocent, Viv. She's super sensitive...and naïve," Nat confessed and shook her head then turned and pulled some fresh vegetables out of the fridge.

"Oh, I know. I commend Jack for being as good as he's been with her. I thought she would never get over that last guy." Vivian frowned.

"Nick! God, I could have beat him to a bloody pulp," Jack growled.

"Now, guys. Kids do that kinda stuff. It's just a part of growing up. We all got our hearts broken at a young age," Nat contended.

"I did for sure," Vivian added and walked around to help Natalie with her task.

"It doesn't matter. When our kids are hurting, we're hurting," Jack said, pulling spices down from the cabinet.

"This is true," Natalie added.

They all dispersed responsibilities as they started getting dinner ready. Jack took to marinating the steaks, Natalie to slicing vegetables for salad, and Vivian to wrapping potatoes.

"He seems like a nice kid," Vivian said absent-mindedly as she placed the potatoes on a baking sheet.

"He's quiet," Nat insisted, cutting up some cucumbers.

"He's got a rough past from what we can gather. Dallie told us that he grew up in foster care," Jack murmured, salting the thick filets.

"Oh, that's sad. Well, I know y'all have welcomed him with open arms. He seems comfortable here."

"We think so," Nat said, smiling.

"Nate and Jordan are coming too, right?" Vivian asked. Nat smiled and nodded. "Good. How are they doing?"

"They're good. Nate and Cole just redid Dallie's truck," Jack added.

"I saw. It looks amazing!" Vivian replied.

"He worked his ass off for weeks. Couldn't wait to surprise her with it." Her handsome husband smiled and looked over at Natalie, who melted again at his gaze.

"You *are* softening to this kid, husband," Nat murmured, glad he was "loosening the reins" on Dallie a bit.

Jack just laughed and shook his head. "I guess so. Everyone deserves the benefit of a doubt, I reckon."

"Agreed," Viv added and popped the potatoes into the oven.

"So, how've you been Viv, really?" It was Jack that asked.

"Good," Vivian responded, tightly. Her dismissal gave Natalie even more suspicion that something was off with her friend. She looked up at her husband then and winked. She would get more out of Vivian later on when they were alone to talk. For now, she didn't want to ruin the mood as she heard Dallie and Cole returning. Jack placed the steaks back in the fridge to marinate then kissed Natalie soundly before coming over to Vivian, patting her arm and kissing her cheek.

"We're glad you're here, Viv. It's about time you came back to see us." With that, he went out the back doors to go finish up at the barn for the night, and Natalie didn't miss Vivian's trembling lip as she watched him go.

Vivian took another swig of her beer and her demeanor changed again as she smiled up at Dallie, who came into the kitchen then with a few bags in her arms. Natalie took them from her and sat them down, pulling various items from them. Cole joined them with more bags of his own. Natalie thanked them, and she and Dallie began putting the groceries away as Cole sat at the island adjacent from where Vivian stood, finishing up the salad.

"Dallie, are you super excited about college, or what?" Vivian asked, eagerly.

"Yeah," Dallie murmured without enthusiasm.

"Oh, c'mon. Why do I hear doubt in your voice?" Vivian motioned to Cole. "Don't tell me *this* guy has you hesitant to go." Vivian winked at Cole, who paled.

"Give me some credit, Aunt Viv," Dallie scolded and smiled over at Cole. "No offense, Cole."

Cole shook his head. "None taken."

"Dallie," Nat muttered, "why don't you and Cole go wash up for supper? I'll re-doctor your scrape when you come back down."

Dallie agreed and she and Cole went their separate ways to shower and change.

Finally, Natalie had Vivian to herself. Vivian tried hard to evade her questions as Natalie eased into de-icing Vivian's hard exterior.

"Viv, something's off. What is it?"

"Oh, nothing, Nat. I'm just super tired lately, that's all. I've been run ragged with these last three movies. The jet lag is killing me. I'm glad I have a few days with you and these beautiful kids of yours." With that, she stepped over to Jackson's baby fence and sat down next to him, busying herself with playing with the toddler, who cooed and laughed at the beautiful actress. Nat couldn't help but smile at her and the baby interacting. It truly warmed her heart that she did indeed have three wonderful children that God had blessed her with.

Perhaps that was it. Maybe Vivian, who had recently hit the ripe age of thirty-five years old, was regretting not having any children… or maybe it was something more.

Jack came back in at that time and smiled at her, immediately lifting her spirits. He headed upstairs to shower, and Nat asked Vivian if she would be alright with Jackson for a few minutes. Vivian gave her a withered, "Of course," and Nat excused herself, laughing as Vivian teased her with, "Don't be too loud; this house echoes."

Jack was already shirtless when she joined him in the bathroom, his hand stilling on his jeans when he looked up at her and grinned. Her heart did a little flip flop as her eyes roved over his hard-muscled chest and well-chiseled torso, his body showing little signs of his age of forty-three years.

"D'you come to join me, wifey?" he asked, his brow cocking as he walked toward her. She gulped as his eyes moved over her, and his hands went to her waist. His voice deepened as he said, "Missed me already, huh?"

She giggled as his mouth came to her neck, making her breakout in goosebumps. "Our daughters are next door, and Vivian is downstairs with our baby," she rasped out as her eyes closed in passion at the feel of his tongue on her pulse point.

"That never stopped you before," he insisted as his hands moved to her bottom and roughly squeezed.

Nat moaned. "I came to tell you that I'm proud of you." She smiled up into his gorgeous face as he pulled back slightly to look at her.

"Yeah, yeah, I'm a sap. What can I say?"

"No, you're a good man, Jackson Edward Kinsen," Natalie murmured. His lips came down on hers then. She savored the taste of him, and the love she felt emanating from her husband in those moments. He tried to deepen the kiss, but she pulled back, taking his face in her hands, wanting him to know how much love she felt for him. "I'm a very lucky woman to have you for my husband, and my daughter is a lucky girl to be able to call you her father."

"And that just couldn't *wait* until I came back downstairs, huh?" He winked, his hands moving back to her waist, and gave her that crooked grin that could melt her panties right off, staring at the lips he'd just kissed. She licked them, her body responding in such a delicious way to the sheer sexuality he exuded—if only they didn't have company downstairs. "Or was it simply my naked body that you just couldn't resist?" His thumb grazed her bottom lip, and she visibly shivered.

"Well, I do *love* seeing your sexy naked body." Her eyes fell over his big shoulders, and she traced the indention of his six-pack with her fingertip as she bit her bottom lip. He smiled knowingly and growled as he pulled her back into him, kissing her passionately again. His big hands and hungry lips were a bit harder to resist this time, and after he kissed her breathlessly, she moaned as his lips descended to nibble at her collarbone. "Jack, I *have* to go back downstairs," she insisted even as she reveled in their passion.

"Alright," he acquiesced and stepped back a little. "But at least let me entice you some, so I can be assured you'll join me in our bed later tonight." She laughed as his hands went back to his jeans. As if she needed much enticing with a man who was as scrumptious as Jack Kinsen was.

She watched, her entire body completely aroused, as he unzipped his fly and lowered his jeans and boxers down over his hips. She gulped as her eyes fell down over his striking, erect sex—the shape and length never failing to impress or excite her—and powerful thighs as he shucked his jeans then turned to cut the water on. She took in the hard bands of muscle on his back and his magnificent rear end before he turned back to her and raised his eyebrows in question.

"Last chance, Mrs. Kinsen. Are you gonna join me or not?" He cupped himself suggestively and Nat sighed, longingly. As tempting as it would be to step into that shower with her achingly gorgeous husband and let him take her breath away, Nat begrudgingly shook her head. "Your loss," he stated, ruefully.

"I know," Nat pouted, "I'll make it up to you, my love. I swear." She blew him a kiss as she moved to the doorframe.

"You're damn right, you will. I'm gonna make you regret every minute you didn't spend in here with me." He winked and stepped into the shower. Nat smiled, thinking of the many ways her husband was going to "punish" her later for not joining him in the shower. She couldn't wait!

She was still smiling when she got back to the kitchen to join Vivian, who had grabbed another beer from the fridge. She turned to look at Nat, phone in hand, as she scoffed.

"God, you two make me sick," she scowled and glanced back at her phone. Nat knew she wasn't serious, but again, was all too aware that something was greatly upsetting Vivian. She'd known her for far too long. Vivian shoved her phone into her back pocket and smiled tightly back at Natalie. "Actually, I want to talk to you." Viv stepped forward to approach Nat just as the doorbell rang. Natalie cursed silently as she looked up at Vivian, regretfully.

"We'll talk later, babe," Nat insisted and patted Vivian's arm as she headed toward the door. She hadn't missed the look of apprehension that had suddenly overtaken her younger friend as she turned away from her.

"Nate, Jordan, come on in," Natalie beckoned to her brother and sister-in-law as she greeted them.

"Thanks for inviting us, Nat," Jordan kissed Natalie's cheek as she came in.

"Of course," Nat retorted and returned her brother's hug.

"Vivian, baby girl, look at you. Gorgeous as ever!" Jordan cooed as she embraced Vivian.

"Thanks, Jor." Vivian laughed.

"It's true. I swear you haven't aged a day," Nate agreed and was next in line to embrace her.

The rest of the crew joined them not much later, and Vivian seemed to relax some as she continued to sip on her beer. She began telling Dallie a funny story about a hunky actor as Jordan played with Jackson and gave him some veggie slices and Nat popped some rolls into the oven. The boys were outside grilling the meat and Savannah painted in the dining room. The room was bombarded with voices as the guys came in from outside then the doorbell rang. Vivian visibly gulped mid-story, and Natalie saw her confidence shake as Jack led Buck into the loud kitchen.

Why would Vivian be anxious to see Buck, of all people?

Buck rounded the corner, and Nat was surprised to see how weary he looked. She'd noted months ago that Buck had lost some bulk within the last year, at least a good thirty pounds of muscle from when he was in his prime. Even though Buck had a couple inches in height on Jack, they had similar athletic builds. In fact, Jack's muscled arms were as well-defined as Buck's, despite that Buck'd had a strict diet and workout regimen just barely a year prior... or maybe she was just biased. Either way, she knew, these past few months had taken a lot out of her friend.

Buck beamed at Natalie as she approached and grabbed his hands. His grin wavered as she asked how he was doing. He hugged her tightly to him and shook his head against her shoulder. She frowned as she pulled back and looked deep into his handsome but pale face.

"Buck?" Nat asked, concerned, cupping his jaw.

"She's home now, but she's so damn weak."

She pulled his big shoulder and led him into the door of her office. "You look like shit, Buck."

"I needed to get away, Natalie. I needed this."

Natalie just pulled him back to her and held him for a moment, feeling him breathe deeply against her and shake as he tried to regain his composure. When Jordan approached, Nat sighed and grimaced. Jordan patted at his back and took her turn consoling their friend. When he finally pulled away, he had tears in his baby blue eyes.

"Buck, honey, are you sure you're alright?" Jordan asked.

"I'm really glad to have friends like y'all," Buck replied. "It's been rough."

They looked to him then back to each other, solemn expressions on their faces. Buck's mother, Laurel, had recently been diagnosed with terminal ovarian cancer and had to be put into a medically-induced coma last month when she'd contracted sepsis.

When they walked back into the kitchen, Buck froze beside Natalie, and she almost gasped from the sudden pull of her arm around him.

He was staring at Vivian, whose cheeks flushed at his gaze.

"Viv?" He gaped at her as if she were a figment of his imagination. His shock soon turned into a big smile as he recovered... but he wasn't the only one who needed to regain their composure, for in that instant, Vivian's eyes turned cold all of a sudden and her chin inched higher as she smiled tightly at him.

"Buck," she murmured, indifferently.

"Wait, y'all *know* each other?" Jordan asked, grabbing the baby back from Nathan.

As much as Vivian had been to visit them, and Buck too, over the years, they had never been in this house together before nor formally introduced...that Nat knew of.

It was Savannah that broke the awkwardness between them as

she rushed at Buck.

"Uncle Buck!" Vanna squealed, and Buck's shock turned into pleasure as he grabbed Nat's middle child and squeezed her for a hug, kissing her cheek and going on and on about how stunning she was. Natalie might be biased since Savannah was her daughter and all, but she *was* a looker with her unique hair color and one of a kind green eyes.

Natalie's eyes fell on Cole, who looked at Buck with wide eyes. Dallie giggled as she too saw his expression as she moved in, next in line.

"And Dallas Kinsen, you're as gorgeous as your Momma, girl! I bet your daddy don't enjoy keeping those boys off a' you." Buck cajoled, and Dallie blushed.

"No, he certainly does *not*." Jack laughed and pulled Natalie against him, quickly kissing her lips. She just smiled back into her husband's perfect face.

"Uncle Buck, I want you to meet Cole." Dallie pulled Buck over to a stunned Cole, who stiffly took Buck's outstretched hand.

"You're…you're," Cole began.

"Buck Jenkins, pleasure to meet you," Buck drawled and tipped his cowboy hat at Cole.

"Holy crap! I can't believe it. You're one of the best defensive ends to play football."

"Ah, don't be goin' and givin' him an even bigger head than he's already got, kid," Nate joked and patted Buck on the back, getting a laugh out of all of them. All except Cole, who just continued to gape at Buck, and Vivian, who suddenly looked incredibly uncomfortable.

A certainty crept over Natalie then and she gasped audibly as she realized what it was that was causing this behavior of Vivian's.

Everyone turned to look at her as she cupped her hand over her face and blushed.

"Baby, are you alright?" Jack asked as he looked down into her eyes.

She started, "Oh, of course. I just remembered the potatoes."

Natalie offered and moved toward the oven.

"Where's my little buddy?" Buck called to Jackson as Natalie pulled the potatoes out and sat them on top of the stove. Jackson cackled and pumped his legs as Buck taught her toddler the art of a fist pump.

The guys made their way out to the back porch then to check the steaks, Buck lingering a little too long to gaze at Vivian as he was the last to amble out. Vivian appeared oblivious to him as she continued her story to Dallie, as if nothing had occurred, but Natalie knew better. Jordan continued to play with Jackson, who had Jordan's number as he lay his head on her ample chest.

"This little stinker is gonna like boobs, that's all I can say," Nat stated.

"What male in *this* family do you know that doesn't?" Jordan laughed. Natalie just shrugged and began making dressing to go with their salad.

She smiled at Vivian, who walked over to them.

"He's the sweetest baby boy, Nat." Vivian ran her fingers through Jackson's curly blonde locks.

"Thank you. He's already like his daddy in a lot of ways."

"Da-da," Jackson called loudly as he reveled in the attention he was getting from the ladies. Jordan and Vivian followed with an, "Aww."

"I'm just glad I could finally give Jack his baby boy. Not that he didn't adore having girls, but I know he was utterly thrilled when we found out Jackson was gonna be a boy..." Nat trailed off as tears came to her eyes, thinking back to the baby they'd lost. He would have been fourteen now.

"So, how do you know Buck, Viv?" Jordan asked, randomly, trying to ease the sadness of the moment.

"You know," Vivian began, her cheeks flushing, "celebrities *all* know each other. What with the various networks and all."

Jordan followed with an, "Uh, huh," that didn't sound convinced.

Dallie joined Nat then and hugged her, asking if there was

anything she could do to help.

"No, thank you, sweetie. I think we're all set."

"Dallie, tell us about this good-looking Jack Kinsen look-a-like you're dating," Vivian stated to get the attention—and Jordan's wondering eyes—off of her.

Dallie blushed then huffed, throwing her hands up. "Oh my goodness. Everyone says that, Aunt Viv."

"What?" Vivian laughed. "It's true. I swear it! It's kind of uncanny really."

"So, is it gross that I think he's adorable?"

"Girl, you'd be a fool *not* to think so," Jordan surmised.

It wasn't long before the kitchen was loud again as the guys came in with the great smell of charred steak fresh off the grill, and they were all sat at the table, saying grace and digging into a scrumptious meal. The conversation was scattered as the girls spoke with Vivian about her latest movies and perfume commercials, and the guys talked with Buck, which mostly consisted of Cole ticking off every great play Buck had ever made, causing Buck to blush and laugh at their star-struck employee. Natalie was grateful, for she knew he needed a good laugh right now.

The chatting was relaxed, and it was good to catch up with Vivian and Buck, who separately spoke of their days and their lives jovially, but once brought into discussion together, an icy chill filled the air between them. Natalie noticed that the arctic blast seemed to come from Vivian, who smarted off each time Buck said something even remotely "Buck-like".

Her husband tried to seem unaware of their turmoil as he asked, "So, how was that charity ball you attended for Helping Heroes?"

Vivian spoke up with a, "Typical," just as Buck said, "Quite eventful!"

All heads shot up then as the conversation halted.

Buck sneered and stared at Vivian, "It was most certainly anything but typical, Vivian."

"Ha! Apparently, it depends on who you ask." Vivian's brow shot up and her lips pursed. Buck's eyes shot daggers into hers then.

"What *exactly* about it was typical, I'd like to know?" Buck crossed his arms over his chest.

"Wait!" Dallie interrupted. "*Both* of you attended the ball?"

Vivian blushed to her toes and glanced back up to Dallie. "Yes, and it was downright drab if you ask me."

Buck scoffed, "Yeah, easy for *you* to say since you're constantly surrounded by the finer things in life! Talk about letting fame go to your head."

"That's not even what I meant, Buck Jenkins, so why don't you stop assuming that you *know* people you barely just met?" Vivian's voice rang out; the entire table stopped.

Jordan gave Natalie a knowing look and Nat cleared her throat then, trying to pull the tension away from Buck and Vivian.

"I think it's about time for my soon-to-be famous apple pie. Who wants coffee?"

Natalie began gathering plates as she watched Vivian tear her eyes from Buck and stand to assist her.

They met in the kitchen, but before Vivian could say anything, her phone rang, and she scowled and motioned to Nat that she had to take it. She exited through the French doors. Buck came over then and apologized.

"I'm sorry for my outburst, Nat. That was rude and uncalled for, and I truly made an ass out of myself. Please forgive me."

"Oh, Buck," Nat scolded. "We know *all* about drama around here. You know that better than anyone."

He laughed, but it did nothing to hide the embarrassment so clear in his eyes. "Well, either way, I didn't mean for that to happen. I'm just tense with all that's going on with Momma."

"Bucko, of course you are. You want some coffee?"

"No, no, I'm gonna head back to Momma's. Thank you so much for dinner. It was great seein' y'all." He kissed her cheek and pulled her to him for a hug.

"Well, you want a thermos for the road?" When he shook his

head, she smiled. "Alright well, don't be a stranger, Buck, and if you need anything don't hesitate to call."

"I won't. Thanks again."

With that, he went back into the dining room to bid everyone a farewell. Nat wasn't long in the kitchen before she was joined by Jordan, who wanted to gossip, only her curiosity was short lived as Vivian came back inside.

"Sorry about that. That was my manager, Jill. She just *had* to discuss a new contract deal with a clothing chain she's been begging for me to do. I swear..." Vivian stilled. "What?"

"Don't 'what' us? You know damn well *what*," Jordan piped in.

Vivian frowned, like she'd been scolded, and crossed her arms over her chest. Before she could get a word out, Dallie and Cole joined them in the kitchen, bringing in dirty plates.

"Aunt Vivian, I was telling Cole how awesome you are at charades. Think we could play a round or two with everyone?"

Natalie saw just what an amazing actress Vivian really was as her face lit up at Dallie, and she joyfully responded with, "Absolutely, I would love that."

Although Natalie knew she was honest in her reply, Vivian had something she desperately needed to get off her chest, and it wasn't long after pie, coffee, and several rounds of charades that Natalie finally got to find out.

She'd seen Nate and Jordan off, gotten Jackson to sleep in his toddler bed, and promised her eager husband she wouldn't be long then joined Vivian out on the back porch with two glasses of their favorite Argentinian Malbec.

"Oh, thank you. I really needed this," Vivian said as she took the wine from Natalie. Nat doubted that as Vivian had a drink in her hand practically since she'd gotten there.

"Alright, Viv, spill!"

"God, I *knew* you'd notice as soon as he got here."

"You slept with him, didn't you?"

"Is it *that* obvious?"

"Well," Nat proclaimed, "if it wasn't after your cold reunion, it was even more so at the insults you threw at him at dinner."

"Dammit, I'm sorry," Viv scowled and sipped at her wine.

"What the hell happened?"

"Well, we met at the Helping Heroes Ball—obviously. I knew who he was right away, despite his introduction, and I did my best not to be the least bit deterred by his good ol' boy charm, handsome swag and egotistical attitude, but by then I'd had several drinks," she indicated the wine, "and with his persistence, we danced and talked. We had a great time, really, and it was truly a beautiful evening. Yet, in spite of what I knew about his reputation with bimbos, I invited him back to my hotel room." Viv grimaced and covered her face with the hand she wasn't holding her wine with.

"You didn't?" Nat hissed.

"I did!" Viv confirmed and sulked. "But, oh my God, it was *fucking* amazing, Nat. Seriously, the best sex I've had, *ever*! We did it so many times... I know *you* can appreciate amazing sex."

"Of course I can," Natalie chortled. *Look at who I'm married to*, she wanted to brag, but knew she didn't need to.

"But then..." Viv sighed heavily. "I woke up and he was gone."

"Gone?"

"Yes. No note, no text, no phone call—no Buck. I was just another one of his one-night stands."

"Oh wow."

"I feel like *such* a fool, Nat. I was so completely mortified. Buck Jenkins made me do the walk of shame from my *own* hotel room.... and the swarming paparazzi the next morning was my thanks for the night of hot sex he gave me. Dammit! I should've known better."

"Oh, Viv. I'm so sorry." Nat reached out and squeezed Vivian's hand then.

"Yeah, not half as sorry as I'm gonna make *him*," she brooded.

It was another half hour of Vivian regretting and moping, and Natalie consoling her before Nat was finally able to join her husband upstairs.

He had the TV on, turned down low, propped up in bed, one bulky arm behind his head, the other on his belly. Natalie's gaze fell over his deliciously naked chest and torso bathed in blue light from the television as she closed their bedroom door. Magnus lay at the foot of the bed sleeping.

Natalie pulled her shirt over her head and smiled as Jack's gaze lingered at her breasts.

"You waited up for me?" she whispered.

"You bet I did." His eyes fell down her body as she pulled her jeans over her hips.

Her husband sighed as he licked his lips. Nat felt her pulse quicken as she stepped forward toward the bed, clad in only her bra and lacy thong panties. Jack's eyes darkened as she pulled the covers back and moved willingly into his open arms. He gave her that crooked grin she loved, and she shivered as his hands moved over her naked back.

"You just wanted to hear the gossip," Natalie teased as Jack's mouth moved to her neck and his big palms cupped her bottom, gripping her flesh and pulling her roughly against his naked pelvis.

He moaned and murmured, "Not as much as I wanted *you*."

He flipped them over then and moved atop her, his soft lips kissing hers. When he pulled back for a breath, Natalie frowned.

"Baby?" Jack asked, concerned, cupping her cheek. "What is it?" Natalie's eyes moved away from his handsome face and she pulled at her bottom lip, begrudgingly. "She slept with Buck, huh?" Jack asked after Natalie didn't respond immediately.

"He turned her into another one of his flings, Jack," Natalie stated, stroking his muscular arms.

"He's too old for that shit."

"Tell me about it. All I can figure is he's just trying hard not to lose his mind while his mom lays dying," Natalie scowled. "But Vivian is devastated."

Jack sighed and moved to her side, pulling her into his arms and stroking her back.

"Nat, I'm sorry, but she should have known better."

"She said that too, but it doesn't make his actions okay. She deserves better."

"Sweetheart, you try to take too much of the world onto your own shoulders."

"I know, I'm sorry... Where were we?" She moved her hands up around his neck, aligning her body with his.

"I'm sorry you're upset by this, darlin', but they'll figure it out, I'm sure. I remember a certain female who *hated* me in the beginning." He grinned again and moved his hand down to squeeze her breast through her bra.

"I never hated you," she murmured then moaned as his fingertips began to make ribbons of pleasure swirl through her center. "My anger was simply misplaced."

Jack belted out a big laugh. "Oh, is that what it was?"

"I only wanted you with such intensity that it frightened me."

"Was it my good looks or were you just dying to see beneath my jeans?"

She didn't have a chance to respond as his lips came back to hers and he pulled her back beneath him. It wasn't long before he had her naked and was loving her with the passion and power she couldn't get enough of. Just when she thought their hunger had been satiated, he flipped them over and settled her atop of him, where he proceeded to show her just what she'd missed earlier in the shower. Later, she fell beside him and lay spent in his arms.

She closed her eyes and tried to take solace in what her husband had said regarding Vivian and Buck, but she couldn't dismiss the uncertainty and distress Vivian had displayed. It had truly disturbed Natalie. She'd never quite seen Vivian's confidence shaken so.

She let the calming sound of Jack's breathing and steady heart-beat lull her to sleep in his arms, only to awaken to the sound of his voice calling to her not long after.

"Natalie, baby," his deep voice pleaded. "Shh, it's ok."

Natalie suddenly realized with shock that she'd been screaming.

She gulped and gripped her husband's strong biceps as she tried to calm her heart and lungs.

"Dallie!" she cried, desperately. "Oh God!"

The horrible nightmare came flooding back into her mind. Dallie had been in danger, grave danger, and she and Jack watched helplessly on as they were ill-equipped to assist her.

"My love, it's just a dream," Jack murmured as he kissed her wet cheek and pulled her tighter into his capable arms, stroking her hair.

The door opened then and the room was flooded in light.

"Mom?" Nat heard Dallie call as she buried her head into Jack's chest and closed her eyes against the rush of tears that came at the sound of her daughter's voice.

"She's ok, sweetheart. It's just a nightmare. Go on back to bed." Jack's big hands splayed across Natalie's bare back, covering her nakedness.

"Jeez, she was so loud. I thought you were killing her in here!" Dallie exclaimed.

Natalie sniffled and pulled her head up to Jack's shoulder, still facing away from her daughter. "Did I wake Jackson up?"

"No, I think I'm the only one. Aunt Viv is out cold." Dallie giggled.

"Dallie, baby, can you give us a minute?" Jack insisted, and Natalie heard the door close.

Jack pulled back and cupped her cheek, scowling. "Natalie, you were screaming at the top of your lungs." She just sighed and fell back into his chest, sobbing. "Oh, honey," he murmured again and continued to soothe her, kissing her forehead and stroking her hair and back until she finally caught her breath.

"Jack," she whimpered gravely, "it was just like that one nightmare before... God, it was *so* real. I was so scared."

"But darlin', Troy is dead now. You *never* have to worry about him ever again," Jack confirmed.

"Jack," she cried and fell into him again. "It wasn't Troy."

CHAPTER 13

Two nights later, Cole woke to the nightmare… again. He was sweating and out of breath as he sat up and tried to recall where he was. He'd been back in his shop, stumbling over the gun, seeing Adam's lifeless body atop a giant puddle of bright red blood. He felt his heart sink in his chest, heard the knocking of his pulse against his eardrums, felt the blood rush from his face. His mind reeled and he felt his stomach pitch. He was gonna be sick!

He ran to the bathroom and vomited, hard and violently. Once his stomach was empty, he flushed the excrement and sat beside the lemon-scented toilet and cried. It was so new and fresh seeing Adam dead again. He remembered the horror and the anger that had overcome him in those moments. He cried for Adam, he cried for himself, but mostly, he cried for Dallas. For the life he would never get to have with her because of the one stupid mistake he'd made two months ago that would define his life. He loved her with an ache that went bone deep, but she would never get to see or feel it…and it was all because he'd hung himself the day he'd blundered onto the carnage of his best friend's murder. Now he would pay severely for it!

Cole sobbed into his cupped hands and cursed his fate. Why was life so damn unfair? This amazing family that had taken him in, that he'd fallen in love with over the last sixty days, the family that had already suffered such great tragedy a decade and a half ago would suffer once again at his hands. The thought of them finding out his deep, dark secret was more than he could bear, and he sensed the urge to vomit again. He didn't want to see the revulsion darken Dallie's beautiful face, the shock that would come, the falter in her smile once she knew who he really was and what he'd been hiding from them all. The betrayal would be almost too much to bear. It was too much for Cole to bear. He hated himself so much in that instant. His self-loathing had become a culmination of disgust that had continually bombarded him since coming to Abundance. Now it was an overwhelming burden that he couldn't escape. It was completely suffocating him, and he wasn't sure how much more of it he could stand.

He got up then and rinsed his mouth out, wiped his tears and walked into the basement media room to check the computer again. He'd done this twice a day now for the last couple weeks, keeping careful track of every move he could. When he typed in his usual wordage, he stopped dead in his tracks as a picture of himself popped up on the screen. He audibly gasped and felt his heart drop. It was the local Denton news, and they had both his name and his picture in the article now. This was it; the day he'd been dreading for so long now. He'd come here to hide and he'd succeeded in doing so, but now there would be no hiding, not for very long anyway. The people of Abundance had seen him and could recognize him from this bad, not quite decade old picture.

Cole sighed. It was time for him to begrudgingly move on from this place and plan his next move. His covert front was over!

∼

"*A*rt!" Art McElroy heard the excitement in his partner's voice. "Yeah, what is it?" He couldn't hide the anticipation he felt in that moment.

"We have a HUGE lead."

"I'm all ears," he boomed impatiently, ready to hear some good news for a change in this tedious game of cat and mouse.

"A trucker from Shreveport says he picked up our guy in Austin —get this—on the day of the murder." Dinging bells went off in McElroy's head as he smiled at the news. "He's positive that it was definitely Cole Callahan."

"That's great news, Trace. Where did he drop him off at?"

Cunningham laughed in triumph. "The truck broke down not two hours into their trip from Austin. Art, you aren't gonna believe this shit…"

"Dammit, Cunningham! Where?" Art practically yelled into the phone; he was hanging on every word.

"Abundance."

～

*N*atalie giggled as Jack pulled her into his lap that Thursday around nine in the morning. His hands rested on her thighs as his eyes grazed over her, making her feel unabashedly sexy. If she hadn't known any better, she would suspect that her husband was trying for yet another baby with the way they'd had marathon sex lately. She wasn't complaining; she loved having his hands—and mouth—on every part of her.

She'd left Savannah with the baby for a few minutes as she came down to ask her husband what he'd like for lunch, to which he'd replied that she would do 'just fine'.

"You, yourself, are enough to satisfy my hunger, my darlin'," Jack whispered into her ear as his lips lingered at her jawline.

She shivered. "Jack, I need to get back to the house. Our daughter is such a space cadet, there's no telling what she'll let our son get into."

He smirked then curved his hands around her hips. "It's been a while since this desk saw any action. I think we need to show it some love." His voice deepened and one hand slid up her back as his mouth descended on hers. She moaned as his tongue slid in and her arms went around his neck, pulling him closer.

That's how Todd found them when he barged in, and Natalie jumped, startled as she pulled back slightly from her husband.

"Do you *mind*?" Jack protested as Todd's face paled. "Todd, why the hell do you look like you are about to die of fright?"

Natalie frowned and bolted upright in Jack's arms as Todd approached the desk.

"Sir, you aren't going to believe what I'm about to tell you. I need to show you something right away."

"Ok, Todd, ok! Just let me have a moment with my wife, please—"

"It can't wait that long!" Todd exclaimed and rounded the desk, pulling the keyboard and mouse to within his reach.

Natalie felt an uneasiness creep up her spine and looked down at her husband's drawn brows.

"This is what I saw on the news this morning," Todd stated and looked expectantly up to the two of them once he'd found what he was searching for online.

As Natalie's eyes fell on the computer screen, she gasped as her hand flew to her mouth.

"What the—?" Jack asked, quickly skimming the article.

"Oh my God, Jack! That's Cole." Natalie felt faint. This couldn't be accurate. It just simply couldn't be!

"No, that's not Cole... that's..." his voice faltered as he continued to stare at the unremarkable picture before them of a younger Cole, clean-shaven, long-haired, unsmiling and empty-eyed.

It was Todd's voice that penetrated their speechlessness. "Sir? Ma'am? *Where's* Dallie?"

~

*D*allie hummed to herself as she dabbed some lip gloss on her lips. She sat in front of her mirrored vanity spending a little more time on her hair and makeup than usual. It wasn't a special occasion or anything, but Cole had seemed a little more despondent now that Vivian was gone and Dallie needed an excuse to doll up. She'd slept in for a change and took her time showering before she would head down to eat then out to the barn. She knew Cole had more than likely eaten already and hated that she'd missed the opportunity to dine with him, but she'd not slept well last night and hadn't been in any hurry to respond to her alarm that morning.

She smiled at the finished product of her rosy cheeks and sparkly eyeshadow and wasn't aware of being watched until she caught a slight movement in the mirror.

She gasped and turned to see Cole standing at the doorframe. He wasn't dressed in his typical cowboy gear but in a polo shirt and jeans, although his hair was hidden by the cowboy hat they'd bought him barely two months ago. She started to smile, but the smile died immediately as her eyes took in the bleakness that surrounded him like an aura. His eyes were red and blood-shot and the sadness etched across his face was overpowering.

"Cole?"

"Shh...don't say anything. This is exactly how I'll remember you from now until the day I die." He moved forward, his eyes roving over her as she stood. "You look so beautiful, Dallie." He looked back up at her face then and his green eyes were cloudy with tears. "Meeting you was the best thing that's ever happened to me. I want you to know that. You are the most amazing person I've ever known."

"Cole, why are you talking like that? You—"

"I have to leave, Dallie. Right now. As soon as possible."

"What? Why? I don't understand."

"I know and I'm sorry for that, I truly am. Just know that these last two months have been the best of my life, and if there was any other way, I would stay… but I simply can't."

Dallie huffed, not understanding what he was saying, trying to take it all in as her heart sank in her chest. She couldn't hide the disappointment of him leaving. She was starting to feel something for this rugged drifter. The thought of losing him tore deep into her so that she winced with the pain it brought.

"Know that my heart will be breaking with each mile that separates us." A tear ran down Cole's cheek, and Dallie fought to control the tears that hit her own eyes as anger and confusion crashed into her.

"DALLIE!" The sudden, loud calling of her name from voices downstairs jarred her from Cole's sorrowful gaze, and she stepped out of the doorway and into the hall.

"I'm here," she called out and came to the landing to look down at her parents, who both appeared distraught. "Guys, what—?"

"Oh, thank God, baby," Her mom said and sighed as her head fell to her dad's shoulder.

"Dallie, sweetheart, we need you to come down here, right now, ok? Don't ask questions, just get down here," her dad commanded.

"Alright, just let me—"

"Change of plans," she heard Cole say behind her and watched her parents' faces fall. She didn't understand exactly what was happening until Cole's arm roughly wrapped around her waist and she felt a cold pressure against her temple.

~

"Cole! Don't do anything stupid," Jack pleaded as he looked up to see Cole holding the very gun Jack had threatened him with to his daughter's head. Jack's heart immediately dropped into his stomach, and Natalie's grip tightened on his bicep.

"I'm sorry, sir. I didn't mean for any of this to happen."

"It's over now, son. Just come on down here and we'll talk." Jack felt bile start to rise in his throat as tears fell down his daughter's cheeks.

"Daddy," she whimpered, and fear seized Jack's heart, then anger.

"It's ok, baby. Just do as he says and everything's gonna be alright." He would tear this boy apart before he let his family go through another tragedy. Hadn't they been through enough already? "Come on down here, Cole. There's nowhere to go." Cole moved Dallie forward to the top of the stairs and stopped. "Take it easy now. One step at a time." Natalie whimpered behind him as Jack took a step back, showing Cole his hands, palms facing out. "It's alright. No one's gonna hurt you."

"I'm sorry that it had to be this way," Cole murmured again as his grip tightened around Dallie and he lifted her as he took the first step down.

"Just take it nice and slow. No hurry."

They slowly moved down the stairs, one at a time as Jack had asked. All the while, Jack's jaw ticked in rage. He would kill Cole West...Callahan, whatever his name was. *No one* came into Jack's home and threatened his family. Cole was a dead man. It was as simple as that! They were about halfway down when Cole stopped suddenly and looked at Jack with eyes full of regret. "She has to come with me."

"NO!" Natalie shouted behind him and shoved against Jack's suddenly outstretched arm. Jack easily pushed her back, his forearm protectively tucking her behind him. He could only deal with one damsel in distress at a time; no need to add two to the list for the moment being.

"Cole, that isn't wise and you know it." Jack had learned over the years that logic and reason were hard to hold onto in times of panic, so he decided that he was going to throw loads at Cole until they won out. "Think about it... Dallie's only going to get in your way, slow you down. You *can't* take her with you."

"Daddy," Dallie pleaded again, and Jack felt his heart split in two. Natalie only sobbed in return, and Jack felt his anger flare up again.

"Is this really what you want, Cole? Look at what you're doing. You've got nowhere to go!"

"DADDY!" Jack heard Savannah cry and looked over to see her standing at the edge of the living-room, teary-eyed, with a pouting Jackson on her hip. He had to get rid of the two of them. Cole was already unstable; another crying bunch could drive him over the edge. Jack had to get Cole unarmed, and Savannah and Jackson were only going to make it more difficult for him.

"Sweetheart, it's ok. Now, I want you to take your brother down to the barn, ok? Go on now, easy. Daddy's gonna handle this." Savannah looked at him only a moment more before turning and fleeing with Jackson. Jack mentally sighed, but the anger had returned to his face as he looked back to his gun against his daughter's head. "Dammit, Cole! Get down here!"

"She's going to come with me," he repeated again.

Over my rotting dead body! Jack thought. Of all the damn days Magnus had to go to the vet, today had to be one of them. Then his thinking drifted in another direction. Intimidation wasn't working. He decided to try something else. "Cole, please don't take my daughter? Take the gun. Take my truck. Take my money. Don't take Dallas. Please?" Jack pleaded. "I'm *begging* you."

"I'm out of options here, sir. Please step back?" Cole was almost to the bottom of the stairs, and Jack's mind and body screamed at him to do something.

"You're putting her in danger, Cole. Think about this for a second; you'll have dug your own grave. Now you have a hostage. The cops are going to come at you with everything they've got. There's no way out of this. Just surrender, here and now."

"I can't sir, I'm sorry. I can't just give up. I didn't do anything wrong."

"Then take me instead!" Jack cried, stepping forward, but Cole only shook his head grimly.

Cole was at the bottom of the stairs now, his back facing the door as he suddenly tightened his grip on Dallie's waist, the hand holding the gun shaking. Jack saw red and just as he was getting ready to lunge, Dallie's eyes held him back. They pleaded with him. He frowned, confused. He knew she had a black belt in karate, and she could take Cole down—maybe that's what she intended to do. Jack waited impatiently, his heart hammering out a cadence of chaos against his breastbone.

"Please, Cole?" Natalie was the one begging now and the sound of her trembling voice cut through Jack's heart like a knife wound, filling his chest with a void he'd only felt once before. "Don't take our daughter."

"I'm sorry, Mrs. K. One day I pray y'all can forgive me for all this."

"This is the thanks we get, huh? For bringing you into our home?" Jack couldn't control the fury that his wife and daughter's distress was causing him. Dallie had better hurry up and decide what move she intended to make before Jack made it for her.

"I can't tell you how sorry I am, but this is the way it's gonna be. Dallie is coming with me." Cole pulled Dallie backward and out the doorframe as Jack stepped forward. Cole's grip on the gun tightened and Dallie cried out, her eyes cutting through his soul. Jack growled.

"Damn you, Cole! You hurt my daughter and I'll rip you, limb from limb, I swear to God! You take one more step out that door and I will hunt you down, I can promise you that. I won't rest until I've found you and *destroyed* you."

"Step back, Jack!" Cole yelled, nervously. "This is out of your control now, sir... I'm sorry. And don't try and follow us. I've disabled the other vehicles. Now don't move. Don't come outside until we're gone. I'm serious." Cole backed away as Jack fought within himself to rush the bastard and tackle him to the ground.

Time was running out. If Jack moved too quickly, the gun would go off right against Dallie's skull. He couldn't let that happen, but he also couldn't let this lunatic just walk out with his daughter and take her to God knew where. He prayed and cursed and tried to reason within himself as he helplessly watched on, and Natalie sobbed into his shoulder. He groaned in frustration as the moment passed, and he watched Cole pull Dallie into her truck. He was too late! He'd done nothing but stand there and let a murdering fugitive kidnap his child.

He angrily rushed out the door once the truck peeled out and ran, screaming in rage, at the dusty trail it left in its wake. He gripped his hat with both hands and squatted to his haunches, trying to contain the rage and pain he was consumed with in those moments. Hot tears ran down his cheeks. He'd never felt more worthless in his life… except when he'd seen his wife covered in blood at the hands of her ex-husband. He stood and sighed as he wiped at his face. He had to go call the police now. They didn't have much of a lead and Dallie's truck would be easy to spot.

He turned and headed back up the driveway. His wife's tormented face gave him pause, and he caught her as she fell to her knees, sobbing.

～

"*D*ammit, I've already answered your questions, Detective. Why aren't you out there *looking* for my daughter? You're wasting time!" The rugged ranch owner grumbled as he sat on the couch, elbows on his knees, holding the tan cowboy hat to his head in frustration.

What this man didn't understand was that they needed as much information as possible and they *were* looking. They had an APB out on the truck and the couple. It wouldn't be long before they were found and apprehended.

"Mr. Kinsen, I know this seems redundant, believe me, but know that we are doing everything in our power and within our capability," McElroy stated.

Jack Kinsen only seemed to become more ruffled with Art's words as he looked over to his wife, who sat sniffling with a toddler in her arms on the opposite couch talking to a uniformed officer.

"I've told you what I know about the kid, what more do you *need*? My wife and children are exhausted."

"I understand. Just a few more questions," Art insisted and flipped his notebook back open. "So, you said that you paid him 'under the table'?"

"Yeah? He was a drifter. Being a ranch owner, you run into those quite frequently," Kinsen answered sarcastically. "It's kind of a nice gesture, so that they don't have the hassle of trying to get a check cashed when they aren't hanging around long enough to open a bank account."

"And quite convenient, don't you think?"

"What exactly are you implying?" Jack's eyes narrowed.

"Not a thing. Don't you worry about your taxes though?"

"Nine times out of ten they don't stick around but for one or two pay periods to begin with, so no. I'm well aware of the tax laws, mind you."

"Jack," The beautiful dark-headed wife called soothingly to him, and he sighed and gritted his teeth at Art. "They are only trying to help, my love, please don't get so upset."

"Mr. Kinsen? At any point did you get the impression that Cole Callahan was hiding something?"

"Murder, you mean? Absolutely not! But then again, what the hell do I know about murderers? You would think Natalie and I, *by now*, would know what to look for." Again, his remark was sarcastic. He was a man who was used to getting his way and now that he'd lost control of the situation, he was furious with himself. Art had seen it at least a dozen times. "He was quiet, shy, sad even, but not malicious," Jack insisted. "If I had any idea this would have happened, he would have never been permitted to be anywhere near my family."

"And you said Cole and your daughter were dating?"

"Yes," Jack grated out.

"He said his name was West? And he was an orphan?"

"Yeah, he lied. He was pretty convincing."

"Well, not *all* of it was a lie," Art corrected. "He was indeed an orphan."

"You said he has a record. What kind of record?" Jack's jaw ticked. Art wasn't usually apt to give too much information regarding an ongoing case, but these people had been through enough that they deserved some type of reassurance.

"Petty theft, larceny, vandalism. Things like that. He started some fights back in high school. He was violent with a few male class-mates, but never any females."

Jack's shoulders seemed to relax some as he nodded. Art could see that no matter the fact, the Kinsens were worried sick over their daughter's whereabouts and for good reason. Dallie had been kidnapped by a fugitive on the run wanted for questioning in a murder investigation. It didn't matter that his record didn't involve kidnapping and murder.

"Did he ever mention his friend, Adam, at all to you?" Art asked, thoughtfully.

"Not to me personally. To Dallie. He told her that Adam was his brother and that he was devastated by his death."

"Thank you for your time, Mr. Kinsen." Art extended his hand, and the younger man took it and pumped it as they both stood.

"Is it possible that this kid didn't murder Adam?" Jack asked before Art turned away. Art frowned and looked back up to the taller man.

"It's very possible, but the evidence against him is mounting, Mr. Kinsen. Right now it's all circumstantial, but if he *is* innocent then why is he running?"

"Maybe he's trying to find a way to prove his innocence?" Jack asserted.

Art laughed, humorlessly. "This isn't Hollywood, Mr. Kinsen. I wish things were easier, but they aren't. People kill one another all the time over the stupidest things. I see it all too often." Jack just nodded at that, not happy with Art's answer. "We're going to find your daughter, Jack. I promise you. And we're going to bring her home… Alive." Jack flinched at the word "alive" and gulped, nodding his hat again at him.

Art ached for this couple and their pain. He'd, unfortunately, worked his fair share of kidnapping cases which frequently involved murder. He prayed that this wouldn't be the case with this family. From what he'd been informed of the Kinsens, they'd been victims of tragedy too many times already. They deserved one hell of a break and hopefully, Art could give it to them.

Perhaps he'd been wrong about this Cole kid. Art still wasn't sure where the young man stood in all this. Just when he was convinced that the kid was a victim himself, Cole had gone and kidnapped his girlfriend from her home at gun point.

Art turned as he remembered he had one more question, after all.

"Mr. Kinsen?" Art walked back to the other couch, where Jack had moved to sit next to his wife. Jack had taken the sleeping child from her and moved the curly blonde-headed toddler to his shoulder. Jack's arm came around his wife and he pulled her into his chest. He motioned for Art to sit, so he took the couch across from them. "I forgot to ask you," Art's voice dropped so as not to wake the child, even amid the chaos of officers and investigators, who ambled about with cameras and equipment of various kinds. "Where did Cole get the gun?"

Jack's face fell then and he grimaced. "It's my gun."

"And how did Cole get access to it, exactly?"

"Well, that's my fault," Jack admitted.

"What do you mean?" It was Natalie Kinsen that asked as her head came off her husband's shoulder.

"Several weeks ago, I threatened him with it," Jack answered.

"You did *what*?" Mrs. Kinsen asked incredulously. "Why would you *do* such a thing?"

"I wanted him to understand exactly who he was dealing with if he messed with my daughter."

"And I see that he *got* the message. Right, Jack?" Natalie huffed as she pulled out of his embrace. "All you did was make it easy for him.

Hell, why didn't you just hand the gun over to him while you were at it?"

"Nat?" Jack's face was surprised as he looked at her.

"No, don't even think about telling me to calm down, Jackson Edward Kinsen! You *showed* him where the damn gun was! How did he have the combination to the safe? Did he find it or did he see you open it?" Damn, this lady could have been a cop herself. She sure knew all the right questions to ask. Art just watched and waited.

Then he saw realization creep over Jack's face as he paled.

"What? What now?" Natalie cried and gripped his forearm in angst.

"I forgot to lock the safe back," Jack stated grimly and his shaded eyes fell back to his wife's face.

"How could you!" She yelled and shoved at him. Art jumped up and came towards her then, pulling her from her husband as she screamed again. "This is your fault! How *could* you? Our baby was taken by a madman, and you could have prevented the *whole* thing!"

Jack's face was horror-struck as he stood and stared at his wife, his jaw clenching and his eyes filling with unshed tears. Natalie crumbled against Art then, and he cradled her head against his shoulder, frowning as Jack's eyes caught his.

The middle child, a young teenager, Savannah, walked in from the dining room at that time, her face red and tear-stricken as she sought her mother. Her aunt, one Jordan Butler, propped herself in the archway and just looked on, swiping at her eyes.

"Mommy?" Savannah croaked out, and Natalie's head lifted suddenly off Art's shoulder.

Natalie gave her a weak smile and brushed at the tears on her face. "What is it, baby?"

"Please don't be mad at Daddy," Savannah pleaded and took her mother's hand. Natalie's lips trembled and she looked up at her husband, who swallowed hard, that tough exterior still persisting as the tears remained bottled up in his eyes.

"Oh, sweetie. I'm not mad at Daddy. I'm just plain mad is all."

Natalie pulled her daughter into her embrace, Savannah's head falling to Natalie's shoulder. "I'm just mad, Savannah. I just want Dallie back. I want my baby back!" As she crumbled again, Jack stepped forward and pulled his wife and daughter into his chest, embracing them in a group hug.

Art turned away then; this family's agony ripped deeply into him, not unlike difficult cases he'd had before, but they seemed like such a loving family. They didn't deserve to have this happen to them—not when they'd already had their fair share of heartache.

Art surmised that he had work to do; Cole Callahan once again had him on a wild goose chase, and this time the stakes were even higher than they'd been just two months ago. Now, he had a young woman whose life might be in danger to add to the mix. Missing person's detective, Al Mitchell, was on the case and he was one of the best on the team, Art knew firsthand.

As he turned to head to the basement to see if there were any clues in Cole's sleeping quarters, he froze as he heard the phone ring. Everyone stopped what they were doing, and Al ran to get the equipment ready to trace the call.

Natalie's head shot up, and she looked to Jack, who nodded. Art moved closer as she ran to answer the phone next to the couch, she again gulped and looked up at Jack. Al nodded at Art who nodded at Natalie.

"Hello?" she cooed, uncertainly, into the receiver.

A soft feminine voice came over the recorder, "Momma?"

Jack's head fell back and his eyes squinted in relief as he practically fell onto the couch next to Natalie, whose face crumbled again as she smiled over at her husband. He leaned in to kiss her and squeezed her thigh.

"Baby," Natalie belted out, "are you ok?"

"I'm ok," Dallas Kinsen stated, sounding more tired than fearful as Art would have expected.

Art caught Al's gaze in the background as he rolled his finger in a circle as if to say, "Keep going."

Natalie looked expectantly up to Art, who simply nodded at her and winked. "You're doing great, keep going," he mouthed.

"Oh Dallie, honey, we're so worried about you."

"I know...but I promise I'm ok."

"He hasn't hurt you, has he, Dallas?" It was Jack who spoke gruffly into the phone then.

"No, Daddy. I'm fine, I swear."

"Dallie, honey, *where* are you?" Natalie asked, gripping the phone even tighter. Suddenly the line went dead, buzzing loudly. "NO!" Natalie cried into the receiver and began to sob, inconsolable. Jack's arm went around her, and he pulled the receiver from her hands even as she cried, "No, please, no", again.

Jordan stepped in to take the baby from Jack, and he pulled Natalie into his chest and murmured to her. Her heart-wrenching sobs stirred everyone, and Art saw Al swirl his index finger around his head, indicating for them to wrap it up for the night. They would keep a crew of two or three there in the house for the night in case something new came to light or another call came in, but Art doubted that immensely. The road crews were ready for any sign of the truck and they were setting up road blocks.

Art once again headed to the basement to look for evidence before he returned to his office. He caught Jack's eye as the cowboy stood and walked his wife to the base of the stairs. He nodded reassuringly to the father of the girl who'd been taken. He set his mind to find Cole Callahan and Dallas Kinsen and bring justice to this poor family.

Art's night was just beginning.

~

*N*atalie stepped from the shower and pulled the white towel from its rack on the wall, drying herself with it. The steam had opened up her stuffy nose and the hot water had soothed her swollen, stinging eyes. She sighed. She'd blamed Jack for

Cole's actions and she'd felt horrible for it. How dare she make him feel even worse than he already did? What kind of woman did such a thing to the man she loved?

She'd been utterly horrified when Cole had taken Dallie and completely helpless to stop it. Afterwards, she'd been mad—mad for being unable to save her daughter and mad that her life was once again turning into a tragedy. Of course it wasn't Jack's fault that Cole had taken his gun. If he'd really wanted it he could have gotten it, Natalie surmised, or he could have found another one; even Nate had guns that would have been easy to get to.

Nate and Jordan had taken Savannah and Jackson to their house, much to Savannah's dismay, but Jack had reassured their daughter that he would come get them in the morning, that they all just needed to rest tonight. He'd then escorted Natalie, who was a blabbering mess, into their room, and she'd wanted a shower to calm her nerves. Once she reassured him she'd be alright without him, he'd left her. After he was gone, she hit her knees and began to pray for the safety of her first-born child, for God to bring Dallas safely home to them, and for her husband to forgive her anger. She'd sobbed until all her tears were spent then she'd let the water soothe her and soaped up her hair and body then rinsed and finished.

She wrung her hair out and wrapped the towel around herself then combed out her hair and covered herself with an intoxicating lotion to help calm her body and mind. She stepped out into the bedroom and felt the cool air from the fan hit her skin.

She stopped in her tracks as she saw her husband. He stood, clad only in his boxers, the arm nearest her propped up against the window pane. She could see his side profile as the bright moon bathed his beautiful face and big muscled body in mesmerizing vivid blue ribbons as he gazed out into the night. He looked so distraught and alone that it ripped out her heart.

She'd only seen that look on his face once before and the memories of that dark time in their lives flashed through her head. She silently winced from the pain it brought her. The anguish on his face was palpable as she watched him stare off into the distance.

"I swore to protect her," he murmured as if in a reverie. "She was just four years old then and I *promised* to keep her safe." He sighed heavily as his head fell. "I failed her...and I failed you. Twice now." He looked up into her face, and she gulped from the intensity burning in his eyes, trying to squelch the tears that suddenly stung her own. He was a man completely torn apart and right now he needed her comfort, not another meltdown. She approached him and shook her head.

"No Jack, my love, you have *never* failed me." She reached for the hand he had propped against the window and pulled it to her lips. He clenched his jaw and tore his eyes from hers.

"I stood by and did *nothing*...as he took our daughter." He gritted his teeth in anger.

"Oh, Jack," she cooed and leaned into him, kissing his big bicep as she took his hand in hers. "What could you have done? He had a gun pointed at her head?"

"I could've *tried* at least."

"And if the gun had gone off?" She shook her head, not daring to think of it. "You'd never have been able to forgive yourself."

He sighed again as those green eyes of his glistened with unshed tears. "I still just stood there and did nothing."

"You tried to reason with him. You were so composed."

"I failed."

"You tried!" she insisted. He looked back at her. "You can't blame yourself." Natalie frowned; she felt so guilty. "I was wrong to say what I did about it being your fault. I *don't* blame you, baby."

His eyes searched hers and he gulped again as he looked away.

"Nat, all I can think about are all the horrible things that he's doing to her right now." His other hand closed into a fist.

"Don't, Jack. Don't do that to yourself," Nat murmured. He scowled then looked back to her. "Dallie is a strong person, despite how innocent she is. She's the best of both you and I. You know she can take him down. She's taken *you* down before, remember? That's why we put our girls through self-defense classes. She is *going* to be ok."

"How can you be so sure?" He swallowed hard as he interlaced their fingers and turned to her.

"Because I don't dare *consider* the alternative." Her resolve faltered then as she held her chin high against the tears that threatened her eyes. She was barely able to keep them at bay as she gazed into her husband's dismal face, so rife with misery, his eyes open pools of sorrow—Natalie's own fears mirrored there. He frowned even deeper at her, silently speaking to her with his stricken green eyes.

Suddenly, he was grabbing her and pulling her flush against him, his mouth covering her own as his arms wrapped around her waist. He kissed her with desperate passion as he backed her against the wall, tilting his head as his tongue plunged deeply into her mouth. His despondent groan was equal parts need and desire as he jerked the towel from around her and his mouth fell on the damp flesh of her neck. His hands squeezed at her breasts and his head lowered. He drew her nipple into his hot mouth and pulled on it, and Natalie moaned hungrily, realizing how much she needed his comfort too. His hand moved between her thighs as her own sought out his raging erection. In a matter of moments, he was lifting her by her hips, his fingers were opening her and his hefty sex was entering her. Natalie's body didn't disappoint as her center responded accommodatingly to him as it always had and her legs wrapped instinctively around him. With one deep, smooth thrust he was fully engulfed inside her and her head flew back as she cried out.

Her husband was one of the strongest men she'd ever known both physically and emotionally. Jack had always been her rock, now it was her turn to be his in the only way that she could at this moment in time. He plunged hard and deep inside her, seeking refuge within her—thrusting all his anguish and fear and pain into her—and she absorbed the dark emotions dwelling within him and expelled them from her throat with each lunge of his powerful thighs. Her back rubbed against the cold, unyielding wall and her hands gripped Jack's shoulders and back as she held herself tightly to him. His vulnerability surfaced as he sought comfort within her feminine embrace; his big, sinewy muscles growing taut as he arched and climbed higher and higher, seeking reclamation as he raised and lowered her body upon himself. It wasn't long before his firm grip on her bottom tightened and he moaned against her neck, his teeth nipping at her sensitive skin as his pace quickened even more.

She gave a soft whimper as his body crashed against hers and the hard muscles of his back rippled like molten steel beneath her palms as he bucked up and roared his release, his rigid body racked in fierce tremors before he finally collapsed against her, exhausted.

His forehead rested on hers and his ragged breath fell on her face.

"I'm sorry," he murmured. "I love you. God, I love you so much, Natalie." He held her for long moments, kissing her exposed flesh as their breathing returned to normal. Finally, he pulled out and stepped back, holding her as her aching legs dropped. They felt like Jell-O as she stood, and Jack pulled her back into his arms. "Did I hurt you, my love?" he asked sweetly as he gazed into her face, his hands cupping her cheeks.

In their entire thirteen-plus-year marriage, he'd never *once* hurt her. Despite his massive size, he'd never really been what Natalie would consider rough with her. Right then was about as close as he'd ever come to that. She shook her head and smiled, reassuring him. "No, darling, you didn't hurt me. Not at all."

"I know I was a bit vigorous." He kissed her lips softly.

"Jack, I'm fine. Honestly."

When he was finally satisfied with her answer, he drew her with him into bed and pulled the covers around them, wrapping his arms around her as tightly as they could go as his pelvis spooned her bottom. He gently stroked her arms as she attempted to close her eyes and try not to think about where her daughter was and if she would ever see her again.

Sleep didn't come easy for either of them as the knowledge that they were truly alone—well, kid-less anyway—in the house kept them awake. Natalie couldn't rest her mind and each time she unconsciously tried to roll over, Jack was pulling her back against him as if he were afraid to let her out of his grasp. Her heart went out to him. He would never stop beating himself up over this, no matter how much time passed. Even Magnus stirred as if he could feel the ever-present fear circling their hearts like vultures to hours-old carrion.

When Nat did drift off to sleep, she woke in a panic, remembering suddenly that Dallie wasn't home, wasn't safe, and had been taken at gunpoint to destinations unknown. It was then that Jack was there to rock her and kiss the tears from her cheeks. This went on for hours before Natalie finally felt exhaustion take her, and she coasted off into a restful slumber where she was back, well over a decade ago, in the barn on her parent's ranch.

Dallie's little curls bounced as Jack picked her up and into his strong, bare arms. He gave Natalie a sexy smile as he looked at her, and she felt her heart soar. Damn, he looked *so* good in that tight black tank top!

"Take me riding, Jack," Dallie insisted.

"Let's ask Mommy first, my lil' darlin.'"

"Oh, Mommy, please, please?" Dallie begged.

He wouldn't tell Dallie no, Natalie knew, no matter what she said. Dallie had Jack wrapped so tightly around her little index finger that it was comical.

Natalie smiled back up into his handsome face and nodded.

"Oh boy," Dallie stated and squeezed his neck, giggling, and Jack laughed along with her.

"Which horse do you wanna ride this time, sweetheart?" he asked and adjusted his hat.

She took her time deciding and chose Jack's own black stallion, Midnight.

"Good choice, Dallie." He winked over at Nat and moved towards the stall.

As he walked away, Natalie's heart strings went with them and a tear came to her eye as she heard Dallie say. "Jack, I wish you were my Daddy!"

CHAPTER 14

*W*ho was this person sitting next to her? Had he ever been truthful with her? Was *any* gesture he'd ever made to her genuine? Had he planned this all along? To trick her? Earn her family's trust then just betray them all in the end? Who was this man who'd kidnapped her? What had he done to Adam? And what did he intend to do with her?

Dallie said nothing as she numbly drove, noting the steady lulling beat of the tires on the asphalt and the headlights shining down on the straight, flat highway in the darkness.

Cole had demanded right away that they head north and park the truck in an old abandoned landfill outside of Abundance. There it hadn't taken them long to walk a little ways and find a vehicle that Cole could hotwire; it was a generic sedan of some kind, pale silver in color. Once he made sure they had enough gas, they headed north on I-35 and went through Gainesville toward Oklahoma City. They'd driven a great distance, through both Oklahoma and into Kansas, and weren't but a few hours from the Nebraska border when he told her that he intended to get a hotel room. That's when she finally broke her silence.

"I'm not staying *anywhere* with you," she said as tears suddenly poured from her eyes.

"We have to rest, Dallie," he insisted, "You've been driving for hours!"

As soon as Cole had pushed her into her old '57 Chevy truck, Dallie's heart had really and truly sank in her chest. Fear seized her body and mind as she froze and robotically did as she was told, her hands gripping tightly to the steering wheel to try and hold herself together. She couldn't afford to panic at that point. The steady rain of tears only made her job even harder as she drove and as much as she knew that she needed to consider how and when she planned to disarm her kidnapper, she couldn't do much beyond stare ahead and let the road take her away. Her disappointment and heartbreak were all-consuming, and she couldn't stop thinking about how scared her family had been. She was also mad at herself for not fighting harder. It had been too tricky in the house, her mom and dad were in the vicinity, and even if she'd succeeded in getting the gun away from Cole, that didn't mean she would have succeeded in not getting someone shot. No, she hadn't thought it was worth the risk. Even her dad had thought he could simply tackle and disarm him, but had hesitated as the gun sat so dangerously close to her temple. It wasn't like Jack Kinsen not to fight like hell for those he loved. He'd known too that it was simply too risky.

So, she'd decided to simply bide her time and once she saw the opportunity, she would take it. But it hadn't come. They hadn't stopped for anything but gas twice and neither time had proven to be a good prospect. No one was around, of course, they were the shadiest of places, and Cole had chosen to make her be the one to pump the gas. He'd been smart about it too, choosing older stations without cameras and he refused to let her go to a public bathroom. She'd had to go in the woods. And those woods had been too barren to afford a decent hiding or running spot. No, she'd simply had to wait and again bide her time.

Now, it was far past dark, her fears were swamping her, and Cole was suggesting cooping her up in a motel room where he could corner her and possibly kill her...or worse. Then again, he *did* have to sleep at some point too and that might be her opportune moment. She finally acquiesced.

"Only if I can call my parents," Dallie contended. She knew they would be worried sick at this point and she had to let them know she was ok. She chanced a look over at the man who'd taken her against her will, for the first time in hours, and the hurt in his eyes seemed to be as great as her own. That couldn't be possible. He was the criminal here, he had no right to feel wounded. "They deserve to know that I'm ok, Cole."

"Yes, they do... you're right."

Dallie just stared back at him, surprised.

They had stopped not much further at an old run-down, ancient-looking, one-story motel just off the highway, and Cole turned to her as she turned the vehicle off and rubbed her aching hands together. She hadn't realized how hard she'd been gripping the wheel.

"Dallie, just bear with me a little longer. Ok? I know this has been really hard. Let's just get a room and rest and I'll explain everything." Cole sighed heavily and motioned for her to exit the car. Again, he'd picked the most barren, unpopulated place for them to stop.

Dallie wasn't sure she *wanted* an explanation—after all, they'd had hours in the car for him to explain himself—she simply wanted to go home. But she knew that if she got herself killed she *never* would, so she tried to calm her rattled nerves as Cole moved beside her, and they walked toward the motel office. She thought about grabbing the gun from his waistband, but again reminded herself that it would be much easier once he relaxed in sleep.

"I'll do all the talking, alright? Just stand behind me and don't make eye contact, you got it?"

Dallie just nodded and bowed her head as a bell attached to the top of the door chimed, and they entered. Cole approached the high counter and asked for a room, pulling out his wallet. The gentleman behind the counter had an Indian accent and took the cash from Cole, no questions asked. Dallie noted a closed-circuit monitor on the other side of the counter and a camera angled down at her. She tried to look up at it, but just as she raised her head Cole turned and grabbed her elbow, pulling her out the door. *Oh well, good attempt,* she thought.

Just as he pulled to a stop, five doors down the alley, Dallie reminded him. "You said we could call my folks."

"Not from here."

"But you—"

"I know, Dallie. And I'm gonna keep my promise. We'll find a payphone."

They turned and walked up the block towards an old liquor store and around a corner where a dirty glass phone booth sat. Dallie sighed as Cole crammed into the streaked glass encasement behind her and inserted the change then she dialed her home phone.

"Hello?" Her mother answered on the third ring.

"Momma?" Dallie's relief was palpable as her shoulders relaxed.

"Baby, are you ok?" The soft soothing sound of her mother's voice gave her strength.

"I'm ok." Dallie reassured. They needed to know that she hadn't been harmed. Their fears needed to be calmed.

"Oh Dallie, honey, we're so worried about you!"

"I know...but I promise I'm ok." As much as she wanted to bawl and tell her mom how afraid she was, Dallie wouldn't give into her tears.

"He hasn't hurt you, has he, Dallas?" Her father's voice called to her then and she felt her lips tremble and her resolve falter. How badly she wanted to be enfolded in his big capable arms in that moment, safe from the world at large. He'd been right all along about being careful; he'd been right to be so protective of her. Now she was paying the price for her own gullibility. But she wouldn't let him hear the fear in her voice. Both of her parents had been frightened enough when Cole had taken her, she wouldn't add to it now.

"No, Daddy. I'm fine, I swear."

"Dallie, honey, *where* are you?" her mother pleaded.

Suddenly the line went dead, buzzing loudly in Dallie's ear.

She rounded on Cole, tears blinding her eyes as she dropped the receiver.

"Why did you do that?" she cried. "I wasn't going to *tell* her!"

"They were tracing the call, Dallie. They are trying to track our location," Cole stated calmly, regret shining in his eyes.

Dallie huffed and robotically replaced the receiver. Cole grabbed her elbow again and steered them back toward the motel. Dallie considered dropping to the ground and screaming, but by the looks of the barred windows and greasy, scary-looking biker eyeing her suggestively from the corner of the liquor store, she felt safer taking her chances with Cole.

He led them through the red door with a golden metal number eight screwed onto it and placed the key on the table. Cole flicked on the lights and locked and bolted the door. He grabbed a chair from the small round table, shoved the top of it underneath the door handle, and sat down in it. He fell forward, elbows on his knees, and took his face in his hands, looking all the world like a man apart.

Dallie felt her heart stir in her chest at the sight of him. How could she actually feel sorry for the man who had taken her captive, the man who'd forced her out of her home with a gun stuck to her head? Maybe she would just never be strong enough for this tough world. She was such a softie. Even now, at the mercy of a man who was running from the law, she felt sympathy for him. What was wrong with her? Instead of being angry, Dallie just felt resolved. It was her plight in life to root for the underdogs, to see the good in all people. It was her fatal flaw.

She tore her eyes from his bowed head and looked around. The dirty shades of the wall sconces reflected shadows on the ceiling. There was only one bed, a queen she assumed, a medium-sized TV on a dresser, an old fridge that droned loudly and a long countertop with a sink at the far wall with a door that led presumably to a bathroom. She sighed and sat on the bed, pulling her knees into her chest. She continued to stare at Cole and wondered what he would tell her. Had he killed Adam? Was Cole really capable of murder? And could Dallie handle the truth of it?

Just when she thought he might have fallen asleep and the roaring silence between them became completely unnerving, he looked up. His green eyes looked hollow and remorseful, and the pit in Dallie's stomach widened, her heart leapt into her throat. He was going to kill her after all. Why else would he look at her like that?

"What are you going to do with me now?" she croaked out, her voice a decibel below panic.

Cole's brow drew and he gave her a confused look as if he couldn't fathom what she meant. When she squeezed her legs even tighter in her self-embrace, he snorted incredulously.

"Dallie, I would *never* hurt you."

The tears returned then as she remembered the feel of the cold metal against her temple.

She scoffed, "You put a *gun* to my head!"

"It wasn't loaded." He shook his head.

"What?" Surely she hadn't heard him correctly.

"The gun wasn't loaded, Dallie. The bullets are in my pocket. The magazine is empty. I would never put a loaded gun to your head." He gazed solemnly at her as her rattled brain continued to try and grasp his words. When he pulled the bullets from his jean's pocket, the thought finally registered, and she lost it.

"You bastard!" she cried and jumped up, charging at him. "I can't believe you would do that to me, to my family! How could you? I hate you. I HATE YOU!" Her fist pummeled his chest, and the pouring of torrential tears blinded her as she succumbed to the panic and fear and hysteria she'd felt for the last eight hours. Her fury didn't seem to be a match for him as she was upended and slammed roughly down onto the bed, a big hand covering her mouth.

"Shh," Cole whispered as he straddled her thighs, shifting his weight over the top of her to pin her arms and legs down. "I know you're upset. You have *every* right to be. I'm an asshole in the most basic form. Trust me, I already know. But, *please*, Dallie...stop screaming?" As quickly as her rage had taken over, it waned. The physical and emotional turmoil she'd been through on this day was starting to wear her down, and she felt her breathing calm as the adrenaline pumped its last dose. His eyes burned into hers. "I'll move my hand, but you must not scream anymore, ok?" Dallie only nodded. He moved his hand, but his body stayed on top of her and despite his obvious physical strength, he wasn't as heavy on her as she expected he would be.

Dallie's anger might have blown over, but torrential tears continued to stream down her cheeks and sides of her face, into her ears.

"We trusted you," she spit the words out at him as the pain of what he'd done clutched her fragile heart.

"I know." He sighed.

"They were so frightened," she murmured, looking away from Cole's intent gaze.

"I'm so sorry, Dallie. I never meant for any of this..." He cupped her cheek in his palm.

"What did you do, Cole? Did you murder your brother?"

"He wasn't my brother. Adam was the best friend I ever had...*like* a brother. And no, I didn't. I loved him. I would never hurt him. I stumbled upon his body." Cole's weight shifted again and he pulled away, leaving Dallie to move freely. She sat up slowly, watching Cole as his head lowered and he dangled a leg off the bed. "I knew something was wrong the minute I walked into our shop that day..."

"Shop?"

"Burns and Callahan Automotives. My name is Cole Callahan. I'm a mechanic. From Austin. Adam and I owned a body and mechanic shop together. His car was there, but he wasn't in the office like usual and something just didn't feel right. I accidentally stepped on the gun as I was walking into the garage. It was dark and

I had a box in my arms. I thought it was a metal tool, but when I picked it up, I knew immediately that something was horribly wrong… then I saw his body, he was lying in a huge pool of blood. He was dead, Dallie. He was dead." Tears burst forth from him then as he recalled the scene. He let them fall and sighed. "I touched him to check. He was cold. So cold. The next thing I knew, there were blue lights shining from under the door and I was running… I have a criminal record. I touched the gun and Adam. My fingerprints are my condemnation. And there's nothing I can do about it."

Dallie didn't speak, just listened intently to Cole's confession.

"So I ran. I hitchhiked to Abundance and decided to hide until I could figure out what to do. Adam had no enemies. I have no idea who would want to kill him. He wasn't a part of anything sketchy. That wasn't him. So, I'm at a total loss here. I thought that I could figure it out, but now I've just screwed things up even worse than I ever intended to. I had planned to head to Canada, but then when the truck broke down, I found your ranch and you, and I just *couldn't* leave. I didn't want to. I loved the feeling I got when I was surrounded by your family. I've never felt anything like that before and I—I fell in love with you," he whispered. "That's why I couldn't leave you back there. I know it sounds stupid. But I had to bring you with me. So that you could hear my side of the story, not what the media tells you about me. I didn't kill Adam, Dallie. I'm innocent! I was a fool to involve you. I know that now. I've spent the last several hours trying to figure out what to do. You don't deserve this, and I'm so sorry I scared you. I never meant to hurt you, Dallie. I never meant to cause all this pain…I just didn't know what else to do. Please forgive me?"

He grabbed her and pulled her to him and held her with a desperation that frightened her. He sobbed as he gripped her shirt, and Dallie felt his fear and sorrow with each shudder of his body. As implausible and unbelievable as his story was, she believed him. She believed that he was telling her the truth. She trusted him and trusted in his innocence. She held him and let him cry it out, for this man had been a loner and alone all his life, and Dallie knew that he'd probably never been able to fully express himself until now.

When he finally pulled back and wiped his eyes, she saw the love shining there in the light emerald depths. How had she not seen it there before and how had she ever doubted him? It was immediately apparent to her that he wouldn't hurt her, despite that he'd kidnapped her. It was also immediately apparent when his lips found hers then that she was in love with him too. The kiss was sensual and frantic with need, and Dallie answered it with reassurance and confidence. It wasn't just a kiss of passion—it was so much more— and when Cole pulled back, Dallie sighed.

"I'm so sorry," he began. "I didn't mean to fall for you. It was wrong. I'm going away for a long time, and I was completely selfish, but I just wanted one more moment with you. One more moment like this." His fingers intertwined with hers. "It's been so amazing knowing what love feels like. To be able to love a woman as wonderful as you are. If I live a hundred years, I'll never forget you."

"Cole, are you sure that they have solid evidence against you? Are you sure they aren't just wanting to question you?"

"From what I've read about the case, I'm the prime suspect. That means that the circumstantial evidence against me will be enough to put me away."

"Not necessarily. If you're innocent then there has to be a way to exonerate you!"

Cole just shook his head, sadly. "Fate is cruel and has never favored star-crossed lovers."

"Oh, Cole. We aren't Romeo and Juliet."

"Aren't we?" He pulled her hand up and brushed his soft lips against her knuckles. "I've seen that movie. I know how it ends."

"Don't be so dramatic. You haven't even talked to the cops yet. You have no idea what they have or don't have against you. Think and stop assuming for just a moment."

"Dallie, baby, your optimism is almost as beautiful as you are. In your world, it would be easy to see a way out of this, but I'm a criminal."

"Former criminal."

"It doesn't matter. In their eyes, I'm guilty simply because I was there. That's just how things have always been for me. Trouble has *always* surrounded me. My record speaks louder than any words I can come up with to claim my innocence. It won't matter what I tell them. I've been in the system. I know how it works. Tragically, this is the end for us, Dallas."

Dallie slept in Cole's arms that night as she tried to think of some miraculous way to get him out of this nightmare he'd found himself in, but she couldn't find any solution that didn't involve him turning himself in.

That next morning, she explained this to him and much to her surprise, he acquiesced.

"Actually, I've been thinking the exact same thing. I'm going to take you home, and I'm going to turn myself in. This has gone on long enough. I've made such a mess of things. I should never have put you in the middle of this, Dallas. I'm so sorry."

She held him tightly to her and cried. Cried for the fate that tore them apart and cried for the sorrow of the situation before him. Cole had been dealt a bad hand at life, and it had only served to follow him like a black cloud over his head. He was a good person, and Dallie prayed with everything in her that somehow, some way God intervened and got Cole out of this predicament.

It was in His hands now.

They ate breakfast at a diner not a mile away as they hadn't eaten all day the day before and despite their despair, they enjoyed their meals and what little time they had left together before Cole turned himself in. Then they headed back home to Abundance.

*D*etective McElroy came to check up on Natalie and Jack the next afternoon and much to Nat's surprise, she felt stronger, more relaxed than the day before, despite not sleeping well, or long enough, and despite the continued anguish on her husband's face. Natalie had faith that God would help them. She held onto hope like a security blanket and let it guide her through the day.

Jordan had brought Savannah and Jackson home later that morning once Natalie called and told her they were awake and about. She'd made breakfast for Jack and herself, and Jack stayed up at the house, refusing to go down to the barn. He hadn't let Natalie out of his sight for more than a minute. They sat around on the couch after their silent meal, her back against his chest as he stroked her and kissed her cheek and shoulder, his fingers laced in hers. When the kids got there, they joined them, cuddling into them, and the house was quieter than Natalie could ever remember it being, even Jackson, who was always playful, just sat solemn. It was as if they were all preparing for a bomb to go off.

Then the excitement began.

Not long after McElroy came in, his phone went off, and he literally ran to the window.

"Everyone stay inside and don't come out until I give you the go-ahead," McElroy stated firmly as he ran out the front door.

Jack looked apprehensively over at Nat, and they all took off towards the front windows of the house to peer out and see what was happening. Natalie's heart hammered in her chest as a pale silver sedan pulled into the driveway. The two officers, who'd been sitting in their squad car waiting all morning, had their guns raised at shoulder level, pointing them at the vehicle, and McElroy slowly came down the porch steps, his own gun drawn.

Nat heard muffled voices and moved her head to see Dallie step out of the driver's side, arms in the air.

"Oh my God," Natalie cried and felt Jack's strong arms encircle her. She heard Magnus's low growl then.

"She's ok," Jack stated. "She's home." His voice sounded so elated that Natalie laughed, tears of joy coming to her eyes.

The two officers swarmed the passenger side, and Natalie saw Cole being shoved to the ground. She heard Detective McElroy laugh as he escorted Dallie up the porch steps.

Natalie's heart literally leapt with joy as the door opened and she threw herself at Dallie, her arms wrapping around her daughter.

"Oh, thank God! Thank you, God!" Natalie cried as Dallie returned her embrace. She took Dallie's face in her hands and looked her over, unable to contain her relief. Aside from red cheeks and eyes, Dallie was fine. Nat's prayers had been answered. She pulled her daughter back into her arms and sobbed with liberation. She felt Jack pull them into his arms then and heard his heavy sigh of satisfaction.

When Natalie finally pulled back, Jack grabbed Dallie and held her tightly to him for a long time, his eyes closed.

"Oh, my sweet girl. I'm so very glad you're alright," he murmured in Dallie's ear as he stroked her long, curly hair. Dallie just continued to cry as Natalie leaned up and kissed her forehead.

Life could go on now, Natalie's baby girl was home... and safe.

~

It wasn't until the next day that Dallie felt like she could talk to her parents about what had actually happened with Cole. Her dad was going to be the tough case, she knew beyond the shadow of a doubt. Jack was as hard-headed as she was at times, and the entire incident wasn't gonna go over smoothly, but she knew the longer she let it fester, the harder it would be to lance. And time wasn't exactly something that Cole had oodles of at the moment.

Once she'd gotten home yesterday, the outpouring of love and pampering had been immense, and Dallie was grateful that she'd been able to return safely to her family. They doted on her, hugged and kissed her, especially Savannah, who hadn't let her wander too far from her sight or grasp. Her Uncle Nate and Aunt Jordan came over and they all had a lovely dinner together. Her grandparents were in Europe or they would have been there too. Her mother had refused to upset their once-in-a-lifetime vacation, she'd told Dallie, until they'd known something definitive. They were thousands of miles away anyway, and informing them wouldn't have served a purpose other than to worry them for no reason, so Dallie was grateful that Cole's little escapade hadn't spoiled her grandparent's trip.

Her mom had seen her up to her room where she'd asked about what had happened. Even though the door was wide open for Dallie to tell her then, it had seemed like an inopportune moment, so Dallie'd just told her the truth—that nothing had happened, that they'd stopped in Kansas, stayed the night, and Cole had decided to bring her home. Then her mom had sighed in relief, and Dallie had taken a nice, hot shower and joined them for dinner.

This morning she would be talking with a Detective Trace Cunningham from the Austin police department about Cole. And her parents would learn that the gun wasn't loaded and that Cole was innocent of the charges against him. Dallie was anxious. She'd never really talked to an officer of the law before, well except for the officers she went to church with, but they'd always been out of uniform then. She was also anxious because she was under the microscope and she didn't want her parents to know all the things that had happened between her and Cole. *What if he wants personal details?* And how would they react to all this?

She was about to find out.

She met Detective Cunningham in the living room. He was dressed in a suit and tie with a brown cowboy hat atop his head and tan cowboy boots. His head was bent as he glanced down at a spiral notebook, a glass of sweet tea sweating in front of him. Dallie immediately relaxed. She'd been around cowboys all her life, and right now she felt she was in the presence of a good 'ol boy just hanging out, not in the middle of an interrogation.

She cleared her throat as she approached, and Detective Cunningham looked up. Dallie gave a weak smile, and he stood and quickly pulled his cowboy hat off his head.

"Miss Kinsen. Detective Trace Cunningham. Thank you for agreeing to give me a few moments of your time."

He shook her hand firmly and motioned for her to take a seat on the couch across from him as he replaced the hat back on his head. Dallie did as he asked and glanced at her parents, who stood behind the couch Detective Cunningham sat on. Her mom smiled reassuringly and her dad gave her a wink and tipped his hat at her. She gulped.

"Now that you've had some time to compose yourself, Miss Kinsen, how are you feeling after your ordeal?"

"I'm fine, Detective. Just tired is all." She smiled and thanked him for asking.

"Good, good. I know your folks here were pretty worried about you," Detective Cunningham stated, turning around to look back at her parents, "and Detective McElroy as well. We're real glad that you were able to get home safe."

Again, Dallie thanked him for his kindness.

"Now, I'm gonna ask you a few personal questions, and if at any time you need more privacy, you just ask, alright?" His eyebrows went up at that, and Dallie knew that he meant if she wanted her parents to leave the room he would kick them out. She almost laughed in relief but simply nodded. "Alright then, tell me, in your own words, what happened Thursday morning that started this whole incident?"

Dallie proceeded to tell him about how she'd been getting ready for her day and had turned to see Cole standing in the doorway and what had been said.

"So, he didn't say *why* he had to leave, just that he couldn't stay?"

"That's right." She then proceeded to fill him in on how her parents called her name and she'd moved to the landing and how Cole had stepped behind her, grabbed her, and put the gun to her head. She told him the exchange between her father and Cole and how they'd all hesitated, how she'd been pulled out of the house and into the truck.

"Did he ever talk to you about an Adam Burns?"

"He never told me his last name, he always just called him Adam and he told me originally that Adam was his brother."

"That's right because he gave you a fake name he made up?"

"Yes, he told me on the first day I met him that his name was Cole West."

"Did he tell you what happened to Adam?" Detective Cunningham's eyes grew more solemn as he asked.

Dallie nodded sadly. She looked up at her mom, who looked to her dad then, and she hesitated for a moment before she said, "Cole only told me just day before yesterday about what happened to Adam."

"Will you tell me what he said?" Detective Cunningham grew excited suddenly, and he grabbed for the voice recorder from his pocket and hit the record button.

"He told me that he and Adam owned a mechanic shop together. They were best friends, like brothers, and the morning of the murder, he walked in and felt that something was off. He said that he pulled in and Adam wasn't in the office which wasn't normal. He said the garage was dark and as he was walking with a box in his arms. He stepped on something. He went to set down the box, knowing he hadn't left a tool out. He said, at first, he just heard the metal and thought it was a wrench or a flashlight, but then when he picked it up, he immediately knew that it was a gun and dropped it then ran to turn the lights on. When he looked over, he saw Adam laying in a pool of blood and he ran to him. He realized that Adam was dead. He said he was cold." Dallie's head fell and she sighed before looking back up at her mom and dad. "He saw the blue lights and knew that he would be mistaken for the murderer. He said, he knew that his fingerprints were on the gun and on Adam and so he ran. He told me that he had a criminal record... Which he'd actually told me before—"

"Oh, he did, huh?" Her mom was the one to ask. "And when did he tell you *that*?"

"About a month ago."

"And you were ok with his *criminal* record?"

"Mom! He was ashamed of it. He said he was a different person back in high school and he stole things and got into some fights. He wasn't proud of it. He said that all that changed when he met Adam." Dallie's eyes moved back to Detective Cunningham's then. "He made Adam out to be like a saint. He said he loved him very much and had no idea who would want to kill him."

"So, he didn't confess to murdering Adam? He told you that he was innocent?" Detective Cunningham asked.

"Yes."

"And you believed him?"

"I had no reason not to believe him."

"Even though he lied to you about who he was and where he was from?"

"He did that to protect me."

"To *protect* you?" her father interrupted. "And how was he protecting you when he put a gun to your head in front of your mother and I?" His tone was acidic as his eyes narrowed at her.

"It wasn't loaded," Dallie mumbled and lowered her head, feeling her cheeks flaming up.

"Say again," Detective Cunningham instructed.

"The gun wasn't loaded." Her eyes flew up to the detective's. His look hovered in between amusement and surprise. "He took the bullets out of the gun and put them in his pockets. He said that he never would have pointed a loaded gun at me." She emphasized the word 'never' and shyly looked up at her father, whose arms were crossed over his chest now. His eyes were dark with anger.

"And you know this to be a fact?" her dad asked.

"He pulled them out and showed them to me when we got to the motel," Dallie insisted.

"And how long were you in the car with this punk?" He drawled loudly. "It never occurred to you that he didn't simply take out the magazine when you weren't looking?"

"I could see him the entire time."

"Even when you went to the bathroom?" her dad countered, sarcastically.

"He didn't leave my side," she assured him.

He harrumphed and growled as he turned around, trying to calm himself. Her mother scowled as she patted his shoulder.

"Miss Kinsen, aside from the gun, did Cole Callahan harm you in any way?"

"No."

"You two were dating, I was told."

"Yes."

"So, would you say that you knew him better than anyone else here on the ranch?"

"Yes. We were together a lot, between work and dating. He accompanied us to church at times and was with us for meals. He redid the engine in my truck and repainted it along with my Uncle Nathan."

"Yes, I actually spoke with your Uncle Nate yesterday." Detective Cunningham nodded, jotting something down in his notebook. "Did you ever get the impression that Cole would hurt you...that he was dangerous in any way?"

"No. Never. He was always gentle and even took up for me at the mall and... well, just recently in fact, when a friend's boyfriend insulted me."

"So, let's go back to the kidnapping for a minute. Walk me through exactly what happened after he forced you into the truck."

Dallie told him about how they'd headed north, dumped the truck, hot-wired the Buick and drove, only stopping for gas and to use the restroom along the side of the highway.

"We were in Kansas, just about three and half hours from Nebraska, when Cole mentioned resting at a motel. I told him I would but only if he let me call my parents."

"And what did he say?"

"He agreed. Once we rented the room, he took me to a payphone."

She told him about the phone call and how he'd hung the line up after just a short period of time, so the call couldn't be traced.

"Why do you think he continued to run even though he claimed that he was innocent?"

"I think he just didn't know what else to do. We talked in the room once we got settled."

"What did he talk to you about?"

"About Adam... He started by apologizing for taking me from my home and for frightening me and my parents." She looked up at her dad, who'd turned and was now facing her. "He apologized and told me about the gun being empty. I got mad and charged at him. He tackled me and—"

"He *tackled* you?" Her dad practically growled.

"Only to calm me down so that I stopped screaming, Daddy."

"So, he got physical with you?"

"No, I mean... he didn't hurt me. He just—" She stopped. The look on her father's face was murderous. "Once I calmed down, he told me about what happened the day of the murder and who he was, and I asked him myself about why he was running. He feels like trouble just seems to follow him."

"Why did he kidnap you, Dallas?"

Dallie sighed. This was the part her dad wasn't going to like. "He just wanted me to know the truth about him instead of what I would hear—"

"Oh, that's rich! So, it made more logical sense to *kidnap* you," her dad grumbled. "And then have you drive for eight hours."

"He just wanted one more moment with me is all."

"One more moment! How poetic."

324

Dallie huffed, ignoring her dad then looked at Detective Cunningham. "He told me that he fell in love with me." Cunningham's eyes raised. Her dad scoffed, her mom sighed, and Dallie just blushed. "I think being around us made him see that there's good left in the world. We reminded him of Adam, and it was hard to let that go."

"So, he decided to bring you home?"

"We slept first then the next morning, he told me that he was going to bring me home and turn himself in."

"How noble!" her dad exclaimed and rolled his eyes. She gave him a withered look.

"Is it possible that he could be exonerated, Detective?" Dallie asked.

"It's tough to say at this point, Miss Kinsen. He's our prime suspect right now, and with kidnapping, assault with a deadly weapon and evasion charges—to name a few—adding to it..." Air hissed between his teeth. "I highly doubt Cole Callahan is likely to see the light of day anytime soon."

"And what if I were to drop the charges?"

"Pardon?" Detective Cunningham stuttered and adjusted his Stetson.

"I don't want to press charges against him, sir."

"Dallas Noel Kinsen!" She heard her dad protest and she looked up at him frowning.

"Well, I mean...that's your decision, Miss Kinsen. I would advise against it, but—"

"Like Hell!" her father said.

"I must confess that it is *her* decision, Mr. Kinsen."

Her dad's moss green eyes burned into hers for a few minutes more before he scowled and turned on his heel, leaving the room, his heavy boot falls striking against the hardwood floors. They heard the back door slam a few seconds after, and her mom's eyes closed as she jerked, startled.

"Thank you for your time. Here's my card, Miss Kinsen. I'll be in touch." Detective Cunningham stood and tipped his hat at them. "Miss Kinsen. Mrs. Kinsen." He smiled and showed himself out as Dallie's gaze drifted to her mother. She just stood there, hands on her hips, shoe tapping with one eyebrow raised.

"So...you went and fell in love with him, huh?"

CHAPTER 15

"*D*addy, we *have* to help him," Dallie stated at dinner that night once everyone was settled in their chairs.

Her father hadn't spoken to her since that morning, even when she'd come down to the barn to try and talk to him. He simply walked away or found something else to do where he wasn't near her. He'd even gone as far as to lock himself in his office. She'd known that this would be difficult, but she couldn't stand him ignoring her like she didn't exist and that this problem didn't need to be addressed, because it did, and soon.

This was the first time he'd looked at her since she'd been questioned and dropped the charges, but she wasn't so sure she was prepared for the wrath that reflected back at her in his eyes as he raised his head and extended his arm to rest on the table, his jaw clenching. The smile on his face was in defiance.

"Help him? And why in God's name would we do a thing like that?"

"Because he's innocent."

"That's what he told you."

"He is!"

Jack sighed and clenched his fist. "Dallie, I'm sure that you want to believe—"

"Daddy, he—"

"Took you from your home at gun point, remember?" His grave voice grew loud.

"The gun wasn't loaded."

"Do you honestly think *that* makes any difference?" he yelled. "He succeeded in traumatizing your sister." He pointed over at Savannah, whose maple head just lowered, sadly. "He scared the hell out of me and your mother, but I guess since you guys had a *moment* together, and he confessed his undying love for you that it just makes it all ok!" His green eyes burned heat into hers, and she gulped.

"No. I didn't say that—"

"Let me say *one* thing, so that you're clear on how I feel about this, Dallas!" her father exclaimed and took a breath in. "That bastard came into *my* home and threatened *my* family. Whether the gun was loaded or not makes no never mind. His intentions were made clear that day. He didn't care about anything beyond himself. Come hell or high water, he was getting out of here and he didn't care what he had to do to get there."

"Daddy, we're Christians. It's our job to—"

"Don't you dare!" Her dad slammed his fist down hard on the table. The dishes and silverware rattled, and everyone jumped. Baby Jackson started wailing, freaked out by his father's outburst. "I brought him into my home. I clothed him, I fed him, I gave him a job and a place to stay. I even permitted him to take my daughter out on dates and didn't even *balk* at the fact that your tongue was rammed down his damn throat not just a week ago, so don't you dare even hint that I haven't done my duty as a Christian! I've probably done more for that boy than anyone in his entire life ever has, but dammit, my hospitality ended the minute he threatened you."

Dallie's shoulders slumped as her father's brows drew in anger. She wasn't sure she'd ever seen him this mad before. He went on, "Kidnapping you was the thanks I got for all I did, Dallie. That's how people are! They use you. They trick you. They deceive you and guess what? That's *exactly* what he did. To all of us! Now I don't want to hear another word about this. The minute he put that gun to your head, the jig was up. I don't want to hear his name in this house *ever* again, do you hear me?"

Before Dallie could sigh, he pointed to her. "I mean it! I don't want to talk about it anymore. I'm *done!* Do I make myself clear?"

She gulped, she knew she'd just lost her chance to convince him. She just nodded and lowered her head.

"Don't you think we've all had just about enough tragedy in our lives?" he said as he stood, not quite done with his vent. "The sad thing is that he *fucking* knew about it. You told him about all the horrible things that had happened to you and your mom...and that didn't stop him from using us and tearing our very hearts out when he took you by force and made you drive him out of here. That's what I can't get over, Dallie."

He leaned forward, his eyes full of sorrow as he grimaced. "I thought the minute he left with you that you were dead. I didn't think I'd ever lay eyes on you again." He pointed to her mother then. "You were too little to remember what happened when Troy came back for your mother, but I was here." His voice changed then, it was softer, wistful. "*I* was the one to put the pieces back together of what that monster tore apart and I was so fearful that I was gonna have to do that all over again. So, *forgive* me if I'm not as quick to forget what Cole did—as you so *obviously* have."

With that, her dad walked away from the table, and Dallie looked over to her mother, who had silent tears running down her face. She wiped them away as she smiled, weakly, back at Dallie.

"Mom, I—"

"It's ok, baby. Your dad's just really upset. He was *so* scared, honey. We all were, so very scared. I've never seen your father like that. Well, I have...*once* before." Her mother's head lowered and she sighed, closing her eyes. "You're going to have to just be patient with him. Alright?"

Dallie frowned and nodded. Now she felt bad for saying anything at all. She hadn't meant to make it seem like she was only thinking of Cole's misery, when in all honesty, she understood her parent's grief too. She'd felt it as intense as they had that day. She'd been scared and disappointed and angry herself and she'd seen the pain in their faces. It had ripped into her so fiercely that it was all she'd focused on as she'd driven through two states.

"Dallie, you know how protective your father is of those he loves. When someone threatens his family, they become the enemy and well, now Cole is the enemy. It's going to take Jack some time to reconsider that."

Unfortunately, Dallie knew that time was something Cole was running out of.

~

*I*t took Dallie three long, drawn out days to get the courage to talk to her father again. She knew that her mother had spoken to him at some point because his looks had softened towards her, and he didn't seem as angry as he'd been that first day. All of which Dallie understood, too well even. She'd felt the same exact feelings the day that Cole took her from her home. She couldn't fault her father for feeling the pain even more than she had. After all, the protection of his family had always been his number one priority for as long as Dallie had known him. She hadn't lived through the same tragedy her mother and father had when Troy came back to take her and kill her mother. Well, she had…but she didn't remember any of it. She wasn't actually there on the front lines like they'd been.

Dallie took a deep breath and stepped into her father's office and shut the door behind her. He turned, a stack of papers in his hands, and gave her a resigned look then he set them down and squared his jaw. He beckoned for her to sit, and she could almost hear a faint sigh as she did so.

She hesitated because she wasn't sure exactly what to say or where to start, so she just spoke from her heart.

"Daddy, I'm sorry!" she began to cry then and although it wasn't a part of her plan, she was glad for it. It was refreshing to get her bottled up feelings out.

"Oh baby, I'm sorry too." He moved and came around the desk to embrace her.

This only served to bring more tears as the fear she'd experienced in the last week suddenly overpowered her. She remembered how frightened she'd been and how much she'd longed for his strong, protective arms around her when she thought she'd never see any of them again. When the tears ran their course, she looked up into his eyes and swiped at her face, ashamed that she was being so emotional. He just gave her that handsome smile that he'd been giving her for as long as she could remember. The one that let her know he was always on her side, always there for her, always wrapped around her finger. He kissed her forehead and pulled her back into his arms, tucking his chin against her head as she rested it against his shoulder.

"Sweetie, I love you *so* much. You know that, don't you?" Dallie only nodded. "And I would do anything for you, for your sister and brother, and your mother. I would die for you all. In a second. Without a thought or regret."

"I know." Dallie sniffled.

"Dallie, I can't describe to you how helpless I felt when Cole left with you. I can't explain to you how inadequate I felt as a man—and a father—that I just allowed him to take you away from us...without a fight. It went against my very nature not to attempt to stop him in some way, but I was so afraid that I would mess up and he would shoot you."

"I know." Dallie nodded. "It's why I didn't do anything either. I was afraid that the gun would go off and shoot you or Mom and I couldn't risk that."

"The fact that Cole is innocent of murder is one thing, darlin'. But he's not innocent of kidnapping you."

Dallie lifted her head off her father's shoulder then and looked up at him. His jaw was clenched again; she knew that wasn't good.

"You might be able to forgive that, but it's going to take me a little longer to do so…and I know what you're gonna say." He pulled away and sighed, moving to sit at the edge of his desk, extending his legs, and crossing his ankles and his arms over his chest. He lowered his head for a moment, his cowboy hat shielding his face. "He felt like he was out of options, he was a man on the brink of panic. I get that, I do!"

"So, you understand how a person could make a *huge* mistake in a time like that?"

"Of course I do." Another deep sigh emanated from his big frame.

"And you've made mistakes that you regretted."

"Of course I have." Her dad lifted his head then and looked at her. "But not for one second would I ever stick a gun to someone's head, not the woman I love or my children. No matter what!"

Dallie huffed and crossed her own arms in defiance. "Daddy, he's not you."

Jack gave her a crooked grin and shook his head. "No, he's not. So how can I understand his frame of mind in those moments? I've never been accused of murder or been a fugitive of the law."

Dallie paused as she took in his words. "So…"

"So, I can't judge him."

Dallie smiled at that and felt her heart soar with hope. "So, you'll help him?"

"I'll help him," her dad grumbled.

"Oh, Daddy!" She threw herself into his arms, and he grunted as she hit his chest.

He laughed big and stroked her hair. "Now don't take me for a softie because you know I'm not." *Yeah, yeah,* she thought. He was like a chocolate truffle with a hard exterior and a soft, gooey inside —well when it came to her anyway. "But your mom told me that you love the man, and I know that love is stronger than anything, so I mean to do what I can to pave the way for you."

"Oh, thank you. Thank you." She sighed against him and felt the tears come back to her eyes.

"Now, I mean to go talk to him. I need to know how he feels about you. And I do have a few conditions..." He trailed off as he pulled back for her to look at him.

"Anything!" she stated, exuberantly.

"You'll go to school and stay there, no matter what happens with this case. You'll finish college and continue your dreams and not allow this guy to affect who you are."

"Of course!"

"And if he's found guilty of murder?"

Dallie hadn't thought that far ahead. She was too convinced of Cole's innocence to put much stock in the fact that he would be found guilty. She felt a burning in her stomach as her dad's eyes darkened.

"You'll cut all ties with him."

Dallie's gut tightened. Could she actually do that? She loved Cole and the thought of him rotting away in some jail cell tore her heart into a million pieces, but she had to stay positive. He was innocent, she knew in her heart he was. So she nodded, praying with everything in her that justice would come forth and save the man she loved.

$$\sim$$

*A*my Burns paced back and forth across her living room. Her trip to Padre Island had been both needed and relaxing, but it had also given her a new perspective and the more she considered her options, the more she knew exactly what she had to do. Jeremy hadn't called, he hadn't written, and he hadn't seen her in months. He was avoiding her, like the plague. Now, the question she asked herself was- What did she intend to do about it?

He had used her. He'd manipulated her. He'd gotten his way... Now he was getting off scot-free. The anger rose inside her like bile in her stomach. She'd murdered her husband, at Jeremy's request, so that they could be together. But they weren't together, and Amy had a burning suspicion that he'd never really intended for them to be. What was he up to? What was his angle in all this?

Her doubts and questions had kept her up at night, uneasy on her vacation to her sister's. And she'd come home knowing that she had to do something before Jeremy pulled the plug on all this. She had to be the one to go to the cops first before he did. He had something, knew something, had some kind of evidence or record of something. And he was about to act on it. She couldn't stop her brain from ringing with this warning. So she'd come home, and now she was staring at the phone and pacing.

She took a deep breath and picked up the receiver and dialed 9-1-1. She sighed as the dispatcher came over the line.

"9-1-1, where is your emergency?"

"I need to speak to the detective handling the murder case of Adam Burns," Amy stated in a shaky voice. She closed her eyes and felt the panic wash over her like an ice water bath.

She would be heading to jail today. She would need a good lawyer, but by God, Jeremy Burns wouldn't be far behind her.

⁓

*J*ack Kinsen sighed as he looked through the thick glass wall in front of him, waiting on Cole Callahan to meet him in the cold and sterile-smelling holding area. He could faintly hear the other conversations going on around him—just two other people seated in the neighboring stalls on either side of him, speaking into telephones to the inmates on the other side.

The building was sealed tighter than a drum and the officers looked grim as they ushered the shackled inmates in and out. Jack couldn't fathom how on earth Troy Cameron had ever managed to escape a place like this.

Just before Jack's thoughts could go further on the topic, Cole appeared before him. He was haggard-looking and his beard was overgrown. It had only been six days since he'd been apprehended, but the dark circles beneath the young man's eyes looked years old. The orange jumpsuit was slightly rumpled and looked out of place on him. Cole literally froze when he saw Jack and his eyes showed a combination of both fear and relief at seeing a familiar face.

Jack simply beckoned him forward, and Cole hesitantly ambled forth, shoved by the muscular black officer behind him.

He gulped when he sat and slowly raised his bowed head to look up into Jack's eyes. Jack could see the misery etched on his face and the bloodshot vessels in his eyes. Cole appeared to be an innocent man, but that was only Jack's opinion.

Jack motioned to the phone as he picked the receiver up, wiped the mouthpiece on his shirt, and spoke into it.

"You look like shit, son," Jack stated, feeling bad suddenly for this kid whom fate had given up on.

"I don't really feel much better than that to be honest, sir." Cole gave him a look of regret then lowered his head before asking, "What are you doing here, Jack?"

Jack gave a humorless laugh. "Well, truthfully, if it'd been up to me, I'd have let you rot in here, Cole. After what you put my family through, I wanted to kill you, painfully and without mercy."

"I understand completely and I sincerely apologize for what I did."

"I appreciate that."

Cole looked back up at him, a flicker of doubt on his face. "You didn't come here for an apology, did you?"

"No, I didn't. I came here because my daughter is in love with you."

Cole gasped and a flash of hope crossed his face, only for a quick frown to swiftly replace it. "It doesn't much matter what Dallie feels for me. It doesn't look like I'll ever be able to reciprocate it."

"And *do* you reciprocate it?"

Cole smirked, lowering his head again, "It doesn't matter."

"It sure as hell does to *me*!"

Cole looked back up. Jack's jaw was set as he just glared at him, evaluating the younger man thoroughly, looking for any sign of deception.

"Dallie is..." Cole trailed off, his eyes looked wistful as he searched for the right words. "She's incredible. She's beautiful and smart...so giving and kind. More wonderful than anyone I ever hoped to love. Too good for someone like me."

"She believes with everything in her that you're innocent, Cole."

"I am. I didn't murder my best friend. I swear it! I would never hurt him."

"The problem is that the cards are stacked against you."

"I know. That's why Dallie and I have no chance. Even if I *could* get out of here, which I won't, I'll still never be good enough for her."

"I used to believe the same thing about her mother. That I would never be good enough for Natalie. She's the most beautiful woman I've ever seen, and there are times when I still feel like I don't deserve her love."

"Really?" Cole looked both surprised and confused.

"Yeah. I wasn't always the family man I am now. I was a bit of a hellion when I was younger, even older than you are now. I was a sorry excuse for a bull-rider when David Butler found me wasted that night at the rodeo in San Antonio some fifteen years ago."

"You? Wow! I can't see that."

"We all have regrets in our lives, Cole. No one's perfect. Even Dallie's not perfect."

"She's about as close as I'll ever see to it."

"Maybe so, but she loves you and that's all that matters to me right now." Jack raised his eyebrows in conviction. "So, let me tell you what I'm gonna do. Here's the deal! It's a one-time offer. Take it or leave it. I've just hired the best criminal defense attorney that the state of Texas has to offer and I only ask for one thing in return."

"Wait. What? Why? *How?*" Cole stammered.

"Because I *can* and I adore my daughter. Her happiness and well-being mean the world to me."

"No, I mean...that's gotta be outrageously expensive. How did you do that?"

Jack just laughed. His daughter was even more of an angel than he already knew she was. "Dallie didn't tell you?"

"Tell me what?"

"Well, now I know you don't just love her for her money."

"Money? What money?"

Jack laughed again and shook his head. Cole just frowned and looked angry. "Sorry, kid. I'm not laughing at you, honestly. I just figured you knew is all." Jack cleared his throat. "Let me put it this way, Dallie is worth an absolute fortune come the day she turns twenty-one. Actually, she's worth a fortune *now*, thanks to her mother and I and her rich grandparents." Cole just looked at Jack as if he'd sprouted antlers. "Her biological father was in the NFL for a time and her mother used to be editor-in-chief for one of the biggest magazines in the country...and yours truly inherited quite a large amount when his own parents passed away two decades ago. That money has only since been invested and multiplied. Dallas Noel Kinsen will never hurt for anything— nor my other two children— even when I'm long gone. Money will never be a problem for my family. In fact, Dallie wouldn't even have to go to college if that's not what she wanted, but she wants to be a vet, and we want our children to know the importance of higher education. Money isn't everything after all."

Cole had paled and looked like he might pass out. "I didn't know. I mean, I knew the ranch did well, but I didn't know y'all were *that* rich."

"That's because we don't value money as much as we value family and God and ethics, Cole. Having money usually only causes more problems. We've had our fair share of those."

"I know."

"Yes, you did and that didn't stop you from causing more."

"I'll never be able to express my regret or apologize enough for what I put y'all through. I wasn't thinking clearly. I was a fool... I don't see any way I can ever thank you for all you've done and continue to do for me."

"You can't do anything about the past, I always say. But you *can* do something about the future. The only thanks I require is that you strive every day to make yourself worthy of my daughter. Prove to me that you deserve her. Dallie is a beautiful person inside and out, who only sees the good in people. She's delicate, but that doesn't mean she's weak, she's one of the best souls I've ever known and I want the man who ends up with her to see the same thing I see when he looks into those sincere blue eyes of hers."

"I swear to you, Mr. Kinsen, if you give me this opportunity, I swear not to disappoint you, or Dallie, ever again. I swear it on my life!"

"I believe you, Cole, because I believe in my daughter. Now, I'm not going to waste any more of your time. Your attorney needs to speak with you, and you have a precious girl who can't wait to see you walk free. I don't like keeping my girls waiting, so I'll take my leave now. I wish you luck and pray that this goes well for you. I'll be here when you walk out the doors. Until then, stay strong for Dallie."

"I will, sir. I promise. Thank you! Truly!"

Jack started to hang the phone up then said, "Oh and Cole?"

"Yeah?" he answered eagerly.

"I expect to shake on it when you're a free man." Jack winked at him.

"Absolutely!"

"*S*o, let me get this straight. You murdered your husband because you're having an affair with his older brother, Jeremy?" Detective McElroy asked the widow Burns as she sat teary-eyed across from him at the interrogation desk. McElroy looked over at Cunningham, his eyebrows raised, as the younger man just shook his head and drew his lips in. McElroy set his coffee mug back down and sighed.

It was an enlightening evening to say the least. He'd been with Amy Burns for the last hour. Amy had called 9-1-1 earlier that evening and had asked to speak with him. The operator had questioned her until finally he'd patched her through to McElroy, who informed her he was on his way to her. She hadn't resisted arrest as he'd cuffed her upon confessing to Adam's murder. He'd brought her straight to the precinct where he'd called Cunningham, and they'd begun questioning and recording her.

"Wow! And you say that it was Jeremy who put you up to killing Adam?"

"Yes, he said Adam was 'in the way' of us and needed to be 'taken out of the equation.'"

"And where does Cole Callahan fit into all of this?" Cunningham was the one to ask.

"We chose him to frame. We knew what his reaction would be when he found Adam that morning. He was the only one of us with a criminal record, and he had nothing to lose, so he was perfect." She sniffled. Cunningham handed her another tissue. "We didn't know he was gonna run. We thought it was gonna be an easy open and shut case and we'd be in Mexico right now on a luxury vacation."

"I take it that didn't quite pan out like you thought, huh?" Cunningham smirked. "When did you figure out that Jeremy was using you?"

"It took a little while. I guess a few weeks after the murder when he practically shoved me out of his office."

"Do you have any evidence of his involvement, Amy?" McElroy asked.

"Well, nothing in writing or anything like that...we've talked on the phone many times though, and his secretary has seen me come and go. I'm sure she's heard some of our conversations as well as... well, ya know?"

"You had sex in his office?" Cunningham asked.

"Oh yeah. Several times in fact. There's *no* way that she didn't hear it."

McElroy's brows went up. Sounded like they had solid case, now to verify the other set of prints on the gun. McElroy knew they would match hers.

He'd had a nagging suspicion about this woman since day one. He'd known she was hiding something even then. Now, he knew what it was.

"You were the only one there when Adam was shot, correct?"

"Yes, Jeremy wasn't there."

"So, was it you who took the tape then?" Cunningham asked.

"What tape? What are you talking about?" Amy looked over at him confused.

"I'll be damned! He was gonna try and use that damn tape as leverage, wut'n he?" Cunningham replied and looked over at McElroy, who frowned.

"Son of a bitch!" McElroy stood and grabbed his suit jacket. "Trace, send a car over there right now and put out an APB out on Jeremy Burns! Let 'em know I'm on my way."

~

"I'm coming," Jordan sang out as she ran to answer the door. Nate was probably getting dressed, as he'd come in from a long day's work to shower not half an hour before that.

She'd been in the middle of making dinner when the doorbell rang. It wasn't unusual for them to have occasional company, but most their guests usually called first; of course, maybe it was David or Corrine wanting to borrow sugar or milk, as they'd been known to do every now and again. Or Nat...

Jordan's thoughts stilled as she opened the door and her eyes fell on a dark-headed young man on the porch. A shiver went down her spine as he looked up at her; his eyes were sparkling sapphires. She literally gasped and dropped the kitchen towel she was holding.

He looked startled as her hand went to her mouth to stifle her response.

"Is this the Butler residence?" he asked and bent down to pick up the towel.

That's when Jordan looked past him to the elderly couple behind him; their faces were grim.

Jordan recovered quickly as the young man cleared his throat. "I apologize. Yes, yes, it is. I'm Jordan Butler. Can I help you?" she asked and took the towel he handed her.

"Does Nathan Butler live here?" the kid asked, scuffling his feet.

He was clad in sneakers, jeans and a ratty looking t-shirt with the imprint of a 90's band. His hair was shaggy and unkempt, not quite shoulder length but thick, his skin was russet-colored, his eyelashes were long and full, his top lip had a perfect cupid's bow. Despite his gangly appearance, he was quite handsome, and when Jordan nodded her head at him, he flashed her an adorable dimpled smile that made him even more attractive... He was the exact image of the child Jordan had imagined that she and Nate would've had had she not been barren.

She gulped as he asked, "Is he here?"

Jordan could do nothing but freeze as a keen realization crept over her.

"Depends on who's askin'," she heard Nate reply from behind her and felt his hand go to her lower back. She shuttered as she turned to look at him, and his face immediately grew concerned. He took an instinctive step in front of her before looking at their guests then he literally recoiled as if he'd been shot. He recovered quickly as his arm went around Jordan's waist, holding her to him. She gripped him like a lifeline as he said, "So, who's askin'?"

The elderly man stepped forward, sensing their discomposure. "Look, we ain't wantin' nothin' from you. He's just wanting to meet ya. This last week's been a little rough for him, is all. He lost his Momma and..."

"My name's Morgan Dean," the boy stated and raised his chin a little higher.

"Hi, Morgan. I'm Nathan Butler. You wanted to meet *me*?" Nate extended his hand to the boy, who looked down at it as if he weren't sure what to do with it. It took him a moment, but he finally gripped Nathan's hand and shook it firmly then looked back up at him.

"Yes, sir. According to this letter my momma wrote me before she died, she stated that you're my father."

Nate pulled his hand away from the boy's as if he'd been burned, and Jordan inhaled sharply at this revelation. They looked down as the young man pulled a crumpled letter from his back jeans pocket. Nate frowned as he handed it over and quickly scanned it then looked from the child back to Jordan. He paled.

"Wow... I can't... I..." Nate gulped. "How old are you?"

"I'll be fifteen in November."

"Holy shit!" Nate swore. "Your mother—"

"Was Joanne Dean. She met you—"

"At the San Antonio stockyards... I'll be damned! Jo, Jo," Nate gave a terse laugh.

"You remember her?" the boy asked shyly.

"Of *course* I do." Nate smiled.

The boy seemed pleased by this and gave them a crooked grin in return.

"Oh, Nate," Jordan couldn't help but be happy for them and gave a stifled laugh as tears flooded her eyes. "You have a son. That's incredible!"

Her husband looked apologetically up at her then, such regret shining in his eyes. She immediately shook her head as if to say, "there's nothing to forgive, my love," and kissed him softly on the lips, feeling a tear slip down her cheek. He gave her a weak smile when she pulled back, and she turned to look at the boy claiming to be her husband's son.

"Morgan, welcome to our home," Jordan stated and smiled brightly at the boy and his assumed grandparents. "Please, won't you come in?"

EPILOGUE

THREE YEARS LATER

ole Callahan took in a deep breath as he shifted the white roses and gift box to his left arm and knocked on the door.

He was as nervous as a long-tailed cat in a room full of rocking chairs. His long-sleeved Oxford shirt collar felt tighter than normal around his neck and the heat in the long dorm hallway made it feel like a sauna. He gulped as he heard the door lock slide and the knob turn. He felt faint as his eyes fell on his drop dead gorgeous twenty-one-year-old girlfriend.

All thought fled his mind as he took in her lovely appearance; blonde curls down and almost to her hips, a silver choker around her neck, her tall, curvy frame adorned in a long-sleeved maroon sweater dress and black leggings. His heart immediately melted and he smiled big at her.

"Hello, gorgeous," he murmured as she gaped at him.

"Cole! What are you doing here?"

"Happy birthday!" he cried as he entered and pulled her into his arms.

She returned his kiss and his embrace then pulled back slightly. "My birthday isn't for another day. I told you I was coming home for the weekend. Christmas break starts day after tomorrow," she scolded even though he knew she was glad to see him.

"Well, I couldn't wait until tomorrow to see you. I missed you." He leaned in to kiss her soft, full lips again, grabbing her and wrapping his free arm around her waist. He deepened the kiss and got a moan out of her before finally stepping back.

"Are these for me?" Dallie motioned to the flowers.

"Only the best for my lady." He handed them over to her, and she smiled beautifully up at him.

God, how he'd missed that smile even though it'd been just a couple weeks since he'd last seen it. Dallie was in her junior year of college and would then be transitioning into vet school after. Cole was so proud of her.

The last three years had been both difficult and amazing, and Cole was thankful for the woman who stood before him. She'd been his rock and his refuge during the darkest time of his life. Cole had been cleared of all charges in the murder of his best friend, Adam Burns, after Amy Burns came forward to confess, and Jeremy Burns had been arrested as an accomplice. He'd been hiding the tape of the shooting in his closet. He'd claimed that he'd planned to turn it over to police, but Cole knew that his plan to blame Amy as the master mind had simply gone south. Apparently, they'd been having an affair.

Cole hadn't been so lucky with the kidnapping charges. Although Dallie and her family had dropped the charges and Dallie had testified in defense of Cole, he'd still been found guilty and sentenced to serve one year in jail. He'd been released at the eight month mark for good behavior and had to serve an entire year of parole, but his record was now clear and he was free to live his life again.

Jack had helped him buy and build an automotive shop in Abundance and also generated some business for him. Nathan came around occasionally too, to tinker, much to Cole's surprise and pleasure. The Kinsens' reputation and popularity in their hometown had only served to smooth over the damage that Cole had done there. It was as if the entire incident had never happened, and Cole couldn't be more grateful for their hospitality, kindness and generosity.

Jack and Natalie had continued to house and support Cole until he was able to get his business established and find an apartment in town. For the most part, when Dallie was home, he stayed with her. She'd moved her room to the basement, so that she had more privacy.

Savannah was in high school now and taking mostly AP classes that blew Cole's mind. She was set to graduate early and had already been accepted into several well-known colleges. She pretty much had her pick of the litter, but Savannah was destined for NASA for sure. She'd attended space camp two summers in a row and she was obsessed. She'd also been asked to perform a featured solo in the Dallas Symphony Orchestra, where she'd made them all cry last Christmas with her amazing talent. Jackson was two months shy of being five years old and growing into a little man every day. He loved being with his dad on the ranch and getting to ride horses. He was a mini version of Jack Kinsen, and Cole knew he would be following right in his Pop's footsteps by the way things were going. Jack and Nat were doing well too, and the ranch was simply flourishing, even with Dallie busy in college.

Nate and Jordan had become impromptu parents following their introduction of Nate's son, Morgan, one surprising day, three summers ago. He now had Nathan's last name and was attending the University of Texas to pursue an architectural engineering degree. Jordan adored the young man who favored Nate, and Nate enjoyed being an unexpected dad, although he'd told Cole many times that he regretted not knowing about his son's existence until he was fifteen. He'd made up for it though as much and as often as he could. Morgan seemed to enjoy the ranch life and had taken to his grand-parents and the Kinsens easily enough, unsurprisingly so. Cole was grateful that the Butler ranch would have an heir after all.

Cole absolutely loved his inadvertent family. *Who wouldn't?* The Kinsens had given him a home, encouragement and love like he'd never known. And now he was about to ask their eldest daughter for her hand in marriage. He'd fallen so deeply in love with all of them and couldn't imagine life without Dallas and her kin. He'd already spoken with Jack about making Dallie his wife, who—much to his surprise— just laughed and hugged him. Cole had also asked to buy some of Jack's land to put a house on. His soon to be father-in-law had loved the idea and had started helping him pick out house plans. Cole knew Dallie would want to be near her family. That ranch was a part of her; it always had been and always would be. Cole got the feeling that Dallie would settle down there with a practice of her own when she finished vet school. She'd practically said it not too long ago, and Cole had jumped at the opportunity.

Cole hadn't taken his promise to Jack lightly. He'd shaken the man's hand once he'd been freed from jail and hadn't wasted a single moment of his time pining for time lost but had started immediately moving forward to earn the trust and respect of the people he loved most. He'd gone above and beyond to prove his worth to Dallas Kinsen and each time he looked into her father's eyes, he saw that it had all paid off.

"Cole?" Dallie's eyebrows went up. "Where'd you go, love?" She giggled, and Cole's heart swelled to bursting.

"I'm sorry, darlin'. What did you ask me?" Cole blushed and moved over to where she stood trimming the stems on the roses.

"What's in the box? Or do I have to wait until tomorrow to find out?" She winked back at him.

"No, actually, you get this surprise now. I have a nice dinner reserved for us."

"Oh, yum! I'm starved. I can't tell you the last decent meal I've had since you were here last." She just beamed back up at him and his heart slammed into his ribs as he nervously thought about how he was going to do this. Now that he was here before her, it seemed even more difficult than what he'd envisioned in his head.

He moved to her small full-sized bed that sat next to a row of windows and sat down, for he felt lightheaded all of a sudden.

348

"Cole, babe, are you alright?" She stopped what she was doing then and moved over to where he sat, taking his face in her hands and bringing it up.

The sincerity in those dazzling sapphire eyes filled him with warmth and the words began to pour out of him like wine.

"Dallas Noel Kinsen, you're the most amazing woman I've ever known. I'm so head over heels in love with you, baby. You've been by my side even in the bleakest moments when I didn't deserve you or your kindness; you were there. I want you to *continue* to be there. Always and forever. Will you complete my dream of having a family? Will you do me the honor of being my wife?" Cole asked as his trembling hand opened the red velvet box and extended it upward towards his beautiful Dallie. Her shimmering blue eyes glanced at the diamond solitaire only momentarily before they flew up to his and her hands came to her mouth as she gasped. He moved then and knelt before her. He took the ring and pulled it from its perch in the box. "Marry me, my angel!"

Dallie pulled her cupped hands away and nodded as her face couldn't contain the smile that broke free at that moment. "Cole, I would *love* to be your wife. I love you! Oh, I love you so much!" she cried as he pushed the ring onto her extended left ring finger and popped up, pulling her into his arms, his lips descending to hers.

Their sweet, loving kiss soon turned passionate and hot and before Cole knew what was happening, they were tearing the clothes off of one another. Their kisses and touches were hungry and needy, their lips eager and insatiable, and soon his naked body was moving atop of hers and he was settling between her legs. He stopped himself before he did something they'd both regret.

"Dallie?" He stilled the hand that moved between his thighs. "Are you sure?"

She nodded. "I'm ready, Cole. I've *been* ready."

"My sweet girl. I've been ready for you too, but are you *sure* you don't want to wait until we're married? You still have college to finish and—"

She gave him a retired look. "Now you sound like Daddy." She took his face in her hands and kissed his nose and cheek. "Cole. I love you. I want to give myself to you. Will you please just let me?"

He wanted to tell her how very much he adored that she'd waited to give herself to him and how undeserving he was of this beautiful gift, but he only gasped as his body responded to her touch—for he knew that once she finally gave herself to him, she wouldn't be able to stop.

∼

"*Mom*, dad…Cole and I are engaged!" Dallie's squealing voice came through the speaker phone, and Jack's heart filled with such love that he almost winced.

"Oh, baby! I'm so happy for you," Jack's voice tightened as he tried to rein in his emotions.

"The ring is gorgeous, Daddy. I can't wait for y'all to see it!" Dallie exclaimed.

He wouldn't tell her that he'd already seen it as Cole had asked Jack just weeks ago for his blessing and his daughter's hand. Although Jack was sad to let her go, he knew his eldest child was going to be loved and taken care of because Cole adored her. Cole had actually cried when he'd presented the ring and proposal to Jack and swore to never disappoint him or Dallie ever again. Jack had to say—he hadn't thus far.

It was as if Cole had a new lease on life following his conviction and sentencing. Jack hadn't been too sure when he'd gone to pick him up that day at the jail when he'd been released. It didn't take long for Jack to see though that his fears were unwarranted. Cole had told him of his plan to get a job, get on his feet and start earning the respect of the Kinsen family he sought to become a part of. He'd proven himself time and time again.

"Looks like we have a wedding to plan," Natalie said and smiled lovingly over at Jack. His heart melted at the tears that sprang to her eyes. For he knew how happy and sad she was in this moment. He felt it too. "Have we thought about a date?" Nat inquired.

"Well, I know that I want to get married in the fall. And I want an outdoor wedding...and I want Aunt Jordan to take our pictures," Dallie rambled on, so happy and in love.

Jack remembered back to the day he married Natalie; how ecstatic and in awe he'd been. What a day that was! How beautiful she looked floating down that runner to him and their future. How utterly delighted he'd been to call her his. His sweet, amazing wife!

Now their daughter would be a bride and eventually a mother... and Jack would be a grandfather. Wow! That thought made him afraid and emotional at the same time. Their name and legacy would live on into the next generation. He gazed back into his wife's beautiful face and grinned back into the eyes that mirrored his. He looked over at Savannah sitting across from them, his almost grown baby girl, and Jackson, his little son, and knew his life was only just beginning.

ACKNOWLEDGMENTS

I just want to give a **HUGE** shout-out to all my family members, my beta readers- Jamie, Brooke, Danielle, and Caterina, my Twitter family- Patty, Katie, Cassie, Jen, Marc, Joe *and* the entire writing community there, who always blow me away with the amazing support and encouragement, my book blogger friends- Britney, Crystal, Emina and Kali, ALL of my indie author friends (who've helped me in *some* way—whether that be retweeting, sharing, commenting, liking, posting, tagging, book photographing— anything and everything you do to help make this indie author biz a little easier) and **ALL** of my READERS for your unwavering support in me!!!

Thank you so very much for your love of my characters and this series!

Without you all, these books would simply be just words on a page… You've helped bring my characters to life and given them an audience. So, ***thank you*** with all my heart!

If you enjoyed this novel, please be sure to review it on Amazon here, so that others can read it and enjoy it too :-) https://www.amazon.com/dp/B07RTRHQL5

AFTERWORD

I am currently working on books 4 and 5 of the *Abundance* saga, entitled *Stars over Abundance* and *Abundance: Legacy,* respectively.

Book 4: *Stars over Abundance* is set simultaneously in the time frame of book 3. It's a side story of Buck and Vivian—yeah, you probably saw that coming after their conversation at the dinner table huh? And a few other characters you might recognize (wink, wink).

Book 5: Abundance: Legacy is the culmination of three stories in one. After reading book 3, you can probably *guess* which characters' stories will be highlighted, but as always, I have a few tricks up my sleeve and I'm eager to introduce you to some fun, new—and lovable — characters :-D

On the following pages, you get a sneak peek into the prologue of book 4— Enjoy!!

SNEAK PREVIEW OF STARS OVER ABUNDANCE

STARS OVER ABUNDANCE: BOOK 4

*V*ivian Alexander sighed heavily and looked out onto the crowded dance floor of the luxurious Austere Hotel. She stood at the bar sipping a dirty martini with extra olives, wearing only a ridiculously expensive black lace Dolce and Gabbana dress, silver heels that were far more uncomfortable than the outrageous price tag claimed, and a matching silver comb that had been used to sweep her long sandy blonde hair up into a French twist.

She'd been dreading this charity ball all week, but her manager had *insisted* that she go. Jill Bradley had been her manager for the last twelve years. And she'd been a good one, so when she told Vivian to do something, she did it—even if she grumbled incessantly about it along the way. But Vivian had actually been right this time. This "charity ball" was nothing more than a stuffy charade for a bunch of pompous jerks. It was all about appearances...and money. That's why she'd wanted to avoid it. Helping Heroes had received a rather large donation from her and all these other celebrities in attendance. Vivian felt that was more than enough a bargaining chip, but no, Jill asserted that Viv absolutely *had* to make an appearance, albeit it be a short one. Jill was accurate of course. After all, it was good exposure and showed Vivian's commitment to the cause of donating and volunteering her time with underprivileged children. Plus, Vivian *had* been super engrossed in her work lately—what with multiple films and projects—and she'd not graced a gala or event in quite some time, so of course she'd found it prudent to acquiesce.

The Ponderosa Ballroom was indeed a lovely one with its fifty-foot ceilings and sparkling, cascading hand-cut crystal chandeliers. There were ice sculptures and bubbling marble fountains, cocktails were overflowing and hors d'oeuvres were being passed around by waiters in white suits and black bowties. The ballroom was dimly lit with circling blue disco balls and the music that streamed out of the speakers was poppy classical. It wasn't unlike any other charity ball Viv had ever attended.

Although she looked like a million bucks, Vivian felt as out of place here as a vegan at a Texas BBQ, but she plastered on that perfect smile that had made her famous, nodded to the stars she knew and tried to keep to herself as much as possible. She wanted to quickly ride this façade out and go up to her room within the hour. Maybe she'd settle into the oversized, jetted jacuzzi tub with a glass of wine and simply enjoy the quiet, or cuddle up and read the romance novel Jill had thrown into her bag to relax her.

Vivian Alexander was an extrovert through and through. She'd always enjoyed being the center of attention and absolutely loved being an actress. Over the last fifteen years, she'd gotten used to being photographed, interviewed, stalked—by the media for every little move she made—and never getting an ounce of privacy to herself. She literally lived in the spotlight almost every single second of every single day...but one thing she couldn't stand was all the phoniness, faking it for appearance's sake. The founders of Helping Heroes were nothing but a bunch of high and mighty corporate bigots, and Viv couldn't stomach them!

Vivian remembered that she was there for the kids and forced herself to move back into the crowd. It wouldn't help for the photographers to come around and see her standing off to herself looking like she was sulking. She could just see the headline now!

Hollywood Starlet found pouting at charity ball— Is it a new beau or is she feeling the effects of **middle-age?**

Vivian had seen a similar tabloid already. She was thirty-five years old now and felt that biological clock ticking loudly as each day passed. Leave it to every media outlet to capitalize on the one short-coming Vivian had so far; her lack of a husband and children.

It had been an embarrassing interview with Naomi Wiley, one of the top talk show hosts on prime-time TV, when she'd asked Vivian when she planned to settle down. It had been a random question; completely off topic for one thing and highly personal for another.

Vivian had been so busy with her career she hadn't had time to think about settling down. She'd absorbed herself in the Kinsen children since she had none of her own and was too busy spoiling them and trying to keep up with their goings-ons. She hadn't really been looking for love; not to mention that the last two men she'd dated had been *total* ass-hats.

She waved to Leonard Palmer, a well-known director and former producer for one of her movies- *Destiny of Promise,* and greeted Trent Mooney, her former co-star. They talked for a bit as he introduced his wife, Jennifer and she began to tell Vivian about their new baby. Vivian groaned internally. It wasn't that she didn't love babies, but it seemed the entire universe was trying to tell her something that she wasn't quite ready to hear.

When she could finally pull herself away from the conversation that seemed to last ten years, she moved toward the frame of the French door and grabbed a glass of champagne off of one of the passing trays, replacing her empty martini glass in its place. She downed it, the bubbles burning in her throat. That wasn't gonna do it!

She headed back to the bar.

"Martini, extra dirty," Vivian murmured to the handsome young bartender clad in a black button-down shirt who'd served her the same thing not just ten minutes prior. He nodded and gave her a grin. He had beautiful ebony skin and blonde hair with big chocolate brown eyes not unlike Vivian's.

"Rough night?"

"You could say that," Vivian flirted and winked.

Once he handed the martini over, she sipped it and immediately turned to avoid his eyes. He was giving her a look she was all too familiar with; not that she wouldn't enjoy a hot night with a young stud such as himself, but he was genuinely *far* too young for her and God forbid, that was the last thing she needed for the media to see— A young college-aged kid leaving her hotel room in the walk of shame. Especially, after she'd been called out for being *middle-aged*.

She thanked him, handed over a generous cash tip from her black Michael Kors wristlet, smiled at him, and walked forward.

She froze in her tracks at the sight of a face she knew well but had surprisingly never formally been introduced to. It was the black cowboy hat that sat on his head—his trademark—that made him immediately recognizable.

"Howdy, ma'am." Vivian shivered at the deep Texas drawl.

"Howdy yourself, cowboy," Vivian murmured back and grinned playfully at the blonde-haired, blue-eyed sex god before her. She felt the mind-numbing effects of the alcohol start to move through her system as she extended her hand to him.

"I don't reckon you and I have ever officially met. I'm Buck Jenkins."

"Vivian Alexander." Her sultry voice rasped out.

He took her hand in his and brought it up to his lips, rubbing her knuckles ever so lightly with their full softness before tenderly kissing her prickling flesh. She gasped internally and bit into bottom lip. Her pulse quickened, and she almost moaned aloud.

Her night had just gotten *exciting*.

ABOUT THE AUTHOR

Shanna Swenson is the author of the *Abundance* series: *Abundance*, *Return to Abundance, Escape from Abundance* and *Starlight Valley,* heartwarming adult romance novels that showcase the healing power of true love in the face of tragedy.

She has been an avid reader all her life and began writing at the age of fourteen. She fits her zodiac sign of Cancer to a T and enjoys the simple things in life. She loves to laugh and is always smiling. When Shanna's not supporting her fellow indies with her face buried in a book or writing her next novel/novella, she enjoys action and horror movies, pro football, hiking, Yoga, and traveling with her own "knight in shining armor".

You can find Shanna on these social media platforms.

Her website is www.shannaswenson.com

facebook.com/shannaswen

twitter.com/shanna_swenson

instagram.com/shannaswen_author

goodreads.com/Shannaswen

amazon.com/author/shannaswenson

pinterest.com/shannaswen

www.ingramcontent.com/pod-product-compliance
Lightning Source LLC
Chambersburg PA
CBHW050912250626
47155CB00001B/198